LUDIK AND THE RUNAWAY MOUNTAIN

JOHN ILHO

ISBN 978-82-693652-3-8

For my grandmother Lurdes.
I wish you were here to see this.

Acknowledgments

First and foremost, I want to thank my wife, Sara, for her never-ending support. Then, I want to thank her again for being the best editor a writer can ever hope for. Truly, this book, or any of my stories, would only be half as good without her.

Huge thanks to Jeff Brown for finding the time to create this beautiful cover. It's truly amazing. Still in the art department, I am also extremely grateful to Chaim Holtjer for his rendition of Aviz in his unique cartography style and Hari Wishnawa for the beautiful symbols he crafted. I may have put the words together, but you guys have made it stunning to look at.

I want to express my deepest thanks to all who have given me invaluable feedback, advice, and support to make this novel even better: Marius Vangen, Winnifred Artemis, Nuno Mendonca, Fabio Augusto, Jason Groves, Paulo Buchinho, Malky McEwan, Eric Wyman and Johanna Stumpf.

Next, I'd like to thank Bryan Thomas Schmidt for his outstanding work developing and copyediting this, as he called it, "Chihuahua Killer," and for his stellar editorial review.

I also want to express my profound gratitude to those who have joined me in this journey at some point or another to help me improve my craft by being crushingly honest and kicking me in the butt when I deserved it: Gavin King, Alison Patrick, Pål Skjønnhold, and Michael Kobernus.

And finally, I want to thank you, dear reader, for being awesome!

Writing careers aren't built by great writing but by great audiences. Without you, all this would've been a pointless endeavor.

SHAttered Mountains
THE SHATTER
Esoin R.
Leothtre
Leotht woods
Snottyfield
ALGirin
Apicaline
Kingdom
OF
AVIZ
Etre R.
Bastard's Horn

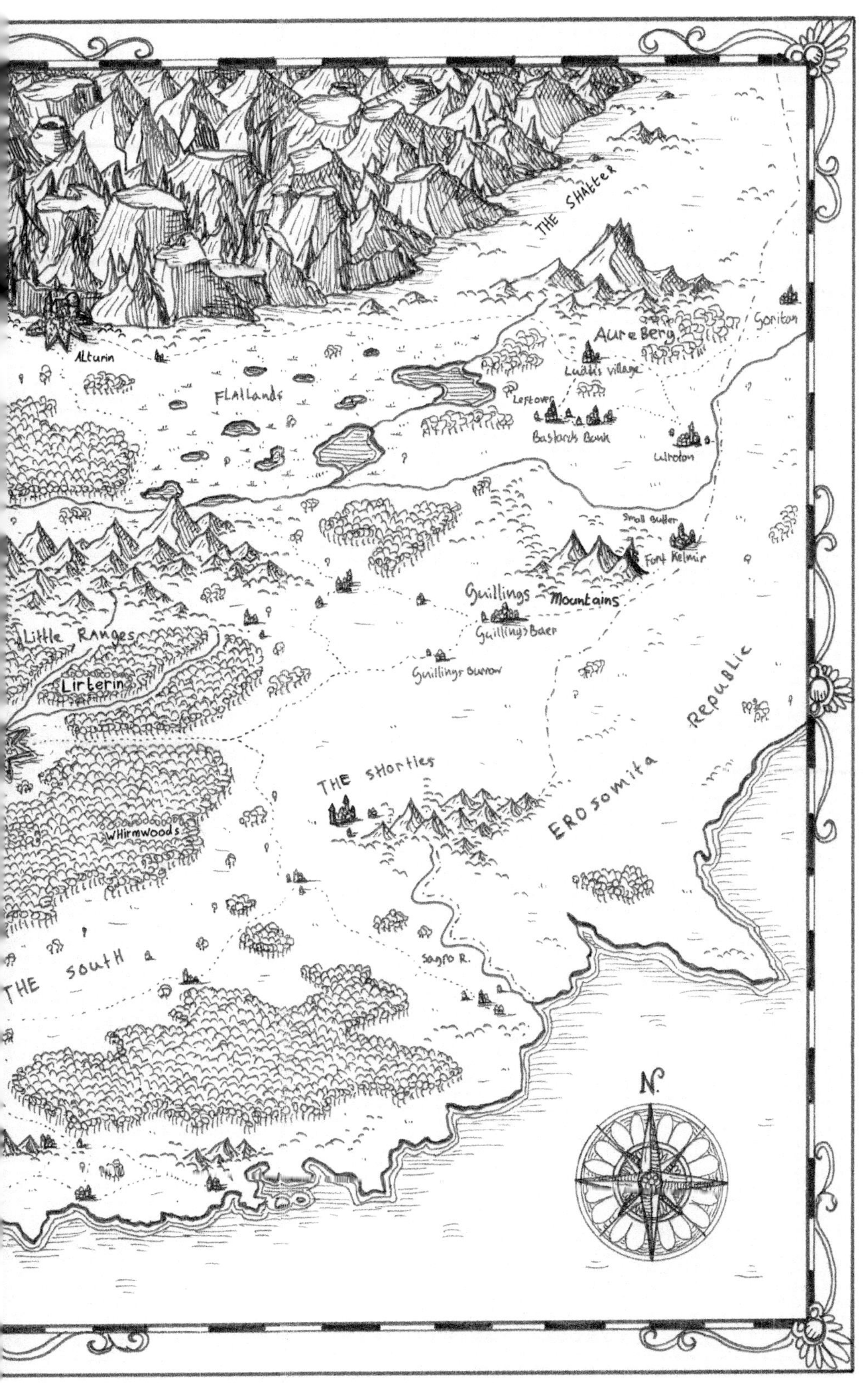
THE SHATTER
Goritan
Aure Berg
Ludd's Village
Alturin
FLATLANDS
Leftover
Bastards Bank
Wroton
Small Gutter
Fort Kelmir
Guillings Mountains
Guillings Baer
Guillings Burrow
Little Ranges
Lirterin
EROSOMITA REPUBLIC
THE SHorties
WHirmwoods
THE SOUTH
Sagro R.
N.

Prologue

Mathew Doller was about to be grounded for life. Maybe spend some time in jail even. Hell, the whole nation would remember him as the boy who destroyed countless books of unimaginable historical value.

All this because he had—*had!*—to stay at the Boston Public Library every day after school. *No arguing!* He was to report there to Aunt Kelly from now on until the end of time.

What a load of crap.

Not the library part—that place was dope. His reservations were more toward the *had* bit. Why wouldn't his parents trust him? He was only best in his class, always respectful of his folks' wishes, and as far as he remembered, he had been an outstanding son. Right? Sure, he had broken an arm or two skateboarding with his friends, but who hadn't broken a few limbs in their childhood? No. All this overreacting simply because he stole Justin's precious bike and dumped it in the river, but, goddammit, he deserved it.

Mathew huffed and pushed his thoughts away as he reached the door. He took one last look over his shoulder. The corridor seemed empty. He slid Aunt Kelly's key into the lock and turned it gently until he heard the satisfying click of an unlocking door. On the other side lay a room yet to be explored. What would he find? Books? Yeah, of course. But of what kind? Suppressing his anxiety, he turned the knob.

A thick hand grabbed his shoulder and spun him around. Aunt Kelly's eyes bulged with anger. Where had she come from? "We've discussed this, Mat. You can't go wherever you want. Some of the stuff here is of extreme historical relevance and away from the public eye for good reason."

Damn, that sounded interesting.

"I don't want you touching anything," Aunt Kelly continued, "especially if it looks old. If you start creating trouble for me, I won't let you stay with me anymore."

"And that would be a shame."

Aunt Kelly slapped the back of Mathew's head.

"Ouch!" he said, rubbing the spot where his aunt struck him. "That hurt."

"Maybe that'll remind you not to be a smart ass with your aunty next time. Don't you have some homework to finish instead of stealing keys from me?"

Mathew shrugged. "Not really."

Aunt Kelly sighed. "Just promise me you won't go around touching books you shouldn't be touching. You know the ones. The older they are, the farther you keep your hands away, you hear me?"

"Older equals farther. Got it."

"Promise me."

"Sure," he said rather petulantly.

Aunt Kelly's stare intensified.

"I promise," he added a little more assertively.

Satisfied, Aunt Kelly relaxed. "Alright, off with ya." She snatched her keys from his hand and walked briskly away.

Mathew shuffled the other way, back toward the stairs and the lion statues, seeking a new set of fossils imbued in the walls. There must be a book somewhere in there to keep him entertained. After all, there were something like twenty-four million books there—what a ridiculous number. Maybe this was better than skateboarding. Fewer broken bones, at least. He could still feel where his arm had snapped like it had happened yesterday. The memory gave him the shivers, and to be honest —he stopped walking. *Aunt Kelly forgot to lock the door.*

He bee-lined back to the door. Surely Aunt Kelly hadn't stuck around. Still, he tried to be as inconspicuous as possible but couldn't help humming the Indiana Jones theme song as he reached the knob and turned it all the way. The door cracked open. Yes! He slipped inside and closed the door behind him. He sat there in the dark, half expecting another heavy hand to land on his shoulder, while his eyes adjusted to the dim light of the emergency exit signs.

He pulled out his phone and turned on the flashlight app revealing a wooden bookshelf with glass doors that stretched across the room. The books looked like ancient relics, so old the paper threatened to flake away if he blew on them. Mathew examined the covers closely when he caught a tiny flash from the corner of his eye. What was that?

He peered into the dark aisle. Was someone else in there with him? Why hadn't they turned on the lights? Could it be another lone kid trying to get a kick out of sneaking around?

A small burst of fire erupted from an open bookshelf at the end of the aisle.

His heart skipped a beat. That was not good.

Mathew dashed toward it, pointing his tiny light everywhere frantically. There had to be fire extinguishers everywhere, so why couldn't he spot any? If a fire broke out, no one would ever believe it wasn't his fault, no matter how much he protested or squirmed. His life would be over. But when he got to the source of the fire, nothing stood out. He let out a long sigh of relief. Had he been holding his breath the whole time? He was sure he saw fire. Wasn't he? Could he have imagined it? The dark can do that sometimes.

A tiny flame, like a lighter's, lit up in front of him. Mathew stood still as it danced and flickered, suspended before a book's spine—*New and Old Worlds and How to Get There*. He could put it out by pinching it with his fingers, but before he reached it, the flame fluttered toward the book and seeped into it.

"Holy crap on a cracker," he muttered.

With a trembling hand, he pulled the book out and turned the cover. Nothing seemed out of place. No burn marks or singes. Flipping back and forth a couple of times he found only blank pages. What kind of book has nothing written on it? Oh! Could it be one of those books written with invisible ink? Like lemon juice? What an odd thing to—

Mathew flinched as fire licked his face, tossed the book aside, and stumbled backward. The flames retreated inside the pages—that was not a trick of his mind. "What the..." Mathew mumbled as he rubbed his eyes trying to wipe the orange smudges from his vision. He approached the book cautiously, light fixed on its open pages. That's when letters began to form right before his eyes.

What is your name, child?

Was it talking to him? Holy Cow. "Uh... Ma- Mathew?"

Hello, Mathew. I have a proposition for you.

Chapter 1

The Mountain

Ludik

Most people call me Ludi, or Lud, even though my name is Ludik. Or they do call me Ludik, but I don't catch the *k* on their lips. No, it doesn't bother me—being deaf, that is. Still, if given the choice, I would've gone with ugly.

There are many misconceptions about deafness, but the oddest to me is that we are void of sound, which is simply not true. Something I know all too well. And it's with a sound that my story begins.

I was eight years old at the time, playing in Dad's shoe shop—a cozy little place if you ignored the macabre shoe molds of all sizes lining the walls like bundles of severed feet. Dad hunched over his work like a frightened roly-poly, meticulously sewing the body of a shoe to its sole. He glanced at me every now and then, saying something with keen eyes, while I played with bootlaces and different leathery materials, testing their textures and flavors. He got up from his bench, cupping something in his calloused hands like it was alive and could escape at any moment—his apron dangling as he walked. It resembled the curtain of an abandoned house more than anything else. Dad extended his hands toward me, unveiling what he had brought. I peered inside and found what seemed to be the clipping of a giant's toenail. Dad rubbed it with his fingertips, suggesting I do the same.

"What is it?" I asked.

A half-smile grew in his sturdy jaw. "This is the future, Lud. And I'm the first one doing it." I loved watching Dad's lips. So confident and excited. He poked my nose with his rough finger. "Maybe one day, I'll teach you all about it."

I didn't know about that. I wanted to be an explorer and go on grand adventures, just like the heroes in the stories Mom and Dad read to me at night.

Dad returned to his workbench, focused on finishing his shoe. Snipping away the extra leather and then branding it with a hot wire—an encircled mountain with three peaks, the right one slightly bent, along a few swirly leaves and flowers at the bottom. He marked every shoe he made that way. That was another thing other shoemakers weren't doing. But Dad always said quality work requires branding until your brand becomes your name.

Intrigued by this new material in my hand, I began to test it further. I pulled and pushed. It was strong yet very malleable. I prodded with teeth and tongue and found it tough and chewy, tasting of oil and hand soap combined. "Can I keep it?"

Dad didn't answer, engrossed in his shoemaking. He had said he needed to get this order done, just like the ones before, so his new product could have a fighting chance in a very traditional market.

I did not wish to disturb him further, and I had other things in mind, too. Careful not to get too close to the bundles of feet hung on the wall, I passed the door leading directly into our home at the back of the workshop. I found Mom folding laundry and did my best to look innocent, heading straight for the kitchen and the door to the garden.

A rolled-up towel hit me on the back of the head. I turned.

Mom had a hand on her hip. "Where do you think you are going?" she asked from the living room. Living room is an overstatement. There were only three rooms: the kitchen-dining-living-room, the bedroom, and the bathroom. Though calling the bathroom a room was another overstatement in itself. I guess I should be grateful it was indoors, unlike most neighboring houses.

My eyes darted between her and what lay beyond the back door.

"You are not to go anywhere, remember?" she continued, her lips moving precisely and deliberately so I could read them while her hands repeated in sign language. Mom's persistence in teaching me how to read, sign, and lip-read would prove crucial in the years to come—though I certainly didn't appreciate it back then.

"Unless you have decided to apologize to Mr. Harin, you are staying right here with me. He is furious about that business with his fence, and I would be too if I had spent all night looking for my stone-hens. I know you are listening. Don't pretend you're not. Here." She pulled a notebook and a pencil from her vest pocket and scribbled something on it. She tore the paper and handed it to me.

Stay, it read. I guess my go-to "but I didn't hear you" excuse had outgrown me quickly.

I slumped on the floor, legs crossed, pouting. Mom got back to her chore. And I got right on with scheming my exit. And as she took a rather large bed sheet from the laundry basket, perfuming the room with hints of mountain lilies and fresh mountain air, I took my shoes off.

Mom grabbed yet another bedsheet, and I found my chance. I slipped away as carefully and softly as I could, reached the door, and tiptoed out into the garden.

Beyond our garden's stone fence, more stone fences mazed endlessly around green farming fields until they ended abruptly at the mountain's foot. The Aureberg mountain conquered the whole northern horizon, its three peaks still covered in winter snow, one slightly bent.

I hopped to the peach tree in the middle of our garden and sat against her trunk, shaking loose more petals, which added to the growing pink carpet covering the grass.

You're sneaking out again, the peach tree said. Not said exactly. Trees can't talk like we do. But if they wish, and if you are willing to listen, they can make themselves heard.

"I want to hear the rest of the story."

Do you, now? Its leaves rustled in the wind preceding another cascade of dying blossoms, from which delicious peaches would soon grow. *Very well. Where did we leave off?*

I pinched my chin, browsing through my memory. "So you told me how in the old days magic was everywhere, right until the Shatter, and then... oh, I know, the Worldroot tree."

The peach tree pondered in silence—an eternity for me. So long, I thought Mom would find me before I could hear a single word of the story. Or perhaps, I should be digging another hole instead. I shouldn't, though, not after all the trouble I got into for digging that hole under Mr. Harin's fence. On second thought, I could not stop feeling sorry about the scaled worm I'd severed in two. Mom says they grow back, the halves becoming two distinct worms, and that what I should really feel sorry for was Mr. Harin's fence. I wasn't too sure about that.

Oh, yes, the Worldroot tree, the peach tree finally said. *Pure magic ran through her roots, deep into the world, binding it with another.*

"Another world?" I couldn't believe it. This world was already so big no one had seen it all, and there was still another?

Yes. Another world. If you held magic in your heart, you could travel between them. Don't give me that look. One world is quite enough for a little boy. Think of me. Unlike you, I will never gaze over more than what you see now. Here is where my roots are. Here is where I'll grow, where I'll blossom, and where I'll wither.

"Don't worry, Peach. One day, I'll take you to see the world."

Don't be foolish. This is the fate of trees. It's how we are. It's what we are—our nature. And to go against one's nature is as productive as fighting a mountain. It does not matter to trees if we move or not. But we do wonder. Same as man dreams of flying.

"What happened to her?" I asked. "The Worldroot?"

A long time ago, so long that this story only survives among roots, passed on by long-living trees to long-living trees. Trees who live far longer than I, or stubborn little boys who disobey their mothers.

I giggled. Giggling always made me feel like I had hiccups, and I could never tell when others were giggling or in need of a scare.

A mage, all-powerful, tried to make this a better world. Using magic given by the old forces that guide the universe, the mage waged a long and deadly war to defeat the evils that lurked in the shadows. But such a war left deep scars in the land and held back the prosperity of life for thousands of years. It shattered the world, all in the hopes of making it a better one.

The problem is, you see, no living creature will ever agree on what better means. Not now, not then, not ever. What is better for some does not necessarily mean it's better for others. They couldn't even agree on which evils so desperately needed to be destroyed.

Drained by the wills of the mad, the Worldroot withered, her leaves fell, and her body was left to rot. It is said she did not die, not completely; that her roots still live underground, waiting for brighter days to come when the Leohirin flourish and once again bathe in the sunlight that is their right.

"The Leo... huh?" I said.

Oh, oh. I think you are in trouble. Again.

"Me?" I spun around and met Mom's glare, arms crossed. "I was just..." I said, failing to come up with any proper excuse. "I wasn't doing anything. I swear."

"I should have never told you that I speak to trees," Mom said. Even when angry, she would take her time and speak slowly and sign to me. "If you thought you were in trouble before, wait and see—" She turned abruptly, head poking back inside the house.

Dad emerged and hastily grabbed her by her shoulders. He hugged her tightly and let her go in a heartbeat. He said something, though I could not read his lips from that angle. His face was white; his eyes desperate. Pointing at the mountain, he said something else, making his lips visible to me. "Borik just told me. They are mad," I think he said.

I could not see what Mom replied. Her hands were all over the place as if seeding a crop or feeding birds.

The ground shook.

Mom and Dad squatted. Then it shook again, breaking their balance, and forcing them to sit down. It shook a third time. So violently that for the briefest moment I wasn't touching the ground.

"Ludik!" Mom said, dimples appearing on her face. Dimples meant she was shouting—that's what shouting sounded like to me back then. "Come! Quickly!" her hands shouted along.

In a quick frenzy of events, we were back inside the house. Mom was in our room stuffing clothes in a bundled bedsheet. At the same time, Dad hastily shoved as many supplies as he could into a canvas bag. Then the floor tossed us up in the air like vegetables in a frying pan.

Oddly, that did not scare me. Almost like when Dad threw me up in the air, and I felt safe because I knew he would be there to catch me.

More questions came to mind than fear. Where were we going? When would we be back? Should I bring a toy? I had some toys Dad made for me, but I always enjoyed playing with plants and dirt much more. I was reasonably sure that wherever we ended up that day, there would be plants and dirt to play with.

I looked back at the garden. I could not leave without saying goodbye to the peach tree. I tried to voice my concern, but no one was listening. So I raced toward the back door, and before I stumbled out into the garden, a massive hand grabbed my shoulder and pulled me back. Naively, I tried to fight it.

"I want to say goodbye to the peach tree," I protested, but Dad slung me over his shoulders as if I weighed as much as a feather pillow.

From there, I got a full view of the back window. I couldn't quite make sense of what I was seeing. At first glance, I thought the house was falling. But falling from where? It's a house; it's already on the ground. Then it dawned on me it was not the house that moved. It was the mountain.

The ground trembled; pushed and pulled; contracted and stretched. The tiles from the walls came loose and shattered against the stone floor, where patterns like lightning trails spread.

Mom ran outside, and we shot out behind her. Aureberg was moving, the snow from its peaks sliding off, leaving a trail like a cloud in the sky.

And the noise. Immense. Unnatural. Terrifying. So loud it broke through my deafness and exploded in my gut.

The ground shook with brutal force—without concern for those who populated it. Wherever I looked, I saw only bedlam and chaos. People ran, tripped, fell, and cried. If I wasn't afraid before, I was then.

The ground waved like water on a lake during a windy day. Dad fell, and I with him, sprawling aimlessly across the dirt and gravel. I scraped my face and my hands, and despite the pain and numbness, I got back to my feet. Dad did not bother with the supply bag and grabbed me by my shirt like I was the bag.

The river overflowed behind us, engulfing the village, gurgling over houses and cattle. We would not escape it. Dad lifted me back onto his shoulder, hurting my ribs. My stomach tightened like a wrung towel. We were going to die. I wanted to close my eyes, but I couldn't. The Wellers, our neighbors, whose son I used to play whilp with, disappeared under the deadly brown froth pursuing us. Their house, our house, Dad's shoe shop, the peach tree... gone.

Mr. Harin sat casually on his porch, walking stick by his side, tea mug cupped in his hands. He didn't try to escape. He sat there as if dying that morning had been in his plans all along. Then the bakery, the smithery, the school... They were there, and then they weren't.

I hated myself for not understanding the urgency. I should have helped Mom and Dad instead of trying to say goodbye to the peach tree. That delay would cost our lives, the water rushing ever closer.

Then, the mountain rose higher, lifted half of the village in the air, and pushed the water out of sight. I don't know if it's the way time distorts memories, but I could swear I saw houses flying like the forces that bind us all to the ground had no say in it. Homes, boulders, and trees kept going up and up until they seemed to hover for a second before they all came crashing down.

We hit the ground hard. I landed on my back and hit my nape against a rock. It almost knocked me senseless. My vision blurred, head woozy. I got up with my elbows, but I couldn't find Dad. The ground before me had parted as easily as opening a cabinet door. I forced air back into my lungs and got to my feet, but as I lurched toward where I'd last seen him, something caught the collar of my shirt and yanked me away. I witnessed in disbelief as the section of land I had just stood on crumbled into the crack, spewing thick columns of dust into the air.

"We have to help him," I cried, fighting Mom's clutching embrace. I wasn't thinking, no longer in possession of a mind. "We have to help him!" I flailed, scuffled, tussled, kicked, and slapped. "Let go of me!" But Mom held on. I struggled until there was no fight left in me. She hugged me tighter, her cheeks wet against mine.

We stood there, beyond the point of uncertainty, watching Aureberg continue its path, unconcerned, inconsiderate as it plowed across the land and everything on it—mountains, deceitful things, lying with their stillness.

"Why?" I said into Mom's shoulder. "Why did it do this? What's it running away from?"

But Mom said nothing. For there was nothing to be said. She just hugged me close, letting her tears fall as we watched our world, our whole life disappear like it had never been.

Chapter 2

Refuwee Cump

Ludik

Sleep eluded us all night, while the northern lights kept us company. They danced and waved, manifesting shades of green, yellow, and purple. And they were also sad, like streams of tears. They did little to appease our souls, but they did seem—at least for a little boy—like the sky was mourning. Like it, too, had lost much of which it held dear.

By morning, a new spectacle took place. Columns of men marched through the dawn, forcing us off the road. They wore stuffy, dark blue armor, swords hung in scabbards at their waist, and carried spears and square shields with the silvery half-start crest of the Alturin city amidst a field of blue. They marched north. *To the mountain,* I thought. Then a group of maybe six ekkuh riders fell behind.

One dismounted, took his gloves off, and said something to our group of survivors.

"Stay here. Don't go anywhere," Mom told me as she got up to meet the man.

The rider was tall and imperial, with a chiseled face, and a perfectly groomed beard. He and Mom exchanged words, but I paid no attention. My eyes were fixed on the marching men as they grew smaller down the road. I didn't know what they could do against a mountain, but I was glad someone was doing something.

I looked at my bare feet as if noticing them for the first time. How ironic, the shoeless son of a shoemaker. There was nothing left from our lives but a bag full of clothes.

Mom took a knee in front of me and pulled up a pair of trousers—Dad's trousers. She ripped them apart and into threads. Next, she folded several layers together, which she pressed against the sole of my feet, then rolled strips of fabric around them, like bandaging a deep wound. "Don't run in these," she signed. "They'll fall off."

We must have walked for hours before the well-groomed soldier decided it was time to rest. I took stock of our group. What a sad bunch. More people than I could count on my fingers and toes, but not many more. The well-groomed soldier didn't take a break like the rest of us. He sat with each survivor, a bespoke smile for each story he heard. Who was he? My curiosity wouldn't remain thirsty for long.

"Nice shoes," I read on his lips as he sat next to me. Mom interpreted the rest. "Saw your mother make them. She's a tough lady; you should always listen to her."

I looked him up and down. "Are you a general?" I asked.

There it was, the look, the awkwardness. Right in his eyes, my accent taking him off balance. But to his credit, he bounced back as if he didn't notice anything. "You can call me Mink. I see you're a tough boy, too. That's good. It's a nice thing when we can take care of ourselves." He winked. "I'm sorry for your loss. It's better to have had a good father for a little while than a bad one all your life. Just remember, always have someone to share your pain with. It can even be me if you ever need to." He patted my shoulder. "It's okay to cry. It means you're not a coward."

"It means I'm weak," I said, shaking my head.

"Takes more courage for a man to cry than you think. If you're afraid of your emotions, they'll corrupt you. That's what my dad taught me." He poked my chest with a strong finger—a finger more suited to wielding swords than to helping little boys.

"Will the mountain come back?"

"The mountain? No. And if it does, the Alturin Guard will protect you. Or Alturin itself. It was built to repel the attack of thousands of men. More than enough to repel a mountain." Mink tousled my air and moved on to the next survivor.

Mom cupped my face. "I'm proud of you. Whatever happens next, I am very proud of you. Do not ever forget it."

"I'm proud of you too, Mom."

Mom smiled with wet eyes and caressed my cheek. "Let's get up. People are beginning to move, and we don't want to be left behind."

Not long after, I found myself running along the column, looking for answers. I tried to find Mink, but failing, I settled for the soldiers on ekkuh-back steering the column. The four-legged animals seemed docile enough, with their honey-colored feathers and kind green eyes, until, of course, you considered their large size, sharp claws, and pointy reddish beak. Those were no regular ekkuhs. They were war ekkuhs.

The soldiers looked down at me, much like I once looked at the scaled worm I had cut in half.

"Can you tell me where we are going?" I asked.

"Hey, what's wrong with him?" said the soldier with a freshly sewn cut coming down from his left eye to the top of his lip.

"Think there's a potato in the mouth. Yeah, that's it. A potato, I reckon," said the other, pointing his small, cracked shield at me.

"I wish I had potatoes to put in my mouth," replied the first. "What do ya want, boy? We ain't got no potatoes."

"There are no potatoes in my mouth."

He eyed me while frowning, twisting his lips. "A peach, then."

I took a deep breath. "I want to know where we are going. That is all."

"Hey, Oddik," said the soldier with the battered shield. "I think he's deaf."

Oddik raised his brow and nodded to himself, then he frowned again and waved his hand dismissively. "Good try. But if he's deaf, how come he can hear us?"

"He can't, he's deaf."

"Well, Hannik, then how is he answering our questions?"

Hannik scratched his chin. "Didn't think o' that."

"That's why I'm the brains here."

"Then where did he get them potatoes?"

They both stared at me questioningly.

"I have no potatoes!" I stomped my foot on the ground.

Hannik and Oddik glanced at each other and back to me, no longer amused with my presence.

"*Refuwee cump,*" Oddik's lips formed. I always had trouble when meeting new words so it took some mental strain to piece that one together. "Stay close to your mom, aight? We can't afford to go out searching for missing boys with potatoes in their mouths."

"Ah, look, Odd, another one," Hannik said, looking behind me.

A boy who seemed to have his face covered with mud specks came running up to us.

"What do ya want?" Odd said.

"Where are we going?" the boy must've asked.

Odd slumped his shoulders and threw his head backward.

"Ask yar friend," Hannik said and turned his attention elsewhere.

The boy turned to me expectantly.

"Refuwee cump," I said.

"Refuwee cump?" The boy moved his lips as if tasting something new. "What's that?"

"It is where we are going," I said, not giving away that I also did not know, and extended my hand to greet him. "I'm Ludik."

"Nice to meet you, Lud," he said, shaking it. "I'm Graze. You talk funny."

"I hear funny too."

We talked for a while, pretending to know things we knew nothing about, and we parted ways only hours later, after the column stopped for another break.

I found Mom exactly where I'd left her. What did I expect? That she'd gotten lost in a single column? "Look at your feet," she said. "Come here."

I looked at my rag shoes. They had gone loose and dragged behind my feet which were bare against the earth beneath. When did that happen? To be fair, they'd gotten wet almost immediately and the sole of folded fabric had offered little protection against the lumps and pebbles on the road.

"Mom," I said while Mom reattached the makeshift shoes, "what is a *refuwee cump*?"

Her attention turned from my shoes to my eyes, a hint of a smile emerging on her lips. "Refugee camp," she said very slowly, signing each letter.

I repeated it a couple of times so I could get the hang of those new words. "Refugee camp," I repeated until Mom was happy with my pronunciation. "Mom," I began again, "what's a refugee?"

"It is a person who seeks refuge."

"Refuge?" I asked, which led to yet another repetitive lesson.

"It means a safe place."

My eyes lit up. "A safety camp!"

Mom chuckled. "I suppose."

"Then we are going to be alright. The well-groomed soldier said so, too."

We camped by the road again for the night. Riders came from Alturin bringing blankets and food. We ate bread and dried meat—a small comfort. The northern lights came back, illuminating the sky and the earth, and up north, a dark, jagged line delineated the horizon.

"Mommy, what is that?"

"It's the edge of the shattered mountains. You have seen it before, but perhaps you were too young to remember," she signed, not bothering to speak, though the light in the sky was more than bright enough to read her lips.

We walked for another full day, from daybreak to dusk. And with each step we took, the shattered mountains grew, a gigantic wall jutting from the ground at least a thousand feet high. It was ragged and rugged, without any linear edges, like a million giant crooked daggers packed together, stabbing the sky. It stretched west and north as far as I could see.

Dusk settled neatly on the horizon as we passed a formation of rocks that resembled giant eggs on a bird's nest. The land was flat and empty of trees, littered with many smooth stones. Some were small, the size of carts, and some larger than houses. Then we came to a village of white tents, and beyond it lay the city of Alturin, carved from the face of the shattered mountains itself. A massive wall, shaped like a half star or a half gearwheel, its cogs biting into the terrain like giant's teeth, protected the city from outside threats.

As we entered the camp, we found Mink standing on top of a stone, asking for us to gather around. "This will be your temporary home," he began, "until a better solution is found for all of you. I understand each case is unique, and I promise to try, to the best of my abilities, to find a suitable future for you in Alturin or nearby villages. Please make an orderly line while we sort out where to place everyone. Supper will be served at the large tent in the middle of the camp. I ask for your cooperation. There are many things left to be done, and any voluntary help will be immensely appreciated."

Some desponded faces stepped forward and raised their arms. I counted seven.

Mink smiled at them. "Refer to Balival here," he said, motioning to a man crossing things on a notebook. He had detached yet penetrating eyes.

I tugged at Mom's skirt. "Can I join them?"

Mom pursed her lips. I swore she was about to say no. But she did not. Instead, she raised a finger in front of me. "But be careful."

I joined the volunteers, my chin raised high and proud.

Mink looked at me with amusement and said, "Now that's the kind of support I'm expecting."

Balival regarded us as if we were a disappointment, but in retrospect, I guess that's what his face always looked like. "Yes," he said. "The latrines still need a bit more digging. You two there, you'll find my men working on them at the back of the camp. Report to them." The men he referred to dragged their feet away. "I need four to help in the kitchens. Do any of you know how to cook?" Two women and one man raised their hands. "You'll do. Report to the large tent in the center of the camp."

Leaving only me, a woman, and a man.

"And you, what do you do?" he asked without looking up from his notepad.

I looked up to see their answers. "Farmer, my lord," the man said.

"You look like you have a strong build. Can you swing an ax?"

"Yes, my lord."

Balival scratched something on his notepad. "And you?" he asked the lady next to me.

"I can sew," she said.

"Excellent. We need help to reinforce the tents' canvases. Follow me," he said, turning around, leaving me without orders.

"What can I do?" I said.

He stopped and looked back, as if noticing me for the first time. "I have no work for little boys."

"Why don't you let the boy distribute blankets?" Mink said. "Many cots are still empty of bedclothes."

"My lord," Balival responded without the slightest hint of bother. He turned back to me. "Follow the aisles between the tents. You'll find ladies carrying clothes, water bags, and such. Report to them."

I was about to take off when Mink, mimicking the movements, said, "Oh, we didn't have time to set the cots properly. The trick is to flip them on their end, place a foot on the bottom stick, tug the canvas a bit, and the last peg should slip right in."

I had no clue what he was on about but did not want to sound rude. "Thank you, my lord," I said, copying Balival's words, and was on my way.

It felt good to be useful, though the only job I got was mostly out of pity. They gave me a stack of blankets and told me to distribute them along the cots. Which I did, perfectly, may I add. Squaring the edges of the folded blankets with the edges of the cots. As I delivered blankets to each tent, I noticed that the canvases that lined the cots were still loose on their frames. Men struggled to stretch them out and failed. Pegs jutted evenly all around the structure, and the canvas had matching ringed holes. But when it came to the last peg, it seemed nearly impossible to fit it through.

"You have to flip it on its end, press your foot on the bottom against the ground and then pull the canvas up. That ought to do it," I said.

A large man eyed me, skepticism exuding from his face. But he did as suggested, and to his surprise and mine too, the last peg on the canvas slipped right in. I tried to hide the smugness on my face. But judging from the lack of gratitude I received, I must've failed.

I went from tent to tent, spreading the news until I got to Mom's tent. Our tent. Like all the other tents, it had space for about twenty people, and I guess the news traveled faster than I did because, by the time I got there, people were already using Mink's trick. I am not going to lie. That annoyed me a little. I wanted to be the one to show Mom how it was done.

Later, we gathered at the mess hall and were served a rich stew filled with many potatoes. Guess I finally did have a potato in my mouth. We ate in silence. Not that I could hear the silence, but I could see the mouths, and all they were doing was biting, chewing, and swallowing.

That night, I pulled my cot as close to Mom's as I could. I missed Dad. And I knew she must've missed him too, so I wanted to keep her company. Mom watched me, and when I lay down again, she placed an arm around me. For the first time in three days, I felt safe again. Right until morning, when a rider from Alturin barged into the camp and decreed, by order of the Duke of Alturin, that no refugee was allowed to leave.

Chapter 3

The Fence

Ludik

The tension was palpable as the refugees gathered before the general's tent. Mom and I stayed in the back, where she found a wooden crate so I could have a better view. I expected Mink to emerge and appease the crowd with his beguiling smile, though I hadn't seen him in well over a month since the rider's arrival. Instead, a man bearing fine armor and an immaculate white cape flowing down to the deck popped out of the tent. He paced in a manner that met all the parameters of someone who had something better to do, much like his hair, which no longer appreciated the company of his scalp. He stopped and examined the people. His eyes were deep, the color of combat, and his jaw was so sturdy and square that I imagined him crunching nuts, shells and all. Breaths grew still in anticipation.

"I am General Munika Muril," he began as Mom interpreted for me. There was no chance I could read the general's lips from afar, and even if I were up close, his overly presumptuous beard would have made it impossible to read them. "The King of Aviz has burdened me with the defense of the northern border," he continued. "I understand some of our measures may seem harsh to you, but I assure you that all was done with the best intentions in mind. The catastrophe hit not only many of our villages but also others on the other side of the border, including the small town of Goritan. For some absurd reason, the Erosomitan government blames us for the mountain's collapse. In a show of good faith, we offered our help to our needy neighbors, but I fear that may not be enough to maintain peace. In response, we are reinforcing the border.

"This, however, means we have to sustain our soldiers at the frontline and will inevitably, due to the full disruption of the entire northern farming region, lead to some rationing."

The people around me shifted uncomfortably.

The general raised his hands as if trying to tame a wild ekkuh and said, "I am here to promise you that King Artumin always puts the needs of his loyal subjects first." He paused to let that sink in. "The Duke of Alturin has made himself personally responsible for seeing that those needs are met and will ensure a steady supply of food, fresh water, and other essentials."

Someone else said something, and I saw a glimpse of rage cross the general's eyes. It was brief, perhaps too brief to notice, but not to me.

"For the last time, it was built to keep you safe," the general replied as if bored by the conversation.

The crowd waved and wobbled again like a stormy sea.

"What a foolish superstition," Munika said. "Wood is as good as stone. Better even." He turned away brusquely and disappeared into his tent. Two guards stepped in front of the entrance like drapes.

"Mom, what does this mean?" I asked her.

She seemed sad, but then again, she seemed sad all the time now. "Nothing new, honey. Why don't you go play with your friends."

"Friend," I mumbled.

"One friend is better than none," she said, squatting in front of me. "Do not go too far. Always stay close. You hear me?"

I nodded.

"I want to hear you say it."

"I will stay close." I stared at her to let her know she had forgotten something and eyed my feet to make it obvious.

"I am sorry, honey. I asked again, but they didn't have shoes for you. You are going to have to keep using—where are the shoes I made you? You should wear them. They're better than nothing."

"They are not. They really are not," I said rather peevishly.

"Nothing is way better. All they do is make sure my feet stay damp and dirty. It is like walking on filthy diapers."

I expected her to argue further, but she didn't. She hugged me instead. Then she pushed me gently away and signed, "I am sorry."

"It's not your fault, Mom," I signed back.

I staggered about the deserted camp while everyone remained at the general's tent as if they had no intentions of going anywhere else that day.

I found Graze playing whilp with other kids. The camp had grown quite large the days after our arrival due to a constant stream of refugees coming from other wrecked villages.

I never liked whilp, nor did I want to risk making more friends. I wasn't being difficult. It's just that you have to sift through so many bad ones before you find one that is worth your time. And I had already done that.

Graze focused on spinning the wheel at the end of his spinning stick. Then he pulled off the spinner at a precise angle and direction, and the wheel shot toward three small poles fifty feet away. He knocked one down, gaining a point. A good move. One that I would have had a hard time matching. In whilp you get three rounds. Each knocked pole only earns you one point on its own but if you manage to down all three you triple the points. The only way to knock all three poles is to loosen the wheel at an angle, or have it curve into the line of poles. It's extremely difficult. And by the looks of it that was precisely what Graze needed to win the match.

A broad kid, taller than any kid at his age had the right to be, patted Graze on the back. Graze responded with a forced smile and walked away.

I waved at him. "That was a good shot," I said as he got near.

He plopped down next to me and threw a hand toward the tall kid who now inspected the wheel he'd won from Graze. "I couldn't get it to bend. Now I lost my wheel. To him, of all people."

I didn't know what to say, I didn't care much for whilp, though I did care about my friend. "We will get you a new one. It is only a stupid game anyway." I regretted the words as soon as they left my mouth. I had played whilp before, with the Wellers' son mostly, whose real name now escapes my memory. He would never play again. And, I mean, if anything makes you happy, can it really be stupid?

Graze's eyes lifted from the dirt and locked on me. "What's the plan? Infiltrate the kitchen? The armory? The general's tent?"

"I thought we'd leave camp."

"Leave camp?" Graze was up in a heartbeat. "We can't leave camp."

I shrugged. "We cannot infiltrate the kitchen either, yet we do it."

Graze's hands rubbed his face. Whenever he did that, I expected his freckles would rub away. "I guess it could be fun. We haven't tried it since they erected the fence."

I thought about it. I didn't understand the fence's purpose, only that, as it was made abundantly clear, it had been built for our protection.

"We shouldn't," Graze insisted. "My mom says we can't leave camp."

"That is just what moms say. I do not think they would be good moms if they did not say it. And we do not have to go far. Just for a bit."

Graze pondered for a second. "I don't know. It could be dangerous."

"They say you can leave camp as long as you are a skilled worker," Graze informed me as we reached the fence at a spot away from prying eyes.

"What's a skilled worker?" I asked as I inspected the tall wood planks at least ten feet high. I wondered briefly about where they had found so much wood to build the thing.

"It's someone who is skilled at something," Graze said as his fingers followed a gap between two planks. "You know, like a juggler. I think this is a good spot."

I inspected the gap. It ran all the way to the top. "Let me go first," I said, and Graze stepped to the side.

"What use can a juggler be?" I asked as I climbed, concentrating half on wondering what it would be like for someone to hear you without having to look directly into your face and the other half on fitting my fingers through the gap, hooking them on the other side, and making sure my feet wouldn't slip. "Do you think climbing is a skilled job, too?" I added as I reached the top and looked down at Graze.

"It does require skill," he said and began his climb. He met me at the top, and we both balanced our bums on the edge of the fence. "But I think they mean other things. Like cooking."

I nodded while inspecting how we would get down the other side. We could use the same technique, but apparently, it was not necessary. Beneath us lay a large beam of wood, one end supporting the fence at an angle and the other buried in the ground. We could easily slide down it. I lowered myself until my feet touched the beam and began making my way down.

"Do you know how to cook?" I asked Graze as he slid after me in a sitting position, looking like he was riding an ekkuh.

"Of course. Well, sort of." He got to the end and showed me his hand. There was a pale, thin line of skin going from his thumb to his wrist with even-spaced dots on each side. It kind of resembled a leaf. "I tried to make dinner once. I saw Mom around the kitchen all the time and thought, 'I can do that.' I grabbed the knife, and the next thing I see is blood all over the place. Do you see these dots? These are stitches."

"Wow," I said. "How many?"

He showed me all his fingers. "This many."

"Think you could be a cook, then?" I asked as we walked away from the fence—the shattered mountains to our left, only the scatter of gray stones and shallow grass ahead.

"It's not the worst idea. Cooks do have all the food."

I nodded in agreement. "How far should we go?"

"Oh, I don't know. Until those rocks over there." Graze pointed to a collection of six or so stones stacked together, none bigger than a wagon.

As in response, I strode in its direction. "I don't think I have any skills. My dad was a shoemaker. Do you think that counts?"

"Are you kidding? Of course, it counts. Everyone needs shoes." He glanced at my naked feet. "You lost him in the Collapse, right?"

"I miss him, you know?" Not wishing to dwell on grief, I asked, "What does your dad do?"

"Pottery," Graze said, hunching his shoulders and averting his eyes like he was ashamed to say it.

"Is it not skilled work?"

He shrugged. "Maybe."

We reached the agglomeration of stones in the comfort of the slightly awkward silence that followed. The rocks stacked and leaned against each other as if someone had assembled them and were far enough from the road to conceal us from curious eyes. As we rounded the formation, we found a tiny cave. Gleefully we squeezed into our great find. It was like a tiny house built specifically for two little boys eager for adventure. I wondered how many kids would have such a place to play in. Not many, I'd bet. We giggled more than talked, sharing "wows" and "how-great-is-thises."

"Think of all the things we can stash here," Graze said.

"Yes! We'll have to find some treasure. It is settled then, from now on, this is our headquarters. I name it Fort Intrepid."

"Intrepid?"

"Yes."

"What does it mean?"

"It means brave, fearless, and, you know, all of the good stuff."

"I can support—" Graze popped his head outside. "Quick," he said, motioning for me to stay low. "The army is moving."

We crawled out, glued to the ground, and poked our heads above the shallow grass of the flatlands. Alturin rose above the camp where a column of men, waving blue banners, poured through its gate.

"Where do you think they're going?" Graze asked.

"To the mountain. To find it. To make it pay." I knew it wasn't true. General Munika had said it. They were going to protect the border. I'd said it more out of wishful thinking than anything else.

Graze seemed amused by it. "But the mountain collapsed, Lud."

"That is what they keep saying, yes. But I saw it. It did not collapse. It ran away. It's like people refuse to believe it because it defies logic. But that is what happened."

Graze looked at the moving mass of men, ekkuhs, and metal, then back at me. "But ran away from what? What could possibly scare a mountain?"

I didn't know, and I didn't care. It shouldn't have moved at all.

Chapter 4

Clear Sky

Ludik

"What did you get?" I stepped into Fort Intrepid, reluctantly escaping the warm autumn sun.

"Not much," Graze said, pulling things from his bag. "Half a loaf of bread and another blanket."

"No shoes?"

He shook his head. My eyes fell back to my new makeshift shoes, more like thick socks. Mom had made them from torn blankets, and I had to remove them every time I ran, climbed, or even walked over damp grass. Still, this time at least, they were better than nothing. But with winter on the horizon... Let's just say I wasn't eager to experience a shoeless winter. Hard to believe more than half a year had gone by... and I still didn't have proper shoes.

"You?" I think he said as he shoved bread in his mouth.

I smiled knowingly and unwrapped my treasure. Graze's eyes widened as if trying to escape their sockets.

"No way!" he said, the bread left unchewed in his open mouth.

"I did."

He spat out the bread and picked up the sword.

"Be careful. It's super sharp."

"Lud, are you mad? Won't they be looking for this?"

"Probably," I said. "Does not mean they will find it."

"Thought it'd be heavier," he said, swinging and thrusting it, as careful as any boy our age could be. "Where did you get it?"

"From the armory. The guard was sleeping on his post, so I just sneaked in. Not that great of a feat if you think about it."

Graze was amazed, his finger sliding down the blade until his eyes fell on the braided blue leather of the hilt.

We went through our inventory: four blankets, three pillows, two ceramic plates, a dwindling half loaf of bread, a jar of pickled green carrots that, no matter how hungry Graze got, remained unopened, two large shirts, at least twenty good sticks, half a shield, three forks, two rusty spoons, and one Alturin sword.

"Do you think you can get a helm?"

"I do not know. They have plenty of swords but not so many helms. Not all soldiers wear them. I was actually searching for a bow. Maybe we could try our luck with hunting."

Graze's hands flew to his belly. "Don't talk about food. I'm starving." He picked up the loaf of bread and bit directly into it.

"I did not talk about food. I talked about game."

He frowned at me. "We should get back," he said, mouth still full. "Lunch will be served soon. Maybe there'll be meat today."

"When we come back later, do you want to visit that rock formation that looks a little like giant eggs?" I asked as we walked back to climb the fence.

He glanced over his shoulders at the barely visible formation of stones further east. "It looks pretty far."

"More the reason to do so."

Graze pursed his lips. "Alright, after lun—"

A flash shone brighter than the sun. We looked toward the city as a trail of lightning faded away. A second later, the ground trembled. We surveyed the sky, heads turning and wobbling, but apart from a fleeing bird, the sky seemed utterly empty. Not a single cloud to be seen. We broke into a sprint as I clumsily kicked off my shoes.

"What was that?" I said, heart racing like a drum as we reached the camp's fence.

"Bastard's bother. Did you hear how loud it was?"

"No. Well, sort of. I felt it."

"It scared the life out of me."

"You are paler than snow; you know that?"

"Me? What about you? I can almost see through you."

We laughed, patting each other's backs for making it out alive.

"Well, now I'm even hungrier," Graze said and took to climbing.

"Still… after lunch?"

"After lunch!"

On my way, I found a rather annoyed-looking face staring right at me.

"You there," the face said. "I know you've been sneaking around. I have seen you, you and all the other brats. Always up to something."

I lay perfectly still, like he wouldn't see me if I didn't move.

"I'm talking to you. A sword went missing tonight. You wouldn't happen to know anything about it, would you?" He stepped closer to me. He was the man who'd been sleeping at his post when I took the sword.

I made my best I-don't-know-what-you-are-talking-about look. How was I going to escape this one? "Sorry," I said. "Could you repeat that?"

The man produced a rather distasteful expression, like he had tasted something profoundly foul. "You're the deaf kid. Bastard's bother. Get on with you."

I didn't know why having a disability aided my innocence, but I wasn't going to contest him. I found Mom waiting in the mess hall with two plates of food. She had gotten thinner, clothes hanging loose as if they belonged to someone else.

I sat next to her, and she slid a plate in front of me. "Mom," I said, noticing how much more food I had on my plate. "Here, have some of mine."

She smiled tenderly, a hand coming over my shoulders. "I already ate, honey. This is extra, so you do not have to eat alone."

I returned the smile. "They were coming with vacancies today, weren't they?"

"Yes, but they already have enough housemaids and cooks." She drew a shuddering breath. “I am not worried. I’ll find something soon. We only need to be patient.”

“I don’t think I can do that.”

She tousled my hair. “It comes as you grow, and you have to be patient for that, too.”

“Did you see the lightning?” I asked, but her eyes were already distant.

“Sorry, did you say something?”

“The lightning.”

“Oh, yes. Odd, wasn’t it?”

I nodded and filled my mouth. Graze would be happy. There were at least two pieces of meat on my plate. I ate eagerly, and as soon as I finished, I was on my way, ready for another afternoon adventure.

But Graze did not show up. I grew restless. Had something happened? I headed to his tent and found him talking with his father. His father looked at me, and even though I did not know him personally, I saw deep relief in his eyes. He patted his son’s shoulders and pointed at me.

Graze approached as if afraid to spook me. “Hey, Lud,” he said, hands locked behind his back. “I can’t go today.”

“That is alright. We’ll go another time. It is not like we’re going anywhere.”

“Yeah, that’s the thing.” Graze rubbed his cheeks with both hands. “Dad found a job. We are leaving within the hour.”

The world spun around me like the ground was torn apart from under my feet again. How could this be? I finally had a friend, and now I had to watch him go. I gritted my teeth. “I don’t know what to say. I-I...” I began to stammer.

Graze hugged me, and I returned the hug.

When he let go, I managed to squeak, “I’m going to miss you.”

“We’ll meet again. I know we will.”

“Where are you moving to?”

“I don’t know. Dad is quiet about it. Just that he found a job and we have to leave now. Guess you were right. Pottery is a skilled job.”

“Perhaps you’ll become a potter too.”

"But it's so boring. Let's not get too hopeful on that front. Take care of our fort for me, will you?"

I nodded.

"I gotta pack now."

I didn't want to linger there any longer, afraid I might start crying and ruin our goodbye. "Yes, of course. Bye, Graze."

I wandered for a while, not knowing what to do with myself. I should have gone back to Mom. But instead, I followed as planned, climbed the fence, and roamed the flatland, one mindless step after another.

Chapter 5

The Stump

Ludik

I LEANED against a boulder while the sun hung low on the horizon, painting the distant tents orange. How long had I been walking?

I entered the circle of egg-shaped stones as high as the fence and found a single tree. I hadn't seen a tree since we left our village. I didn't know what kind of tree it was, but it looked sickly, and I could not accurately describe the stench around it. Latrines and rotten wood?

Are you here to pee on me?

"Uh?"

You foul thing. Probably while saying something like, 'Just watering the plants, hey?' If I could move, I'd make skewers out of you all.

"I won't pee—"

You understand me? It has been too long since I have spoken to anyone, much less a filthy human. Do you know what the last human who spoke to me did?

I shook my head.

She lifted her fancy skirt and peed on me.

"I'm sorry," I said, too melancholic to care. I found a small stone and sat there.

Someone peed there, he said. *Not even two days ago.*

"Then I'll share your pain."

The tree went silent for a while, then, in a burst of anger, spat, *Now you listen to me. Don't make me like you. You are a human, a piss-pooping monster, incapable of empathy or love.*

"I lost my house," I began, "my dad, and today I lost a friend. So I wish you were right."

The tree considered my answer, its dead branches and feeble leaves rustling in the stinking breeze. *So you won't take a leak? Change the olive's water? Drain the main vein? Squeeze the lemon?*

"I won't pee on you!" I shouted. "I knew a peach tree; she was my friend. And I would never pee on her."

She? That's the correct pronoun. What was her name?

"Her name?" I never asked her name.

And you know treespeak.

I shrugged. "Mom does. Guess I caught the habit."

Ah! Treespeak's no habit. You either can or cannot. It is a gift and a rare one at that.

"Fine, what's your name?"

Tarilin. You know, you are only the second human I've spoken to in my tormented existence. If it turns out the first one is your mother, could you do me a favor?

I waited for Tarilin to continue.

Tell her to pee herself.

"My mom would never pee on you."

Are you sure? Are you sure your mommy would not? What if she had to press them apples?

"Shut up! She has been through enough."

I thought Tarilin would finally let me rest, but, of course, he didn't.

Do you see that stump?

I looked at it. A tree had lived there once.

She was peed away.

I sighed heavily and regretted taking such a deep breath. The urine stench burned sour in my mouth. "I'm going now," I said. As I rounded the large stone, I saw the camp up in flames.

My feet were running before I knew it, heart in my hands, Graze completely out of my mind. I had to find Mom. I was up and down the fence as the first stars began to twinkle in the sky.

It was all too reminiscent. People ran back and forth in panic. Men set fire to tents. Soldiers formed lines and shield walls. Madness.

"Mom!" I yelled as I darted through the turmoil. "Mom!"

I rushed to our tent and found only a balefire in its place. What happened? Wasn't this supposed to be a safe camp? I spun on my heels, breathing erratically, eyes darting into anything that moved, but everything was moving. I was out of breath. How could I have been so thoughtless? Was this why Mom wanted me to stay close? Could she have known this could happen? But if she knew, then why were we still there?

Something touched my shoulder, and I jerked forward, nearly tripping.

"Where have you been?" Mom asked, her skin sweaty, forehead dirty with soot. She took me in her arms. "We have to move." She pulled me by the hand toward the front gate. A soldier stabbed a refugee with his spear. I turned my face away.

"Mom, what is happening?"

She stopped and looked at me. "We need to get out."

A soldier shouted something from the top of a barrel.

I squinted to catch his lips. "You fools, think about winter! What will you do then? Little food is better than no food at all!"

I surveyed the scene. The shield wall in front of the gate prevented the fleeing refugees from escaping. People were on their knees, praying to the Bastard or to the Light, fear and dread drenching their eyes.

"Mom, Mom! I know another way out," I said and began pulling her in the opposite direction. She did not protest.

"What is happening?" I asked when we made it to the fence.

"The lightning... the duke died. The people, they... they demanded to leave. They got scared, I—" Mom choked on her words. "I don't know. It was all so sudden, and I kept looking for you, and then... the soldiers wouldn't let them leave and—"

"Mom, can you climb this?"

She looked up the fence, then back at me.

"Here, I'll show you. Just hook your fingers in and then push with your feet. See? It's easy."

"For a little boy, maybe."

"Quick, Mom, before someone comes," I said as I reached the top.

Mom took to the wall and, to my surprise, and probably to hers too, she reached the top with relative ease. "Fine, I am here now. How do we get down? We jump?"

I slid down the support log and looked back at Mom. She blew air out, puffing her cheeks, and slid down behind me. When she reached the ground, she contemplated the fence, fury in her stare. "So it's true. Those bastards," she mumbled. "Let us get out of here."

"This way, Mom."

"I'm guessing this is where you come every day," Mom said, inspecting Fort Intrepid. "I doubt we can hide here."

I passed her the bundle of blankets and the sword.

"Why would we need that?" Mom asked, her eyes tired but still managing to whip out some disappointment.

I shrugged. "We might need it. Trade it for something. I don't know."

That seemed to satisfy her a little. "Any other stash we need to visit?"

"I know where we can hide for tonight."

"Of course you do."

We scampered through the flatlands. Behind us, some of the fires in the camp had died down, but an amber hue lingered like a halo around it. What had happened there? How was any of this possible? What would we do now?

My feet were so numb I couldn't feel the grass, lumps, pebbles, or even the cold under them. When we reached the rock formation, winded and exhausted, I said, "Here, Mom."

Mom had her hands on her knees and nodded. When she straightened, she signed, "What is that smell?"

"Pee," I said. "You get used to it after a while."

We made a bed with the blankets and decided to hide there until morning. Though the sky was clear, there were no northern lights. For once, I was grateful for it. Snuggling against Mom, I closed my eyes.

When I opened them again, it was morning. And something not much like a voice said:

You! You peed on me.

Chapter 6

Barber Baker

Ludik

Winter fell around us with all its usual drama. The air grew colder, the trees naked and dumb, and snow flurries worsened our days. And that's when it wasn't raining. Not much happened besides camping in the wilderness and constant hunger. We had no food other than pickled green carrots and whatever else we found on the turf: winter berries, edible roots, soggy mushrooms. And the trees weren't much help.

You shouldn't eat that, one told me. *The mushroom season has ended —it's maggot country now.*

I caught a spike-mouse once. Not much meat, but it was something.

Mom suggested crossing the border. But why should we? One side would consider us traitors and the other spies.

As the days dragged on, Mom got weaker. My stomach gained a life of its own, clawing at my abdomen and lungs. The pickled green carrots didn't help much. They were only slightly worse than eating live, vinegary slugs.

Sometime later, we came across a village, if one could call it that. Its name was Leftover, as faithful a name as any place could ever hope for. Leftover consisted of a dirt road with about twenty houses lining each side and a tavern that was part grocery, part butchery, part bakery, and part barbershop—a very *Leftover-y* mix.

"Sir, I beg of you," Mom said to the man in a white apron and white hat behind the tavern counter, his hands powdered white, clunks of dough clinging to his fingers and fingernails as he received money from another customer. "I can do anything—bread, stew, pies. I can clean, and I ask only for some food for my son and me."

The man regarded Mom from the corner of his eye and jutted his chin out to another customer. The customer pointed at the rack of bread loaves.

Mom waited while the shopkeeper fetched the bread, chunks of dough flaking off his hand, and extended it to his customer. She laced her hands. "Anything you need, sir. My son can help, too."

"Lady, do you know how many refugees have gone through here asking for work? If what I heard about the refugee camp in Alturin is true, soon, there will be hobos begging in every corner of the kingdom. And this business up north—Northern Death, they're calling it. Keeps me up at night—I'll tell you that much. With the mountain, so went the north's future."

Another man entered the shop and took a seat by the barber's chair.

"I'll be with you in a minute, Lorik," the barber-baker said.

"But surely, you could—" Mom began, but the barber-baker cut her off.

"You see that man?" he said. "He wants his hair cut. Leftover's a small place. As you can see, I do pretty much everything around here to make ends meet. I'm sorry, but you came begging to a town of beggars." He covered the dough with a wet towel, rubbed his hands off most of the dough, and snatched a pair of scissors, heading for the barber's chair. "Will it be the usual, Lorik?"

We knocked at every door. The village, however, had a severe case of refugee fatigue, and we were met only with "scram," "get on with ya," and shaking heads.

One of the doors we knocked on did not shoo us away. There was no one inside to do the shooing. It was way down the road, at least half a league from Leftover. We peered through the windows like stalkers. It looked like no one had been there in months. I wondered briefly if something awful had happened to the owners. Then I remembered that something awful had happened to all of us and was still happening, and it wasn't like we were going to destroy the place. Right?

So I broke a window with a rock. Inside, it smelled of dust and mold. But it would do. I helped Mom in, and we made ourselves at home. There were mattresses and blankets in the bedroom, which we dragged in front of the hearth. And there was some food in the pantry, not much, and mostly pickled nastiness. But beggars can't be choosers, so we ate nastiness with the appropriate delight.

As night approached, the wind pushed wandering flakes of snow through the broken window. I went out to gather deadwood and started the hearth, and there was even a flint over the mantle to start the fire.

I watched the flickering flames, warming my hands and face, my stomach rumbling like a wild beast. "I'm going for a walk," I said, but Mom was already fast asleep. I skulked in the cover of the night. The shop was still open, the dim light from the oil lamps shining on the unsold bread loaves. I sneaked closer, observing the barber-baker's every move. He turned his back and went inside the kitchen. I skipped across the street, heart lodged in my throat, slid behind the counter, and snatched a loaf right off the shelf. I even grabbed a couple of honey-apples from the stand on my way out. A manic grin crossed my lips as I hopped back to Mom like a little shortnose-bunny.

"We are not thieves, Ludik," Mom scolded me after I woke her up and told her what I had done.

"This is not our house, either." I wasn't going to apologize for trying to survive. Mom was getting ill, and I needed to do something.

Reluctantly, she ate. "What has become of us?" she asked, while we stared at the flickering flames of the hearth. She sighed. "What will become of us?"

I scooched closer to her. "It's going to be alright, Mom. I'll grow faster."

"I don't want you to. I want you to have your childhood back."

"But I can't have it, can I? The mountain made sure of that."

Mom averted her eyes. "If anything happens to me," she began, but I would not listen and shook my head.

"Nothing is going to happen to you—I won't allow it."

She cupped my face in her hands. "You have to forgive the mountain."

Rancor brewed in my heart, feeding on the grief that kept me company. I clenched my jaw.

"I'm too weak. I need to know that you will be alright if I... Just tell me you'll forgive it."

"Stop it. Nothing bad is going to happen to us." I pointed to what was left of the bread. "See, I got bread. I'll find more." Mom took me in her arms, but I pushed her away. "I'll gladly steal all the loaves in the world."

"Ludik. Anger, grudge, revenge. They won't suit you. They will bring you nothing good."

I looked away. How could she ask that of me? How could I forgive Aureberg after the misery it had plunged us into? Wasn't it enough that it could not be stopped nor reasoned with, now I had to forgive it, too?

But as I looked into Mom's beseeching eyes, the lie slipped my tongue, "Fine. I'll do it. But that doesn't mean anything will happen to you."

The next morning, I walked the two leagues that separated Leftover from Bastards Bank. I sat by the crossroad, right at the center of the village. An improvement over Leftover but not by much. Maybe three times bigger, judging by the number of shops on the main road. There was a tavern and a bakery (two distinct establishments, not one) and a pawnshop.

I observed the pawnshop, wondering what it was all about. Heaps of junk piled outside, and through the window, I could only see more garbage.

A pair of honey-apples appeared before me, and I followed the arm holding them.

"Do you not want them?" the lady asked. She had a kind face and a fancy dress. Well, maybe it was an ordinary dress. After seeing nothing but rags for so long, it looked like the best tailor in the kingdom had sewn it.

"I don't have any money," I told her.

She set the bag in front of me and took a step back. My voice has that kind of charm. "You are begging, are you not?"

"Begging?"

"Oh, sweety," the woman said, pity in her eyes. "You're slow, aren't you?"

"Lady, what's a pawnshop?" I asked, ignoring her stupidity.

"It's where you buy and sell used items, of course."

I squinted at her. "Will it sell shoes?"

"I don't see why it wouldn't. You have a fine day now, you hear?"

I watched her stride away, almost giddily. I bit into one of the apples and decided to beg for the rest of the day. All I got was the tiniest little coin, dropped in front of me like someone tosses away a peach pit after eating.

I walked back to Leftover and the barber-baker. His apron was a plethora of brown handprints, dough, and human hair. I showed him the coin and asked, "Could I have a loaf of bread, please?"

The barber-baker looked at me as if looking at a dead mouse rotting on the floor of his shop.

"That's a half-guilling," he said as if that would clarify something for me.

"It's all I have."

"A loaf is three guillings," he explained. "Come back when you have five more of those."

"Is it enough for a pair of shoes?"

The man stood motionless. "Shoes? Even the cheapest shoes would be two gollings, at least. That's thirty guillings. Get out of here, you rump. Go on, shoo."

I waited for nightfall, and when the barber-baker went into the kitchen, stole another loaf.

That night the temperature plummeted, and in the morning, it was like waking up to an alien world. From the window, the light reflecting from the ice-covered view hurt my eyes. I used to love winter mornings like that. Mom and Dad would throw me outside, and we'd play in the snow for hours. Now the sight was but an echo of another life.

"I'm going out."

"Ludik," Mom began, but as she rolled on the bed to face me, she fell back asleep.

I kissed her forehead, her skin cold and wrinkled against my lips. I added a couple more logs to the hearth and grabbed my Alturin sword.

The snow-covered road was a chore to walk on, but I reached the pawnshop with my feet still attached to my legs.

The pawnbroker eyed me with discontent at first, then with slight amusement as he prepared to shoo me away. At the same time, I navigated around the tables, chairs, lamps, sculptures, rusting farming equipment, brooms, mops, cutlery, and pottery, among hundreds of other items.

"Young man, please be careful on your way out," were his first words to me.

I smiled and, from my cloak (which was nothing more than a blanket covering my shoulders), produced an Alturin sword still in its simple blue scabbard and belt. I unsheathed it halfway and presented it to the pawnbroker.

"Where did you get that, you little thief? Come here, I'll have you arrested," were his last words to me.

I knocked more than a few items over on my way out and fled the village so fast that I barely touched the frozen road—so much faith in my plan, so foolish and so naive.

Back at Leftover, people reinforced their windows with iron bars and wood planks. *These people are so weird,* I thought. Would the barber-baker be interested in the sword? It was a risk worth taking.

I found him busily lugging produce inside the shop, yet it was only the middle of the day. Perhaps he needed a day off or something. He looked me up and down. "Did you find the other five half-guillings?"

I shook my head. "I found this. Can we trade?" I presented the sword somewhat cautiously.

He looked at the sword with disgust. "Hide that thing away. Don't show it to me; don't show it to anyone. Are you daft? If they find you with it, they'll cut your hands off. Did you know that? Do you want to be both deaf and handless? Aren't you miserable enough?"

I hid the sword. "Then what? Tell me, what can I do? Should I just die and be done with it?"

The barber-baker sighed, slumped his shoulders, and motioned for me to come closer. He grabbed a loaf of bread and handed it to me. "Here, today, you don't have to steal."

The compounding shame bore a hole in my heart and called it home. "I—"

The barber-baker held a hand up, and I watched him stuff vegetables in a bag: potatoes, green carrots, kaffom-plums, and sweet beans. He looked from side to side as if he was doing something illegal and slid jerked meat into the bag. "Stay out of trouble, kid. The winter is still long, and this one will be longer. If you want to make it, you'd better start getting smarter. And don't go anywhere for the next few days. In case you haven't noticed, there's a storm coming. It'll be here by nightfall. Without the mountain..." he trailed off. "May the Bastard help us."

"Thank—" the barber-baker stopped me again and used his eyes to indicate the way out.

"Look, Mom," I said after gently pushing her awake. "The barber-baker knew I was the one who stole from him before, yet he still gave me all of this. Here, have some meat."

"It's a small village." Mom's hands toiled the signs. "Everyone knows everyone; it doesn't take long to know who did it."

I fumbled with my thumbs. "Should've thought of that."

"We either learn from others' mistakes or our own. I hope you learned not to steal again."

"Unless I'm starving," I added.

Mom tried to sigh but fell into a coughing fit instead.

I helped her find a better position and brought her a cup of water. "I am going to find deadwood for the hearth."

It's easy to find deadwood. All I had to do was ask the trees, and they would tell me where to go. They preferred it; even welcomed it. It was better to see their dead limb and friends turn to ash and have that ash fertilize new soil than to watch them decompose, eaten by creepy crawlies or funky fungi.

I roasted some vegetables in a skillet over the fire. We ate well that night, though our shrunken stomachs couldn't fill up with much. After dinner, we watched the wind build up outside, so I pushed a tall cabinet in front of the broken glass and stuffed a blanket in between.

The night would prove long, so we snuggled by the fire, covered in blankets, and waited for the storm to pass.

Chapter 7

The Storm

Ludik

The storm lasted three days. Had it lasted only two, maybe things would've been different. Life, however, doesn't work that way. It didn't matter how much wood I fed the fire—the house refused to warm up. I braved the storm to fetch more wood, hearing the trees' wailing songs for their toppled friends, whose roots had been ripped from the earth that sustained them—that's pretty much it for a tree. The brutal wind battered my face and forced me to fight for each step—a fight that I lost more times than I won, forcing me back inside.

We watched the hearth burn, greedily consuming everything we tossed in it, and we prayed to the Bastard for the storm to end soon.

Then, in the evening, it happened. A tree branch rammed through the window. I tried to fix it with blankets; the only cabinet in the room was already plugging the other broken window. I unhinged a door and pressed it against the window, but wind gusts kept toppling it, allowing the creeping snow in, painting the floor white.

The wood ran out.

I tore furniture apart, starting with the dining table. I hacked it to pieces with my useless sword. Afterward, I moved on to the chairs, then the beds. I preyed on every little scrap of wood, wicker, or paper. Knick knackery, spoons, bowls, and hairbrushes were scavenged in our battle against nature. Clothes, towels, cloth. Anything that caught fire was conscripted to the war effort.

The constant work forced me awake, but in the end, there was nothing left to feed the gluttonous fire.

I shoved our last picture frame and the picture in by the end of the third day. The storm mellowed during the afternoon, and I managed to collect wood outside. Despite the exhaustion, I soldiered on and did it. I restocked the wood.

Lulled by the warmth, I leaned against Mom. Something in the back of my mind warned me against it, but I was so tired I wouldn't listen. I had worked continuously for days, and I deserved to rest a while. I had earned it. Mom took me in her arms and kissed my forehead. I had done it; I had won; we would survive the storm after all.

Safe in Mom's arms, my eyes began to shut. Drowsiness came over me like a heavy blanket. Even the trees had gone silent. The worst was over.

When I opened my eyes, the hearth was dead.

Frost grew in the windows like mildew, and snow spread across the entire floor, glittering with the first rays of sunlight. The air was still and thick, sharp against the teeth. Breathing came as easy as drowning; my joints cracked, and muscles cramped; the blanket rigid and brittle to the touch.

Mom's arm around me was cold and stiff.

Something broke inside of me.

I didn't want to turn. I didn't want to know. I didn't want to see.

I forced my eyes shut, forcing sleep to return. If I managed to go back to sleep, perhaps I would wake up, and the hearth would still be burning, and Mom's heart would still be beating. But my eyes refused to close.

The sun trailed across the window.

All I had to do was remain still and wait for the cold to claim me too. Yet, I'd failed at that as well. Why couldn't I just die? How was I supposed to go on without Mom? I should've kept the hearth going. I should've stayed awake. Every cell in my body screamed in agony, pushing me to stand up, to face reality, to start pumping blood again.

I unclutched Mom's arm and sat up, pushing the blankets away—

every movement an ache, like a thousand ice-cold needles raking against my bones. My fingers were stiff, unbendable, my head a lump of cast iron. I braved a glance. Mom was pale and serene. She was so beautiful. Every breath, every movement brought forth the worst pain I have ever felt. I hugged her and cried and cried and cried.

Time drew by, heart too stubborn to quit. My throat came unstuck. My fingers thawed.

Then the sun was gone, and night settled again. I didn't bother with fire—it had failed me enough. I curled up against Mom and waited, wishing she'd come and take me with her. To the Bliss, to where the cold is denied entrance, and mountains are only mountains—a place with mirthful trees where the Bastard tells his tales. And I would never have to wake up again to remember how much I lost.

I'm not sure if I slept or not, but when morning came a shadow loomed over me. I forced my eyes to focus and found the barber-baker crouching, extending his grimy hand to me. I took it, and he helped me up. Then, gently, he covered Mom and lifted her in his arms.

"I should've known when you didn't show up to steal from me. Just stay there, alright? I'll take care of it."

The way he said "it" provoked all kinds of nasty reactions in me. That *it* was my mother. I found myself hating that man. I hated him as much as I hated the entire world and its unfairness and callousness. I wasn't being fair to the barber-baker, but to the Ordeal with fairness. I needed to hate something like I hated the mountain.

But in the end, I was the one to blame. I got comfortable and lazy, and I fell asleep, and Mom, my mommy, died. I hated the world because I hated myself.

The barber-baker built the pyre behind the house. Some of the other Leftoverians came to lend a hand, but I don't remember their faces. It all became a big blur. They came to me with their condolences. Why? What use did I have for strangers' condolences? I hated them. I hope they saw it in my eyes.

The barber-baker laid Mom on the pyre. I wanted to tell him not to do it. That I wasn't ready to say goodbye. When I opened my mouth, however, nothing came out. I watched the fire until only dying embers remained, and Mom became ash and memories.

I followed the barber-baker to his shop. The storm had left a path of destruction across the city. How many trees had toppled, and how many windows had broken? People cleaned the streets from debris. The barber-baker gave me hot soup and forced me to eat it. His heart was in the right place, but he was not a patient man. I have a lot to thank him for, yet I never learned his real name. I couldn't stay there. Of that, I was sure. I just couldn't. Everything reminded me of everything I'd lost. And everything I'd lost reminded me of Aureberg. Guilty and wronged, I wasn't going to stick around feeling sorry for myself. I had to do something. I had to start moving.

After the barber-baker went to bed that night, I searched the room for winter clothing. I found a wool sweater and a sheepskin jacket so large it hung over my feet. I took my useless sword and strapped it over my shoulder. I tiptoed down to the shop and stuffed some food in a bag I found along the way—one last theft from the man who'd saved my life. Outside, northern lights painted the sky, undulating like a river flowing upstream.

"I'm sorry, Mom," I said to the sky. "I'm facing the mountain, even if it's the last thing I do."

Chapter 8

Compost Walking

Ludik

My teeth teetered; my body shivered. Walking kept me alive. Whatever lay ahead could not be worse than what had come before. Something deep inside me had snapped, the parts that made me whole broken, rattling miserably with each wobbling step.

Faces came and went, shadows on the road. People, I think. They eyed me with incredulity, and on their lips: "Are you deaf?"

I am. But I couldn't answer. I could only keep going.

Go home, little human, the trees said. *Do you have a death wish?*

"I don't care."

Don't underestimate winter. It'll kill you.

"Shut up."

Where's your mommy?

"Shut. Up."

Look here! Compost walking!

"SHUT UP!"

The stars hid behind clouds. The sun hid behind clouds. The moon hid behind clouds. The blue sky tainted gray. The pain was gone, or had my body dissolved into a ditch somewhere? That could only be a good thing. Was I thirsty? When was the last time I drank? Yesterday? I bit snow. Had that been yesterday? Was I hungry? No, I ate. Jerked meat. Was that yesterday? No, yesterday was...

I was still moving. Wasn't I? I don't remember my feet at all. I floated, coaching above the road. Or was the world simply turning around me, and I was the one who stood still? Were those stars? Empty houses. Empty lands. Despondent trees. Why won't they shut up? Victims of the mountain, singing songs of sorrow as they faced the looming darkness.

It has never been this windy,
It has never been this cold.
Summer days will have me,
With our wild Light to hold.
My leaves will be gleaming,
In Leohirin's might to glow.
Darkness a stream, Life a show.
New beginnings of a story long told.

The moon came up, full and bright, surrounded by streams of dancing lights. The trees were gone. Finally. My former village formed around me. I could barely recognize it. *No, it was no longer my village*. It was a geological feature, a dent in the world.

A tree stood alone, broken, and dying.

"Which way to the mountain?" I asked.

Ludik?

I regarded the poor creature. Frostbitten, blight-afflicted leaves, broken wood, she would not survive long.

Don't you recognize me? Well, I suppose I am very different these days. The cold... it has never been this cold. The trees are singing. We only sing during the darkest hours. I'm so happy to see you. I'm so happy you survived—makes my end a little more bearable. I'm so tired.

"Peachtree!" I lumped to her side and sat against her. "I'm going to find the mountain. It'll make amends. I promise you," I said. Why was I so hot?

What a foolish little boy you are. I'm too weak to change your mind. Where is your mother?

"She's gone. Aureberg claimed her too."

But you'll die. The winter will kill you. Even if you survive the journey, the mountain will kill you. You don't look more alive than I do.

"I will find it, or I will know I tried. Bastard, I feel so hot."

What are you doing?

I shed my jacket and sweater.

Ludik. You'll freeze.

"I'm fine." Only a shirt and undergarment covered my skin, every fold, seam, and crease, a branding iron. "Peachtree?"

Yes?

"What's your name?"

Oh, even in the end, you make me smile. Laurin is my name. Will you stay with me for a little while?

"Laurin, I need to keep moving. If I stop too long, I won't be able to get back up. Tell me, where do I find the mountain?"

Follow the lights; they'll lead you there, to the northern death, beyond the shattered mountains. Follow the broken trail. I'm afraid all roads are broken. The cold can be deceitful—you won't get far without clothes.

"Goodbye, Laurin. Thank you for all the stories."

Go in Light, then, my stubborn little boy who disobeys his mother.

I was on the float again. The Shattered Mountains loomed closer, making me small and insignificant, like a grain of sand. The lights blurred, and the world became fuzzy. I could not stop. I would not stop. *I'm coming for you, Aureberg.*

I am coming!

A damp and swampy smell tickled my nose. My hand touched something wet and lumpy. It wasn't ice or rock. I cracked my eyes open. Stacks of turf and wood lay by my side while a thick white canvas flapped gently above. Something else bothered me. I was warm and cozy. Moreover, the abundant aches that populated my body were gone, and soft, yellow blankets wrapped me in a bundle.

Was I moving? There were bumps and shimmies. And the light coming from tiny holes in the canvas above me shifted as it moved through shadows. I was on a cart. But how? I was just with Laurin, saying goodbye to her, wasn't I? Where was I being taken to? Who was taking me? And what were they doing with blocks of stinky turf? I shifted carefully so as not to announce my awareness and crawled on all fours to the end of the cart. I peeked through the gap between the canvas and the box.

A pair of eyes stared back at me, piercing, and fed up. The man began to say something, but before I could see what it was, I scrammed off the box cart through the rear end, and the bright light of day dazed me.

Something was odd in how the breeze touched my body. I groped my chest and slid my hand down to my legs. I was naked. I shaded my eyes with my hand, trying to make sense of things. The snow was gone, and so was everything else. There was a road, some hills, a dilapidated house, and endless meadows. Where in the Bastard's name was I?

A thick finger poked my shoulder. I turned and found the cart driver, his beard gray, his hair grizzled, his demeanor grizzlier. His lips moved as I stepped backward. What was he going to do to me?

"Are you deaf?" he said. I almost got mad at him. How dare he? Again with the "are you deaf" crap. After all that I had been through—wait! He hadn't specifically *said* it. He signed. When you sign "Are you deaf?" it means something completely different.

I stared at his rough hands forming words. Then I looked him up and down—a frowny face, rough and edgy, body dressed in all shades of rock and stone. Muddy shoes covered his feet, and a tattered beanie hung over his hair. He had the patient look of a mother bear protecting her cub or an angry anthropomorphic piece of limestone.

"Who are you?" I asked.

"*Hums*," he said with his mouth, his hands unsure if they should step in to translate.

"Hums?"

The man frowned. Apparently, he wasn't frowning before. He spelled it with his hands, "Heimee Heims."

"Heimee." I nodded to myself, half convinced he wished me no harm. Not because he didn't seem threatening, he could probably kill me with his eyelids if he so desired, but he hadn't killed me and knew sign language. "What do you want from me?" I signed back to make sure I wasn't dreaming up his gestures.

"Why would I want anything from you?" Heimee signed.

I glanced at the cart. An old broken thing, on its side, large white letters read HEIMS DISTILLERY. A large stone-ox, with long, large horns and a bored expression, waited to continue. "Why... then... uh?" I mumbled.

Heimee shuffled through the cart and produced a bundle of clothes. He tossed it at my feet. Shirt, sweater, trousers, and a pair of old, worn-out shoes. All gray like his. Who was this man who gave me shoes just like that? Like they're as easy to have and give as giving stale bread to birds.

"Had to guess your size," he signed. I stared at the clothes, then at Heime as he climbed into the driver's seat. I picked up the clothes and ran after him.

"Where are we?"

"Halfway between Ullroton and Guillingsbaer."

"What? Ullroto... Gui... what?" I had never heard of such places. "Why are you transporting dirt?"

"Not dirt. Peat," he signed, his forehead and eyebrows folding in on themselves. "You're very lucky. I don't travel north so often. My peat supplier stopped his shipments. What an oat. You can't trust anyone these days, I tell you. Everything's fine until one day, they fail you and die. That's why I came this way, to find a new supplier."

"Yes, lucky," I signed, though luck was not a friend of mine.

"Was about to burn you—built a pyre and everything. I even tried to light it—the fire wouldn't stick. That's when you decided that being dead wasn't suiting you—wish my former supplier had your grit. Where was this place?" He rubbed his scruffy beard. "Who cares? All the names here are dumb, anyway. This absolute oat gave you those clothes and asked if I needed a haircut while he chopped a lamb—one of the weirdest moments of my life."

"The barber-baker," I mumbled in disbelief. "I stole a jacket and food from him."

Heimee made something with his face. I think he was laughing, but it was hard to say. Can rocks laugh? "I sold him Heims at a discount. With the money he saved, he can buy a new one. The ordeal with that, he can buy two. Maybe even afford soap."

So I never left the Leftover? The whole event zoomed around me, making me dizzy. But Peachtree? I surely couldn't have made that up. Could I?

Heimee snapped me out of it. "Are you going to put those on?"

A thousand thoughts raced through my head while I dressed, only to end up looking like a mini Heimee. The big novelty was the shoes. They weren't perfect, too big for my feet, but what did I care? The barber-baker had shoes to give the whole time. Despite all the help he gave me, I hated him. But that didn't matter now—I had shoes on my feet.

Heimee observed me and said, "You look good for someone who was dead three days ago. Do you need a ride somewhere, or are you okay here?"

I looked around again. There was nothing in sight. "I don't have anywhere to go. I failed, I—"

Heimee curled his lips. "Alright, bye." He hit the reins, and the ox looked back at him as if to make sure it hadn't been just another whack of his tail and began to pull the cart.

I watched him go, my mouth agape. "What? Hey, wait!"

The cart came to a halt.

"Do you need something else?"

"I don't have anywhere to go."

"You said that. It means you don't have a *where* in which I can leave you. Thus, *here* is as good as anywhere."

"But... but—"

"But what? I already wasted enough time with you; I still have at least two weeks of travel ahead."

"But you helped me."

"And I haven't heard a 'thank you,' but that's alright. You're welcome." He hit the reins again.

"Wait!" I said.

Heimee pulled the reins.

"Thank you," I signed.

Heimee slumped his shoulders. He looked ahead, then back at me, then ahead, then back at me. "Fine, hop on."

I hurried to his side. "What are you going to do with the, *uh, pee*?" I said as Heimee hit the reins again.

"Peat, boy. Peat." He dropped the reins to sign. "Man has been using it for thousands of years. Every hearth, every stove, every kiln. Don't you know what peat is?"

"I thought it was called turf."

"What a tasteless word. Start saying peat, or I'll leave you right here."

"What do you need peat for?"

"Whisky."

"Ah," I said. "What's that?"

"You talk too much for a deaf kid. Whisky's a spirit. I burn peat to smoke malt in the kiln—there ain't no better peat than the one found in the flatlands—has a mineral character."

What a load of gibberish. "Interesting."

"You're not a good liar. Why were you butt naked in the middle of nowhere?"

I shivered, the memories still fresh, horrible, guttering, unrepentant. To Heimee's credit, he stared blankly at the road and continued as if having little boys about to cry on his cart was part of the job. I held tightly to my hate for Aureberg and stopped the tears from pouring out, gritting my teeth.

"The Collapse left its fair share of orphans. Guess I was unfortunate enough to stumble upon one. Can you use a spade?"

"Anyone can use a spade."

A wide grin dashed across Heimee's lips. "Spoken like someone who never held a spade in his life."

Chapter 9

Heimee Heims

Ludik

Heimee tugged at my sleeve. "That's Guillingsbaer."

To our left, a strange city perched on a hill, garish spires sprang from the center, some blood-red, others green and yellow, surrounded by a meager wall, especially compared with Alturin's. What purpose could such a wall have? Windbreak?

"Why does it look like a pin cushion?" I asked.

"It'd take a while to explain. We'll be home in a few hours."

I thought about how he'd phrased it, "*We'll be home*," as if his adopting me was a done deal. I wasn't going to say anything; after two weeks of camping, bed-sharing, checking Otto's—the ox—stools to see what had made it sick, and having a numb bum, I was happy to get off the road, but I guess Heimee saw it in my face.

"I'll tell you this," he signed. "There's plenty to do in the distillery. If you stay, I have work for you. I'll give you food, clothing, and a place to sleep. It beats living as a beggar—I can promise you that. And if you're a good hand, I'll even pay you."

I wasn't in the mood to discuss my future. "Where did you learn sign language?"

Heimee frowned, gave me a lingering, searching look, and looked away.

I crossed my arms and considered his offer. The not-having-much-of-a-choice bothered me—angered me even. If I accepted it, I would also have to accept what had happened to me—that I was an orphan, and I wasn't ready for that.

I could not stay with him for long. I just needed to get a little stronger, wait for the spring to come, then find that ordealing monster.

Heimee glanced back at me, then at the city, and sighed. "They're proof this world is a sad, sad place, mostly populated by idiots."

"What?"

"The pin cushion." He nodded in the town's direction. "For reasons only known to them, the Bastards and the Leohts think whoever has the highest building is the holiest of the lot. The Bastards build a Palrik, and the Leohts roll up their sleeves and build a taller Dendron. Like I said, idiots. Though that might be a euphemism on my part."

"I see." But of course, I didn't.

Afterward, we reached a small village called Burrow (I would later find out that its actual name was Guillings Burrow, but no one ever called it that for obvious reasons), and everything looked alien: the muddy houses, the hilled countryside, the thick trees, and even the dirt looked more poop-ish. Then the smooth road turned to solid rock, forcing the cartwheels into grooves carved from years of use. The trepidation made my teeth clatter and my numb bum number.

That's when things got a little familiar. Large rocks scattered here and there as far as I could see, though not as abundant as the ones found in the flatlands near the shattered mountains.

"When my grandfather bought this place," Heimee explained, "he thought he had hit the jackpot. It was unbelievably cheap. He dreamed about making a living growing cereal. Poor fool. Little did he know the plot was entirely made of bedrock. The only things that grow here are moss, shallow grass, and frogs. It's a good thing you're deaf; I can tell that much with all that croaking. Pops tried to sell it back, of course, but no one wanted it. Then my mother had the brilliant idea to produce ale. And for a while, that's what they did. They managed to make the grossest ale in the whole continent. They even got famous for it." A nostalgic smile crossed his face. "You see those large rocks? Whatever caused the Great Shatter tossed them all the way here from the shattered mountains. Impressive, if you think about it. We called them frigates. See, because they look like ships."

They didn't look anything like ships to me. For one, they had no sails. Sure, some were larger than a house, but that alone doesn't make them ships. Also, I should mention I had never seen a real ship before, only on the cover of books Mom used to read to me. Still, it made you wonder: what kind of force could have tossed such immense rocks so far away? Not even a mountain could do that.

Shortly after, a complex of several stone buildings began taking shape. One was long and tall, at least three stories high, with white letters reading HEIMS DISTILLERY across the façade, and ended on a large frigate, coming out of the far wall like a stone tumor. The other building was shorter and boasted a sizeable odd-looking chimney that reminded me of a mushroom growing on top of a larger mushroom that sprouted from the dark shingled roof.

"The long building is where we steep and malt the barley. The one with the chimneys is where we have the kiln and the still pots. The other small houses are a barn, bottling area, storage—among other stuff."

I didn't ask any questions since I had the hunch I was about to embark on a whisky-making tour. Then, as we cleared the larger building, a house came into view made from two large frigates joined together by a roof and clumsy stone walls. It looked like the two frigates had gotten together one day and decided to squeeze a house between them for fun.

"I have to take Otto to the barn. But you make yourself at home." Heimee fetched a long iron key from inside his jacket and gave it to me.

The shingled roof was slanted and undulated, the windows crooked in odd angles like the drawing of a six-year-old, and moss and lichen grew on every surface, giving the house a greenish tinge.

"The front door is on the left frigate. Take your shoes off before you enter."

I circled the larger of the two frigates as Heimee drove away, discovering a stone porch and a door carved into the frigate. I unlocked the door, which led into a burnished tunnel, dug through the stone with carved shelves on each side, filled with shoes, tools, and bowls. Jackets and sticks hung from the wall. I tip-toed across the corridor, finger sliding across the stonework—smooth as porcelain. It led me into a tightly packed living room with a wicker couch and a tiny support table by the hearth. The kitchen had been dug out from the frigate, too, including the oven, stove, bench, and even the dining table. The angled window offered a view of the distillery, and from the kitchen's window, far in the distance, the edge of a thick forest fixed the horizon.

On the far end, rows of books covered the wall from top to bottom, leaving only enough space for a framed glass cabinet. Inside it, I counted ten bottles of spirits which got older the higher the shelves went.

Heimee entered the room before I could finish my inspection. He pointed to the shoe prints on the red-tiled floor and gave me a miffed stare. "Thought I told you to take off your shoes."

"Sorry, I got distracted," I said, pulling off the shoes. "I'll clean it up."

He nodded in acknowledgement then said, "Well, I'm soon going to get some rest. Your bedroom is upstairs—left door."

I followed his stare to the a metal spiral staircase, at least a thousand years old, at the end of the room which led to two short doors above.

With but a couple of steps, Heimee reached the cabinet and took out an odd bottle. The label said Heims 15, single malt. At first glance, it reminded me of apple juice, but it behaved differently, thicker somehow. "Finally," he said.

He rummaged around the cabinet and produced a thumbglass, hopped to the kitchen to get a small terracotta pitcher, then popped the cork as he sat heavily on the wicker couch, filling his glass ceremoniously. He added a few drops of fresh water from the pitcher, and swirled the glass before sniffing it like someone smelling their lover's hair. Then he sipped it gently, relaxed, digging his back into the wicker, and let out a prolonged sigh.

"Is that whisky?"

"No, it's peach tea. Of course, it's whisky."

I regarded the cabinet again. With each shelf, the numbers on the bottles went up until my eyes landed on two modest square bottles. "Heims 39," I mumbled. "Why not drink that one?"

Heimee chuckled. "I wouldn't dare. Too expensive."

"But you made them, no? Can't you always make more?"

Heimee's eyes narrowed. "That number represents how many years the spirit matured in casks. I only produce a dozen bottles or less a year, depending on the Bastard's share. I keep them as insurance. You never know when you might need an expensive favor or *an expensive friend*."

Thirty-nine years? That was insane. That brown liquid was older than me fourfold.

"If you're thinking about stealing them, know that the whole country will be after you. Maybe a foreign nation or two as well."

"I wasn't," I said defensively, though the thought had occurred to me. "Why stop at thirty-nine? Why not forty?"

"That's the age my wife was when the Bastard took her from me. No whisky of mine shall outlive her."

I drooped. I couldn't handle hearing about losses. Mercifully, Heimee continued, "Care for a sip?"

"Can I?" I'd always wanted to try Dad's spirits. They looked yummy, but Mom and Dad always insisted I was too young.

He extended the thumbglass. I took it, swirling the liquid as Heimee had, noticing the trails it left on the glass like loose syrup. Would it be sweet? Candy-like? Or mellow like tea? I leaned my nose and took a whiff. My nostrils burned like I'd breathed the fumes above a campfire, and tears welled in my eyes—my curiosity lay brutally murdered. But I didn't want to disappoint Heimee, who watched me intently. Every instinct warned me not to drink it. But once the burning sensation eased, it left hints of sweet apple biscuits and nutty woods. Those are good smells, right?

I took a sip.

Hot embers and dish soap cauterized my tongue, cheeks, and throat in one go. I both gagged and gasped at the same time. It took all my strength not to be sick, hand plugging my mouth. I coughed through my fingers as my eyes tried to escape my face—the liquid rampaging across my innards, forcing me to curl.

Heimee took the glass from my hand before I dropped it. "Good stuff," he signed.

"People pay money for this?"

"Much money." Heimee smiled widely. "You're a tough kid; I'll grant you that. I'm afraid whisky is an acquired taste and one not suitable for your age. Now, don't forget the floor."

I cleaned the floor and went upstairs, feet wobbling with each step, my gut still tingling, and left Heimee to make love to his cup of acid in privacy. The room was small, and the ceiling was low. It contained a single unmade bed, a tiny chest of drawers, and an even smaller bookshelf. I browsed the books. *The History of Aviz and Algirin*—that could be interesting. *The Secrets of Ancient Casks. Tales of Salamorin and the Great White Aramaz.* No way! A Salamorin book? Score! *The Light of the Wild.* And *Great Scotch: Steep, Peat, Distill.* I guess I was lucky not all of them were about whisky, and I vaguely wondered if all the books downstairs were. But that didn't matter because I was about to read the *Tales of Salamorin.*

I grabbed the book and sat in bed. Oh, it was severely comfortable. From that angle, the slanted ceiling seemed like it could crash down on me at any moment, and the crooked diamond window, revealing the day's end, threatened to fall off at a moment's notice.

I opened the book, and the walls began closing in on me. Dad used to read me Salamorin's tales come bedtime. At least a year had gone by since the mountain took him, and I missed him so much. So damned much. Him, Mom. I missed—

I balled my fists and gritted my teeth. Somewhere beyond that bedroom, there was a mountain I had to find. But first, I had to grow stronger. Taller would be a plus. And I had to wait for the right time. It'd be foolish to face the shattered mountains unprepared again. Meanwhile, what could be the harm in helping Heimee? I owed him, did I not? Besides, how hard could making such a vile beverage be?

Chapter 10

Shovel, Pump

Ludik

Heimee put me to work the very next day—my first day as a master distiller's apprentice. From the very beginning, I wasn't too fond of my new title, especially after Heimee introduced me to a mountain of barley, a couple of spades, and two wheelbarrows. I had never seen so much cereal in my life, and I grew up around farms. To make matters worse, despite the wintery day outside, the air inside the malting building was thick, humid, and sweet.

I yawned as I reached for the spade and regretted it instantly. Breathing made me feel like a bee drowning in its own honey. "I'm alright," I lied. I had, in fact, spent the night lost in the adventures of Salamorin and his white aramaz—a four-legged bird that can summon storms. Salamorin gathered a large army to face the hordes of evil demons at the service of the treacherous Queen of Sandar, who had ordered Salamorin's family executed. When everything seemed lost, he rode the white aramaz into battle and summoned the biggest storm the world had ever seen, only to... oh right, whisky.

"Sure you are. Normally, we have a team to do this sort of thing," Heimee signed, "but since there's so little barley this year, I thought, why not do it ourselves?"

I pondered how the mountain of barley in front of me could ever be considered 'little'. I mean, how much barley did it take to be considered a lot of barley?

"First, we need to fill the steep tanks, then pump water in." Heimee pointed to two large tanks occupying the end of the room. "The water temperature needs to be precise. I'll show you how we do that later. What do you say? Since you're so fresh, why not make it a race? A little competition always makes this more fun. I'll make it easy on you; if you manage one barrow in the time it takes for me to take two, you win."

I could do that. I took the spade into my hands and shoved it into the barley. "Prepare for defeat, old man."

I lost miserably.

For starters, I couldn't even fill and toss a spade full of barley. Heimee dug through the heap like a wild beast, while all I managed to do was watch helplessly as all the barley poured from the sides of the spade before even making it to the wheelbarrow. Once I finally filled the damned thing, I couldn't even lift it. In a short while, my arm muscles turned to overcooked rice, and my back muscles decided they'd had enough of being soft and squishy and turned to stone. Soon Heimee was ahead by four wheelbarrows. "This is stupid," I said, shoving the spade aside. "There must be a better way of doing this."

"Don't be such a sore loser."

"Urrghh." I nearly turned my back on him and left. Maybe that's what I should've done. But he had been nothing but nice to me, and it was my duty to stick it out. A couple of hours later, we were done, and I had lost thirty-two to three-ish. After that, it was time to fill the tanks. Fortunately, that part was a little easier.

I'm kidding. It was excruciating.

The water had to be pumped, and Heimee promptly volunteered me for the job. If my arms had become a soggy mess, now it was my shoulders' turn. But to my credit, I didn't quit. So I pumped and pumped and pumped until the blisters I'd earned from all the shoveling popped.

"This is a nifty invention," Heimee said, holding a wood rod with numbers carved on the side like a ruler. A glass tube ran up the middle, ending in a bubble of red liquid. Heimee tapped the bubble. "That's alcohol. It expands when heated and shoots up the glass. These numbers here tell us how hot or cold something is. It's called a thermometer. The cretins who make these haven't agreed on a universal scale. They keep coming up with new iterations, which they name after themselves—what a bunch of idiots. So I call these numbers: Heimees. Why not? Five Heimees is the temperature we want."

He dipped the red bubble into the water and waited. The red line went from room temperature—about 4.5 Heimees—to 0 Heimees from the frigid, toad-infested pond at the back of the building. Heimee poured pots of hot water he had been heating up, while I stirred the tank with a giant metal spoon.

"We come back here in a few hours," Heimee signed. "We drain the water and refill the tanks."

"Can't wait."

"Don't fret; it builds character."

As soon as my prickling back touched the soft mattress, I passed out.

Come dinner time, Heimee shoved me awake and signed, "Bastard's bother, close that damned window."

Blissfully he didn't wake me for the second round of pumping, and I didn't protest. But what I was ready to protest about was dinner—pork and barley stew. After getting acquainted with barley all morning, I wasn't too eager to shove it down my mouth. But boy, was I wrong. As it turns out, a full day of heavy labor turns you into a gobbling machine. I barely chewed the food, gulping down spoonful after spoonful.

"Easy there," Heimee signed. "There's more where that came from."

"What joy awaits us after steeping?"

"We spread it on the floor."

I nodded sagely, having no idea what to make of it.

After supper, I headed back to my room. It was nice and warm, so I opened the window. Since Leftover, I couldn't sleep right in a warm room. I hoped to finish the Salamorin book but ended up reading the same sentence a dozen times before drifting into a deep sleep.

When I opened my eyes, Heimee stood above me, frowning. Daylight flooded the room, and my brain had turned to molasses. "It's freezing in here," Heimee signed and closed the window. "You are going to fall ill. It's winter, for Bastard's sake."

I groggily sat up and regretted every single second of it. I had experienced much physical pain until that moment in time and had been sure that nothing could surprise me. I was wrong. Leaving the bed took a feat of inhuman strength and willpower. Even my forehead muscles ached.

After breakfast, we were back at the steeps. Heimee dug his hand into the barley and pulled out a handful, feeling its weight and generally considering it. "See how puffed it got?"

I nodded.

"Means it's ready."

We drained the tanks and grabbed a couple of spades. I assumed it would be easier this time around, with the added experience and all, but that turned out to be plain wishful thinking. Not only did my sore muscles refuse to keep up, but the soaked grain was much, much heavier. The only advantage seemed to be that it clumped together instead of falling out from the sides. Although, I'm not entirely sure if advantage is the right way to describe it. Afterward, we pushed the wheelbarrows up ramps, all the way up to the third floor.

"If you're going to be sick," Heimee signed once we reached our destination, "do it in a bucket, not on the barley."

I shook my head. "I'm fine," I signed, pressing my lips together to plug my mouth. "You do know there's plenty of floor space next to steeping tanks. Why not drop the barley there?"

"You see that hole in the wall? That's a chute that leads directly to the kiln. After the barley germinates, all there's left to do is to push it in."

I wasn't entirely satisfied with his answer. How would less work later help me now?

"The trick is," Heimee continued, ignoring my moping, "you tilt the barrow and pull it in one smooth motion." Heimee exemplified, producing a perfectly even barley line like a painter's brushstroke.

I tilted my wheelbarrow forward and watched as all the barley clumped in a heap in front of me. I began to suspect Heimee had taken me into his service so that I could amuse him.

"Don't be so grumpy," he signed. "You'll get the hang of it. But for now, here's a rake. Also, stop being so pale. You're sucking the joy out of the room."

So, I raked the barley heap into a somewhat even layer and went back for more. I'm not going to lie. I didn't want to look weak in front of the man who'd saved my life, but I took every chance I found to dawdle. Raking was a great excuse to take a break from shoveling or pushing the wheelbarrow up the ramps. It took the whole day, but we got it done. And I have to say, I was grateful for it, regardless of how sick I felt. It got my mind off things. I went through the day without thinking about Mom and Dad and the other terrible things that had happened to me. That night, I slept like a rock, leaving me no time to weep or feel sorry for myself. But most of all, I felt proud for doing something hard and not giving up.

The following day, I woke up with Heimee at the foot of the bed again, closing the cracked window. "If you want to freeze, that's on you, but this sucks the heat out of the whole house. At the very least, clog the door with something."

"Heimee," I said. "I don't think I can move. Can you help me out of bed?"

Heimee smirked. "Quit whining. We need only to rake the barley today to let it breathe. It'll feel like a day off."

Chapter 11

Burrow's Friend

Ludik

"You have to go to town," Heimee said over breakfast.

"Why?"

"Otto's sick. You need to buy medicine."

"Again? He was sick for days on our way here."

"He's not a bright ox. Keeps his mouth where his butt should be. Here, seven bolts should cover it," Heimee extended seven guillings to me over the table. "There is an apothecary in *Bum-hole*, a sweet old lady. You're going to love her. She knows what Otto needs."

I happily strolled down to town, the sun caressing my face. For one, it was much better than spending the day raking; for another, walking has a way of soothing the spirit.

An hour later, I entered Guillings Burrow. It wasn't much bigger than Bastard's Bank. It was, however, much filthier, its streets paved with mud-baked hay and dung. Where I came from, the stonework was straight and symmetric, unlike Burrow, which was crooked and ugly. My guess is that construction only began after the stonemasons visited every tavern—of which I counted six. Six! One tavern for every tenth household. I wondered how much of Heimee's business was done right at his doorstep.

One such building had a wooden plaque bleached by time reading:

APOTHECARY. I passed through the bead curtains inside. The dim light forced my eyes to adjust. A funky smell like a bog mixed with jerked meats, cheap perfumes, and spices terrorized my nose.

Jars of pickled things lined the walls: vegetables, animal claws, animal tails, ears, whole animals, herbs, and hearts. One contained baby ekkuh's heads tightly packed together. The ceiling was a plethora of dried things: all kinds of leaves, several types of chilies, whole skinless jerked animals—of what kind I could not tell—hens perhaps. Perhaps human babies. It creeped the caboodle out of me. Large open bags revealed several ground spices, leaving little room to walk on. One of the labels read ground giregaro genitals: suitable for headaches.

No, thank you.

I tiptoed around, afraid to stumble upon something and touch something by accident. *Were those eyes in a jar?* A wrinkled, frowny face followed me from over the counter. The old lady wore black robes, her skin pale and hairy, and generally looked as if she was a thousand years old. "Uhdo matcha be?" the old lady said. I had a hard time reading her trembling lips.

I pressed on. "Heimee said you'd know what Otto, our ox, needs. He ate something bad."

"Him, uh, oh haw. Sneerarup."

I didn't even try making sense of that. So I shook my head and touched my ear. "I'm sorry I'm de—"

"Arya retarded?" Now, that's a sentence I can always pick up.

I sighed. "No. Just deaf."

"Cannya talk normal?"

I stared at her.

"Ya look retarded to me. What we ol' stinky trunk wanagan?"

"Our ox, Otto, is stomach sick."

She regarded me over her pointy nose. "Ugon. Who matcha be?" I think she said.

"Ludik."

My name provoked a heavy frown as if she disliked it dearly or suffered a sudden stroke. "Shada getcha something foya?" She leaned over the counter in a conspiratory manner. "I'veroot here, poisonous efeatan raw, bah cooked, kamakya whole."

That conversation was making my head in. "You mean, cure my deafness?"

She shook her head. "Just the retardedness."

I blinked. "Just the ox medicine, please."

She creased her wrinkles, chewed air with her toothless mouth and disappeared behind a bead curtain.

While I waited, I continued to peruse the bizarre collection further and noticed a girl queuing behind me. Her lips moved. Was she talking to me? Oh. Not again.

"I'm sorry, I didn't catch that," I said.

She had beautiful almond eyes. Freckles spotted her tanned cheeks, and her dark braided hair fell over a long pale-blue jacket. She stepped toward me.

Was my mouth open? Was I staring? I glanced away. She was saying something again. Why couldn't I read her lips? I was looking right at them. Then I felt a bit invasive. How long had I been staring? Why was my face getting so hot? She said something else. Boy, her lips were pretty. As she rolled her eyes and gestured toward the counter, I panicked.

I squinted, trying to make sense of what she was trying to say. She stepped even closer, grabbed me by the shoulders, and spun me. The old lady gazed at me, shaking her head slowly.

"Retarded," she said, followed by a bunch of stuff I couldn't be bothered with.

I tossed the seven guillings on the counter and took the herb jar in my arms. The apothecary slid two bolts back, and I pocketed them, turning to the girl. I wanted to say something, anything—since when was I mute? Oh, Bastard's bother, what was wrong with me?

She tilted her head slightly and smiled. Her lips were moving again. This was my chance. Sweat formed on my brow. Bastard, I was hot. Then she gestured with the palm of her hand in front of me like she was pressing it against an invisible pane. Oh, I knew that one, "Stay."

I nodded.

She stepped around me and addressed the mean old hag behind the counter. I couldn't look away from her—the girl, not the old hag. She was mesmerizing.

The old hag brought her a jar of gray gunk of some kind.

The girl's hands shot around as she spoke with that dehydrated piece of human composite who'd crossed her arms, giving the girl an unconvinced look. The girl repeatedly landed her fist on the counter, and the apothecary sneered in return. Arms flailed and arched in the air, and somehow things were exchanged.

The girl swiveled on her feet, a cocky smile on her lips as she held her jar. She motioned for me to follow her outside the museum of revolting grossness.

Her lips moved again. "You must be new here."

Yes, I did it! I read her lips. Now what? *Uhhh.*

She waited for me to react and then extended one hand to me. "I'm Brinn."

I puffed my chest and shook her hand. "Ludik. It's a pleasure to make your acquaintance." Who was I?

She bit her lower lip. "Lud, huh? Are you well?"

"Yes, you have excellent lips." I wanted to slap my face. "I mean, I read lips. Yours are excellent." Much better.

She tilted her head, her mouth producing an oh. "You're deaf. Never met someone deaf before. What's it like? To live without sound, I mean?"

"It could be worse. I could be legless. But I guess that's what the legless say about the deaf."

Brinn giggled, or maybe she had hiccups. It's hard to tell. "You have a nice voice."

Did I read that correctly? Nice voice? Was she deaf as well? "I'm often complimented about it."

"What brings you to Burrow?"

"Heimee—"

"The master distiller, huh? Oh, so you're the one he found up north."

"How—"

"Small town," she offered.

"I see. Listen, I have to take this to our ox. But I would like to meet you again."

"Why don't you come ice skate with me tomorrow? We have to make the best of it before the snow comes."

"Great. Thanks."

Brinn smiled politely. "You can always find me at the bakery if we miss each other."

I bowed for some reason, then awkwardly tried to make up for my clumsiness. I walked home like there was no ground beneath my feet. I'd made a friend, and she didn't find me weird. That's an absolute win in my book. I wondered how Graze was doing. Suppose he was learning pottery with his dad. I wish I could tell him I was learning to make whisky. I bet he would get a good laugh out of that.

CHAPTER 12

FROZEN LAKE

LUDIK

"HEIMEE?" I asked as he grabbed a handful of barley from the floor and examined it closely. "I met this girl yesterday, Brinn. Do you know her?"

"No girls in the house. Now look, see that?"

I looked at the grain: it had sprouted. "Uh?"

"This malt's ready for the kiln," Heimee said. "So let me get this straight, you stroll around town for five minutes and just happen to stumble upon another orphan? Do you have a special calling or something?"

I stared at him.

"No girls in the house."

"I met her at the apothecary."

"Oh, oh. Oh. Oh, no. You're fond of her. You're gonna go dumb on me, aren't you?"

I crossed my arms. "That's not it."

"Then why are you asking?"

I pursed my lips. "Is it time to shovel again?"

Heimee smirked. I think. It's always hard to tell with a face like his. "Start pushing the grain down the chute."

We fetched our trusty spades, but before we got started, Heimee continued, "She lives with her aunt. Mean old hag. If you liked the apothecary, you're going to love her aunt. Bakes a mean loaf, but if Brinn's anything like her, I don't want her anywhere near here. Is she pretty?"

I blushed. "You said she's an orphan. Did she lose her family in the Collapse too?"

"Worse. Her village was raided." Heimee contorted. "Stupid war. If only people stopped reacting to every little provocation, this world would be a far better place."

"War?"

Heimee squinted at me. "You do know there's a war going on, right?"

I kind of did. I heard about it at the camp, though I failed to grasp its dimension or severity.

"It's unfortunate what happened to the Kallaks," Heimee continued. "Then again, there's plenty of injustice going around. Just keep pushing the green malt."

"Are we safe here?" I asked.

Heimee stopped shoveling and shrugged. "This is more a pissing contest than anything else. An absolute moron sits on the throne, and this is the crap he churns out. The king's as clever as what comes out of Otto's ass. It's Munika who runs the country. Do you think a man bred for war will file for peace? I'd bet you he's the one poking the wasps' nest. The Erosomites aren't interested in an all-out war. If they were, we would all be speaking Erom by now. That doesn't mean they won't invade if we give them a chance. There must be at least one warmongering idiot in their assembly, and that's all it takes. But trouble will only find us here if Fort Kelmir falls. Guillinsbaer's garrison will protect Guillinsbaer, sure enough, but the surrounding villages—

"You know what? This conversation is hard enough with a drink in my hand." Heimee clutched his spade and began shoving barley down the chute like he was mad at it.

The chute led to the kiln on the adjacent building, the one with the mushroom chimney.

Once the malted barley or green malt—it had changed its name though I could not figure out why—was in the kiln, we spread it evenly across the floor. The room smelled of smoke, no surprise there, but not the wrong kind of smoke that hurts your eyes and throat, but pleasant, nutty, and woody. It reminded me of breakfast: toasted bread, tea, cookies, and fresh butter. A long rod with paddles stood on raised rails. Its purpose was to stir the barley to ensure even smoking and drying.

Fortunately for me, Otto was up and ready to operate the paddle rod. Later, Heimee attached Otto to a wheel that rolled the rod from end to end in the smoking room, airing the barley.

Next, Heimee and I fed the furnace with a precise mix of peat and deadwood that he meticulously calculated by frowning a lot and scratching his chin.

"I was planning on meeting her tomorrow," I said.

"Who?"

"Brinn."

"We should be done after lunch. Don't fall in love! There's nothing worse than a love-struck boy. Or any love-struck buffoon. Love strikes you dumb."

After the smoked and dried malt cooled down enough to be worked with, we shoved it down another chute that led to an Otto-operated mill to grind the grain into coarse flour. Heimee pulled a crank, and the barley poured into a huge copper pot called the mash tun to be mixed with water. And so, it was time to pump again; pump until my arms turned to overcooked noodles.

Then it all got very technical. So I'll sum it up. We heated the mash tun to about twenty Heimees by burning more peat beneath it and stirring it constantly for about half an hour, pulling on a rod that turned blades inside. That was another great exercise, let me tell you. We collected the resulting decoction by opening a tap and draining it through the perforated bottom into another tank. We pumped fresh water into the mash tun and repeated the process at twenty-three Heimees. And a third time at twenty-five Heimees.

Then came the really fun part: shovel the spent grain out of the tank and clean it. It was moist and damp, and the air inside the tank was even sweeter than before. According to Heimee, the spent grain was great cattle feed. We kept some for Otto and would sell the rest to nearby farms.

Ah, then we pumped the decoctions from the temporary storage tank underground into one of two huge tanks called washbacks. There, Heimee mixed the product of our labor—now called wash—with yeast coupled with a big initial stir to dissolve it. After that, we only had to stir it from time to time.

Heimee cleaned the sweat off his brow. "Got a brand new batch of barley this morning. What do you reckon? Should we get to it?"

If I had to do that again, I would surely die or, worse, puke.

Heimee laughed. "Tomorrow it is."

In the evening, I found two more of Salamorin's tales hidden among a sea of whisky books. One was even a book Dad used to read to me when I was little. It made me feel close to him. I missed them so much. I wanted to devour them in one breath, but, of course, I didn't read a single word. I opened the book, vaguely saw some letters, and woke up the following day.

Heimee wasn't too pleased about the icicles hanging from the drapes, but it was so cozy snuggling under the warm blankets knowing the world was cold and austere outside of them. I just couldn't help opening the window and invite the cold in.

"If you sleep out, you'll find the door locked," Heimee signed to me after we steeped the new load of grain. It was surprisingly easier this time around.

"I'll be home before nightfall," I assured him. I had no doubts about my timing; it's not like I'm a great conversationalist after dark.

The lake was bigger than I expected, mostly frozen, with sparse trees surrounding it. It wasn't full of kids like I feared it would be. I counted ten—some playing whilp, some ice skating. I found Brinn sitting on a rock, tying skates to her shoes.

"Lud, you came," she said. Then she continued to speak while tying her skates, so I couldn't see her face. I didn't want to look like a fool, so I nodded. She smiled and passed me a pair of skates.

It dawned on me that I shouldn't have nodded. Well, how hard could ice skating be?

A big kid, older than me, eyebrows bent on consuming his eyes, came over. "Hey," he said, "heed on more pay wilb, wanna-oh?"

Some people just don't know how to move their lips properly. Time to investigate. He had a whilp stick in his hand, and he casually nodded to his friends who waited with a whilp wheel. I processed that information in my brain and—

"What's wrong with ya?" the kid said. That sentence was always an easy one to translate, and as he said it, my brain decoded his previous statement: *need one more to play whilp, wanna join?*

I wiggled the skates and shrugged. "Sorry, going ice skating."

His eyes emerged from his overcast eyebrows, and he promptly called his friends while wiggling a plump finger at my face. Even at the refugee camp, I didn't have to endure this kind of behavior. Two kids came to his side.

He moved his lips with exaggeration now. I bet he was talking loudly too. Like a jerk, but I got what he said. "He sounds like he swallowed a hot potato."

"I'm deaf," I said patiently.

The boys all cracked up, hands on their bellies, slapping their knees. I gritted my teeth. Why do people like them exist? What's the point?

"You'll never need an umbrella with eyebrows like those."

The laughter subsided, and I got punched in the eye.

I stumbled, falling on my bum. The big kid stepped closer, ready to kick me, but Brinn got in the way, arms flailing. She cocked a finger at the kid's face, then at me before pressing it into his chest.

"He started it," I read on his lips with one eye closed and in pain—a near-impossible feat. I was kind of proud of it.

Brinn slapped Eyebrows across the face, and for a moment, the big kid appeared to deflate, hand rubbing his reddening cheek. He looked at me with fury and turned away, taking his friends with him.

Brinn extended her hand to me. "Never mind Moreen. He's a moron."

I touched my sore eye lightly, it felt bloated and hot, before taking her hand. "Yeah, but friends call him Moreen, for short."

"You should put some snow on that," Brinn said and scooped a handful of snow, pressing it to my eye. "Keep it there for a minute or so."

"I never skated before."

She took my hand and led me out onto the ice. "It's easy. I'll teach you." She skated backward, holding my hands. "Are you related to Heimee?" It was hard to concentrate on her lips long enough without losing balance, and I had already fallen so many times my bum was as sore as my eye.

I shook my head and fell. "He saved my life," I said, wincing.

Brinn pursed her lips as she helped me back up. "He seems nice."

"That's a strange way to spell grumpy."

She looked down and tapped the back of my knees. I think she wanted me to bend them. I couldn't be sure. It would be easier if she faced me while she talked. It's always very frustrating when people do that, but somehow, when she did it, it was kind of cute.

"Brinn, would you like to learn sign language?"

She blinked. Then she regarded me for a very long time. That's the sort of question you should never ask someone you just met. You know, you should always start small and talk about the weather for a month at least. Get to know her full name, maybe even her favorite color. Then, if the time is right, you can drop the, 'Hey, would you mind learning an impossibly challenging language because lip-reading is a bit of an inconvenience to me? Thanks.'

"Sure!" she said.

I was taken aback. What? Was it that easy? I should've done this with everyone I've ever met.

"Then we can share secret messages!" Her eyes glittered with joy.

"Yes, that," I said, scratching the back of my head, which made me lose balance and fall again.

Brinn laughed as she helped me up. "Is it hard to lip-read? You always take some time before you answer."

"It is very hard. It takes all my attention. And I can only read about a third of what people say, and I have to guess the rest—take clues from context, facial expressions, and such. Then some people talk like this," I open my mouth as wide as possible, "and others like this," I remained placid, barely moving my lips.

"But my lips are easy to read, right?"

"You are a great enunciator," I said. "But you kind of move a lot."

"Oh! I was talking to your knees just now, wasn't I? Do you want me to talk slower?"

"No, talk normally. I hate when people do that, or when they talk louder. Actually, I don't hate it. It makes it super easy to tell if they're idiots."

"Were you born this way?"

I shook my head. "It happened slowly. I'm lucky in a sordid way. If I had been born deaf, I don't think I would've been able to lip-read."

Brinn looked over her shoulder. A commotion brewed at the edge of the ice shelf. "I think someone fell in the water," she said and pushed me on my skates over to see.

Some appeared to shout, while others covered their mouths in horror. I followed their stare. A boy splashed about in the frigid lake, desperately trying to hold on to a chunk of ice, but it kept flipping on him. The current pulled him away and his soaked clothes weren't doing him any favors.

"Take off your clothes!" I shouted, but my voice must've drowned in the noise. I guess that was a poor choice of words.

Why was no one helping him? Couldn't they see he was in shock? I untied the skates, took my shoes off, and removed my jacket.

A hand grabbed my shoulder. "Ludik, the water is freezing," Brinn said.

I shrugged her off and continued stripping until only my breaches remained.

Brinn clutched my arm. "You'll drown too."

I wrenched my arm free and jumped in the water. The shock hit me like an old friend with a knife in his hand. The lake was deep and so murky I couldn't see the bottom. I surfaced and spun around but couldn't find the boy. On the ice, the kids pointed, and I followed their directions.

"Yes, there," they seemed to say.

I dove under, deeper with each stroke. Dad had taught me how to swim in the river in our old village. The one that almost killed us. He said it was important that I learned how to swim, that a lot of kids are curious about the water and drown because no one's watching. A quick and silent death would not be his son's fate.

I saw a brownish blur squirming in the murk. I swam to it and got hold of his jacket. I kicked hard to push us up, but his clothes made him too heavy. When we breached the surface, my lungs burned for air. Whenever I tried to rest my legs, the weight of his clothes dragged us back down. I pulled his jacket off while we sank. The boy offered little help in his rescue, shivering uncontrollably. I swam back to the surface, arms stiff from all the hard work. "Help me get him up," I shouted as I reached the edge of the ice.

The kids inched forward a little but not enough to reach me, afraid to step on thinner ice. I couldn't hoist the boy by myself. Were these his friends?

Then, Moreen got on all fours and neared the edge. His massive hand reached out and grabbed the kid by the collar of his shirt, pulling him out of the water while his friends held him by the waist. I pulled myself up, sliding like a salamander, while the ice cracked and wobbled under me. When I reached thicker ice, Brinn met me with my jacket and rolled it around my shoulders.

I glanced at the boy while Moreen shook him like a rattling toy. The boy had stopped moving. Moreen then slapped him so hard across the face that I thought I heard it. The boy gulped for air as if that was the first breath he'd ever taken, arms and legs spasming, and began to shiver frantically again.

"Take his clothes off," I said. "Get him warm."

Finally, the remaining kids began to offer help in the form of scarves, beanies, and jackets that Moreen used to wrap the boy in. Then he lifted the kid in his arms, stared at me with his ugly face, and gave a simple yet respectful nod, as if he was the one who had to forgive me. There are some people I will never understand. Some words escaped his lips, but I was too tired to put any real effort into reading them, so I nodded back. Nods get you very far in the deaf world.

"That was intense," Brinn said. "Aren't you cold?"

I didn't want to get sicker than I had to, so I turned around, removed my wet breeches, and dressed up my clothes.

"Don't worry," Brinn said when I turned back to her. "I only peeked a little."

I don't know if I blushed. I didn't think it was possible to blush at that moment, but I felt like I blushed. "You know, I don't think ice skating is for me."

"How are you even talking after swimming in that water? I am happy that Poleen is safe, but Bastard's bother, you could've died."

I gave her a faint smile. "I'm used to being cold. Want to meet up tomorrow?"

"Only if it is this exciting."

"I'll do my best to live up to your expectations."

"It's nice to see you're making friends." Heimee stared at my purple eye after passing a cup of warm tea. "I hope you deserved it."

I told him what had happened. He heard me without interrupting, cranking his jaw and drinking his glass of snake venom.

"Ah, Ludik, the deaf hero of Bum-hole," he signed at last and raised his glass in my honor. "You could've died too, you know. Did you somehow forget how I found you?"

"What was I supposed to do? Let him die?"

"That's what the other kids were doing."

"Then why didn't you leave me on the side of the road? That's what the other grown-ups did."

"Hardly a day goes by I don't regret it." Heimee took a sip from his glass and smiled. "I'm glad you have a kind heart, kid. A dumb and stubborn heart, but kind. That counts for more than you know. You still look as cold as a mountain top. Do you know what warms you right up?"

"Whisky?" I took a guess.

"Whisky," Heimee said, raising his cup. He took a long draught and passed the glass to me.

"I'm fine, thanks."

"Suit yourself. I find this won't be an excuse to skip work tomorrow?"

"I wouldn't miss it."

The next day, the first brew was ready. The sweet wash turned into a kind of ale. Heimee gave me some to taste. It didn't kill me, not like the twenty-year-old Heims, but I concluded that alcohol was not for me.

We sieved it several times until we got a clear liquid that we transferred, via pumping, into the wash still. The wash still is this very tall wizard's hat, entirely made of copper that ends in a large copper tube where the alcohol condenses and collects. Alcohol evaporates at a lower temperature than water, so Heimee was very careful about the temperature inside the still. To be honest, it all sounded like magic to me. We put a gross but not so deadly liquid on one side, and it comes out the other ready to dissolve metal.

To my astonishment, we repeated the process in a second, smaller still, called the spirit still.

The spirit went in the still and out came a liquid Heimee treated with the utmost respect. He didn't offer me a sip, and he didn't try it himself. Apparently, if you don't know what you're doing, it can turn you blind.

Heimee studied the temperatures and turned a crank dividing the pouring spirit into cuts. He mumbled something about foreshots, hearts, and tails. I didn't pay attention; I wasn't taking any risks involving blindness.

"You won't go blind by simply being close to it. I know what I'm doing," Heimee said as he dropped some kind of floating device into the fresh spirit. "Perfect. Now all we need is to pour it into barrels."

"Why do you do this?" I asked. The whole process dumbfounded me.

Heimee regarded me for a long time, nodded to himself, and sat on an old wooden stool he usually used to reach high shelves. He motioned for me to sit next to him.

I felt a harrowing lecture coming but did as told.

"That's a good question," Heimee signed. "Do you know what it's called when someone doesn't give up and, despite grueling adversity, still gets what they want?"

"Stubbornness?" I prodded.

Heimee chuckled. "Close. But not quite. The word you're looking for is perseverance. This land was supposed to be utterly worthless. But it's my land. Bequeathed to me by my parents. Any other fool would have sold it for a bolt and moved on." Heimee looked around from the washbacks to the stills before nodding to himself. "But I turned it into a household name. I didn't give up. Through sweat and hard labor, I produced one of the most sought beverages you can find. Sold on every establishment. Present on every worthy spirit shelf across the kingdom. It wasn't easy. Perfecting this art took many attempts. Many, many failures. But I did not give up. I persevered. Every bottle I produce is proof of that.

"If what you're trying to accomplish doesn't involve hardship, sacrifice, pain, if it doesn't require determination, if it's so easy anyone could do it, is it really worth it? No. But if you want to make something known, something great, something right; if you want to make this a better world or leave something behind that did not exist before you set out to do it, you can only do it with perseverance. Am I making sense to you?"

"I guess," I said. "But why whisky?"

Heimee smiled. "I kind of stumbled upon it. Maybe that's what the Bastard wanted and saw in me the right man for the job. He certainly drinks his fair share. But mostly, I do it because I love it—because it feels right. It wasn't always the case, though." He placed a hand on my shoulder and looked me in the eye. "You're stubborn. That's a good quality. Annoying but good. Don't let anyone tell you otherwise."

I nodded, of course. But in the end, I concluded that Heimee had to be insane. You have to be properly mad to make whisky—turning barley into a lethal mouthwash and then having it mature well into puberty in oak barrels stored in a damp, dark cellar is utterly insane.

The worst part was that I was beginning to enjoy it.

Chapter 13

Agricultural Consultant

Ariel

ARIEL SAT on the barley field, collecting soil and seed samples.

"I did as ye said last season," Billy said, crossing his arms over his voluptuous belly. "Nothin's workin'."

It was a foggy morning. What did she expect, a sunny day in Scotland? That would be shy of absurd. "Weather's unpredictable," Ariel said, "and the soil's chemistry changes over time. It's alive, you know, so each season is bound to have a few surprises."

Billy glanced at his old tractor, rust collecting around the frame. "Thought I'd save a penny, that's all. Lamby there needs a few repairs."

Ariel regarded Lamby. Repairing that jalopy would cost him at least a few thousand quid; it was only a matter of time until it flopped belly up and died. Billy needed a new tractor, and a good one was as expensive as her Aston. Ariel was not in the business of ruining farmers' lives unless, of course, they proved to be a boggin dobber like Mickey McDougal, in which case she would gladly watch his crops die. But not Billy. She liked Billy. He was honest and humble and polite—her kind of person.

"So what do ye reckon? The wee bastards all dyin'. It's this global warmin' nonsense, I tell ye. It's too hot, too humid, too wet, too dry, there's never balance."

Ariel stowed her samples in a plastic bag and got up, buttoning her yellow tweed jacket. "Let me get this to lab, and I'll get back to ye tomorrow. And Billy," she said in the most comforting voice she could muster. "It'll be alright. Have I ever let ye down?"

"S'pose not," Billy said, suppressing a pout.

"Tell ye what, fix Lamby up, and I'll subtract the amount from my fee."

Billy's eyes glittered like a cat's after smelling a freshly opened food can. "Yae'd do that?"

"Of course. Honestly, Billy, Lamby's a fine lass, but it's time for her to retire." Ariel's bank accounts had enough money to live comfortably, and Billy was only one of her customers. In the end, she would still make more than enough. Agricultural consultants, the greedy bastards, charge astronomical amounts of money to poor farmers. Ariel didn't like that, but she couldn't afford to harm her credibility by being cheaper. God no. Despite none of the other consultants ever coming close to her results. And that was something Billy Prentice, like all her other clients, was well aware of. "If ye decide to buy a new tractor, I'll even consider waiving my share this season. With one condition," Ariel lifted a finger before Billy could protest, "I expect Maggie to bake me one of her butter tarts."

Billy wobbled, unsure whether to jump or crouch, and stayed somewhere in between. "A tart? She'll bake ye a dozen tarts. Hundreds. Tarts for life, I say."

They walked back to Lamby and drove back to the farmhouse, where Ariel had parked her car, but Billy told her to wait before she could bid him farewell. He rushed inside the house and popped back out, holding a bottle. Ariel knew what it was—the sensual contour of the green glass, the humble white label. Ariel could taste the smokiness already; there was always room for one more bottle in her collection.

"I know yae're fond of them peaty," he said as he presented her with a bottle of Laphroaig 18.

"I try not to hide it just for such occasions." Ariel accepted the box. "This is very generous. Thank you, Billy."

"Nah. Had that bottle there for months collectin' dust. It's like lickin' an ashtray if ye ask me. I'm more of a Dalwhinnie man."

Hmm, Dalwhinnie, Ariel thought as she considered the bottle. "Well, then. Lucky me."

"When you return, yae'll have Maggie's butter tart waitin' for ye."

"Send her my regards, will ye? I have to run now."

Ariel got into her Aston Martin DB9, nestled in the white-leather seat and turned on the seat warmer. She had bought it second-hand to add seriousness to her profile as a prosperous agricultural consultant. Although that was one part of her appearance she didn't mind maintaining. Didn't mind at all. She drove straight home, stopping only a mile or two away to dump her collected samples in a trash bin. There was enough garbage at her place as it was.

Her house wasn't fancy by any terms, but most would call it idyllic: a stone house perched at the edge of a lake, like the cottages she used to ransack back when she was a runaway. The only thing she wanted from a house was seclusion and enough comfort for her and her cat, Bubbles. And seclusion is something one can find in abundance in rural Scotland.

Bubbles strutted to her as she opened the door and brushed up against her legs.

"Stop that! Ye know how much trouble I have removing fur from my pants every day?"

Ariel had never wanted a house pet; too much trouble. But she found a stray cat at her doorstep one morning, fur flaking away like a dilapidated house, skinny legs, and snot bubbling out its nose. What a poor excuse for a creature. Ariel had no choice but to take the thing to the vet and give it a name. And to be fair, Bubbles wasn't so bad—long golden fur, yellow eyes like hers and a tendency for nibbling her fingers when she stroked its chin. Stupid cat.

Ariel checked her schedule. She would have to devise some cockamamie excuse to fix Billy's crops. Would sprinkling sawdust over the soil be too absurd? Maybe. She could sleep on it; besides, tomorrow's first order of business would be visiting the McLennan's farm. Nothing should grow at the McLennan's, but they supplied a friend's distillery with some of the best barley in the land for an above-market price, thanks to her. For some reason that perhaps a true agricultural engineer could explain, if the crops survived the highly rocky and acidic soil of the McLennans' farm, the yielded barley would come out plump and sweet. Perfect for whisky-making.

The only problem was that Colin McLennan didn't like her very much. He had been suspicious of her from the moment they met years before when Ariel told him she was twenty-seven. In reality, she had been only a couple of months shy of turning twenty. Still, you can't have a degree in agricultural engineering and field experience at the age most teenagers are out getting heavily drunk and smashing their parents' cars or spreading STDs. Or both. Not that she wasn't much different from said teenagers, but at least she wasn't as stupid. Or so she liked to believe. Now she was twenty-six, which meant the McLennans thought her to be thirty-five. In time, Colin had tamed his incredulity and reached the profitable conclusion he didn't mind being lied to. After all, Ariel had turned unfarmable land into a prosperous one. And at the end of each year, he raised Ariel's bonus, afraid she'd wander off to greener pastures.

Ariel opened a can of food for Bubbles and tossed a ready-made meal in the microwave. "Rats," she muttered as she noticed her house plants. "Why are ye always like this?" she rebuked the potted daisies and Japanese lilies. "Dandelions flourish in concrete pavements, but if I forget to water ye for a few days, ye pull this tantrum."

Ariel dropped a glass of water on each vase, then placed her hands over the plants and poured light over them. The sagging leaves absorbed the warm glow, and a moment later, the plants returned to full vitality. "That's better, innit? Now, let's drop the drama, shall we? Look at Bubbles. If I forget to feed him for a day or two, he goes out to hunt mice or pillage a dumpster or something."

Bubbles purred as he munched his heavily processed food when the microwave beeped. Ariel opened the door, and the scent of chicken tikka masala filled the room. She put the food and cutlery on a tray and took a beer from the fridge.

Ariel brought the tray to her bed. She had no use for the bedroom and had never bothered to buy a couch. What for? She didn't have many friends, and the ones she maintained weren't the visiting kind. If now and then a love affair came through the door, he would have to love her for who she was, wouldn't he? A king-sized bed in front of the largest flat screen she could find—now that was the dream.

Ariel wasn't fond of public television broadcasts and would rather watch small independent videos on YouTube—today's choice: Second World War's Operation Fortitude, narrated by an overly sarcastic bird. Ariel enjoyed war documentaries, often fantasizing that had she been alive during the war, she would have hopped to Germany and laser-waxed Hitler's mustache off. Hide under her light weaving and shave that silly thing off. That would have certainly ruined his morale and brought the war to a rushed end. Imagine the Fuhrer explaining to his generals that someone had entered his chambers and shaved off his mustache. The war would have been over on the same day.

But whenever she questioned herself about getting involved in today's political belligerence, she always found some excuse not to. More often than not the reason was that there simply wasn't one all-evil person to blame it all on, and when there was, creating a power vacuum could prove more harmful than beneficial. So what would she do about it? Cut down entire armies of people who believed in what they were fighting for? No. Also, she wouldn't have the guts for it. At least, that was her reasoning.

She ate her food while watching dummy versions of Sherman tanks, landing crafts, aircraft, entire airfields, and regiments being inflated or built. *Remarkably ingenious,* she thought when she noticed a slight rattle from the kitchenette.

Bubbles growled, hissed, spat, and dashed under the bed. The temperature dropped, and the lights dimmed as if being sucked by an invisible source. Something was terribly wrong.

"Leohirin."

Ariel jerked on her bed while making herself as invisible as she could. Someone was in the room with her. She could match her clothes, hair, and skin color to her surroundings, but it required much attention and focus. Try to recreate a photo-realistic painting, and you'd see how hard it can be. No, the best she could do was to make herself darker and hide in the gloom. She sucked all the light from the telly and the windows, but it proved pointless in the end as the room brightened up suddenly as if a portable sun had replaced the ceiling lamp.

A robed figure stood by the kitchenette, although stood might be the wrong word, since his feet weren't touching the floor. The figure pulled back his hood with pale hands, unveiling his face or whatever was left of it.

Ariel suppressed a gasp. His face was as pale as a cave-dwelling creature. Why was there only half of it? Where there should be flesh and bone was only a vague, shadowy outline and dust particles floating like a swarm of tiny flies.

Ariel tried to hide again, but her power proved worthless. Could it be? He had to, right? *A leoht like me. Another leoht. Here, in my house.* Ariel took stock of her situation. This person was immensely more skilled at light weaving than she ever was. The living room window was only a couple of meters away. She could daze him with a bright flash and jump through it. Would the glass cut her? In the movies, that never happened, but she had the feeling the movies were lying.

"You can call me Alfred."

Ariel balled her fists to stop her hands from shaking. Alfred floated closer to her, robes flapping as if blown by an empty wind. His eye was sad, while the other belonged to a different dimension. This man wasn't alive, not in the word's true meaning. Ariel clutched the fork in her hand. "What do ye want from me?"

"You'll want this for yourself."

Ariel jumped off her bed and got into a defensive position, a fork as her only weapon. Light wouldn't work against another leoht. The best she could hope for was to slow him down. Her thoughts raced. *He had at least a dozen opportunities to strike, but if he wishes me no harm, why does he have to look so evil?* "For myself? You must be missing more than half your head." *Yes, Ariel, please offend the demonic apparition. What harm could come of it?*

"You know who I am. You've seen me in her memories."

Ariel reached for the pendant around her neck, fingers rubbing the seed it carried. "How do ye know about her?"

For a brief moment, Alfred's face came to life—whole, colorful, two eyes, a wide smile, and happy. Not handsome, he had a chubby face, puffy cheeks, and his brown hairline had begun the usual man-in-his-thirties migration. She had indeed seen him. But what of it? Those were not her memories, and like all her foreign memories, they lacked context. Knowing her friend had known this man did not soften his menacing figure. But she did learn that they had a nickname for him. They called him Half. Well, that was a little too on the nose. "Why didn't ye help her?"

"I did. I hid her."

That sparked fury in her. "Yeah, look at how well that turned out."

"Miranda," he said.

A shiver ran down Ariel's spine at the mention of the name. She knew that name well, yet it was the first time she heard it with her own ears. "What about her?"

"She's back."

The words filled the room with all the joy of an abandoned graveyard or a deep-sea shipwreck—the words and that man's poor wardrobe choice. Ariel had to do something about that. She flicked her wrist and willed Half's robes to turn pink. Bright pink, like the one you might find on a Barbie set.

Half didn't object nor even react in the slightest to the tempering of his garments. "Does that help?"

"A little." Ariel pursed her lips and, with a wave of the hand, added bright yellow circles to the pink robes. Again, if this outfit adjustment made him upset, he made no protest. "How do ye know?"

Half stared at her.

It was a dumb question, and Ariel knew it. From her memories, she knew he and Miranda shared a deep connection. So she continued, "Where is she?"

"At the Worldroot."

"What? She can't move about willy-nilly. Didn't ye turn her into a book or something?"

Half flinched as if the recollection hurt him. "She has made an acquaintance, and he's helping her find her other parts."

"Could ye be a little vaguer? It'd be tragic if ye made sense."

"An American boy found her and is helping her."

That wasn't much better. "Why would this boy help her?"

"What do all men want?"

"Alright... answer me this, will ye? Why come to me? Can't ye stop her yaerself?"

"No."

Ariel waited for him to elaborate, and when he failed to do so, she pressed on. "And ye seem to think I can?"

"You are a leoht. You can travel the roots, and you've seen Scae in your memories. Stealing a book from a boy should be easy for someone of your skill and ability."

"Oh, give me a break. Having a tree share her memories with me when I was a child hardly makes me an expert in the tales of desperate house witches. Why won't *ye* stop her?"

Half sighed a long sorrowful wheeze. Ariel hoped he never did that again.

"A long time ago, I helped to stop her, and this is what's left of me. I loved her with all my soul and betrayed her so all of you could live. Every day is agony. Every day forever, unwhole. You haven't the faintest idea of what that's like."

"Oh, boohoo! So let me get this," Alfred disappeared, "straight... Rats!" she muttered as Bubbles exited his hiding place. "Do ye believe this? If what he says is true, I..."

Ariel wandered around the kitchenette. Hands fumbled for a glass from the cupboard, opened the bottle of whisky, and poured a healthy amount, her meal forgotten over the bed. She wasn't hungry anymore. "Rats! Rats! Rats!" She drank her whisky, the peatiness soothing her temper.

Bubbles rummaged around the room, still clearly startled.

"He's gone, stupid." Ariel let out a deep breath, mouth overcome by the lingering notes of floral accents and oak nuttiness and took another long drag of her whisky. "Rats!"

She pulled the seed from under her blouse and regarded it. "I'm guessing ye want me to do this. I'm pretty sure yer mother would. *Typical.* Maybe *Halfred* is right. I mean, it should be easy. I just need to steal a book from a kid, and we'll be back in no time. What do ye think?" The seed seemed to stare back at her. "Helpful, as usual."

Bubbles searched around a corner and hissed at a shadow.

Ariel observed him. "Guess I'll have to find someone to care for ye while I'm gone. Probably Maggie. The Prentices have kind hearts; they'll take good care of ye, though I doubt they'll let ye sleep on their bed."

Chapter 14

Three Heads

Ludik

"It's a beautiful night, isn't it?" Brinn signed as we sat by the lakeshore. Well, she tried to sign, at least. She wasn't very good at it, her gesticulating habit always getting in the way. But after nearly three years of lessons, I expected her to be further along.

Of course, I didn't tell her that. She didn't have to learn sign language in the first place. So I wasn't going to jeopardize our friendship by saying something stupid like, "Why can't you be better at sign language?" On the other hand, lousy sign language is better than no sign language at all. And it made it possible to talk with her at night.

"I guess," I said as I peeled calluses off my fingers.

"I can't stay long tonight. People need to have their bread early in the morning. Bastard forbid fresh bread in the afternoon."

"Ask Heimee if he'll hire you next time you visit."

"I already have. I ask every time I visit. He says he doesn't want to quarrel with my aunt, then offers me his condolences."

"That does sound like him. Well, I'm pretty sure tomorrow I won't leave late. Tomorrow's all about bottling. That never takes too long. I don't think Heimee likes it. He gets too attached to the casks; having to empty them feels like he is killing a pet or something. Aren't you afraid Era will wander away?"

Brinn considered her aunt's ekkuh. Slender, her dark brown feathers glistening in the moonlight, big eyes, pupils the size and shape of an egg. "We have an understanding, her and I. She knows I'm her getaway pass from aunt-villainy." To this, Era bent her legs and lay down next to us.

"Can I ask you a weird question?"

"I hate when you don't. Please, weird away."

I considered my question while taking a deep breath, watching the lantern-swillows blinking their chest green while flying high among the stars, migrating north. It was a beautiful night. "Do you believe mountains are alive?" I asked.

"Alive?"

"Yes, do you think they can move? Think, have a will?"

"Sure. Look at the moon."

I looked at it, so full and bright it could be the sun warming spring into summer. "The moon?"

"Yes, think about it. She moves across the sky, never stops, never rests, keeps going and going, and has phases like moods. What else can she be if not a flying mountain? Dead things don't move or fly. Not as far as I'm aware."

I played with the thought in my head. "That's nonsense."

"Why? Did you know the moon tugs on the world? That's how the tides form. Which means she is also magical. Can dead things use magic?"

"I suppose not."

Brinn smiled with smugness known only to those who pull a meaningful analogy out of their bums. "Why do you ask?"

My eyes sank back into my callouses. My hands had gotten so rough I barely recognized them. "One murdered my family."

"What, a moon?"

I picked up a pebble and tossed it into the lake, watching the ripples spread through the surface. "No, silly, a mountain. Aureberg."

"Oh, you mean the Collapse?"

"The mountain didn't collapse. People keep saying that, but it's not true. It rose from the ground as if it had legs to walk on and tore the world apart."

Brinn waited for me to continue, and before I knew it, I'd told her my whole story. It was the first time I shared it with anyone. I told her about my father, the refugee camp, and how my mother joined him in the Bliss. "And that's when Heimee saved me," I concluded. "I have to find the mountain. I have to. I need to know why I had to become an orphan. But how can I leave Heimee? I owe him so much."

Brinn laid a hand on my shoulder. "Mere men butchered my parents. If I found them, I would do much more than ask them why. So much more. I can think of a thousand different ways I'd drain their bodies out of their pathetic little lives." Brinn's eyes lit up with fury as she signed. Then the anger faded, and she smiled. "Talk to Heimee. Tell him you need a vacation or something."

"He'll say I'm nuts." I gazed at the moon again. Could the moon be a living mountain?

"I'll tell you this much. If you decide to go, I'll go with you."

"Don't be silly," I said.

"I'm not. Every day I live with my aunt is pure agony," Brinn explained. "I hate her, and I hate bread. Can't stand the smell, can't stand the way flour brushes against my hands or swooshes against the marble. Can't even eat it, so sick of it I am. Why do you think I'm always at your place even though it is so far away from me?"

"I like to think it's because I'm there."

Brinn laughed. "That too. But mostly to get away from her. You're just a perk."

"Thanks."

"She slapped me yesterday." Brinn tensed at the recollection. "I left the bread in the oven too long. It wasn't burnt, just a little darker and crispier than usual. We still sold the lot, and no one complained. But she slapped me anyway. Said the bakers' guild would give her a huge fine if she sold bad bread. But it wasn't bad. I wanted to kill her. Grab my peel with both hands and whack her stupid head off her neck. One good swing, and I'd be free. I think I could do it. My shoulders are as thick as a man's from all the kneading. So, in a way, you'd be saving me."

"How come?"

"I wouldn't have to become a murderer. Offer me anywhere to go, any excuse, and I'll follow you. I just don't want to go alone. I envy the moon, you know. She gets to see the world every day. Wouldn't that be amazing?"

"Is it, though? She can't come down to visit or touch or experience the world. Maybe that's why she keeps pulling at it."

"That's a weird way to look at it."

"Wasn't that the point? To 'weird away'?"

"I did say that. But this weird is a tad depressing. I'm not going to lie to you; I expected fun weird."

"Would you really go with me to find Aureberg?" Even to me, it sounded absurd.

"In a heartbeat," she said.

When I got home that evening, I found a half-drunk Heimee singing to himself in the kitchen. I wish I could hear him when he did that, but I couldn't. I wished I could learn to play an instrument, but something told me I wouldn't be very good at it.

"Where's the girl?" he asked when I came in.

"Her aunt keeps her busy. I barely see her during the day anymore."

"Pity, I was getting used to having at least one pretty face around here."

I went to the kitchen for a glass of milk and a cheese sandwich. Heimee had bought freshly churned butter, and it always tasted best eaten on the same day. In the following days, it would develop a tang that I wasn't so fond of.

"When are you going to tell her you like her?" Heimee asked as I sat on the wicker couch.

I almost spilled my milk.

"You've been her friend," he made quotation marks with his fingers, "for how long? Two, three years? If she's still putting up with you, it's because she likes you." He rubbed his chin contemplating something above me. "You know what, perhaps you're right. Not to mention that you're too young to have a girlfriend. Better let some older boy conquer her heart."

A block of ice seemed to form in my stomach. "What older boy?"

"She is a little older than you, isn't she? Girls often prefer a little maturity." He amused himself with the expression of panic I tried and failed to conceal before continuing, "But considering the competition in

Bum-hole, you still have a chance. I suggest you don't waste it. Why don't you take her to Guillinsbaer?"

"That's three hours away."

"Yes, but it's also the only place in the region where you'll find a reasonable market."

"Burrow has a market."

"*Bum-hole's* market has the romantic appeal of explosive diarrhea."

"Heimee," I said, dropping my sandwich. "I'm eating."

"Then why does crap keep coming out of your mouth?" Heimee wiggled a hand in front of me, warning me not to respond. "I know you think I'm old, that I belong to a completely different species, a homo-geriatric or something, but I can assure you that I know what I'm talking about."

"Alright, suppose I take her there. Then what?"

"Buy her lunch and a gift. Girls love to shop—the more useless and shinier the object, the more they crave it. Don't try to understand it."

"I don't think Brinn likes useless things."

"She's a girl. She likes pretty things, even if they're useless."

"With what money?"

Heimee filled his cup of Heims. He usually drank in moderation, but judging by how his fingers dragged, this wasn't his second glass.

"Are we celebrating something?" I asked.

His hands opened, then closed. Opened, then closed. Opened again and closed. I waited, afraid to move like someone watching a morning bird.

Heimee drew a breath and began to sign, "I lost my wife ten years ago today."

"I'm so sorry. I didn't mean to—"

"It's alright. Funny, my father was against our marriage. 'My boy, marrying a daft girl, I won't have it,' he'd say. He wasn't a bad person, only ignorant."

I shifted in my seat.

"Yes," Heimee said. "Gabinn was deaf. She died of some invisible sickness that made her every breath a torment. We had two boys together. Lord Louree Guilling drafted them to fight in the last war, not two months after the Bastard took her. I told the lord that I needed them to help me in the distillery—that I didn't have anyone else. He duly reminded me that in times of war, everyone must make sacrifices, and anyone who refuses would be considered a coward and executed. Can't tell you how happy I was the day he died. Praised be the Bastard, for He pointed his mighty finger right down at the lord's head and cracked it open with a bolt of lightning. I wasn't even religious until that day.

"Every night, I dream of them, Beneen and Horleen, that they'll come back to me one day. But the letters stopped coming years ago. They were only sixteen and seventeen when they left. If they're alive, they'll be grown men now. Be happy that you're deaf, and no one will take you to war. You'd be useless there. That's the best kind of useless one can be." Heimee took the glass from the table and gulped its contents down without any of his usual rituals.

He refilled the glass.

"But it's a good thing to protect our country, isn't it? I mean, soldiers helped us after the mountain—"

Heimee pounded his glass against the table, spilling most of the whisky. "War is a stupid, meaningless affair! It's done only for the benefit of those in power. If we had done nothing, if we'd let things be, I'd still be a father." Heimee clenched his jaw, and I could see how much pain those memories brought him. "And that damned refugee camp you talk about. I heard the stories. They locked you all up there, feeding you scraps, afraid you'd get away and infest their streets with beggars. I heard about the revolt and how so many died. For what? Do you know why you don't have a mother? That's why. That's what soldiers do!"

I averted my eyes, and the room went still, broken only by Heimee's shuddering breaths, hands pressed to his face. I had never seen him so fragile, so naked.

He was a beautiful man.

"I'm sorry," he signed at last. "You didn't have to see me like this. It's the Heims talking. Some idiots think it numbs their pain, but that's not true. They're addicted to the pain—not the drink." He took the bottle from the table and examined it. "This is how they find more of it. What am I saying? Don't mind the rants of an old man."

He flopped on the couch.

"Heimee," I said, "thank you for everything. Thank you for everything you've done for me."

Heimee's stern lips cracked, revealing the faintest smile. "Don't go all soft on me now. One of us is enough for an evening."

Heimee inspected the bottles—square, faintly green, *Heims* written in relief at the sides. We stenciled the labels onto the bottles. Heims. Ten years, thirteen years, fifteen years. Single malt whisky. We rolled barrels out from the cellar under the steeping room. There were over a thousand barrels there. I didn't like going down there often. It was dark and spooky, though in the summer it was quite refreshing. We rolled the selected barrels to the bottling room.

I loved those days. I may not like whisky, but it was a magical event every time we uncorked a barrel, and the fumes inundated the room. I grew curious about each particular batch. Every barrel produced a unique whisky with different shades of amber, scents, and flavors; some casks were emptier than others, even though we always filled them with the same amount.

"See how empty it got?" Heimee asked. "Every year, as the wood contracts and expands—breathing with the seasons—part of the spirit evaporates. We call this the Bastard's share."

I found the thought quite amusing, imagining the Bastard drinking from the casks when no one was looking.

Also, if you're wondering, Heimee only bought barrels made from coppiced wood. Most trees are defenseless against insects and elicit deforestation. Coppiced trees, however, are protected and well cared for. Trees lose branches all the time, and underwood is basically a vertical branch. This way, the trees produce wood and, in return, are kept alive and healthy. It's not a bad deal.

"Here," Heimee signed when we finished bottling for the day. He reached into his pocket, produced three coins, and tossed them to me. "You haven't been completely useless this season."

I caught the coins and inspected them. Smooth silver, one side read,

3 Gollings, and on the other, three stars hovered above a tall tree enclosed in a wedge shield, the nation's coat of arms.

"Three heads," I muttered to myself. I had never held so much money in my life.

"Have I overpaid you? Oh well... Just remember, if you spend all your money on a girl, you're a fool. You should save some of it."

I clutched the coins in my hand, determination flooding my eyes.

"You're not going to save it, are you?"

I wasn't. I knew exactly how to spend it.

Chapter 15

Flying Letter

Ludik

I WAS GOING to buy shoes. Not loose, raggedy shoes, nor tight shoes prone to callusing. No second hands, either. I, Ludik, son of a shoemaker, would have my own shoes. Bespoke, if the money allowed it.

It wasn't even lunchtime when I headed to Burrow. I woke up extra early to finish my chores and give Otto a bath. You'd think that would be a fast chore, but Otto had the surface area of a jousting arena.

Down the dungy street, Mr. Aree loaded his wagon. He was a kind old man Heimee usually hired to transport Heims to Baer and whose sense of humor I would never understand. Not because I didn't get it, but because his lower lip was bent on consuming as much of his face as it could, making it impossible to lip-read.

"Ouch!"

Something pointy hit me on the side of the head.

I rubbed my temple where it struck me. Was it a pebble? I turned around, expecting to see kids ducking behind a haystack or something but found no one. Men sprawled on the tavern's benches, dozing off after their mid-morning aperitif. And the non-alcoholics generally went about their own business. Nothing seemed out of place.

I looked down at my feet and found a piece of paper folded to look like an arrowhead stuck in the hay. I picked it up and tapped the crumpled tip with my finger. That's what hit me. There was handwriting on it, so I unfolded it, noting the straight and deliberate creases, forming symmetrical triangles. The handwriting was delicate, feminine, and precise. The sort of calligraphy found only in old books and—

It was addressed to me.

What, in the Bastard's name, was I reading? I reread it, but it made no sense. I rubbed my eyes to ensure I wasn't dreaming and read one more time, carefully examining each word.

Dear Ludik.

I could tell you why I, Mathew Doller, am currently dangling off a cliff, rope tied to my feet, but I'm afraid that if I tell you why too soon, you might leave me hanging. Or cut the rope to see if I can fly. I can assure you, I will. However briefly.

But Miranda says you're cool, so here we are. Now listen, forget about whatever it is that you're doing.

There are three mountains east of Guillingsbaer. Bang to the left one. Only two roads lead there. Take the right road... as opposed to the left one. I don't mean the correct one. Well, I do mean the correct one, and the correct one is the one to the right. Sigh. After about two miles—what do you mean he doesn't know what a mile is? No suh! Jesus, why did you bring me to the medieval ages? Okay, okay, I get it. After one and a half league, more or less, there will be a tree perching on the cliff edge. There's only one. Ya can't miss it. I'll be about ten feet below it.

Please hurry.

Seriously,

Mat.

My mind raced to find a plausible explanation.

As far as I knew, there weren't any other Ludiks in Burrow. No, that's not accurate. As far as I knew, I was the only Ludik in the region. Of course, I could be wrong, but the '*ik*' in my name is very northern.

And even in the north, it was not a common name. What were the chances that I lived so close to another Ludik my head just happened to intercept his messages? The rest of the letter didn't make much sense either. How could this Mathew fellow have written this letter while upside-down? And how had it reached me from so far away?

It had to be some kind of prank. But who could be behind it? I didn't have many friends in Burrow. I'd been careful that way. Also, the letter was too imaginative for the average Burrow kid. I snapped my fingers. Brinn. It had to be an elaborate prank of hers. But it wasn't that funny even. She usually had a better sense of humor; upon closer scrutiny, the handwriting couldn't possibly be Brinn's. Her calligraphy was as smooth as a handful of gravel. She could've asked for someone else to write it. That, or she had been hiding some serious calligraphy skills from me.

But if it was her, then where—

I saw her coming up the street, a basket full of bread in her arms. Any doubt as to whom was responsible evaporated. I folded the letter, trying to follow the creases, but gave up and ended up with a neat square. I stashed it in my pouch, tucking it in a small compartment so it wouldn't touch the honey apples I had brought.

I waved at Brinn, but she didn't see me—or pretended not to see me. That was fine. I didn't have time for this anyway. If I didn't hurry, Mr. Aree would leave without me, and I would have to walk, turning a one-hour journey into a two-hour feet-blistering trip, which meant more time without buying shoes.

"Hello, Mr. Aree," I said as I reached him.

Mr. Aree scrunched his face in what I can only assume was his way of greeting, his lower lip covering everything beneath his nose.

"Would you mind giving me a ride?"

He showed me two fingers. At first, it seemed like a rude gesture, but then he rubbed his pointing finger against his thumb. *Two. Money. Oh yes, Two bolts. Of course.* It had to be a bolt. No one in the right mind would charge two heads for a ride to town.

I reached into my pocket and produced a full head, glistening in the sunlight. It was as if I had shown him a severed limb. He snatched my hand, and for a moment, I thought he'd steal the coin; instead, he bent my fingers over it. He shook his head and raised his hands in a "Are you mental?" gesture, then motioned to the general area around us.

Were there rules about money? I didn't know it wasn't socially acceptable to display money publicly. And how could I have known? I never had any.

Mr. Aree sighed, relaxed his shoulders, and invited me aboard anyway.

"Thank you, Mr. Aree. I'll pay you after I get change, I promise."

He waved a hand dismissively.

An hour later, we reached the giant stone pin cushion called Guillingsbaer. Heimee and I often traveled there on official business, so I knew the lay of the city pretty well. The city's very religious, and preachers infest every corner. "You're lucky you're deaf," Heimee had once told me. "You don't have to hear these lunatics preach about how miserably you should lead your life." He shoved a preacher aside. "Yeah, I get it, the Bastard's an idiot. Get out of my face before I put you in contact with Him."

I prayed to the Bastard every now and then, but I seldom visited a Palrik. No, that's a lie. I've actually never been inside one. Both religions were the same to me. They both prayed to the light and the Tree of Life. One, however, had a nameless Bastard who had led a miserable and perilous life and spent his late years preaching his findings on the streets until they found him dead in his meditation pose, and miraculously his body did not decompose. Ever. It is said you can still see him meditating into eternity in the first Palrik in Polis, the capital of the Holarmo Empire. A city so far away it could very well be imaginary.

I often wondered if I ever went nuts, would someone start a religion after me?

Mr. Aree left me at the beginning of the shopping street before it became too narrow for any cart to continue.

If you want to buy anything, Baer's shopping street is the place to go. It had everything you could possibly need. And everyone went there. Not by choice, though, but because the nearest market was leagues away in Lirterin.

The street bustled with chaotic activity. I don't have to be able to hear to know how loud it was—I felt it in my skin. People gathered in packed, tiny esplanades or haggled with street vendors. Some held the flow of the crowd chatting in the middle of the road, ignoring everybody else's insults. Soldiers marched up and down on endless patrols. Well-dressed people perused what street vendors had to offer or admired showcase windows, happily ignoring the beggars lining the curb.

I pitied the beggars, maybe because I had been one myself. Granted, not for long, but still. I wanted to share my money with them, but I'd worked so hard for this money. And if I shared, I might not have enough for my shoes. Was I being selfish? I remembered the apples in my pouch, noting the weird note that stuck my head earlier next to them, and decided to offer them to a kid sitting on the curb. It was like seeing a younger reflection of me.

"Great, more apples," he said and promptly forced a smile, revealing pristine white teeth. "Do you have money?"

"What?"

"Listen, kid," the kid, much younger than me, said. "I can steal as many apples as I want. What I need is money, so I don't have to steal apples."

It was tricky deciphering that, but he had easy lips. "But if you have my apples, you won't have to steal more."

The kid blinked as if what I said was truly moronic. He lifted a blanket at his side, revealing a bag full of apples to which he added mine. "Thank you so much for your kind help," he said, adding the most forced smile in the history of forced smiles.

Despite that, I felt good about myself. I had done my part.

A year or so ago, I stumbled upon a shoe shop. Heimee had told me he wouldn't spend money on new shoes since he had already given me "a perfectly good pair," but he also mentioned that Danilee Shoe Shop was the best in the region. So there I went, up the narrow busy street, heart pounding in my chest until I found a showcase widow with *Danilee Footwear, Buy and Repair* stenciled in golden letters.

I reached for the shoe-shaped door handle and pushed the door open. A familiar smell of treated leather welcomed me. Like I was opening the door to Dad's workshop, like returning home. I quickly shook it off my mind and took notice of the room. Two rows of chairs divided the shop into men's and women's sections, each facing shelves packed with incredible leather shoes: work shoes, hiking boots, riding boots—you name it. They came in all shades of black, brown, and white. Different patterns, too—pointy, round, or square toe caps. Long quarter, short quarter. Thick heel, slim heel, tall heel. Fancy or humble brogues, or no brogues at all.

"May I help you, my young man?" the cobbler said with the passion one might show for cheap dish soap. He wore a spotless, olive-green apron. He had an oval-shaped bald head, and where he still had hair, he'd shaved not so long ago—a razor-cut scab hung above his right ear—and observed me with unimpressed eyes over his thin spectacles.

"I'm here to buy shoes," I said.

"How unexpected," the cobbler said, straightening his apron and measuring me with his eyes. Fortunately, his lips weren't hard to read, but I did struggle. "We don't sell second-hand shoes, I'm afraid."

"I came here to buy new shoes. Heimee Heims told me this is the place to go." I often used Heimee's name as a greeting card. Everyone knew him or his brand. Well, anyone who drank knew him or his brand. And everyone drank.

"Very well. Don't touch anything unless I give it to you." The cobbler reached for the top shelf and produced a pair of beautiful boots —dark brown, thick-soled, modest, perfect lines. He produced a pair of clean socks and a shoehorn. "Please put these on before trying any shoes." He passed them to me. "Did I guess your size correctly, young man?"

I put on the boots; they fit perfectly. I got up, taking a few steps. That's what walking should always feel like. Like stepping on fluffy pillows. "How much for these?" I asked.

"Fourteen heads."

"Fourteen heads?"

He shook his head and showed five fingers on his hand. "Fifteen heads."

"Fifteen heads?"

"Fifteen heads."

Blood drained from my face as I took the boots off carefully. I don't know how I would ever pay them back if I damaged them in any way.

Heimee would be furious at me. Trying not to get my hopes down, I asked, "What do you have for three heads?"

"Old shoes," he said, words like daggers.

I didn't mind them being old. "Old but never worn, right?"

"As I said, I don't sell second-hand."

"Can I have a look?"

"Wait here." The cobbler shuffled through the storage room and came out holding four boxes. "These are all I have left in your size within your... *budget.*" He settled them down in a line and opened the lid of each box, one by one as if revealing a treasure. The first three were very unremarkable. Flimsy sole, thin body. Turnshoes, they called them. Only good because the seams were turned inside and hidden from view. You would think that's good, but you'd be wrong. The seams would rub against your skin, and because the sole was but a thicker layer of leather, they were only marginally better than good winter socks. I remember Dad telling me he had stopped making turnshoes because no one paid for them anymore, not even himself.

My hopes vanished like a blown-out candle. Until the cobbler opened the last box, and my heart sank to my stomach. A tingling sensation spread across my skin like static. There, in that box, were a pair of thick-soled boots, and branded on the side of the creamed color leather was an encircled three-peak mountain with swirly leaves and flowers.

I was petrified—the air in the room became as thick and dense as water.

The cobbler waved a hand in front of my eyes.

"How much for these?" I can only imagine how cracked my voice was. I felt the vibrations when I spoke and knew I didn't sound right.

"Four heads."

I felt gutted. Of course, I couldn't afford them. How foolish was I to think this would be easy? But the boots had to be mine. "I don't have four gollings," I said. "I told you; I only have three."

The cobbler inspected me as I forced my eyes dry. "Then three is the price."

"Three?"

"Three."

"Three heads?"

"Three heads."

I hugged him.

The cobbler held his hands up, peeled me away like someone getting rid of a dirty tablecloth, and adjusted his apron and spectacles.

I reached into my pocket and eagerly passed on the money.

"Don't you want to try them first?" he asked.

"It doesn't matter."

"Then may I suggest baking soda and dried woodberry leaves," he said as he pinched the coins off my hand. "For the smell."

I put the boots on. Oh, my dear Bastard. How was this possible? I was so elated I had to leave the shop in a hurry to get some fresh air. Every step I took was a flood of childhood memories: playing with laces, scraps, and rubber. I touched the sole, feeling its unusual texture. They weren't as soft or comfortable as the first pair I'd tried, but they were perfect for long hikes. They might even be perfect for work.

And I walked—walked in my dad's boots. When I took my eyes off my new boots, I was back in Burrow. Already? The sun was on its way down.

Brinn should be off work! I had to show her my boots. My new boots! I headed for our spot by the lake, and sure enough, there she was. I started blabbing about my morning before she could say, "Hello."

"Are those?" she signed and pointed at the brand on my boot.

"They are!" I exploded with excitement. Hours passed, and I still couldn't believe it. "Isn't it amazing?"

"But how?"

"I don't know. The cobbler just had them stowed away at the back of the shoe shop. He never sold them. I guess people weren't ready for rubber soles."

"But isn't that the mountain you want to kill or something?"

"Yes," I said, unphased. Who cares about Aureberg? My dad had made those boots. And now they were mine.

"But isn't it a little like walking around with a picture of your worst enemy?"

"I don't care. I'm never taking them off."

"I'm very happy for you."

I couldn't stop grinning. "How was work?"

"As good as it can be expected. I didn't kill myself nor anyone else."

"I hope that business with the flying letter helped. But I must be honest with you; I didn't get it."

"Uh?" she said. Well, I think that's what she said. It's not like I can read 'uh' on someone's lips, but it was a fair assumption judging by her contorted facial expression.

"You know, Mathew Doller hanging from a tree, asking for rescue."

She furrowed her brow. "Buying those shoes really affected you, huh?"

"Here," I said, fumbling in my pouch and passing it to her. "You're telling me you don't know what this is?"

Brinn took the letter and unfolded it; her lips moved, and her brow furrowed as she read. "What am I supposed to do with this?"

"Bastard's bother, you are still trying to trick me."

"Yes, I'm a mastermind of boring pranks." She handed me back the letter.

I read it:

Dear, Ludik.

I'm thrilled about your shoes. They're wicked pissa. Now help me, ya burger head!

P.S.: I really need to pee.

Chapter 16

Small Butter

Ludik

I was stunned. The words had completely changed, and then... It happened again. Right before my eyes.

> *Okay, I promise I won't call you burger head anymore. Have I mentioned I need to pee? And that I'm upside-down? Do the frickin' math there, buddy. I'll wait right here.*

"It changed again?" Brinn asked.

I showed it to her. "I don't know what to think of this."

"What is there to think? We are going, right?"

"Are we?" I mean, I had never been summoned by a magical flying letter before. Was I supposed to trust it willy-nilly? "What if we get there and he reaps the souls out of our bodies or something? He has the power to know where we are from leagues away but not to pull himself up. Makes no sense."

Brinn pinched her chin, then tossed her hand in the air before bringing it back to sign, "And why did he choose you? I mean, there's a whole city filled with, you know, people who can hear." Brinn began to walk again and stopped abruptly. "Do you think he can hear us?"

I opened my mouth, then closed it. The truth is, I didn't consider it. Hearing isn't one of my fortes. "I don't know. Can you hear us?" I asked the letter.

Brinn and I stared at it as if looking into a deep well after throwing in a rock, waiting for the splash.

The letter didn't change.

"Maybe we should tell someone," Brinn suggested.

"Who? Heimee? I don't think he'll believe us."

The letter shifted.

If you show this to anyone, I swear it will turn into a cake recipe.

"It can hear us," I noted.

"Amazing," Brinn said then frowned. "And disturbing."

I mulled it over in my mind. Part of me was scared, and the other part felt extremely lucky. How would I be able to go on with my life without satisfying this much curiosity? Brinn was right. We couldn't just pass on the opportunity to meet an actual mage. He was asking for my help, wasn't he? Who was I to deny help to anyone? I drew a deep breath.

"We're going," I said, then to the letter, "We're on our way. Just hang on."

A pun? Really?

More letters formed on the paper.

By the way, there are a bunch of Erosomite raiders coming up. My guess is that they are going to raid Small Butter. Kelmir Fort fell last night, FYI. I can stop them. If you ever decide to get here.

Brinn's eyes went from giddy to stern within an eyeblink. "We'll get there faster with Era."

Dusk was on its final breaths when we reached Brinn's house at the bakery. Brinn's aunt waited at the door leaning on the door frame, arms crossed. The look on her face was enough to prickle my skin. I gave her the politest smile in my arsenal. "Good evening, Ms. Kallak."

Ms. Kallak didn't bother acknowledging my existence, eyes fixed on Brinn.

"She doesn't like you very much," Brinn said. "You should wait here. I'll be right back."

Except she wasn't right back. As soon as Brinn reached the porch, Ms. Kallak straightened herself and began rebuking Brinn for reasons I could not catch on her lips. I turned away. This is one of the perks of being deaf. You can always shut the world off by not paying attention.

Pssst. Hey, Ludik. Pssst.

I turned to face the large Ulmaro tree calling for my attention. I neared him.

"Hey, Ulmarin." Yes, he was an Ulmaro tree named Ulmarin. Trees aren't known for their creativity.

So, are you going to help him?

That caught me off-guard. "You know about him?"

Of course, he knew about him. Mathew was tied to a tree. One tree tells another, and that tree tells another, and in a matter of minutes, the whole region knows what's going on.

Sure do.

"Uh..." I said. "Do you know who he is?"

We don't. He arrived today, being chased by that blue-haired girl. We think it has something to do with the attack on the fort last night. We're not sure.

So the attack was real.

It has been quite an exciting story. Always cheers my day when humans hurt each other.

I held back my tongue on that remark. Humans didn't treat trees as fairly as they should, so trees held a lot of resentment. "What blue-haired girl?"

You don't know? Humans are so slow with information. We should run the world, not you. The Erosomites saw an opportunity and made a move. Then this girl pops up right in the middle of the action. And from what I heard, I like her a lot. We are betting she's Leoht. Isn't that crazy? A Leoht!

Was it? I mean, there were plenty of Leohts in Guillinsbaer alone. I glanced back to see if there was any progress. Brinn's arms flailed left and right while her aunt spoke with bloodshot eyes. I could go there and help Brinn, but what could I say? Brinn told me her aunt didn't like me; going there could make it worse. "Thanks, Ulmarin. I have to go."

So you are going to help him? I bet against Teerralin, you were. Don't make me lose here. She's already smug enough as she is.

I looked to the other side of the road, where a much smaller tree was saying, *Oh, I'm the smug one. Sure, sure! Keep telling yourself that.*

"Yes, I'm going."

Yisss. Take that, Teer!

Brinn tried to force her way into the house, but her aunt did not budge. Brinn threw her hands in the air and circled the house. Her aunt shot after her and snatched Brinn's arm. Brinn spun on her heels, and her aunt slapped her.

I spun and ran toward her. "Leave her alone," I shouted.

Ms. Kallak eyed me for the first time. She was menacing, tall, and broad-shouldered, her blue eyes were colder than ice, piercing and mad, her gray hair cut short and without care. "This is all your fault," Ms. Kallak said, cocking a finger at me. "Go home, you little worm. Leave my niece alone."

Brinn managed to wring free from her aunt's clutching hands and began to shout at her, tears forming in her eyes. Ms. Kallak slapped her again. Then something caught my attention. My pouch—it glowed. I lifted the flap, and it was as if a summer's day hid inside.

Ms. Kallak's eyes fixed on the light. Then the light went off. It was coming from the letter. I picked it up.

Give me to her.

I didn't know what else to do, so I followed instructions.

"Ms. Kallak, here. This will explain everything." I extended the letter.

She nearly killed me with her stare, yet she snatched the letter from my hands and read it. "A cake recipe?!" she blared, hate exuding from her face. She looked at the letter again, and for a brief moment, Ms. Kallak's face was as white as the sun. I had to squint, and tiny prickles of light infested my vision. Brinn's aunt curled to her knees, hands on her eyes, dropping the letter. I hurried to retrieve it—the sentences had a light of their own, glowing fluorescently in the night.

What are you waiting for? Get the horse!

I briefly wondered what a horse was before pulling Brinn along. "We should go."

Brinn, however, knelt by her aunt. Ms. Kallak rubbed her eyes, opened them wide and blinked repeatedly. Brinn placed a hand on her shoulder, but her aunt shoved it away. Ms. Kallak shouted something and pushed Brinn back and kept doing so even after Brinn was no longer close to her.

Brinn walked backward, snarling something back to her aunt.

We cornered the house and found Era, the ekkuh, resting on the ground. Brinn pulled her to her feet and patted her neck while saying something to me.

"Sure," I told her without having the faintest idea what she was saying. It usually saves time.

The letter lit up like a lantern. We stared at it for a moment, then Brinn took advantage of the light to saddle Era. She equipped her ekkuh with the dexterity of someone who had done the same action a thousand times, tightened the straps, and climbed on top. Brinn held her hand out to help me up, and I took it.

I'd settled behind her when the letter began to pulse again.

I peed myself. Hope you're happy.

Also, Small Butter is being raided. As in right now. How anyone can harm a place called Small Butter is beyond me... pfbrrt. But what do I care? I now know what pee tastes like.

P.S.: I hate you more with each passing minute.

A knot formed in my throat. I shouldn't have been so distrustful. Had I believed Mathew from the beginning, innocents probably wouldn't have gotten hurt. I passed on the message to Brinn.

In response, she hit the reins hard, leaving behind a despondent Ms. Kallak, knees to her chest, still holding her face.

Chapter 17

Mathew Doller

Ludik

"I'm not sure about this," Brinn signed as we reached our destination, Era following behind. It's not wise to gallop uphill, especially when dual riding, which was only possible because Brinn and I didn't weigh that much.

I sucked in a breath. I wasn't sure of anything either. "We came this far."

"I know, but something's not right. He could be lying about the fort. I mean, we haven't heard this from anyone else. Someone would have raised the alarm by now, don't you think?"

I knew for a fact that the fort had been attacked, and if that was true, why wouldn't everything else be? I couldn't tell Brinn that I'd heard it from a tree, though. She would find me mad.

"And, again, why you?" Brinn looked at the letter in my hand and snatched it. "Hey! Answer the question, or we'll leave you right where you are."

How did I not think of that? I could've asked any question I wanted, and I didn't. I guess I was too stunned and baffled to think clearly.

"Really?" Brinn glared at the letter. "Are you really not going to answer?"

The letter went dark.

Brinn moved about and yelled, though I could not tell what she was saying. I slumped my shoulders, unsure if disappointed or relieved. The letter shone bright again, a single word on display.

Sigh.

Then four more popped. A coldness grew in me, and like walking into a terrible nightmare, I understood.

I'm looking for Aureberg.

I took two steps back. Brinn eyed me, a curious expression on her face. "Isn't that the mountain—"

"What do you want from it?" I asked.

Save me, you doorknob, and I'll tell you everything you want to know.

Well, Small Butter is now We're All Out of Butter. The raiders are on their way here. Stop wasting time!

Brinn and I shared a startled look, bolted up the road, and soon found the tree in question.

'Finally! Quick, pull me up.

From there, we could see the whole Guillings region: the distant lights from the city and surrounding villages like orbiting stars.

I nearly jumped to the edge of the cliff, lying flat on my belly so I could look down without the risk of falling. There he was, just like he said he would be, dangling by one foot, swinging from side to side. I know that talking with a magical letter should be proof enough, but you'd be amazed at how skeptical you can be when reality doesn't make its usual sense. "He's real," I said.

Unfortunately, said the tree in a weary tone. *What an annoying fellow. Why couldn't he have tied himself to a rock instead?*

"Wait? He did this to himself?" I said out loud, forgetting about Brinn.

Yes. I don't think he's too clever. But at least today wasn't boring. Oh, he is asking you, how could you possibly know he did this to himself?

What could I tell him? Hey, 'I'm not talking to you; I'm talking to this tree here.' That was no good. "Hang on; we'll get you out."

There was a hand on my shoulder. I turned to find Brinn, a glowing letter in her hand. She had a confused expression as she leaned over to see. "You can understand him? Is he signing?"

"Uh..." I said and quickly changed the subject. "Can we use Era to pull him up?"

"He doesn't sound happy," Brinn said. "We didn't bring rope. How is Era supposed to help? The two of us should be able to pull him up, no? He doesn't look too heavy." She then stopped in place as if something had spooked her. "Lud, I can hear ekkuhs coming. Many of them."

My heart began to race. Brinn settled the letter on the ground to shed light on what we were doing, and we both jumped at the rope.

Due to his weight and the fact that we had a tree in the way, I could barely wrap my hand around the rope. I twirled my hand around it and felt my bones squeeze. "Pull me instead," I told Brinn. She hugged me by the stomach and pulled hard. I placed a foot against the tree and pushed against it.

Hey, be careful! The tree protested as he bent slightly.

The bones in my wrist complained with each pull, and the pressure prevented blood from reaching my fingertips, making them tingle and prickle as if tiny bugs had decided to call them dinner. The rope nearly slipped from my hand, peeling away some skin and forcing me to grit my teeth to fight the pain. If it hadn't been for the years of hard work, I don't think I could've held on for as long as I did. Still, it was no use. Despite Brinn pulling my chest with all her weight and strength, I wouldn't hold it much longer, much less hoist Mathew.

A beak appeared in front of me and bit the rope. I thought Era would snap it free and Mathew along with it. I held my breath as the rope became lighter and easier to tug.

"Good girl, Era," I said. "That's it."

We hauled until a shoe popped up from the ledge. Even in the dark, I could see it wasn't like any shoe I had ever seen. Brinn let go of me and grabbed Mathew's jacket hoisting him onto the road and to safety.

Mathew was maybe four years older than me, wore strange blue pants unlike any fabric I had ever seen, and his shoes were even stranger —checkered black and white, and like mine, they had a rubber sole, except the rubber was painted white. Could my dad have made those shoes? He wore a white shirt under a jacket made from a similar fabric to his pants. He clutched a large book in his arms and had an equally weird bag on his back strapped around his shoulders and belly. Unlike anyone I had ever met, his skin was as dark as the inside of a whisky barrel. His lips were thick, his face round with strong cheekbones, and his hair resembled a black sponge helmet.

So that's what a mage looks like.

He looked at me with his bloodshot dark eyes, frowned, and stumbled to his feet. He took two wobbling steps, dropped to his knees, pressed strange buckles on the straps of his bag, and pulled it in front of him. Grabbing a tiny flap on the side, he ripped the bag's top apart, put the book inside, and sewed it back instantly by pulling back the flap.

Magic.

Mathew placed the bag back on his shoulders, held his stomach, and curled.

"What was he saying?" I asked Brinn.

"I don't think he feels very well," Brinn said. "Mathew, ekkuhs are approaching. I think it's the raiders. What do we do?" Brinn glanced at where the road curved behind the hill, then at me. "Should we run?"

Mathew raised a finger. "Wait!" I think he said. Then he stood up, wincing.

The letter pulsated with light by the tree, so I fetched it before a gust of wind threw it down the mountain. It read:

Give me a moment; I've been upside-down a lot.

"Mathew, I don't think we have a moment. I can feel road shaking! They're close."

Mathew frowned at me again. Then there it was. Even in his strange face, I saw the cringe. "Deaf!" I read on his lips, followed by a cascade of words, from which all I gathered was "all people." I read the letter for clarification.

Can't believe you got a deaf kid to save me out of all people. Is this the best you can do? Are you actively trying to kill me?

Then Mathew curled again, turned around, and puked.

Uh? Did he not know I was deaf? That couldn't make sense. Could it? The thoughts escaped my mind as a mass of ekkuh riders cornered into view. Twenty—no. Fifty, more following from behind. Mathew was on his knees, still vomiting, and despite his dark complexion, he was much paler than when we'd pulled him up. The riders raised their spears and pointed them at us. The vibration was so intense it tied my innards into knots. The mass of raiders approached like a wild river after a storm.

Brinn clutched my arm. I glanced at her and saw the fear in her eyes. All this trouble so that we could die trampled. Mathew spat on the ground, rose to one knee, and wobbled to his feet.

You guys just don't learn, do you? popped up on the letter.

Mathew raised his hands, the raiders barely a few yards away from him, and the road burst into flames. The riders in front took the full blow, riding right into the fire, scaring their rides and sending them galloping right off the cliff. In the panic that followed, many more followed suit, their clothes and feathers ablaze.

The heat reached my face as if I was working the kiln. Mathew poured more and more fire up the road. Between the flames, I glimpsed ekkuhs coming to an abrupt halt sending their riders tumbling to the ground and into the fiery road.

Hope you have good health insurance, the paper read.

Mathew turned to us, lips moving.

I squinted; the figures on ekkuh backs were moving away. They were retreating!

I regarded the paper. *Alright, Deafo, now let's skedaddle.*

Was he talking to me? Skedaddle? What in the ordeal was that?

Mathew then took two staggering steps and collapsed on the floor.

I regarded the letter. No more words came up. Brinn and I stared, jaw dropped, at the man sprawled on the road, a sea of flames behind him, slowly dwindling. I glanced at Brinn for help, but she looked as stupefied as I was.

That was amazing! said the tree. *Praise be the light! For a moment, I thought I was going to die. I hate fire, but Leohorin's wrath, that was great! The other trees spoke of this, but I didn't believe them. What a thrill. What a day! So many men killed.*

Brinn tugged on my arm. "We should get him on Era and get out of here. Just in case those raiders change their minds."

I closed my mouth, tongue dried from having my chin hanging loose for so long. "Mathew?" I spoke to the paper. Nothing. Guess he needed to be conscious to use it. That made sense, I guessed.

We pushed him on top of the saddle, Era lowered her back to help, and we did our best to ensure Mathew wouldn't fall off tying him with the same rope he came with. We would have to walk all the way back. My new shoes were amazing, but when you buy new shoes, you don't want to use them for that long—you want to ease into them—and I had pushed them pretty far already.

"I can hear drums," Brinn said. "The garrison must have been alerted."

I looked at Guillinsbaer in the distance, fires dancing around the city like lantern-swillows. "We did it, Brinn." I hugged her, and she hugged me back.

She sighed in relief and signed, "That was stupid scary."

We had barely reached the bottom when we crossed a column of soldiers, marching with conviction, holding lamps and spears, ready for battle. A rider approached to inspect us while we casually covered Mathew's face, just in case.

Brinn led the conversation for obvious reasons, but the soldier didn't seem too convinced. His stern, angry eyes fell on me, but despite the torchlight, there was little chance I could read his lips. However, I couldn't look away from the deep scar on his chin.

"I'm sorry, sir, I'm deaf."

The soldier cringed, frowned, shook his head, and trotted away as if he wanted nothing to do with me. I don't know why deaf people are so trustworthy, but I wasn't about to start complaining.

"What did you tell him?" I asked once they were far enough.

"That we ran from Small Butter. What else was I supposed to say? That we have a fire wizard passed out on our ekkuh? Don't think he'd take kindly to that."

"Good thinking," I said.

"That's my genius at work," Brinn said with sunken eyes and ruffled hair. "How do you think Heimee is going to react to this?"

He'd probably give me a hard time. Not just for bringing a strange fire mage with me but for not returning home that night without any warning. Well, nothing to do about it now but to face the consequences.

Chapter 18

Unwelcome Guest

Ludik

"That's quite a smell," Heimee signed, wrinkling up his face as he contemplated the unconscious man on his couch. "I don't know what you cretins were up to last night, but if that's the story you chose to go with, Bastard, help me. I don't think I want to know the truth."

"We should've lied," Brinn said, "I mean, I don't believe our story, and I was there."

I gave her a side-eye. "We both know I'm a terrible liar."

"You're not great at telling the truth either."

"I think he's waking up," Heimee said. "Let's see what he has to say."

Mathew shifted on the couch and groggily sat up. He said something while pressing his hand to his forehead. Then he said something else, massaging his temples. I looked at Brinn for translation.

"His head hurts," she translated.

Heimee fetched a glass of water.

I sat by Mathew's side while Heimee arrived with the water glass and handed it to Mathew. Mathew reached into his bag and produced a small white bottle with a red label where white sharp letters read TYLENOL. He popped it open and poured an elongated piece of chalk, smaller than a fingernail, onto his hand which he then tossed in his mouth and gulped down with some water. "Thanks," he said, placing the flask back in his bag. He said more, but his lips were impossible to read. I remembered the letter and pulled it out of my pocket.

My head feels like a basketball after a Boston Celtics game, I read in the letter.

"What's a Boston Celtics game?" I asked.

"Or a basketball," Brinn added.

Mathew ignored us, extending his hand to greet Heimee. *Mathew Doller. Thank you for*—I read as he stopped to inspect his surroundings —*letting me crash on the couch.*

Heimee shook his hand. "Heimee Heims."

I checked the letter to find Heimee's reply.

"Blabadu," I said and watched as my words also popped up in the letter. Then a new line appeared: *Brinn: Are you alright?* Was the letter going to transcribe everything everyone was going to say? That was brilliant. I looked incredulously at Mathew. "How are you doing this?"

"Doing what?" he asked. I know he asked it because it came up on the letter like a regular conversation. No more headache-inducing lip-reading! This was fantastic.

"The letter is transcribing what everyone is saying," I clarified.

Mathew peered at the letter as if he too was surprised about it then shrugged and nonchalantly added, "Magic." His eyes then grew stern. "Boy, you sure took your sweet time, didn't ya? I thought I was a goner." He extended his hand for me to shake it. His skin felt normal—though I don't know what I expected. I had never seen skin that color and regarded my hand half expecting to find it smudged.

"Are you...?" Mathew frowned deeply. "Are you checking your hand for dirt? Oh, for crying out loud, you knucklehead. I knew I'd regret coming here. Listen here, you moldy corn cracker," he rubbed the skin on the back of his hand, "this is my skin. My skin is this color. Do you understand that? I'm going to give you a pass. You probably have never seen a black person before, but—"

Brinn also touched his skin.

"Get off me!" Mathew blurted. "Were you even listening?"

Brinn shrugged, inspecting her fingers. "Had to check."

"If you pat my hair next, I'll burn yours."

Brinn raised her hands. "How did you know that's what I was thinking?"

"Just drop it. Okay?"

Heimee got himself a glass of Heims.

I looked at him intriguingly, and he shrugged.

"I get the feeling I'm about to hear plenty of nonsense, so I'm taking precautions," he signed, though he didn't have to. His words were written right in front of me. Then he wiggled the bottle to Mathew. "Care for a glass? On second thought, fire and alcohol might not be the best match."

"Was that a pun? You know, *match*?"

Heimee stared.

"No? It would've been a good one," Mathew said. "So they told you everything, huh? Good, then you're all caught up."

"Mathew," I said. "You said you were here for Aureberg. Did it kill your parents, too?"

"My parents? No, no, no. They're fine. Are you hungry? I am starving; I don't suppose you have something to eat?"

Heimee cut bread and cheese and smelled the stew pot to see that it hadn't gone bad. He served portions for everyone and set them on the kitchen table, where we watched Mathew gobble his food faster than Otto ate spent grain.

Heimee looked cautious. I assumed he would pose a heap of questions, but he sat there, observing.

"Mathew," I tried again. "Why were you tied to a tree, and what do you want with Aureberg?"

"This stew is amazing," he said. "What is this, some kind of rice? It's very thick."

I showed Heimee the note. Mathew's words popped as he spoke.

Heimee answered Mathew's question without lifting his eyes from the letter, and on it, his own words appeared:

Pops: It's barley.

Heimee regarded the letter with wide eyes. I don't think I had ever seen Heimee impressed with anything before. He rubbed his chin regarding his guest with new interest.

"Barley, huh? I don't think I've eaten barley before." Mathew shoved another spoonful in his mouth. "Nope, never. But it's delicious. Would you stop looking at me like that? I haven't eaten in days. And what I did back there consumes a lot of calories, you know? I need them back."

I was growing restless. Why was he avoiding the subject? And what in the Bastard's name were calories? I needed answers, or I would burst. I looked at Brinn as if her image alone would help me. Her blue dress, dirty and grimy from the night before—oh, right! That's it.

"Who's the girl with blue hair?"

Mathew gulped down the contents of his mouth and stared at me.

Well, that did it. Yes, I also know things.

"What girl with blue hair? I didn't say anything about a girl with blue hair."

"What are you talking about?" Brinn asked, her words also showing on the letter.

"It was on one of the messages you didn't read."

Brinn squinted at me. "You forgot to mention a girl with blue hair?"

"Yes, Ludik," Mathew said. "Explain that."

Heimee leaned in with the kind of calm you'd expect from an executioner. "Either start talking or start walking."

"Damn it, Pops, don't be so scary," Mathew said. "Alright, deafo. I don't know who she is. Happy? She came out of nowhere and tried to kill me a couple of times. No biggy. Maybe she likes being the only mage around here, and I'm stepping on her turf. Except she almost succeeded yesterday. I had to think fast—so I did the only thing I could think of. I tied my foot to a tree and jumped off the cliff. Ah! Before you start, it's not stupid if it works. And as you can see, I'm alive. The little moron scampered down the road and didn't even see me. *Phew*, I naively thought. Only then did the flaws in my plan reveal themselves."

"Why are you in Aviz?" Heimee sipped his whisky.

"I'm looking for something."

"Aureberg?" I said.

"Well, yes. Here, have a Scooby snack." Mathew tossed me a piece of bread crust.

"A what?"

"Who's Miranda?" Brinn asked, brushing me off.

Mathew raised his eyebrows. "Who?"

"Ludik told me you said Miranda chose him to save you. Who is she? Can't be the girl with blue hair."

"Oh, Miranda." Mathew ate another spoonful of barley stew and stared out the window.

"Yes, Miranda," Brinn said, crossing her arms.

"Alright, gee, calm down with the belligerent stares. It's what I call my powers, that's all. I know it's silly, and I shouldn't have told you, but as I mentioned before, I was upside-down a lot."

"You call your powers Miranda?" Brinn asked, crossing her arms.

Mathew bobbed his head with another spoonful in his mouth. "Why not? Then I can say, 'By the power of Miranda!'"

"Well, Mr. Doller, fire mage or whatever," Heimee said.

"Fyr," Mathew corrected. "That's what a fire mage is called. Fyr."

"Yes, that's very entertaining," Heimee replied, "but you should leave now."

"I know this is probably too much to take; I understand that. But I've had such a rough couple of days. Can't I rest here for a little longer? I'm tired. My head is throbbing, and my feet feel like cheese graters—you know what I'm saying, right?"

"The thing is," Heimee began, then paused to sip his whisky. "At my age, you develop a strong sense of smell, and your stench is overpowering my whisky."

"Wait, Heimee," I said. "Mathew, why are you looking for Aureberg?"

Mathew gave me a willful smile. "I need it to save the world. Well, my world. Or at least have a chance of saving it. You can come with me if you want. I know you know where the mountain is. That's why my powers of intuition chose you."

"Miranda?" Brinn said.

"Hmm?" said Mathew.

"Your powers. Weren't they called Miranda?"

Mathew tapped the tip of his nose.

And that's when it clicked in my head. *A fire mage had chosen me to help him find Aureberg.* I stood up, one hand on the table, the other grasping the letter. "I'm going with you."

"Are you mad?" Heimee's eyes bulged.

"The mountain killed my parents, Heimee. If he's going to find it, I have to go with him."

Heimee grabbed me by the sleeve, shaking me roughly, then let go of me and began to sign. "He lured you into saving him because you're the only gullible moron who would be dumb enough to get involved. Can't you see he's having a laugh? Aureberg collapsed, Ludik. It doesn't exist anymore. Weren't you there?"

"I was, and I remember it well," I signed back. "It did not collapse. That's what people say, but it's not true. I saw it, Heimee. The mountain—it, it ran away."

Heimee fell still for a long moment, eyes penetrating mine. "And here I thought you weren't all that rotten in the head. Maybe the fumes have been getting to you. Let me tell you this. I don't know what goes on inside that little brain of yours, but mountains only move in fairy tales. In reality, they are inanimate objects—geological features. I know you were young when the Collapse happened, and to see all that misery through a child's eye—well, you were bound to fabricate some story around it. That's what people do when they can't comprehend what's happening. But you're older now, and this man's a charlatan. Whatever he's after, he is not being honest with you." Heimee glared at Mathew. "I don't know what kind of tricks you played on them, but you have to set them straight. You set them straight right now."

"Heimee," I began, but I didn't know how to say what I wanted to say. There's no easy way to make someone believe you when you say things like, *I am going with this stranger to find the living mountain that killed my parents.* But when would I get another opportunity like this? A fire mage, able and willing to take down a mountain. They don't land on your head every day. "Heimee, I'm going with him."

Heimee blinked. "You want to abandon your life to follow the first lunatic you find dangling from a tree?" He glanced at Brinn, beseeching her help.

Brinn glanced between Heimee, the floor and me. "I'm going too."

"Oh, for Bastard's sake! No, you're most certainly not. This man is a liar and a buffoon! Can't you see that? I don't know what the trick is with that stupid piece of paper, but it's only an illusion."

Mathew raised a hand in front of him, and it caught fire. "I'm not lying, Pops. These are not tricks."

"So you can use magic," Heimee said, slapping Mathew's hand, dissolving the fire into wisps of smoke. "That doesn't make mountains living or you a good person."

"Heimee—" I said, but he cut me off.

"Uh! Idiots always attract more idiots, don't they? You're not going anywhere," he signed. "You are staying right here. And you," he said to Mathew. "Leave."

"Heimee—" I tried again.

"NO!" His eyes were red, demanding, enraged. "I didn't save you from the ice to see you walk out that door on some fool's quest. I..." Something in the window caught Heimee's attention. He walked closer, peered outside, and let out an exasperated sigh. "Bastard's bother."

"I'm sorry we got off on the wrong foot," Mathew said.

Heimee pointed at the window. "Why don't you tell them that?"

Out the window, nothing seemed out of place at first. The meadow ruffled in the wind, the distillery stood still and quiet, and the sky was blue dotted with sparse white clouds. I walked closer to the window for a better view, and that's when I saw the large column of heavily armed men marching up the road.

Chapter 19

Fire Rain

Ludik

What were so many soldiers doing there? And what were they wearing? Brown and bulky, it wasn't like any armor I had ever seen.

Constipated cow! appeared written on the letter as Mathew took several steps back so he wouldn't be visible from the window. *How did they find me? Alright, think, Mathew. What to do? What to do?*

Brinn's hands flared. "We saved your life, and you forgot to mention that the army is after you?"

Mathew paced to and fro, pinching his chin. He muttered, barely moving his lips, but his words still showed on the letter. *I shouldn't fight them. Why are these barbecue lobsters so eager to die?*

"Mathew!" I shouted before Heimee's patience ran out.

Mathew shot me a look as if seeing me for the first time. "You have to understand. I'm new here. I didn't think they knew who I was. I walked up to the fort to tell them I was a weary traveler on my way to Algirin, and they attacked me. They didn't even let me talk. Arrows started raining; men ran after me with spears. I had to fight back. Then Laser-Pointer Girl got all hot and bothered as well, and, uh, well, it was a mess. Complete mess. Barely got away."

"Kelmir fell because of you?" I was in disbelief. But in hindsight, what was I expecting? The fort fell mere hours before I got a magic flying letter from a fire mage.

"No, no, no. Not because of me. The Erosomites saw the commotion and decided to take advantage of the situation. I swear it wasn't my fault. I was just passing."

Mathew produced the book from his bag. Leather-bound, tinged red, though the color had noticeably faded from years of use. On the cover, large serif letters read *New and Old Worlds and How to Get There*. He opened it at random, then as if remembering something, his eyes shot to Brinn and me. "They saw me?"

We shared a look.

"Oh, this is bad. For all that is holy and covered in Nutella, this is bad. They'll think you're with me."

"We crossed some soldiers," Brinn explained. "It's not like there are many roads out there. We told them we ran from Small Butter."

"And they saw me?" Mathew asked.

"We covered you with a blanket."

"All of me?"

"I covered your head. He could only have seen your hand, but it was dark."

"This hand?" Mathew showed his hand. "Tell me, Brinn, does this hand look like other hands around here?"

Brinn covered her mouth with her fingers. "Do you think that tipped them off?"

"Could you do me a favor and have a look outside?" Mathew said. "What do you think, Frisky Freckles?"

"This isn't their fault," Heimee said. "This is your fault." He turned to me and shot me a *this is your fault* glare.

"I didn't know," I protested.

"You ought to have known."

There had to be more than a hundred soldiers nearing the distillery. Some held long wood spears, some brought bags over their shoulders, and some carried bows and quivers. On a closer look, I realized their armor had no metal; it was all wood and thick blankets.

"What are they wearing?" I asked.

"Fireproof armor," Mathew explained. "I know, right? It caught me off-guard, too, the first time I saw it. It's like they knew a fyr was coming."

I mulled the word "fyr" in my head, but before I could ask anything more, Heimee said, "If you have any decency, you'll tell them the kids have nothing to do with you."

"Hold on, Pops," Mathew said. "It's not that simple. I can't allow Munika to capture me. Imagine the horrors that would follow if that megalomaniac easter bunny got hold of my power. Yeah, I know about him. And I don't think that's in anyone's best interest."

"You seem to know a lot about Aviz for someone who's only passing through." Heimee loomed over Mathew. "Traveler, my ass." Heimee stared him squarely and then glanced at the soldiers gathering outside. "To the Ordeal with you, Mathew Doller."

"Is that like 'go to hell' or something? Never mind. Ludik, don't lose the letter I gave you. We can talk through it. And I'm really sorry about this all, Pops." Mathew stuffed his book back in his bag, wang-jangled the kitchen window open, and hopped out.

Heimee regarded the soldiers as they divided into two groups; one surrounding the distillery while the other half approached the house fast.

What were they doing?

"Wait here. I'll talk to them," Heimee said and walked out.

We followed suit.

Heimee greeted the soldiers; though I could not see what he said, I read the letter, *I'm very sorry, but we don't sell whisky on Cifesbordin, nor tomorrow, but you are more than welcome to come Leohdin.*

A couple of soldiers walked forward, chests in the air.

"Are you the owner of this house?" one said. His armor was no different from the rest, except for a red band around his arm, which probably indicated his rank.

Heimee nodded.

The man next to the commander whispered in his ear, and I saw the deep scar on his chin.

"Seize them," the commander said placidly.

"What? No!" I said. "You can't do that!"

Two soldiers marched straight to Heimee and jabbed the butt of their spears into his stomach. Heimee curled and fell to his knees, wincing in pain.

"Leave him alone!" I dashed toward Heimee, but a soldier caught me by the arm, threw me to the ground, and pinned me down with his heavy foot.

Brinn tried to fight back, but they slapped her so hard she flew backward, sprawling on the shallow grass.

"Stop," I pleaded. "Mathew left. He's not here anymore!"

The man in command twirled his hand signaling something to his troops. The soldiers by the distillery began to shuffle. Sparks flashed under their hunched bodies then tiny flames came to life. Were they lighting candles?

Heimee rolled on his back and onto his feet in one smooth motion, jammed a shoulder in the soldier's ribs, spun on his feet, and punched the other's throat. The second soldier staggered backward, hands clutching his neck. Heimee, mouth open like a roaring beast, kicked the first soldier in the solar plexus.

His defiance was short-lived. The second soldier regained his stance quickly and whacked Heimee across the back with such force the spear snapped in two. Then both soldiers ganged up on him, punching, kicking, and hitting until Heimee was back on the ground, curled into a ball.

The men beside the distillery tossed their candles against the windows. But those were no candles—*they were bottles.* The bottles broke through the glass and exploded, setting the malting barley on fire. Flames erupted and spread fast. In moments, the malting floors were all ablaze.

"No!" I yelled. "You can't do this! He's not here! Why are you doing this? He is gone. Can't you hear me? Stop! He is not here!"

The man in command glanced at me as if I were but a bug. "You might be right," he said. "But how else are we to lure him back? He has a heart; he'll try to save you. Personally, I hope he's hiding inside. He may not be so easily burned, but my guess is he still needs to breathe."

"And what if he doesn't return?"

The man smiled hauntingly, "Don't worry. One day, I'll face the Bastard for all my crimes."

A coldness grew in me like winter from within, my breath

condensing and visible. Why were we being punished? All I did was help someone.

Heimee was back on his knees. Spearheads pointing at his torso. His head hung low, averting his eyes from the fires consuming his life's work. No. Not his life's work. His *life*.

I glared at the man in command. "If Mathew returns, I hope he burns you all to ash."

But why would he? He was in the clear and away from danger. Did he really need me to find the mountain? Sure, I would make it quicker, but that was all. He could probably find it all on his own.

The man stared at me with an infuriating calmness while flames spewed from every window in the distillery behind him. "Burn the house, too," he commanded.

I held my breath.

The soldiers behind him produced the same clear glass bottles with a rag stuffed into the bottleneck, a clear liquid slushing inside. They set the rag on fire with flints and swung the bottles at the house. Another home I would have to see destroyed. I thought of my bed and clothes, the Tales of Salamorin, of Heimee, and what was left of his possessions, all about to be consumed by greedy flames.

The bottles smashed through the windows, but apart from broken glass and the stench of alcohol, nothing happened.

The soldiers shared puzzled glances and tried again. And again, no fire.

That's when a shadow moved across the rooftop. Mathew stood on the frigate, hands on his hips, a broad grin stamped on his face.

Did you miss me? the letter read.

The commander called his archers. But nimbly, Mathew slid down the frigate and out of sight. He reemerged from behind the house, shooting fireballs from his hands indiscriminately.

Covering their faces as the flames licked their skin and charred their hair, the soldiers fled, leaving their bags of fiery spirit behind. Mathew stopped, bent his knees, and engulfed the meadow in flames. I couldn't see past the fire, the heat biting my face.

Sweat formed on Mathew's brow as he gritted his teeth. With a flourish of his hands, men burst into human torches, scampering in every direction, trying to extinguish the fire clinging to their armor. Mathew fell to one knee, panting. "What are you waiting for?" he said. "Get to cover!"

Arrows missed him by no more than an inch, breaking apart against the house wall and the frigate, some getting stuck in the gaps between stones. "Alright. Time to return all the fire you gave us."

I helped Brinn up, and we, in turn, helped Heimee. Bruises and swelling sprouted across his face and neck, even his hands.

Mathew sprinted past us, mouth open as he shouted, but I had no time to read the letter. I had other things to worry about. The sea of fire vanished in a heartbeat, revealing scorched grass, ash, and smoldering bodies.

Then a dazing light, like yellow lightning, flashed on the gray stone.

I turned around. Fire poured out of the distillery and malting building like giant snakes slithering across the field of fleeing men. No one cared about us anymore—only survival. The meadow filled again with flames and fiery monsters, consuming everything it touched. No amount of fireproof armor could save them from that.

Another flash. The distillery's roof exploded, sending the mushroom chimney and thousands of incandescent orbs flying in every direction like a blossoming flower. The chimney landed on the side of the structure, pulling down the wall with it, revealing the flaming stills and tanks inside.

The remaining survivors fled across the fields aimlessly, some partially on fire, some completely on fire, until all those that could still run ran out of sight.

Once he felt satisfied that the fray was indeed over, Mathew put out the fires one by one, pushing them toward the sky, where they dissipated into whirling clouds of black smoke.

We observed him despondently, and I nearly jumped at his throat when he approached, wiping his brow with the back of his sleeve, and said, "*Phew*, didn't think this was gonna be such a hot day."

Chapter 20

Goodbyes

Ludik

"You have gone mad." Heimee gritted his teeth, anger flaring in his swollen eyes. "Why are you so eager to waste your life? I can forgive this. You didn't know better, and you're just a foolish kid with a kind heart. You wanted to help. I get that. But after what we witnessed here, you still want to go with him?"

"I have to," I signed, unable to meet his eyes. "The mountain killed my parents."

Heimee threw his arms in the air and winced from the pain it caused him. "What is this obsession with the mountain?"

"The day you found me," I pressed, "that's where I was going."

"And how did that pan out for you? Did you have a pleasant time at the summit? Did you enjoy the view? No, you almost froze to death. And I saved you. I took you in. Is this how you repay me?"

My head sank lower. How could I make him see? "I'm older now, Heimee. I'm smarter, and after all the whisky we made, I'm also stronger."

"Smarter, you say?" Heimee scoffed and glanced at his scorched distillery. Half of the malting building had completely collapsed and the distillery lay in ruins. He took a deep breath and spoke gently. "Listen, Ludik. We can still get out of this. I'll tell the army we have nothing to do with this dung bucket." A thick finger jabbed in Mathew's direction. "We have no reason to run nor hide. We are as much victims as those poor kids outside. But if you go with him, they will hunt you down. You'll be fighting battles you can't win. I know you're strong, but you're still just a kid. And deaf."

That hit me like a bag of bricks. "Thanks for reminding me. It's easy to forget sometimes," I spat.

"No wonder you don't listen. To the Ordeal with you. To the Ordeal with all of you!" Heimee fumed, got up, and walked away heavily, dragging one leg behind.

Those words hurt me more than I could bear. But I would regret it forever if I didn't go with Mathew. How could I refuse it? "Why can't you understand?" I said, watching him go.

Heimee kept walking.

"We do need to hurry before they come back with reinforcements," Mathew said. "It's a long way to Algirin."

"Algirin?" Brinn asked. "The capital? Shouldn't we go north?"

"I need to get a book from the Aviz library. We're gonna need it to fight the mountain."

"I'm going after Heimee," I said. "I can't leave him like this." I chased him through the soot and embers of the distillery. The whole place was eerily unrecognizable. And if not for the inclination, I wouldn't have noticed he stood on the cellar's door clearing the debris.

The doors to the cellar were scorched but otherwise intact. Heimee pushed a smoldering log out of the way and used his fingertips to pry the door open. He managed to crack one open enough and squeezed through and I followed. Inside, the cellar seemed oblivious to the tragedy that befell the surface, as if it had never happened. Even the odors of wet stone, old wood, and dried alcohol remained unchanged.

Heimee heaved a sigh of relief. I can't hear sighs, of course, but his shoulders sagged, his head drooped back, and his hands, previously jammed into fists, relaxed.

"Heimee, I—"

He held a hand up to silence me and sat on an old wooden bench that had probably stood there since his grandfather bought the land decades before. Heimee was obviously in a great deal of pain but didn't complain about it other than the occasional wince. “Have I told you I ran away from home when I was just a boy?” he said.

I sat on the floor in front of him, like a little child eager for a bedtime story.

“I wanted to see the world, but my old man wanted me to work. I felt wronged and betrayed by my own flesh and blood. I asked him if I could leave for a month or so and see the whole of Aviz. Maybe a little of Erosomita, too. Before I even finished, he started berating me, saying I hadn’t a clue about how expensive traveling was; that I was a fool to think I could live off nature and people’s goodwill; that my duty was to him and my family; that if I abandoned them, it was the same as proving that I bore them no love. He made me so mad, so angry.” Heimee smiled through broken lips with the memory, hands continuing the story. “I seethed in my anger in the very room you sleep today. That night, I climbed out the window, slid on the frigate, and was off into the world. I was gone for months. When I returned, I expected my old man to be livid. But he didn’t say a word. My mother hugged me to an inch of my life and sobbed relentlessly. She’d had to live for that long, not knowing if her child was safe or sound. It’s an unbearable feeling for a parent. I know that now better than anyone. But my old man stood before me, searching for something in my eyes, commanding my attention for what seemed like an eternity. When I finally opened my mouth to apologize, he cut me off. ‘Do not apologize for that of which you meant,’ he said. ‘Your choices are who you are, and a man should not apologize for who he is.’ Those words haunted me for years. Since then, I have learned they aren’t true. They hold a certain pride, a certain grit. They nurture boldness in one’s actions. But I’ve come to realize that I had acted cowardly. I should’ve told them I was leaving, even if it was against their will. One must first be regretful to learn from one’s mistakes. It is quite possible to have unintentional intent. In fact, I’d say those are the most common.”

“Heimee,” I said once it was clear that the story was over. “I need to face Aureberg, or I’ll be the coward in my story.”

His eyes sank. “You’re braver than I was. Make sure you come back.” Then he drew a shuddering breath and said, “In this house, you are no orphan.”

I sprang like a locust and hugged Heimee and felt his thick arms return the hug. His clothes smelled of dirt and smoke and blood. "Come with us," I said.

Heimee snorted. Never a snort held such relief on a heavy heart. "I'm too old for a young man's folly. No. Have your stupid adventure. I'll stay right here." He looked around the cellar to the vastness of barrels stacked on top of one another. Rows and rows of them. "Once people hear about what happened here... I don't believe they'll risk losing their only source of Heims. Bastard help us all; it might start a civil war if I stopped producing completely." He patted my shoulders. "Take a couple of the 39s with you. You know the ones. It's alright. I have a couple more hidden away in case I ever got robbed. They are worth more than gold. Especially handy for buying friends or favors."

I nodded and didn't try to protest, though I didn't like the idea of walking around with such prized possessions. "I'll come back."

He gave me a weak forlorn smile. "I'm sure you will. Just be careful and watch out for that lunatic. He's hiding something; it's as clear as freshly distilled spirit."

"Don't worry, Heimee. I have Brinn with me."

Chapter 21

Dark Nights

Ludik

Please don't hurt me. I make very poor tinder, the tree whimpered.

"I won't hurt you," I said. "I just want to talk."

You know treespeak? I don't think I ever met a treespeaking human before. Uh... well... my branches are extremely wet. They don't burn properly, and when they do, they make a lot of smoke. Toxic smoke! Yes. Your eyes will melt, your lungs will burn, and you'll pee splinters for weeks.

I was out in the forest collecting dead wood for our campfire in the fleeting light of dusk. Being on the road after living the comfortable life Heimee had provided disagreed with me. From the lumpy, itchy floor of the forest, the damp mornings, and the days without a bath to smelling like a tramp, it was proving harder to adapt than I'd imagined.

I ignored the tree and looked down at my boots. The mountain logo on the side of the heel, soothing and encouraging, reminding me of my purpose. I tried another tree for help. These were the Whirmwoods, a large forest extending from Lirterin to the edge of the Guillings region, so trees were hardly a scarce commodity. "Can I ask you something?"

I'm poisonous, said the other tree.

I sighed and massaged my temples. "No, you're not. You are a common milk tree. You both are." Milk trees may look bad at first because their sap is... well, milky, but they're harmless, and their timber does make great firewood even if wet. I waited, but after getting no response I pressed on, "I need to know. A building burned down a few days ago in—"

The Heims Distillery?

"Uh, yes. How do—"

Oh, please, it's fire. We're terrified of it. When there's one, we speak of nothing else for days. As soon as the littlest wisp of smoke rises, that's all we care about.

"So have you seen—"

Although, the tree continued, *this fire was mostly entertaining. No trees around to be harmed, you see?*

A light murmur of agreement spread across neighboring trees.

"Entertaining? Men died!"

Yes. Trees don't chuckle, but I'm pretty sure if they did, that tree chuckled heartily. *It's nice to know trees aren't fire's sole prey. Especially if those who fall under it are vicious Munika's men. He has no regard for our kind. The only downside is that we didn't start it. Oh, if we could, we'd cover man's vainness in ash and soot.*

"They were only soldiers following orders; thinking it was their duty."

You can't spread your roots to both sides, my dear boy. You have to stand by your beliefs.

I mulled her words around in my head for a moment and found them utterly dumb. We don't have to be mean just because others choose to be. But I wasn't about to argue with a tree. "Please, just tell me about Heimee."

Heimee?

"Yes, the master distiller. A grumpy old man; probably grumpier now that his distillery burnt down."

Oh, Muttering Man, yes. He's gained quite a bit of our attention. There it was again, it was not a chuckle, but I swear it was chuckle-like. *From what I gather, he loaded a wagon full of Heims and headed south, muttering all the way.*

My eyes lit up. "So, he's alright? The soldiers didn't come back?" The thought had haunted my sleep ever since I'd left.

I wouldn't go that far. No 'alright' living thing mutters that much. If he weren't driving an ox cart, I'd call him a tree. The soldiers returned but to no avail. The whole region showed up in weight. There are no trees near the distillery, but it was quite the showdown, even from afar. In the end, the soldiers had to retreat—no point in fighting an entire region for one old human.

"Thanks," I said and left the trees to their endless gossip of all things mundane.

I brought dead wood back to camp, feeling marginally better knowing that Heimee was safe. Brinn emerged from the trees a moment later, cradling a bloated water pouch.

Mathew motioned to the circle of stones he had made and said something. "Boycott," I think. Probably nothing worth the trouble. I dropped half the timber carelessly in the circle and set the rest to the side. The wood heaped in such a way no one could light it up without rearranging it.

I took the letter out.

Like being back in the Boy Scouts, I read. *I'll start the fire.* He lifted his hand, the fire lit up, and he dusted his hands off. "Done," he said smugly. "Another three days, and we should reach Lirterin. I don't know about you, but my back could really use a spring mattress. Not that we'll find one in this universe, but anything other than sleeping on the ground will be a gift from the heavens. I always wake up with moss and twigs inside my pants. Does that happen to you, too?"

We didn't answer him. In the past few days, we'd suffered Mathew's weird monologues about cola drinks and cheeseburgers and had learned to tune him out. "I hope Pops is okay," he continued. "If it's any worth, I do regret what happened back there."

"Me too," I answered.

"Well, it was them or us," Brinn said as she sat next to me. "If I had power, I would have used it too. Bastard's Ordeal, if I had my peel, I would have whacked a couple of heads off."

"Is she always this aggressive?" Mathew asked.

"It's only talk," I said.

Brinn shot me a wanna-test-me look.

"I think," I added carefully. "I was never inclined to find out."

Mathew chuckled. "You two are funny."

"Tell me," Brinn said. "Why Aureberg?"

"Power. That's the short answer. It's a living mountain. Imagine the power it possesses. If I could tap into that, who knows how powerful I will become? I could collect huge amounts of heat and blast it all off into space."

"You say a lot of weird things," I said. "What's space?"

"It's what's up there, or what's not up there. It's the space outside the planet. It's ridiculously empty, even of air."

Brinn and I shared a quick look, shrugged, and changed the topic. "How did you get here, anyway?"

"There's this place in Scotland. It wasn't easy getting there, I can tell you that much. I really don't like flying."

"Flying?" Brinn frowned so deeply that for a moment, she only had one eyebrow. "You can fly too?"

Mathew dismissed the question. "My book talks about this old root system."

"New and old worlds..." I said, voice trailing off. "This root system, you mean the Worldroot tree?"

Mathew met my eyes with surprise. "You've heard about the Worldroot?"

"From an old story. Is it real?"

"Well, yes. And no. I stood on the ground where it allegedly stands, said some incantation, and used my power. Then I was here. Well, not here, here. I was three countries away. In Kourr, I believe. A lot of grumpy people over there. I think it's because of the weather. Anyway, then I crossed the overly large and flat Ormandy before reaching Erosomita. Been walking for a while."

"A tree?" Brinn said. "How does that work?"

Mathew shrugged. "All I know is that it felt like I was being liquified and then sprayed on a roller coaster. A crazy roller coaster or maybe a fighter jet."

"For Bastard's sake," Brinn spat. "I haven't the slightest idea of what any of those are. Do you have any clue what he is referring to?"

I shook my head.

"See?" Brinn snapped. "Could you keep your descriptions a little more, uh, let's say, comprehensible?"

"Alright, alright, no need to get angry about it. A rollercoaster is like a railway that—"

"Oh, a railway, of course, why didn't you say so in the first place?"

"Hmm, you don't have those here, huh?" Mathew scratched his head for a moment. "Well, in short, it was a helluva ride."

Brinn sighed in frustration.

"This book we're looking for, what's it about?" I pressed.

"It's a book like this one." Mathew tapped his bag. "It's about magic, and it knows how to take the mountain's power. Or so my book says. We'll go to Aviz's library and take it. Then we'll find that mountain of yours."

A book that could teach us how to defeat a mountain. I couldn't believe it. "A book has that kind of knowledge?"

"Yeah! And the best thing is that I know exactly where it is, so all we need to do is go there and get it."

The conversation went on past dinner and into the dead of night until it was time to get some sleep. Mathew took the first turn in keeping the fire going. You don't want the fire to die during the night while you sleep and wake up frozen or eaten by a borint. Borints love to eat sleepy travelers. I think I'd heard that somewhere. I've never seen one. Nor have I ever heard about anyone being attacked by one. Still, one should err on the side of caution.

A hand pressed against my mouth, breaking my sleep. The campfire had dwindled to a few embers. Mathew stared at me, a finger crossing his lips.

"What—" I tried to say, but he dug his finger harder into his mouth while covering mine a little harder.

I nodded. Mathew lifted his hand slowly, leaving the taste of dirt, burnt wood, and sweat on my lips. I forced my tongue still and lips shut, and sat up, pulling the letter from my pocket. Its letters glowed faintly allowing me to read easily and engage in conversation normally.

"There's someone out there," Mathew said. "We need to move."

Unable to resist, I whispered. "Who?"

I rubbed the sleep off my eyes with my sleeve and peered into the darkness. I could only see the vague outlines of the trees lit by the little starlight escaping the canopies. Then my eyes fell on a form unlike any tree. Could it be a person? The dark tends to play tricks on the mind—no, there was definitely a silhouette hiding among the trunks. My mouth went dry, and my stomach turned cold.

"She found us," Mathew said.

"Brinn?"

"She's up already. Let's go. No sudden moves."

"What can she do?"

"She manipulates light."

"Why is that so dangerous?"

"Let's hope you don't have to find out."

Her shadow—whomever he meant—lurked, making the hair on my neck stand on end. "I think she's closing in." In the back of my mind, something else was troubling me. The trees hushed conspiratorially, too soft to make out their meaning. "What's the plan?"

"We invite her for tea and ask how she's been—what do you think we do?! We run."

Blinding light came from everywhere at once—white light like staring directly at the sun during high noon. I flinched and probably yelped. A hand grabbed me by the arm and pulled me along. I covered my eyes to shade from the intense brightness. Squinting, I noticed Mathew wearing a coal-dark pair of glasses. But before I could think about them further, the light went out abruptly, leaving me utterly blind, with an orange tint trailing across my vision and my heart pounding so hard I felt it on my face. Coldness brewed up my fingertips, and my chest grew warmer. The letter in my hand, I could feel it, but looking at it was as if it didn't exist at all, even though the letters usually glowed at night. But I saw nothing. I looked up and found no canopy outline, or stars beyond it. Even the embers from the fire were nowhere to be found. The world had simply vanished—this was no ordinary darkness. Had I gone truly blind? A small panic grew inside me. I couldn't be both blind and deaf. How would I even—

My hand, I could see it now, holding the glowing letter. Mathew, Brinn, and Era came into being as if a veil had been pulled away, puzzled expressions on their faces. I looked down and saw my legs slowly reveal as if the darkness was draining away somewhere, then my boots, followed by grass and pebbles. The bubble of visibility grew wider, cutting through the forest floor until, fifteen yards behind, it revealed a woman with blue hair and a long yellow jacket.

"Ariel," Mathew said, hands suddenly ablaze. "How've you been?"

Chapter 22

Beautiful Whisky

Ariel

Ariel found herself in Guillingsbaer, washing down her disappointment in herself with the local ale, when she heard a man bellow, "All is light, and Light is all."

Great. Another one. The preacher's hair was gruffy, his beard gruffier, but his bright yellow and green tunic was immaculate. Ariel didn't want to raise attention to herself, though her mug was made from metal and wouldn't break on impact.

Luckily, the taverner shot outside, wielding a broom with both hands. "Scram or I'll wack your head off!"

The preacher, unsurprised by this, waited for the remaining folk at the tavern to intervene. And intervene they did, by flinging their own metal mugs at him. The preacher made himself scarce after that.

She drew the mug closer to her and contemplated it. That explained the bangs and dents all around it. Yet, her disappointment remained rather disappointing, much like the withered potted plant in front of her. Ariel patted its brownish leaves. Poor thing, another day or two, and it would die. Her day was ruined beyond repair, but at least she could do something about that plant.

Ariel drained the last sips of her beer over the plant and covered it with her hands, channeling pure light, imbuing the plant with energy.

As if someone were waking up and stretching their arms, the plant bristled, ruffled, and prickled. Ariel uncovered the poor thing and found a vibrant, green plant with thick succulent leaves and a flower bud rushing to blossom. The petals unfurled and stiffened, revealing a purple flower with a white rim around the orange disc florets.

Ariel contemplated her work; she expected it to bring some satisfaction to her, but none came.

"Rats," she muttered to herself. "I'm gonna need something stronger than ale."

So much work. So much sacrifice and that maniac still got away. But how? Miranda couldn't control that much light in her current form. Could she? Well, Ariel could deny it all she wanted, but the truth was clear—Miranda had done it. Otherwise, she would be in Ariel's hands by now.

Yet. Ariel had failed. Again. Oh, God, what if she never succeeded? Would the world end? *The Worlds,* she corrected herself.

The thoughts brought her back to the morning Half showed up in her room. He could've mentioned that the American boy was a fyr and saved her a lot of trouble. She'd have been more careful with her first approach had she known in advance.

The taverner came to collect her empty mugs and wipe the table with a cloth so dirty Ariel wondered if he was making the tables dirtier on purpose to add to the tavern-*y* ambiance.

"What's the best drink ye have?" Ariel asked him.

The man wasn't fat per se—no one in Scae truly was—perhaps because they lacked dearly in burger joints and pizza places, yet he still managed to present himself as a human blob.

"Heims," he said. "Got's a sixteen-year-old, but it's gonna cost you."

Ariel had no idea what Heims was, but in her mind, any beverage old enough to attend high school couldn't be half bad. "Make more assumptions about me, and it's gonnae cost *ye*." As soon as she said it, Ariel pondered how wise it was to antagonize the barkeeper of a medieval tavern. Or any taverner, for that matter.

Luckily the man didn't seem to take it to heart. However, she prepared herself for quite a bit of tampering with her beverage. Perhaps a little cloud of spit or flecks of rat poop. "Alright, miss."

To her surprise, the amber liquid came in a pristine glass and, as far as she could see, contained no sediment nor any other kind of specks floating in it.

"This is the pride o' the region, miss. The finest drink around; I wouldn't dare spoil it. Especially today, given recent events," he said as if reading her mind. He settled the glass on the table with a thump and returned inside.

Ariel took a whiff. Its scent was all too familiar: it smelled of home, smokey and sweet as breakfast. Could it truly be? She took a careful sip. It was! Her eyes widened. Whisky. A damn good one at that, too. Maybe it had been too long since she last had a proper drink, but she could almost say it was the best whisky she had ever drunk.

"Excuse me, sir," she bellowed so her voice would reach inside the tavern.

The barkeeper emerged with a face full of indentations and a hard stare. "Yes, miss?"

"Who produced this? And where? I'd like to pay them a visit."

The man's stern eyes turned grievous and somber, his shoulders slumped as if Ariel had mentioned his whole family had died in a crazy car accident. "Wouldn't you know it? It burnt down this very morning."

"Really?"

"A terrible, terrible tragedy. Baer's garrison attacked poor Heimee," the taverner said, scowling at the two men sitting at the following table.

"Now, now," one of them said, raising his hands in surrender. "We're on leave, not on duty, so we wouldn't have nothin' to do with it."

The one next to him slapped him on the back of the head. "We wouldn't have anything to do with it. Or we had nothing to do with it. May the Bastard bless ya, Oddik. Ya're as dumb as a mop. Please, we'd like another round."

The taverner took their empty mugs and went back inside.

"So yae've heard about this?" Ariel asked.

The two men shared a look, and one leaned in. "Soldiers talk, and bad news travels fast."

"Ya suck at telling stories, Hannik," Oddik said, clearing his throat before continuing, "The king's men were after this dark fellow, ya see.

Word around town is that he's a sorcerer who can manipulate fire. The same fellow who attacked Kelmir. Munika sent a whole regiment to the distillery, a thousand men strong."

"A thousand?" Hannik interrupted, "A thousand, ya say? Why do ya always have to exaggerate so much? T'was barely one hundred."

Oddik continued as if he heard nothing. "May the Bastard take a shit on me head! I'm telling ya the way I heard it." Oddik leaned further toward Ariel. "This sorcerer roasted the lot like hens in the fire. A thousand men."

"About ninety," Hannik intervened. "Most survived."

"All charred, bone and ash. And the distillery! Gone."

The taverner came out and settled two ales on the soldiers' table. "I'd be there protecting what's left if I didn't lose business," the taverner said. "Heimee Heims is a beautiful man. A great man!"

"I hear he's always grumpy and ill-mannered," contributed Hannik. "Like true men should be."

"Hear, hear!" they chanted.

"Anyways," Oddik continued. "He makes the finest drink this world has ever seen, and now it may be lost n' gone."

"Aren't those synonyms?" asked Hannik.

"Not in this context."

"Especially in this context."

"Shut up. I'm the one telling the story. I'll tell it any way I please!"

"I would've told it better."

"Then why didn't ya?"

"Because ya never let me."

"Gentlemen," Ariel intervened. "Would ye be so kind as to tell me the way to the distillery? I would like to pay my respects."

A few hours later, Ariel reached the charred remains of the Heims distillery. The place was bustling with heart-wrenching activity. Soldiers did their best to collect the remains of their comrades while a mob of aggravated civilians armed with pitchforks, spades, and rakes berated them. The soldiers were vastly outnumbered, and two hours later, they called the retreat.

Smart move, Ariel thought.

Once the commotion ended and the place cleared, Ariel walked to the strange house built between two massive boulders that clearly didn't belong there—perhaps brought over like Stonehenge. Ariel rounded a boulder, found a wooden door, and knocked.

"What now?" came a grumble from inside. The door swung open, revealing a man with a large square face and angry eyes; his skin was a mosaic of different colors. Ariel winced at the sight. That man had taken quite the beating recently.

"I'm sorry to bother ye, but I traveled for months to get here and am a huge fan of yer work. I almost didn't come after hearing about this morning, but at the same time, I thought, maybe in a weird way, this would be the best time to visit."

"That's the dumbest thing I heard today, and half of the region came by. How far did you say you traveled from?"

"From Kourr."

Heimee frowned. "You're much too polite and much too pretty to be from Kourr. Ah, come on in. It's not like you can make my day any worse."

Ariel decided she liked Heimee, maybe because he had a welcoming Scottish warmth about him. She began taking off her shoes, but Heimee stopped her.

"Keep them on. There's glass everywhere. And if you were from Kourr, like you say, you wouldn't anyway."

The house smelled like the inside of a hospital. The window was broken, and shards of glass indeed populated the floor. Yet, she liked the place. It was cozy, like her own little home. Heimee motioned to a stone table, and Ariel took a seat. He reached for a bottle from a large cabinet, walked across the room to get a small pitcher, and joined her with a couple of glasses.

"What's your name?" Heimee asked, filling Ariel's glass.

"Ariel."

"Now, Ariel, where are you from?"

"Scotland."

Heimee stopped pouring for a moment and regarded her apprehensively before resuming filling the glasses. He pushed one toward her, then added a few drops of fresh water into his glass.

Ariel reached for the jar and did the same. "Cheers." She leaned her nose to the glass and took a whiff. It was strong. Very strong, the peatiness completely overpowering the rough alcohol. And dark, the amber so intense it almost looked artificial. In all her years, she had never seen a whisky quite like it. She sipped it and allowed the whisky to cover her whole mouth while Heimee downed his without ceremony. What an experience it was. Not for the faint of heart and definitely not for a beginner. It was like consuming dark chocolate and hardwood. The aftertaste was of orange peel and anise with hints of vanilla. It reminded her of her Christmases with Bubbles and how alone she was—a perfect companion for the broken-hearted. "It's beautiful," she said at last.

Heimee observed her intently. "So you're looking for the dark-skinned boy?"

Ariel shivered at the way Heimee said it. So matter-of-factly. "How do ye know?"

"Until two seconds ago, Scotland was a mythical land where *aqua vitae* was first produced. Well, so were fire mages and women with blue hair. Then that boy entered my house, and everything changed. Will you do me a favor?"

Ariel took another sip from her glass. How could a whisky taste so melancholic? "If I can."

"Don't harm Ludik. That dumb kid. He has a good heart; it's only a little misplaced, that's all."

"Ludik?"

"Blond deaf boy, he and his girlfriend left with that Doller fellow this morning."

Ariel was entirely perplexed by this. "Why?"

Heimee shrugged. "They're teenagers. Sometimes we must let them make dumb mistakes and hope for the best or risk their resentment. See that he comes back safely, and I'll share with you all the whisky you can possibly drink."

Ariel sipped her whisky. "Is he yer son?"

"Yes."

Taken by the intensity of Heimee's eyes and his spirit, she found herself nodding. "I'll do my best. Do ye know where they went?"

"Algirin."

Ariel unfolded a map she took from inside her jacket over the table. "They'll have to pass through Lirterin. If I hurry, I may be able to intercept them in these woods here." Ariel refolded the map. "Why would ye trust me?"

Heimee contemplated the whisky swirling in his glass. "I made this whisky after I learned my boys wouldn't return from the war. It's the first time I have opened this bottle in many years. If you were a heartless wench, you wouldn't have called it 'beautiful'." Heimee refilled their glasses, then raised his. "Cheers."

Chapter 23

Night Hearing

Ludik

"Ariel," Mathew said, dancing flames reflecting in his dark glasses. "How've you been?"

"Oh, ye know—a little distracted sightseeing here and there," the woman, Ariel, said, her words also popping in the letter. The skin on her face was pale and freckled. Her eyes were of an impossible yellow-green, bright as a beacon. Her shoulder-length hair was indeed blue, lighter than the sky, and unnatural. "Let the boy and the girl go; this is between the two of us."

"What?" Mathew replied.

Ariel brought her two hands together and shot a beam of light before us, slicing clean through roots, leaves, and rocks, stopping only after our blankets and supplies lay in smoldering pieces at our feet.

We glanced at them briefly, and in the next heartbeat, Mathew put out his flaming hands and vanished into the blackness behind us. Brinn and I dashed after him, entering a world where even nightly colors refused to exist. How did she do that? And what was I supposed to do? I couldn't see! Brinn groped my arm, then clutched it tightly.

Both relieved and fearing I'd slip from Brinn's grip and be left stranded at the mercy of Ariel, I slammed face-first against a feathery wall, bounced backward, tripped, and splattered on the ground. I groped around the wet moss, trying to find my footing, but the dark was too disorientating. Brinn stepped on my hand, and I let out a yelp. Well, I must've yelped. She found my hair and used it to pull me up and closer to her.

Before I could protest, intense heat licked my face as if I stood too close to a hearth.

Oh, no! I thought. "Mathew!" But before I could panic, the trees panicked first.

FIRE! FIRE! OH, LIGHT, WE'RE ALL GOING TO DIE. Then all at once, the trees burst into singing. I didn't have time to listen; something about it gave me the beginning of an idea.

"Mathew, put out the fire right now! Do it! I have an idea," I said, and nothing happened. "Tap on my shoulder or something."

Brinn shook my arm, then clumsily slapped my chest several times.

"Is the fire out?" I asked the trees, but in response, someone, most likely Brinn, patted my chest, and it did feel a little colder.

"Get on Era, and, uh..." Would they find me crazy? Before I could continue doubting myself, Brinn and Mathew became visible. I glanced at the note in my hand.

"Ye don't know what yae're doin'!" Ariel said. "And ye can't escape. Besides, if ye continue to use fire like that, yae'll only hurt yaerself. Ye can't possibly think ye can control a forest fire."

I used the opportunity to climb on top of Era under the confused stare of my friends. "Get on. I know how to get out of here. I'll explain on the way."

Brinn and Mathew looked at each other, shrugged, and lacking better ideas, climbed on after me. Era flinched and buckled slightly under the weight of three people.

"We only have to escape her, Era. It'll be fast, I promise." I patted her neck. "Would you stop singing?" I yelled at the trees. "The fire's out!"

The singing gave way to a sudden silence.

"Guide us out," I told the trees.

Why would we help you? She's a Leohirin, a rider of the light. She's one with the trees.

"Suit yourselves," I said, imagining the befuddled stares of my friends piercing my back. "But she doesn't seem too concerned about whether my friend burns down this forest. I am. And I know he will. He's pretty stubborn about not being caught. So, please, I beg you, help us now."

I didn't wait for a reply, dug my heels into Era's torso, and she leapt into the void. Well, a void filled with trunks, branches, rocks, roots, ridges, and ditches, that is. Death traps galore. Brinn's arms wrapped firmly around my chest. I'm not going to lie; that bit felt pretty good and gave me the courage to carry on.

"We're utterly blind here. Tell me how to avoid you!" I winced at the thought of slamming at that speed into a tree, and the trees' silence did nothing to help my fears.

You're going to get yourself killed, said one tree, rather unimpressed. *We can't see either, you slab of mobile incompetence. If you continue like this, you'll smash against one of us.*

"But you can feel where we are through your roots!"

I was sure we were about to experience unimaginable pain as Era raced valiantly across the darkness when a tree finally screamed:

You're going to hit Horin. Turn left. Left now!

I pulled Era by the reins, veering left. I hoped.

You turned right, you fool! Can't believe you miss—DUCK!

"Duck!" I bellowed, and as I did, branches grazed my head.

That was too close! Oh Light! Right, right, right, right. Right now!

And so, the most frightening minutes of our lives went by, avoiding head-on collisions while galloping blindly through the thick forest. Then, wisps of light, like tendrils of smoke from a blown-out candle, diluted the darkness until my dark-adjusted eyes made out the faint starlight evading the canopies under a moonless sky.

I sighed with relief. "We did it!! I can't believe we—"

Era stopped abruptly, rose on her hind legs, and dumped us off her back onto the bumpy forest floor. My stiff back cracked with the impact, but it hurt surprisingly little since Brinn and Mathew softened the fall.

Mathew shoved Brinn and me to the side.

She's not far behind, several trees warned.

"Alright! We can't stop here," I said, clumsily getting up and helping Brinn.

Mathew winced, clutching his chest tightly. "*Uuughhh, eehhhhiiiii,*" read the letter.

Brinn shook her blue jacket with her hands, then punched me in the shoulder. "What in the Ordeal was that? Who were you talking to?"

"I'll explain on the way," I said. "We can't stop now. She's right behind us."

"How do you know that?" Brinn asked me as she grabbed Mathew by his shirt and helped him up. "Oh! Will you stop whining? Never had people fall on you before?"

"I'll explain everything. Let's go!" I looked at Era, but she shook her head as if warning me that riding her now wasn't in our best interest.

"Start talking, or I'll knead you into a loaf," Brinn said as we moved, "that was terrifying, and now I'm all pumped up."

"That's the adrenaline talking," Mathew said, breathing easier now.

Brinn grabbed him by his jacket. "I'm not in the mood for your nonsense."

"It's not nonsense. It's a hormone your body produces—"

Brinn pulled him closer to her face and silenced him with a glare.

"Yeah, Ludik, what was all that about?" Mathew spat. "Gee, you're like a Russian doll of surprises."

They both glared at me for an answer.

"Okay, okay," I sighed. "I have night hearing."

Brinn's glare became so intense I thought she would be the one to set the forest on fire.

"Alright! I'll explain everything. Just start moving." I took to a brisk pace, unsure where to go next. "Which way should we go?"

Left. Like a hard left, offered a tree.

I nodded and turned left. "This way." Then I took a deep breath and said, "I can talk with trees."

Chapter 24

High Fever

Ludik

"And that's why I'm a superhero," Mathew finished saying as we continued wandering through the forest.

With my attention divided amongst hunger, drowsiness, tiredness, and the constant chatter of the trees, I only tuned in now and then, glancing at the letter to see if Mathew had finally stopped rambling. He hadn't. It wouldn't have been so bad if we still had our supplies, but alas, they were lost, not to mention sliced in half. Not that it mattered much because we couldn't afford to stop and rest anyway. We walked restlessly, day and night, hoping we'd make it far enough to lose Ariel. Fortunately, Lirterin wasn't too far away.

"Superhero, huh?" Brinn said. "Let's check the boxes, shall we? You're responsible for the fall of Fort Kelmir, the subsequent invasion of an Erosomitan force, the raid on Small Butter, and, let's see, ah yes, the destruction of Heimee's distillery. We all remember how that went. And just yesterday, you almost burned down the whole Whirmwoods, which apparently is home to self-aware and intelligent *trees*. All of this in as little as a couple of days. You are, certainly, at the height of heroism."

You tell him, girl, said a tree, to the hums of agreement of every other nearby tree.

Mathew raised a finger. "Hey! How could I have known?" he said.

"You didn't. Besides, I don't remember hearing any complaints after my *friend* tried to make sashimi out of us."

"You're the sashimi!"

"I really gotta stop using modern references."

"Among other things," Brinn muttered.

Ludik, a tree said. *We're confident you'll leave the forest before she turns around and realizes you're not on the same road.*

"Thank you so—" I began, but the tree interrupted.

Don't thank us. We're not happy about this. Orin and Kellin were on fire, even if for only a little, because of your friend's carelessness.

"I'm truly sorry—"

Oh, he apologizes instead. Hear that, Groovies? He's apologizing. That must mean we're all good now.

"Sorry," I muttered.

You're not very bright, are you?

"What are they saying?" Brinn asked.

"Ariel turned north," I said. "Mathew's right; she thought we'd try to stay clear from the main road."

"Ah! See! I told you so," Mathew said. "She thinks she's so smart. God! Feels good to outsmart her for once."

"Well done," Brinn said, clapping slowly. "You outdid yourself this time. Why don't we take this opportunity to look at some more of your heroic accomplishments? I mean, if it wasn't for Ludik and the, uh—and I still can't believe it—trees, we'd be dead. If you had been honest from the start, we could've avoided the whole fire at Heimee's. Or even if you understood the meaning of discreteness, Fort Kelmir would still be up, Small Butter would still be a nice little village with a mountain view, and many lives would have been spared from misery. You should feel very heroic."

"Gee, Brinn, what a fountain of joy you are," Mathew said, rolling his eyes.

"You're welcome. There's a cart over there. Cover your face."

"Is she always like this?" Mathew asked me. "Or only when she's hungry?"

With Lirterin so close by, traffic wasn't unusual. But something was clearly wrong with the woman hunched over the back of the cart, hands on her face.

"Good day," Brinn said.

The woman looked at us, startled. There were bags under her eyes, her skin was pale, and her haggard demeanor suggested she'd been awake longer than we had.

"Is everything alright?" Brinn asked while glancing at Mathew, who hadn't covered his face.

"Don't give that look," Mathew answered. "There's a kid in there. Ill by the looks of her. She won't give a damn about how beautiful I am."

"Why can't you be even a little circumspect?" Brinn made a snappy gesture and glared at him.

"I'm the very definition of *circumsect*."

"It's pronounced *circumspect*! You don't know what it means, do you?"

While they bickered, I approached the cart and found a girl wrapped in blankets like a cocoon shivering uncontrollably. Gummy, gray skin, purple lips, and droplets of sweat slid down her forehead.

"Her fever is so high," the woman said, not taking her eyes from the little girl. "I don't know what else to do. I tried to reach Lirterin, but oh, Bastard help me; what if she doesn't make it in time?! Oh, Bastard, please help me." She looked back at her daughter. "Inesa, my dear, I'm sorry, I didn't mean that. You're going to be fine, hun, I promise." She grabbed her hair so tightly I thought she'd rip it out, held it for a moment, and faced me again. "I was going as fast as I could, but she began to shiver so much she rattled the cart." She covered her mouth and suppressed a sob. "Please, please help her. I beseech you."

"Mathew?" I said.

He turned away from the finger Brinn held on his face. "What?"

"You have medicine, right?" I prodded. "You kept saying you wouldn't have come here without a full pharmacy on your back."

Mathew clutched the straps on his backpack tightly. "Yeah, but I didn't bring that much. Besides—"

Brinn pressed her finger firmly in Mathew's chest, poking it with each word she uttered. "Spoken. Like. A. True. Hero."

Mathew considered Brinn for a moment. "You know what? I just remembered I might have something for her. Let me have a look." Mathew approached the back of the cart and peeked at the girl. "Oh, god, what if this is a disease my body has never met before," he muttered as he leaned in, but the letter, faithful as ever, transcribed what he said. "Death by medieval virus. What a sad way to go." After no more than a glance, he said, "Looks like the flu."

He reached inside his backpack, pushing aside the Heims bottles and Miranda to get to the bottom, and produced a small white bottle with a red label. The same he'd taken for his headache the day we found him. He poured five chalky pebbles and extended them to the woman. "Give her half a pill every six hours."

The woman only then seemed to notice him as she reached for them, eyes bulging, her hand hesitating slightly.

"He's a healer traveling north from the deep south," Brinn explained. "There aren't any better healers in the whole world. You can trust me on this."

"I'm so sorry," the mother said as she accepted the pills. "I didn't mean to be rude."

"You should unwrap her," Mathew said. "She needs to cool down."

The woman hesitated, glancing at Brinn. Brinn nodded assertively, and the mother removed the blankets around her child. The girl's clothes were soaking wet.

"Remove her clothing and clean her as best as you can," Mathew instructed. "Then change her into something dry. And, most importantly, have her drink plenty of water."

The woman shook the despair in her eyes and dutifully complied.

"See," Brinn said, arms akimbo. "It's not so bad to actually save the day for once."

"Thanks. Brinn," he replied. "I have to say. It does feel good. Like it brings a warm fuzziness to my heart." But his expression said the opposite.

"How long until—" the woman began but stopped herself. "I'm so sorry. I'm Kala." We made our introductions, and she continued. "How long until the medicine works? Her fever seems to be getting stronger."

Mathew's eyes sank a little. "I'm not gonna lie to you; it could take a while. Just make sure she's taking her pills and drinking plenty of fresh water, and she'll be hunky-dory in no time."

I peered at the girl, feeling pity for her, strong fevers being so much like hypothermia. I touched her forehead to measure her fever and found her skin was so hot it seemed to seep into my hand like an open fire.

"Don't touch her," Mathew rebuked me. "The flu is highly contagious. If you get it, we're all gonna get it." He shook his head and produced a transparent bottle, unlike any glass I had ever seen, which contained a transparent gel. "Give me your hands."

I extended my hands cautiously. "What is it?"

"Disinfectant," he said, squeezing a blob onto my hand and then his. It was cold and slimy and smelled of distilled spirit. "Rub your hands together until it dries completely."

I momentarily pocketed the note to rub my hands. "Do you drink this?"

He replied but I had to wait until the note was back in my hand. "Not unless you're stupid."

"You say many strange things," Kala noted.

"So I've heard. There's not much else we can do for her," Mathew said, then to us, "We should get a move on."

"There's space in the cart," Kala said. "I'd be happy to take you."

"Great," Mathew said, slumping his shoulders. "We're definitely gonna get ill." Then, after glancing at Brinn, he added, "Dibs on Era."

Brinn rolled her eyes. "Sure."

"Don't look at me like that," he protested. "You're likely immune to this strain, or at least have a better resistance than I do."

"Sure," Brinn repeated.

I carefully got on the wagon so as not to perturb Inesa, but she was already looking much better. The sweating had stopped, and her lips were a much better shade of purple.

Kala cradled her daughter's head to help her drink some water from her flask when her eyes widened. "Her fever... It's- it's gone."

Mathew looked as surprised as Kala, furrowing his brow. "Tylenol doesn't work that fast."

Kala jumped from the wagon and lunged at Mathew, hugging him tightly.

Mathew held his arms up in surrender, yelping, "Medieval viruses!"

Kala let go of him, "How can I ever repay you?"

Mathew scratched the back of his head. "You don't have to. It's nothing. Just don't hug me again." But I could see the glint of pride in his eyes.

"You're traveling to Lirterin. I presume," Kala said as she loosened her hug. "Do you have a place to stay?"

Mathew shook his head.

"Then you're staying with my sister, Kola. She might be a bit much, but she'll make you the best food you'll ever eat."

My stomach trembled at the mention of food.

Kala looked around our sad little group. "Is this all you're bringing with you?"

Mathew scratched his head, "Yeah, we were attacked by—"

"By a borint," Brinn intervened. "We lost most of our supplies in a creek. Very unfortunate."

"A borint, you say," Kala was shocked. "I have never seen one. And we live in the middle of the Whirmwoods. I heard the stories but always assumed they were tales meant to keep little children from venturing too far. Bastard knows I tell the same tales to Inesa all the time. What was it like? Does it really have four eyes?"

"Oh, it was very dark," I said. "All we saw were antlers coming right at us."

Kala looked at me, and there it was, the pity in her eyes. "You're an odd group, aren't you?"

Mathew gave her a polite smile. "You don't know the half of it."

Chapter 25

Star City

Ludik

As soon as we crossed the forest's edge and Lirterin came into view, glittering in the afternoon sun, I was a kid again, running around the refugee camp, contemplating the star-shaped walls of Alturin.

I knew Lirterin had similar architecture, but there's a difference between knowing something and seeing it with your own eyes. *Would I be allowed to enter the city?* Refugees were strictly forbidden to enter Alturin; that was the whole reason they'd built the camp—to keep the unwanted out; to let children and mothers starve and freeze. *And die.* I seethed, fury for all the past tragedies bubbling back to life. I could see the mountain as if it were right in front of me, destroying my life along with so many others, forcing us into begging and stealing and—

My chest trembled, a coldness brewing inside. I clenched my jaw and balled my hands into white-knuckled fists. I wanted the city gone like the mountain and the hearts of evil men. Let it rain fire and raise it to the ground and—

Brinn took my hand, eyebrows drawn together under a wrinkled brow. "Are you alright?"

The torment vanished as if I'd awoken from a bad dream. I nodded. "Yes, I... I remembered something awful, that's all."

Brinn squeezed my hand. "You want to talk about it?"

I shook my head and gave a reassuring smile.

Soon we were at the gates, yet there were no guards, no hurdles, no deterrents—no obstacles of any kind. We passed the vine and moss-infested bastions carving the landscape into submission as if they had long ago retired from their true purpose of fending off attackers. The city gates were so tall and wide that Heimee's house would fit with room to spare. And none of it held the littlest meaning, burden, foreboding, or threat to anyone else but me. To them, it was a quotidian business. The city existed in the same way the sky does or the forests or the lands.

Not to me.

I held my breath as we crossed the gate, heart thumping in my chest, and, unceremoniously, we rode inside.

Mathew adjusted the scarf over his face. Even he saw it as a wrong move to enter the city, as he put it, willy-nilly. Lirterin was bound to have a large constabulary, and all its members would be on the lookout for the dark-skin mage at large.

We passed a large square, bustling with commerce and simmering with people. I couldn't hear, but the boisterous activity produced a shimmy in my chest.

Kala led us deeper into the city, away from the walls and busy streets and closer to the castle occupying the very center. The castle perched on an immense rock formation, looming high and casting its imperial shadow and authority over the city and surrounding country. The castle itself did not look like a castle but an extension of the rock it stood on, with smooth surfaces, impossible to climb, and narrow windows no man could squeeze through—a solid block of stone and power.

"It's quite ugly, isn't it?" Mathew said, looking at the monolithic castle.

"I don't think they were worried about looks when they built it," Brinn said.

"It's very old," Kala said. "T'was built to defend against mages, or so the legends say."

As I got used to the city and its streets filled with regular people just going about their lives, my nervousness faded, a little at a time. My contemplations ceased when we entered a narrow street leading away from the main road. The buildings were different there, tall and narrow, the stonework sand-colored apart for one exuberantly pink building, and infested with fluid greenery. Climbing plants slithered across the walls, surrounding the whitewashed door and window frames, all the way to the red-tiled roofs. And potted flowers inhabited every other nook and cranny as if we were surrounded not by buildings but by vertical gardens.

Inesa sat up, wrapped so tightly in blankets that only her face was visible. She was no longer pale. Well, at least her nose wasn't, resembling Heimee's after he had one too many thumbglasses of Heims, minus the snot, that is. And, although she was up, she had not spoken a word, but it was evident she was happy to have arrived.

Kala headed straight for the tall wall of pink, knocked on the white door adorned with pink flowers, and as if she had been standing behind that door all along, a large woman with an ample bosom and arms thick as logs burst out and squished Kala in a fierce embrace.

"Sis! So good to see you! What brings you here?" the large woman said. She wore a loose white dress under an aggressively red apron, her hair tied in a bundle behind her head, while her cheeks wobbled as she moved, giving a certain lifelike character to the mole near her chin.

"Nice to see you too," Kala said, doing her best to breathe. "Inesa is sick, I brought her to see the physician, but she seems much better now."

Kala's sister nearly dropped Kala on the floor and trampled over her to reach her niece. "Sick, you say?"

"Hello, Aunt Kola," Inesa said. "My body hurts, please be gen—"

Before Inesa could finish her sentence, she, too, was crushed by her aunt's immense hug, followed by a complete physical examination.

"Careful," finished Inesa while Kola tousled her hair.

"Poor thing," Kola said. "Nothing a good cup of your auntie's tea won't fix."

"She's better now," Kala explained, "but if you saw her this morning... she was..." Kala trembled with the memory. "Let's just say I'm very fortunate to have met these lovely people. They saved Inesa's life."

Kola gave each of us a quick, piercing look as if staring over some invisible lunettes.

"I told them they could stay with you," Kala said. "I'm in their debt."

Kola's inspection broke, replaced by a rumbustious wave of her massive arms. "Your debt is my debt! Thank you so much for helping my niece. She's a lovely child, you know? Once you get to know her, that is. One time, a kid stole an apple from a local vendor and Inesa saw him. So she walked right up to him, pulled his ears, twisted them, and took the apple right back, I tell you. I've never seen such bravery in a child," Kola said in one breath.

"That's quite..." Brinn started, then fumbled, prodding for something with which to finish her sentence before finally deciding on, "brave, Ms. Kola."

"Oh, none of that. Kola is just fine."

Brinn smiled politely. "Your niece is a fine young lady for returning the apple to the vendor."

Kola was stunned. "Give it back to the vendor? No, darling. She ate it right there and then."

"Oh, that's... huh..." Brinn stammered.

"Now, that's exactly what I would have done," I said.

"Oh!" She gave me a pitiful look, the one people always give me after hearing my voice. Kola lumbered to me and patted my hair, her touch as soft as being hit with a mallet. "I see. Don't you worry, child," she said slowly, making full use of her lips. It was like watching two slugs go at each other. I hate when people do that. They would be ashamed of themselves if they knew how ridiculous they looked. And it's not like I could explain to her I held a magical letter transcribing everything everyone said.

I gritted my teeth and answered as politely as I could, "Thank you. You can speak normally."

Kola's lips twitched. I had seen that, too. People often get aggravated when they do something annoying with the best intentions and then learn about their annoyance as if it's my fault. "Is it better this way, dear?"

I nodded. "My name is Ludik. These are my friends, Brinn and Mathew."

"Pleased to meet you, ma'am," Mathew said.

"You are way off your stomping grounds, aren't you, mister?"

"Oh, you would not believe it."

"Come in, come in," she said, heading toward the door. "You all look like you're starving." She stopped abruptly and raised an eyebrow at us. "And in dire need of a bath. Come, come, let Aunt Kola take good care of you. You can tie your rides there. I'll ask my neighbor, Bolo, to tend them. Need not worry. He's a good man and very gentle with animals. And, well, if he's not, Aunt Kola will also take good care of him."

We filed in to get through the door, which was no easy feat, with Kola's massive figure obstructing it. She continued to speak before anyone else had a chance to. "I used to travel too, you know," she said while ushering us to a large living room with plenty of crockery hanging on the walls in all shades of pink. "I even went as far as Alturin. I tell you, quite a lovely journey. I was in the company of this handsome young man, see? Ah, yes, I was young once, you know. And thin. Just like you lot. Pretty too. All the boys in Lirterin wooed me. You wouldn't guess that, now, would you? This young man, oh, was as handsome as they come. And strong too, but more importantly, very wealthy. He took me on vacation to his hometown, Alturin. Have you been there? Oh! It is lovely, I'll tell you. We had the most wonderful time. Oh, yes, Oddik was a fine man indeed."

Brinn's mouth became just a thin line on her face. "And—" She attempted to say more, but before she could, Kola carried on.

"Ah! You're wondering what happened to him." She made the briefest pause. "I dumped him!" she said gleefully. "Right there and then! He was too handsy, you see, and I'm a very respectful lady."

"No doubt," Mathew confirmed.

Kola nodded firmly, doubling down on the affirmation.

I did my best not to laugh. I didn't know if this story was meant to be funny or not, but Kola must've spotted my bloated cheeks.

"It's alright, dear; you can laugh," she said. "He was an imbecile. Trying to take advantage of me. Can you imagine that? I slapped him and rode all the way back home by myself without the comfort of the carriage, but I had my pride. In the end, all I wanted was a bath! And wash his adorable smell off my skin." She took a deep breath, sighed nostalgically, then burst, "And all the dirtiness from ekkuh riding. *Humpft*!"

I know I can't hear *humpfts* and other types of onomatopoeias, but I didn't have to look at the letter to know she said *humpft.* And she was right; I did crave a bath. We all did.

Kola served us a wonderful meal she called *leftovers.* After living with Heimee for so long, I was an expert in leftovers, and this was not it. What Kola served was a beautifully made meat pie, served with roasted vegetables and black rice. I had never tasted black rice before; gooey in texture and livery in taste. And it was only after we ate that Kola revealed she'd prepared it all with fresh black pig's blood. Yummy.

Brinn instantly turned green, and Mathew cautiously settled his fork down on the plate. I didn't care. Having nearly starved before, I took food for what it was, and right then, I was famished. Besides, if you're killing an animal, should you be so picky as to waste any part of it? That's disrespectful, at best.

Afterward, we all took our turns in the bath. Kola tirelessly fetched bucket after bucket from the backyard's common well and repeatedly heated the water on the stove, all while denying any offered help. The whole thing made me slightly embarrassed, but I did not complain, especially when my turn came to get in the warm, soapy water. Ahhhh, that was probably the best bath of my life.

To top it all, Kola washed our clothes and gave us long, comfortable nightgowns.

"Really, this is too much," Brinn said. "How can we ever repay you?"

"You already have," Kola said as we sat drinking tea in the backyard lit by candle lamps. "But you'd repay me even more if you stopped offering to repay me."

Brinn blushed and meekly pulled her knees to her chest, nestling on the wicker couch and closer to me. She looked so cute in that oversized gown, her soft skin gleaming in the candlelight. She caught me beaming at her. "What?" she asked, smiling.

I fumbled with my thumbs. "Uh, nothing, I just—"

"I think what Ludik is trying to say," Mathew said, "is that he has a crush on you."

Now was my turn to blush. "I... uh..." What could I say? What is one even supposed to do? I mean, I liked Brinn. Like, really liked her. Heimee even said she liked me back. But then what? Do we start walking while holding hands all the time? That's such an inconvenient way to walk. Besides, I was sure Brinn was perfectly happy with how things were between us. Bastard help me, she was so pretty.

And, for reasons I still can't fathom, the situation made me uncomfortable. I couldn't say, *No, I don't have a crush on her.* What if she took it the wrong way? And was there any right way to take it?

Before I could torture myself any further, Brinn kissed my cheek. If I wasn't blushing before, I then became a ripe tomato.

"Oh, there's nothing more beautiful than young love," Kola said, then took the opportunity to embark on yet another story.

Brinn then leaned on me, and I just stood there, afraid to move, afraid to do something wrong and ruin the moment. The evening went by in each other's comfort, and I even managed to put an arm around her shoulder. Yes, I sure did.

Still, had I known the miseries that lay ahead, I would've made sure to savor that night so much more.

Chapter 26

Old Worlds

Ludik

Kola showed us to a room with two bunks. After a quick sorting of who slept where, we settled in for the night. I wanted to open the window, but both Brinn and Mathew argued against it, saying they had slept through enough cold nights for a lifetime, thank you very much. I wasn't used to sleeping in a warm bedroom, and the concept of a warm night had become foreign to me and profoundly uncomfortable.

Despite being exhausted, I kept turning in bed, trying to see which side of the pillow was coldest, when I noticed Mathew's book peeking from his backpack.

I craned my head to look over the top bunk, where Mathew lay sleeping heavily after stating the top bunk was his because he had called *dibs*—whatever that was. Brinn slept across the room on the other bunk, sprawled as if someone had carelessly thrown her there. She was also definitely sound asleep.

I knew I shouldn't touch others' belongings, but curiosity had the best of me. Tiptoeing, I reached for the book. It had been so long since I read something. Well, how long had we been on the road? A week? Two? Let me rephrase that. It had been too long since I'd read something new. Eager to read, the anticipation wiped away the remaining drowsiness. I slipped the book out of the bag, left the room, and headed for the candle-lit backyard, fearing it might be too dim to read comfortably, but my fear turned out to be unfounded.

I sat on the same wicker chair and stroked the leather cover, fingers contouring the title's golden letters.

New and Old Worlds and How to Get There

With fingertips teetering with anticipation, I flipped the cover and shot past the index, skipping the starter and going straight for the introduction.

Introduction

Little is known about space, time, or the universe itself. For thousands of years, across various civilizations, cultures, religions, political affiliations, and scientific discoveries, man, despite his belligerent nature, never ceased his valiant efforts to uncover the mysteries of reality. Few, however, glimpsed at the ineffable vastness that is the cosmos.

Twelve thousand years ago, one civilization, located in what is now known as the northern African country of Mauritania, Terra (Earth), came close to reaching farther into the truth than any of its predecessors or successors, including the highly advanced conglomeration of scientific advancements of the XX and XXI centuries.

With magic on their side, they reached for the stars, toward the infinite variety of worlds suspended in the whole of creation. Sadly, the stars answered, in the form of a very large ray of energy, which bubbled the very ground they stood and obliterated any trace of their existence to such an extent that all which remained was a scar in the earth. No name, no structures, no language, no culture, no knowledge. No evidence to suggest they ever existed. And worst of all, no magic.

Except for one last bastion of hope—the Worldroot tree. The last residue of a powerful and ancient organism, stubbornly feeding Terra with the vibrant energy of Scae. As long as there is Magic in Scae, there is hope for magic to return to Terra. And he who possesses magic within can use that connection to travel between worlds.

As I read, I couldn't stop remembering Laurin's tales. My first friend, now lost, like everyone else from my old life. The memories flooded through me, and a tear came to my eye.

I turned the page.

It was blank. So was the next page, and the next, and the one after that. I opened the book in the middle.

Nothing. Not one single drop of ink.

"What?" I muttered.

Then dark smudges formed on the page like drops of oil in a cup of water, dissolving into the paper and then reshaping into organized letters.

If you are going to be this mopey, the story ends here.

Was Mathew up? Was he messing with me? I nearly ran back to the bedroom but decided to peek through the window instead. Mathew slept soundly in a way that was hard to fake.

I sat back down. "Who are you?" I whispered.

The trees must be right about you. You are not very bright. I am the one who has been transcribing what everyone says to that little piece of me you hold.

"Mathew?"

Not very bright, indeed.

Then it hit me. Mathew's powers. Could they be a person? "Miranda?"

Oh good, he can think, after all. I should not be so hostile, I suppose. You did very well escaping Ariel, using the trees to guide you. That was rather cunning, I must say.

"Who, uh... What are you?"

Is it not clear? I am a book. And have been a book for a very long time. Much like a cooking book, but instead of recipes, I conjure deadly spells. And at this point, I do so to your benefit, so I kindly ask of you not to refer to me, ever again, as 'What' but as 'Who' or 'Whom.'

"What?"

Sigh. I am a person. Much like yourself, only shaped like a book. Act accordingly.

"Oh."

And please, do not pity me. You pity yourself enough for the rest of us. I am quite fine, I assure you.

"So, you're helping Mathew save his world?"

It is more of a symbiotic relationship. I help him, and he helps me. As you can see, I have appalling mobility.

"So, Mathew got his power from—"

Yes. I shared my power with Mathew. Fyr is by far the least powerful of the mage classes when wielded by humans. Although highly effective against ordinary men. Perfect for self-defense or intimidation. Its performance, however, dwindles dramatically compared to any other mage class. And, alas, it is utterly useless to me, paper being the flammable substance it is. I regard self-immolation as a somewhat undesirable prospect.

"Could you give it to me as well?"

No.

"Well, why not?"

There are plenty of children playing with fire already. Best to keep it contained. Would you not agree?

I wasn't happy with the reprimanding tone of her words but held my tongue and changed the subject. "Why didn't Mathew tell us the truth about you?"

I expect telling a couple of children you have in your possession a living and talking piece of literature does not come with the ease of comprehension one might expect.

I considered it for a moment. She made a valid point. Although considering the weirdness of everything else that happened, what was one more living and talking book?

I expect, also, that he concealed my nature to protect me from unsolicited hands.

I pursed my lips, unsure how to respond, so I continued, "What did you mean by mage classes?"

There is leoht, obviously, and fyr.

"You're a leoht, too, aren't you?"

Again, obvious, given the magical light I have displayed through the little piece of me in your possession and the way in which you can read perfectly well despite the dim candlelight.

"Why didn't you give that power to Mathew? Wouldn't it have been better if he too was a leoht?"

He does not have the heart or the imagination. Leoht is not an easy thing to be. The colors of the world mingle and fade and lose their meaning. If you are not ready, it could drive you mad. What was the color of the sky? Which shade of blue were your eyes? What was the tone of your mother's skin? And in the dark of night, every night, you feel drained and powerless. A leoht's power needs to be constantly replenished. Under sunlight, they are nearly invincible, but at night, a smart leoht must show restraint. A quality I am afraid Mathew does not possess.

I had a hard time following all this new information, but curiosity kept me going. "Please, tell me more."

The powers you have not encountered are togian, lighten, and dwinan. A Togian has the ability to attract and repel objects—considerably the most dangerous of classes. A wrong move and you could destroy everything you have and everything you are. Better to leave it untouched.

"Are you a togian?"

I am not. A lighten has electromagnetic powers; to you, that translates as lightning, I would say. However, you would have to be incredibly dim of imagination to use it only for lightning. It can do so much more, especially in conjunction with other forces. And no, I am not a lighten either, nor am I a dwinan, the most powerful of forces and, some would argue, the laziest. Contradictory, I know, like so much in our universe. A dwinan has the power to absorb energy and does little else.

"I'm confused; you said togian was the most dangerous."

Dangerous is not the same as powerful. Dangerous things have to be handled with care and restraint. And sure, a dwinan would also need to be careful, but no more than any other force. Power and prudence should always walk hand in hand. And while prudence can be rather scarce on a togian's soul, as a dwinan, you are nearly impervious to damage. I consider an invulnerable foe the most powerful, even if less dangerous. Would you not agree?

"And do any of them give you the ability to speak to trees?"

No. That is something special. One must be intrinsic to their nature to listen at such profound levels. One such as yourself or me.

"You?"

That is how I found you. The lesson is over for now. I know I am a book, but I also get tired. And bored. I presume you will have plenty of questions for Mathew when morning comes. I suggest we retire. There is still a long way ahead of us until Algirin and Aureberg.

"Miranda?"

Yes.

"Thank you for the letter."

You are welcome. May I ask for something in return?

"Sure."

Do not fuss about this. Mathew means well.

"Alright. Brinn, however, might have a few words to put in before the matter dies down."

I do hope so. Few things have been more entertaining than observing that little kettle pot fuming.

Chapter 27

Old Friends

Ariel

"Rats!" Ariel kicked the dirt, then stomped the ground with both feet while grumbling. "I had them! How could they have gotten away?" She arched her back and growled at the sky.

Were they that bold? Was Mathew so incredibly arrogant he'd taken the main road? Were they more afraid of her than of Munika's soldiers? That's crazy. The main road was probably full of spies. It would be impossible for them to cross it and not be seen.

"They must be in Lirterin by now. Or in jail. *Hmm*." A thought occurred to her. "That would work out great for me, wouldn't it?"

If they had been caught, all she had to do was sneak past some guards. Much easier than dealing with a fyr who somehow could see in complete darkness. Wait for the cover of night, make it darker still, and bam! The book was hers. Easy-peasy.

Would Mathew use his power in a confined space? So far, he had shown the level of restraint expected from a four-year-old on Christmas morning. If she required more evidence about Mathew's character, she only had to remember how he had handled things thus far. Maybe he wasn't only a foolish kid after all. Perhaps he was simply a homicidal maniac. And those two gullible idiots probably hadn't a clue about who they were hanging with.

But why would Mathew accept their company? Ariel had endlessly scratched her head about the subject and always came up empty. She simply couldn't find a single reason for Mathew to drag two kids around with him. Was he planning on using them as hostages should the need arise? That was dumb. No constabulary or army would give a damn about two lost kids playing adventurers.

Ariel peered through the canopies. Lirterin was close now; she would've seen the smoke if it were burning. At least that was reassuring. But what itched her most was how they'd escaped through her fingers. There was no way any of them could've seen through the darkness she had cast on them. Even Miranda shouldn't have that kind of power—although she had assumed that before and Mathew had escaped through her fingers right after Kelmir. Even if Miranda had used her power, Ariel was sure the darkness hadn't been tampered with; it had remained consistent throughout. If it hadn't, Ariel would surely have noticed. Wouldn't she?

She reviewed the night in her mind's eye. The boy, Ludik, had shouted at the trees to help them. But that was absurd. Trees can't talk, can they? This was a different universe, after all. Was that the reason why Mathew kept dragging them along?

Doubts festered about her mind all through the rest of the day and night. When the next morning came, as she closed in on Lirterin's massive gate, some of her foreign memories started to fill in the gaps. In her memory, the trees understood each other. Ariel did not know how she knew that or even how the trees communicated, but there was a distinct feeling they did. Her friend had known how. But her memories failed to contain that information, like so many other things. Ariel couldn't piece it together—like a smell you are positive you smelled before but can't pinpoint where or when—yet it lingered with its familiarity.

Lirterin was a pretty enough city but failed when compared with modern cities. For starters, Ariel wouldn't find a movie theater or a pizzeria. *Hmmm, pizza,* her stomach growled. She could very well go for a movie and pizza. And a bottle of Old Pulteney. Yes, she usually wouldn't go for it, but the situation called for a more relaxed whisky—one of those golden amber whiskies they put out—briny and citrusy with hints of apples and honey.

Ariel forced herself to relax. She may have lost their trail, but it was only a matter of time before Mathew did something stupendously stupid and gave away their position again. Besides, Algirin was still a long way ahead; she would have more than enough time to catch up. So why not rest for a while? Enjoy a glass of Heims somewhere? Who knew? Maybe some of Heimee's whiskies sold there bore a more mellow smokiness. Oh! And a warm bath!

That settled it. Today would be an Ariel-day. Who said you couldn't take a break from saving the world?

Lured by the savory smell of street food, Ariel headed to the closest market, where she bought a couple of stinging-honey meat skewers despite her misgivings about medieval street food. But as soon as she took a bite, all reservations about food poisoning and general hygiene disappeared from her mind. "Oh, this good," she mumbled as droplets of sauce ran down her chin. She caught them with her palm. The taste reminded her of chicken teriyaki but made with rich applesauce and super-strong honey. She bought two more before being drawn to another vending cart by the aroma of what appeared to be caramelized apples. Water welled in her mouth as the vendor handed her one. She bit into the red orb. It was like biting into a mango cheesecake covered in crispy maple syrup, juicy and not too sweet—absolute heaven in Ariel's mouth.

She bought another and was about to dig into it when the strident voice of a large woman wearing a red apron caught her attention. *Who would wear their apron out in the market like—no way*. It couldn't be this easy, could it?

The woman had an impressive girth to her and spoke as if she was about to beat the crap out of the vendor, which despite the drudging conversation, kept the polite smile of a man contemplating murder.

Ariel listened intently as she faded the colors of her clothing and hair to the same drab colors that everybody in that backward place was a victim of—all shades of brown. There's nothing she could do about the shape of her jacket, but tweed is timeless. Most people lack the necessary observing powers to notice such minor details. And if someone cared to ask, she could just berate them; nothing drives people away faster than a haranguing woman.

"Oh, I tell you," the large woman was saying. "Did I tell you they saved my niece?"

The vendor nodded his head so vigorously that Ariel expected it to fall off at any moment.

"Twice," the vendor replied, his smile uncompromised.

"Oh, without them, who knows? I don't even want to think about it, my niece could've died. Died! Imagine that! I wouldn't be able to live with myself. You should see them, they are so cute. One of them is deaf, you know, but he seems quite normal, apart from being a little reserved. A little arrogant too, and a touch ungrateful, may I add. But he is in love with the girl, and they just make the cutest couple. I just want to smother them and gobble them altogether."

Deaf. Ariel's ears really perked up now. Could it really be them?

"Please, don't forget your groceries." The vendor pushed the bag closer to the woman.

"Then there's the dark one," she continued.

There! She had found them again. How could Mathew be so careless? Well, it did not matter. Ariel wasn't going to start complaining about her luck and a plan began to form in her head.

"He's very polite and well-mannered, although he has the strangest mannerisms. Handsome too." The woman backhanded the vendor's chest. "If I were any younger, I might've gotten a little frisky."

The vendor's smile faulted, nearly revealing the snarl underneath.

"And mysterious," the woman continued as if it was nothing. "Always making references about absurd things. Half of the time, I have no idea what he is on about. And the clothes he wears! Strangest fabric I've ever seen—strong and blue. Hard to wash too, became heavy as a stone after wet. And the looming, done so precisely. I know no tailor of such skill."

"Wait," Ariel said, jumping in. "Are ye referring perhaps to Mathew Doller?"

The woman's eyes bulged as they found Ariel, inspecting her from top to toe. Then slapped Ariel's shoulder with such vigor Ariel had to take a step back. "You know Mathew?"

From the corner of her eye, Ariel noticed the vendor's disappearance. *Well, there's my good deed for the day.*

"Funny little fellow isn't he?" the woman said.

"Oh yes, ye don't know half of it." Ariel forced a giggle. She began mimicking the woman's moves in order to become more likable, though she suspected it wasn't necessary with this person. Ariel extended her hand, "I'm uh..." what would be an appropriate local name? She hadn't the faintest clue. "Deidre," she picked at last, "pleased to meet ye!"

The woman regarded her for the longest time. "The pleasure is all mine, hmm, Deedee. You can call me Kola. A friend of Mathew is a friend of mine. You know, you remind me of someone I used to know. Jules was her name. We were friends, you see, but she had an almost bizarre tendency to steal all my men. There was this young boy she stole from me. He could've been my husband if it wasn't for her, or perhaps she did me a favor there... well, I'll never know now, will I? Where was I going with this? Oh, yes, his name was Ulvik, a horrible name if you ask me. But that's how they name folk up north. One night, Ulvik and I were at a Ball. Jules came and asked if she could have the next dance. Well, wouldn't you know it? They ended up doing very naughty things that night. So I told her, 'Jules, we are no longer friends,' and broke up our friendship right there and then. They got married, then he died of a heart attack after they had their second child. Sad story. Yes, yes."

Kola's eyes grew distant while Ariel began to wonder if this had been the worst idea she ever had. How could someone talk like that? Before Kola could regain momentum, Ariel took her hands. "Yes, yes, sad. It's just that, uh, listen. I haven't seen Mathew in a very long time. And isn't it the most wonderful coincidence that he would be here in Lirterin at the same time as I am?"

Kola's eyes widened with understanding, and an enormous grin left her mouth wide open. Then she slapped Ariel's shoulder with such force something in her neck cracked. "I tell you what! You are having lunch with us. Your friends are very tired from traveling. Poor things have been walking for days and were attacked by a borint. A borint out of all things. I didn't even know they were real."

"A borint, ye say?" Ariel said. "I can hardly believe it."

As Ariel followed Kola, she immersed herself in serious scheming, ignoring the woman's nonstop chatter. Kola hadn't been quiet for more than two seconds since Ariel met her, and Ariel was stretching her ignoring powers to an absolute maximum, delivering a constant stream of, *hmms, is that sos,* and *yeps,* that kept Kola happy all the way to her front door.

Ariel wasn't pleased about it and already disliked Kola enough that she wouldn't mind if her house burnt down. Not that that was her plan. She would get in, locate Miranda, void the room of light, grab the stupid book, and jump out. Easy and quick. It had to be quick. Any longer, and Mathew might create such a conflagration innocent people would get hurt.

How can someone like pink this much? Ariel thought as Kola reached for the door handle. *Yellow would've been a much better choice.*

The door cracked open before Kola could open it, and Ariel's heart skipped a beat as she slid behind Kola's back. If she weren't careful, her plan would crumble right there and then. *Oh great, now I sound like Kola.*

A little girl came out with a pouty face. "Auntie, what's for lunch?" the girl said. "I'm starving."

Ariel's stomach squeezed at the sight of the child. "Oh, who's this lovely wee lass?"

Had Kola talked about her? Of course, she had. She had talked about her whole life in the last fifteen minutes. That had to be her niece, the girl Mathew apparently saved by administering paracetamol. But all Ariel could think of then was *what if this little girl gets hurt?* She couldn't have that on her conscience.

"I know, I know, sweety. Aunt Kola's is going to make your favorite dish."

"Blueberry pie?"

Blueberry pie for lunch? Now that's a nice aunt.

"You know it! Inesa, this is my friend Deedee. She's a friend of our guests. Deedee? I told you about my niece, haven't I? She is a delightful child." Kola hunched and pinched her niece's cheeks to Inesa's visible displeasure. "Aren't you the sweetest of things? She was ill, you know. Very ill, indeed. With a very high fever. Your friends found her and saved her, you see? They gave her some medicine, and she got better, right there and then! I have never heard nor seen anything quite like it, I tell you." She turned back to Inesa. "Will you help me with lunch?"

"No!" Ariel said.

Kola seemed hurt. "Well, of course not. I wasn't asking you—you are a guest, and I would die of shame if I made you work." She looked directly at Inesa when she spoke to let her know this was a valuable lesson.

"I mean," Ariel said, "she's a young girl. Shouldn't she be out, playing with her friends?"

"Oh, dear! Haven't you heard a single word of what I said? She was sick yesterday. Very sick, indeed. She shouldn't be out and about. What if she gets worse again? Have I told you about when my mother told me that if I bathed in the lake during winter, I would get sick? No? Well, you're in for a good one."

Ariel would be totally fine if Kola got hurt. It would probably be another story for her to tell: the time two sorcerers set her house on fire—no one in town would ever hear the end of it. But she couldn't be responsible for hurting an innocent girl.

"I'm so sorry," Ariel said, "I just remembered something. I have to go."

"Nonsense," Kola said. "Whatever it is, it can—" Kola frowned as a thumping sound grew louder. It came from the end of the street, and soon it felt like a freight train was heading their way. "What is this ruckus about? I tell you, some people have no respect for their neighbors."

Ariel's face turned white as a mass of men in tight formation, bearing that ridiculous fireproof armor she had seen in Kelmir, came into full view.

Of course, Ariel thought. Kola had been babbling about her guests for the whole town to listen. And guess what? The town listened. What were the chances the army would have skipped on that opportunity? None, it seems.

Behind her, she heard a gasp. A *what now?* crossed Ariel's mind as she turned. A girl with an impatient air about her stood at the door gaping at the approaching soldiers and gaped even wider when her eyes found Ariel. Despite Ariel's urban camouflage, the girl took only a second before recognition lit her face.

"You brought them here?!" she said. "Are you that insane? These are innocent people!"

Ariel quickly realized how this must've looked to her eyes, but what did she care? A far more pressing issue marched steadily up the road.

Chapter 28

What Now

Ludik

"What else have you been hiding?" Brinn said, pointing an accusing finger at Mathew over breakfast.

Kola had left our clothes, clean and dry, beside our beds, and after we'd gotten ready, we found honey milk and a wide assortment of local pastries waiting for us on the kitchen table.

I had time to mull it over in my head and decided that I would've most likely hidden Miranda's true nature too, were I in Mat's shoes. I also had my eye on a puff pastry cake filled with egg cream, which was much more deserving of my attention.

Mathew scowled at me. "This is all your fault. Who told you to rummage through my stuff? A man can't turn his back for a minute, Jesus."

"Don't blame him," Brinn blasted, sweeping an arm over the table. "We have given you nothing but our absolute trust, the least you could've done was to return the favor."

Mathew sighed, and his shoulders sagged. "Alright, alright. But you have to understand that I'm the one with all the responsibility here. I must protect Miranda, and I've only known you two for a little over a week. I had to play it safe."

"Oh, sure! You have been doing nothing but *playing it safe.*" Brinn scoffed, then muttered to herself, "playing it safe," and, with that, her rage was renewed. "You are so full of it! It's a wonder you're not covered with flies!" Brinn slammed her hands on the table and rose to her feet. "I'm going to get some air. The stench in here is a little overpowering."

I watched her walk away. From experience, I knew she required some time and space, so I focused on the crackling pastry in my mouth. Puff pastry might just be the best of human inventions.

"Women. Am I right?" Mathew said after Brinn was out of earshot.

I shrugged, mouth too full of deliciousness to answer.

Then something startled Mathew. He turned his head abruptly toward the front door.

"What?" I asked with a mouth full.

"Something's off," he said, eyes still fixed in the same direction. Then he looked back at me, concern in his eyes. "Get your stuff. I think we're in trouble."

Mathew leapt off the table, heading toward the front door. I followed suit and found Brinn there, then Kola, her arms planted on her hips, body wiggling. Kola shouted at someone while Inesa clutched at her skirt. To Kola's side was a familiar face that I couldn't quite place. She had brown hair, brown eyes, and strange brown clothes, yet her face was so familiar.

When recognition hit me, my heart sank. *Oh, no. This is no place to fight.* My feet took a life of their own, moving me out the door. Then everything came into view. Soldiers in bulky brown armor blocked the street on both sides. Ariel had brought company. Kola shouted furiously at the soldiers, but I was too enthralled with the scenery to read the letter. This couldn't be happening. Not again. One false move and many people would get hurt, and to make matters worse, we were cornered.

Maybe we could escape the army with minimal collateral, but the army *and* Ariel? It was doubtful. No matter how I looked at it, we were doomed.

A hand touched my shoulder. Mathew's eyes came into focus. *The letter!* I was so dumbfounded I'd forgotten about the letter in my hand.

"Snap out of, kid," Mathew was saying. "We need to run."

"Have you no regard for anyone?" Brinn said, her hands shooting in every direction. "Are you happy with yourself?"

"I didn't bring them here," Ariel answered. "Let's talk somewhere where bystanders won't get hurt. I can conceal yer escape. Ye have to trust me."

"Trust you? You nearly cut us in half!"

"If I wanted to cut ye in half, yea'd be halved."

Next to Brinn Kola continued to berate the soldiers. "This is an outrage! I pay my taxes! Leave my front door at once! These are good kids. Inesa, I won't tell you again. Get inside now! You found the wrong suspects!"

"Is that a threat?!" Brinn spat at Ariel.

Ariel rolled her eyes. "No, it's the opposite of a threat, ye ignorant bampot!"

"You're the bampot!" Brinn retorted.

"What's a bampot?" Mathew asked me.

I shrugged. How was that the important thing in the middle of all this? The sentences scrolled down the paper faster than I could read them.

Then the rapid flow of words came to a sudden stop.

"SILENCE!" someone in the line of soldiers bellowed, or so said the letter.

The shield wall parted, and an imperious looking man walked through. I had seen him before—a long time ago, in another life altogether. In front of us stood Munika Muril, commander of the armies of Aviz. "You are surrounded. If you choose to fight, you will lose. And die. And so will countless innocent civilians. You can die with that on your conscience. Or you may surrender. Life as a prisoner may be tough but certainly more pleasant than being dead."

Then Miranda wrote, *trust the leoht.*

I looked at Ariel. Could she really help us escape? How was I supposed to trust a woman who attacked us and sliced right through our belongings with a light beam? I hesitated.

"This is a limited-time offer, of course," Munika added, almost like an afterthought. He waved his hand, like a grandparent patting the back of an invisible grandson, and in unison, the soldiers lowered their spears and took one step forward, banging their shields on the cobblestones.

The vibration spread through my feet as if the building in front of us had collapsed.

You had to be impressed by Munika. Either Mathew or Ariel could've struck him down, unprotected as he stood. But the fact that he showed no fear whatsoever made both mages hesitate at making the first strike.

Ludik. It is the only sensible move left. If Munika captures me... Miranda left it open as if the repercussions were too severe to mention.

The soldiers took another earth-shaking step and engulfed Munika.

"So be it," he said as casually as one might order breakfast at an inn.

I balled my fist, "Ariel," I found myself saying.

Ariel turned to face me, confusion and surprise on her face.

"You're right. Let's take our conversation somewhere else."

She smiled at me, catching me completely off guard. Then she shed her brown color and was vibrant anew. Blue hair, green-yellow eyes, yellow jacket. The soldiers, taken aback by the power display, hesitated with their next step, but only slightly.

Ariel spun, and a beam of light slashed through the shield wall, leaving many soldiers holding on to half shields and half spears.

Kola fell backward in shock, looking like a beetle on its back struggling to right itself.

Brinn and I went to her aid, and as we pulled Kola up, Ariel sent a flash so intense that as it radiated through the soldiers the world turned white for a moment. I repeatedly blinked to shake away the haze when I noticed Mathew and his fiery stare.

"Mathew, help us here!" I shouted, knowing full well what those eyes meant.

Mathew flicked his wrist and flooded the street with fire. He took a moment to observe his work, grabbed Inesa by her arm, and pulled her inside the house.

There was no time to argue. Brinn and I pushed Kola through the door.

I read the letter.

"Ye bloody eejit!" Ariel said from the other side of the fiery curtain. "I'm gonnae kill ye!"

Mathew threw blistering fire out the front door.

"Stop it!" I bellowed. "Are you insane? You're going to burn the city to—"

Brinn slapped Mathew across the face so hard it felt like the soldiers had struck the ground with their shields again.

"What was that for?" Mathew said, rubbing his cheek.

Brinn slapped his other cheek. "We're in a confined space! Can't you see how dangerous that is?"

"Relax, sister. I can always move the fire out of our way. Besides, this will hold them out longer. Do you want to get caught? Is that it? Because if we surren—"

Kola slapped him so hard she toppled Mathew to the ground and said, "In my house? And to know I've defended you; given you refuge! Get out! Oh, my poor flowers. Inesa, find your mother. We need to leave quickly." She dragged Inesa by the arm and dashed toward the back of the house with surprising agility. "Kala? Kala!"

Mathew got to his feet, shaking his head. "Stop slapping me. I'll fix it."

The fire now consumed the door and its frame, the heat licking my face. Mathew pushed some of the fire back into the street. But I doubted it would make much difference.

We ran out the back and found Kola, Kala, and Inesa, all three shouting, "Fire! There's a fire! Leave your things behind! Get to safety," to their neighbors. People poked their heads out of windows, fear exploding in their faces once they noticed the rising thick smoke.

Soon the backyard flooded with frightened people trying to reach the street as orderly as possible, given the circumstances.

"Let's mingle," Mathew said, taking his scarf from his backpack and rolling it around his head. "How is it?" he asked, pointing at his wrapped head.

"It's like you're invisible," Brinn said.

"Sarcasm? At this hour?" Mathew turned and bumped into Ariel.

The light mage held a ball of light in her hand. "Give it to me, and I'll make sure it doesn't fall into the wrong hands."

A lumbering woman came behind Ariel and slapped the light out of her.

"No more fire!" Kola said. "I can't believe this. I meet mages like in fairy tales, and they burn my house down. Shame on you!"

Mathew pointed at Ariel while she tried to recover. "Ah! How does it feel?"

Kola raised the back of her hand, but before she could strike Mathew down, he flinched and cried meekly, "Don't hurt me. I'm leaving. I'm leaving."

Mathew pushed through the crowd with Brinn and me behind. We reached a large door where soldiers inspected the inhabitants and ushered them to a spot on the other side of the street where another soldier stood on a cart saying, "Point out the intruders. One has dark skin, impossible to miss."

At least twenty fingers pointed directly at Mathew.

"Guess there's no point in wearing this," he said, removed his scarf and rammed the crowd, shoulder first, creating a corridor as people fell left and right.

Brinn and I dashed right after him when darkness fell around us again.

"No fire!" I shouted pre-emptively to the gloom. Then a hand grabbed me by the arm and pulled me away. Brinn pulled me through the void bumping and pushing people out of our way until we crossed the threshold, and the street was visible. I looked over my shoulder. A black sphere of nothingness engulfed the whole neighborhood like a giant obsidian marble had materialized there.

Mathew waited but a few steps away, motioning us to follow him. This time, I pulled Brinn by her arm, breaking her out of her stupor as she contemplated the black ball.

We took the first street on the left and found another wall of shields, spears, and men wearing thick, fireproof armor. Mathew drenched them with fire, and we ran in the opposite direction.

Miranda understood how hard it is to read while running, so she made her letters as big as possible.

"I don't want to hear it," Mathew said. "If they catch us, it will cost us much more than a lousy city."

It pained me to my core to agree with him, and every time I looked over my shoulder, I was sure the smoke was thickening. A beam of light slashed through the cobblestones slicing a cart in half. The stone ox at the front end jumped into a run dragging the remaining half across the ground, dumping the slowly burning straw on the street.

"This doesn't have to get any uglier," Ariel said from the top of the building to our left. "But I cannae let ye roam around burning cities. I have to stop ye right now!"

"Oh yeah?" Mathew said, and the building Ariel stood on became a pyre.

Mathew stumbled with his next step and panted. "Holy smoke on a cracker," he said, leaning on me. "That wasn't easy."

Men, women, children, and pets ran and leapt out of doors and windows while Ariel landed in front of us, mouth agape, hands dug in her hair. "Clear that fire, ye monster!" she screamed. "Ye bastard, clear that fire right now!"

Mathew drew in a sharp breath and shot Ariel with a fireball. Ariel countered with a thick beam, and the fireball exploded mid-air, sending her flying backward and tumbling over the cobbles. She rolled and shook the flames off her jacket, trying desperately to regain her balance as Mathew shot fireball after fireball as if punching at an invisible man, but with every punch, another fiery orb homed in on Ariel. Ariel dodged, rolled on her back, planted her feet on the ground and jumped to her right, dodging Mathew's attacks, using her momentum to get back on her feet when a fireball struck her shoulder, sending her into a spin. The next blow exploded on her back, hurling her body across a window.

Mathew hunched, hands on his knees, wheezing. "We gotta find a way out. I can't do this much longer," he said between breaths.

I searched for a clear path but saw none. Every possible exit was either filled or filling with soldiers. Only then did it occur to me that this must have been planned from the start. The army knew where we were, and they deliberately chose that moment as their best opportunity to trap Mathew—completely disregarding civilian safety. That was the only explanation for the number of fireproofed soldiers chasing us.

Mathew faced another group of soldiers head-on, pouring fire like a madman. But with each attack, he grew weaker, the fire less bright, less intense. "Come on!" Mathew bellowed. "Is that all you got?"

As he poured fire, the soldiers at the front retreated and were quickly replaced. Flames spread across every building with each wave. Muril would send man after man until they'd drained Mathew completely.

Ash and glass fell all around us as the fire rampaged and blew out windows. I caught Brinn's eyes, fear flourishing in her stare. I could not stand the thought of her getting hurt, but what could I do? Then something else caught my eye. A few yards away, someone waved from a tiny square hole where the street met a burning building, but the hot air smudged the person's face. Who was that?

"Inesa," I muttered. "Look, Inesa is there, in that gutter!" There was no hesitation as I hurried toward the tiny hole. "Follow me!"

Mathew stumbled, but Brinn caught him before he fell and helped him along as my heart pounded in my chest.

A building collapsed behind us; the air and dust it displaced knocked me off my feet. I hampered the fall with my hands, scraping them on the ground. Brinn and Mathew slid through the hole, but Inesa ran toward me.

I tried to warn her, "Get back," but dust and smoke burned my throat as soon as I opened my mouth. Then time slowed to a crawl as the hot wind fed the remaining fires like giant bellows, shattering windows and shooting shards of glass and splintered wood in every direction. I felt my skin sizzle, and without thinking, I threw myself over Inesa to shield her from the brutal heat. My sleeve crinkled and ignited spontaneously. I shut my eyes, squeezing Inesa as best as I could, hoping that at least she would make it. In those last moments, as the heat threatened to melt my skin, I thought about Mom and the night she'd left me to join the bliss, and I found myself walking across the cold end of the earth, across the devastation left behind by Aureberg.

Then in a flicker of blue light, a reassuring coldness washed over me.

When I opened my eyes again, I laid in a black puddle, still clutching Inesa. The little girl looked to her sides, confused, probably wondering the same thing as me, *How come we're not more dead? And where did all this water come from?*

The fire was gone. My clothes lay scorched, tattered, and somehow wet, but I was unharmed. Mathew had somehow diverted the fire before it harmed us.

The street had become a desolate sight, scorched, broken, dead. Soldiers approached cautiously as a unit—one step at a time. There was no point in fighting back; I was about to be captured.

Something wriggled out of my chest. "You're a mage," Inesa said, looking up at me in awe. Well, I think that's what she said. Her lips weren't hard to read, but you never really know when lip-reading after being completely engulfed by fire.

"No, Mathew is." Talking felt like vomiting, acid searing my throat. "Tell your aunt that we're very sorry for everything." The soldiers were now within arm's reach, and spears pointed at my chest. "You should go home now."

Only then did Inesa seem to take notice of them, her lips forming an 'O'. In the next moment, she snuck spryly away between thick legs and singed shields, leaving me behind, watching her scamper while a rough, heavy hand grabbed me by the shoulder.

Chapter 29

Dark Cell

Ariel

When Ariel opened her eyes, she wasn't anywhere she'd expected to be. Had she been sleeping? If so, it'd been a horrible sleep. She wasn't on the street where she'd passed out, but she couldn't remember leaving it. What she remembered was people running from the fires; the ear-shattering sounds of structures buckling and collapsing; the calls for surrender; the shouts for control; the severity in which brave men faced the flames to save what was possible; and the screams—the continuous and relentless cries of panic reverberating across the city as it burned.

Ariel balled her fists. That lunatic. What was wrong with him? Then a disturbing thought occurred to her. She could've stepped aside. She should've stepped aside. Yes, if she had, they would have run away. Maybe the city wouldn't have suffered as much. The outcome was as much on her shoulders as it was on Mathew's. No! She couldn't afford to think that way. Ariel had a mission. An important mission. She wasn't the person best suited for the job. She knew that much. She was an agricultural advisor. She didn't like people that much and was perfectly happy spending her days in bed, reading, watching telly, eating junk food, and tending to her house plants. Occasionally she had to do some work—scam farmers into the best crop yield of their lives. But mostly she liked to be left alone.

But her life had been put on hold because she had to stop a megalomaniac witch from saving the world or whatever that meant. Why did the world always need saving from misguided people trying to save it? If everyone would just mind their own business... Where was she anyway? Was she naked? She couldn't be sure. Her whole body was numb and there was no light anywhere. She'd know if there were, she was leoht, but her bed—was it a bed? She probed around with her fingertips. Straw. Wet straw. Then her fingers ran down her aching body—definitely naked.

Her hand shot to her chest, searching for her pendant, heart racing as pure panic brought her wide awake, fingers sliding across her oily skin, proving her worst fears true. Her seed was gone.

Questions queued up in her mind. Where was she? Why naked? Who had stripped her? Why weren't her wounds healing? And why was it so darned dark? Her first order of business had to be to tend to her injuries. Her power allowed her to recover to a certain degree, except she was exhausted, sore, and her soul drained of light.

"Rats," she mumbled. How long had it been since her skin touched sunlight? Her eyes were open, weren't they? Ariel blinked, making sure she could feel the movement of her eyelids. She could. Her eyes were definitely open.

Ariel raised her head, trying to make out her surroundings, but saw only vague outlines. Squares? She reached further inside of her and found a hint of light, just a wisp of it. She could use it to reveal where she was, but she knew not to waste it unnecessarily. Best to save it in case her wounds festered or some other emergency. There would definitely be a next emergency.

She sat up on her wet bed of straw, wincing and grunting. Ariel tried to speak and regretted it. Her voice was hoarse and her throat so dry it felt like she had drunk a cup of volcanic rock moments after it ceased to be lava.

And she was thirsty.

Clank.

What was that? It sounded metallic. A creak followed, amplified by what sounded like a long hall. Was it a door being opened? Ariel tried to adjust her vision again, and right before she used the little light inside her, a vague orange hue outlined a rectangle—a doorway. The orange became brighter, closer, along with approaching footsteps.

The light from the doorway began to paint her surroundings, glittering on wet surfaces. And that was when she saw the bars caging her. Her eyes were so perfectly adjusted to the dark that the slightest light revealed her shady world.

Her cage was made of thick canes interlaced like a net. Ariel grabbed it by the square holes and tried to lift it. It didn't look like it was attached to the ground by any other means except for gravity. But it was no use; it was too heavy for her, and the oil made it slippery. Straw lined the floor, and all of it was glittering wet. Herbal notes, which reminded her of the orphanage's toothpaste, assaulted her nostrils. Her tongue slid across her front teeth. When was it she'd last brushed them? Ariel touched the ground rubbing the oil with her fingertips. It was milky-white and pungent. What was it, eucalyptus? Minty-like. In and around the cage, the floor glittered with the stuff.

To the side of her bale bed lay another bale, a simple white gown resting on top, along with a glass of water. Ariel took the glass and sniffed to make sure it was indeed water. It was, and she drank it as a man holding a torch appeared at the entrance. The awful reality of her situation became clear.

The soldiers had found her and stuffed her in a cage, which by the looks of it, had been specifically built to contain a fyr. Any attempt at escaping, the fyr would ignite his own death. The fyr wouldn't be harmed by the fire, of course, not directly, but the room had no ventilation she could see, which meant he would suffocate quickly enough. And yet, the man at the door held a flaming torch. If only a spark fell off, a flicker, and Ariel would—she swallowed dryly.

"Leoht," the man said, square face, bald head, and bulky shoulders. "I apologize for the accommodations, but it's what we could do on such short notice." His voice was slow and deliberate, like waves crashing on the seashore.

Ariel squinted. She knew that man. That was the madman who'd stood face to face with a leoht and fyr as if invulnerable. How should she play this—no. She was too tired to play games. She would not play pretend. She would be herself. Whatever was going to happen next, she had no say in it until that man in front of her—who literally held all the power in his hands—gave her some options. She sipped the torchlight slowly, building up her reserves, but it was a meager thing, unable to sustain her. "Not at all," Ariel said. "I quite enjoy the herbal aroma." Every syllable she spoke stabbed at the walls of her throat like rusty daggers. "Ye really shouldn't have gone to such trouble."

Munika smiled. "It was my pleasure. This chamber wasn't designed for someone like you, but I think it will suit you rather well. What shall I call you?"

"Does it matter?"

"I supposed it doesn't. But names for a conversationalist are like directions for lost travelers, so I'll keep calling you Leoht."

So he knew what she was. Ariel didn't know if that put her at any further disadvantage, but it might, and definitely added to her frustration. "Are ye here just to gloat, or there's a point to all this?"

He smiled again, fake and condescending, an infuriating smile that inflicted further pain on her damaged soul. Munika Muril waited a long moment before speaking again—a moment where he bobbed his torch up and down in deep consideration.

Ariel understood the game. *Tell me what I need to hear, or yer next words will be yer last.*

"Why are you after him?"

"Oh, the pronoun game," she said, but in her head, she thought something completely different, *Don't play dumb with him, ye bampot. He'll burn ye like a witch at the stake. What a fitting end for this medieval setting. There is no way out of this cave. Ye have to play along.*

Munika lowered his torch almost at knee length. "Milktree's oil. Highly flammable. For some religious reason, people are superstitious about hurting trees. They believe trees are sapient beings. If they only knew the resources they are. But that's the way," he raised the torch back above his head, "the common folk are. Dependent on the comfortable lies of religion and hope. Ignorant that hope is an affliction fed by weakness, like a fungus or mold or disease. A parasite feeding on the will of the weak and making man lazy. Power, on the other hand,"

Munika bobbed his torch again, the flames dancing and flickering, moving shadows around, "needn't hope. Tell me, Leoht, how hopeful are you?"

"Mathew hurt my brother," she said, recalling those Sunday movies starring Chuck Norris or Jean Claude Van Damme. "I want revenge."

Munika's laugh echoed around the dungeon like rocks sliding off a mountainside. "A pitiful lie. Entertaining, but pitiful." Munika studied her with his eyes. This man had tortured people before. He knew the look of truth as well as the face of desperation. "If you wanted him dead, you'd've killed him. I doubt he would even see it coming. No, Leoht, I can see through you. You have a kind heart."

Ariel met his eyes. Dark blue, as dark and deep and mysterious as the bottom of the sea. Untamable and unbeatable. She could use that. A thought occurred to her. "I can help ye," she tried unsurely. There was no haggling with this man. But what else could she try? "I can help ye catch him. I have no quarrel with ye. All I want is his book."

"Ah!" Munika smiled again, making Ariel's knees tremble. "Honesty, at last. Isn't this much easier?" He waved the torch in a circle in front of him, bits of ash coming free, floating, and waving down to the oil-soaked floor. "You make a generous offer. If only you had waited until we had built a stronger rapport." He stroked his massive chin. Ariel wondered how many fists ended up broken trying to punch it. "A rookie mistake. Either you are naive, which I find difficult to believe, or you are in a hurry."

Rats. "That's all I can offer ye," she pressed.

"I heard leohts can heal with sunlight," he paused, regarding her mischievously, then looked past her into a spot behind her. "I'd be happy to provide it."

Ariel turned around. It was dark, but she saw it. A narrow window about head height: narrow but wide enough to fit through, had it not been plugged with a thick wood plank, with two ropes for handles. "I'm listening."

"Who's the blond boy?"

"The deaf lad?"

Munika kept staring at her. What could he possibly want with a deaf kid?

"Uh," Ariel stammered. She knew very little about the boy. "Why do ye ask?"

The general's eyes became colder, his expression solemn. Ariel held her breath, had she insulted him? Munika swooshed the torch so close to the ground she felt her heart skip a beat. And, right before the flames licked the oil, Munika swung the torch back up, turned around, and left, leaving Ariel in total darkness, heart pounding in her chest.

Chapter 30

Odd Conversation

Ludik

I STARED at my bare feet.

The soldiers had taken all my possessions, including Miranda's letter, and stripped me naked. I couldn't remember their faces and never bothered to read their lips, but I remembered their glee as they shoved me into a tiny cell. I was scared, terrified. But my one job was to wait until my friends came back for me. And I was sure they would. Mathew wouldn't leave me behind, or, at least, Brinn wouldn't let him leave me behind.

Yet, the sun set and rose again. I expected someone to come at any moment, but no one came. The cell was humid and cold; blotches of mildew flourished in the ceiling and walls and stank up the air. A window barely wide enough not to be classified as a hole faced a stone wall allowing the daylight or the dark of night in and the cold, though the cold did not bother me much.

My boots...

The second night, I cried. Someone should've come for me by now. Even if Mathew and Brinn were delayed—probably arguing between an all-in assault or sneaking in—someone from the castle should've come to me. What was the point of taking a prisoner and letting him rot in a cell? Outside, the day brightened again. It occurred to me that Mathew probably couldn't find me without Miranda's letter to point out exactly where I was. There were no trees in the castle as far as I had seen. Fear seeped through my skin as much as the humid air.

On the third day, I got a visit.

I fumbled with my fingers, knees pulled to my chest, and I couldn't be bothered to look when the door crept open and Munika Muril walked in. I watched him from the corner of my eye as he sat on a small stool, inspecting me.

A woman with long black hair and a velvety dark-red dress stood at his right shoulder. Hands hung over her stomach, her back as straight as a support column. Then her hands moved.

"Hello," they said together.

"I'm thirsty," I answered out loud.

The general shouted something. His thick, graying beard made it impossible to read his lips. Or even see his lips.

Another person came in, carrying a water pitcher and wooden cups and stood at the door, unsure of what to do next.

Munika gestured to the damp floor. The other person did as suggested and promptly left the room.

Munika's mouth moved, and so did the woman's hands. "Show it to me."

Blood drained from my face, hiding somewhere inside of me where it was mostly useless. Was I about to be molested? No. That made no sense. If that were the case, why bother with an interpreter? *Where are you, Mathew?*

"Do you understand sign language?" the woman asked.

I nodded timidly. I had been left naked and alone in a dark cell for two days and nights, and for what? So we could chitchat? I wanted to say something. Tell them to let me go or threaten them. *My friends are coming for me, and they won't be as careful as last time.*

But my lips did not obey.

Munika poured water into a cup and extended it to me. My hand, almost involuntarily, reached out to grab it—too thirsty to be defiant. Munika pulled the cup back before I could reach it. His chin bobbed up and down, and the lady's hands moved again with long slender fingers one might find in a lute player. "Do you know who I am?"

I could only stare at the water, reminding me of the persistent headache hammering my head.

"Your friends aren't coming," the hands said. "Even with all their power, they can't breach this castle, not without one-hundred-thousand men willing to lay down their lives. Men have tried to storm this castle throughout history. Mages included, yet they all failed—a tried and tested wonder of war engineering. So if you wish for some comfort, you'll have to cooperate with me. Now, please. Show it to me."

Could he be telling the truth? Was there no hope for a rescue? And what could I possibly have to show him? I literally had nothing on me.

Munika smiled, a cruel and disdainful smile as if death itself grinned and handed me the cup. I reached for it apprehensively, but he did not withdraw it this time. The water was cold and stung at my teeth, but I didn't care and drank all of it.

"More," I croaked.

Munika shook his head. "Too much water could harm you. Best to drink with moderation." He said something else, a command of some kind, but the hands did not move.

The servant came back in, holding a blanket. It looked brand new, fluffy as they come, all brown without any pictures or patterns like only the warmest blankets are. Munika himself got up and covered my back with it. It felt like a hot shower after a day out playing in the snow.

"I have nothing to show you," I said.

"You should be dead, you know?"

I closed my eyes and saw all the fire and smoke: the spears, the arrows, the light beams that sliced cobblestones like a hot knife through lard, and the fire that engulfed Inesa and me in the end. Yes, I should've died.

Munika continued, "Do you know how cold it has been for the last two nights? The short answer is, very. No clothes, no fire to keep you warm, no blankets, and this might be the most humid room in the whole castle. No normal person would have survived one night in these conditions. And I would know, I've seen it before. In this very room, actually. Yet you not only survived one night but two, unaffected. How, I wonder?"

Was that it? Was I an experiment? What kind of sick game was he playing? Did he enjoy watching people die of hypothermia? "I'm used to being cold, that's all. There's nothing extraordinary about it."

Munika nodded, his eyes piercing and inquisitive, scrutinizing my every move. "Oh, but you're wrong. Your display of perseverance is most extraordinary." He drew in closer. "Oh, I see. You don't know."

"I don't know what?"

The general slapped his knee and laughed heartily. "Remarkable! Isn't this just remarkable?" he asked the interpreter, but she translated as if it had been intended for me. "Then we both must see it. I think this calls for a demonstration. But first," Munika stroked his chin and, after a long moment, gave another command. A second later, the servant came in, handed Munika a pouch, and excused himself again.

Munika stared at me intently as he produced a book from the pouch. My eyes widened as I read the cover: *New and Old Worlds and How to Get There.*

Had he captured Mathew? That didn't make sense. He had told me they weren't coming because the castle was impenetrable, not because they had been arrested or killed. "Miranda, help me, please. They're hurting me!"

"Miranda," he said as if tasting the name. "Interesting. Have you read it?"

Utterly confused, I was more disoriented than found. Questions flooded my thoughts, trampling and overlapping each other.

"I presume you have." He extended me the book. "Please, read it back to me."

I took it and opened it. Blank. It was all blank. "Miranda?" I said tentatively, but no words formed. I stared back at Munika, stroking his chin, eyes growing tedious.

"It tried to manipulate me," he explained as he took the book from my hands and stowed it back in the pouch. "No one manipulates me; I'm the one who sells rancid meat to the butcher. Yet, it lied well, but not well enough. After that, it went silent. But not before it told me things too absurd to be real. And that's why I knew there had to be some measure of truth in its words."

"I don't understand," I said. "I don't know what you want from me."

"I believe you, Ludik. You're not a liar." The way he said it was almost fatherly, tender and caring eyes, then he added, "I know where your friends are. Mr. Doller is probably the least inconspicuous item on this land. I will have them both killed soon."

I froze, short of breath, heart palpitating in my chest. "You're lying."

"Oh, my poor refugee boy. You are, of course, allowed to believe whatever you want."

Refugee boy.

"Gone are the days you stole swords from my armory. Yes, I read those reports about a deaf child in need of discipline. What a rascal you were. Probably the only living thing in that miserable human gutter for which I had the slightest respect. It's only because of me you weren't punished. You might be the reason why I didn't burn the whole thing with everyone in it when I had the chance. It would've been so much easier. Well, you and that idiot, Katunik. You have grit. Resilience. I admire that."

He paused, as if reading me, before continuing. "It's probably best if you don't believe me. I wouldn't want you imagining the corpse of your dear girlfriend, a spear through her heart after my men had their way with her. How would you be able to sleep at night?"

Fear and rage made me twitch. "Don't you dare harm her!"

He smiled lavishly. "Yes. That's the grit I'm talking about. Keep the blanket; I'll come back for you shortly."

Chapter 31

Peach Pit

Ariel

Servants came in and left a terracotta water pitch and nothing else. No one spoke to her despite her cries, or even dared a glance. Ariel understood it very well—hunger was part of the torture. But understanding it didn't make it any better, and in some ways—many ways—it made it much worse. It meant it wasn't over, and it wouldn't be anytime soon. Or perhaps it would, but not due to hunger. Her wounds were festering. Her oil-soaked prison was a large-scale Petri dish, and she was the bacteria's main course. Ariel used some of the water to clean her scratches and burns but knew very well they wouldn't get better without medical care or sunlight. And a mild fever had already settled in.

She couldn't be sure of how much time had gone by or what time even meant. Her mind had become sluggish and brittle. A sweet scent of spices and roasted things broke her stupor. She hadn't even realized her eyes had been closed, but now she opened them, torch light illuminated her little dungeon. A table had been set at the entrance. When had it been brought in? Had she slept through it? Ariel couldn't tell; the hours bumbled and mingled into one another.

On the other hand, the unmistakable smell of freshly roasted poultry overpowered even the pungent oil. Did she imagine it? Her stomach growled. Maybe the hunger was playing tricks on her mind. A tray with a roasted bird of some kind surrounded by steaming potatoes and carrots occupied the center of the table. And beside it rested a bowl with fresh, succulent-looking peaches. How could she have missed that entrance?

Munika sat at the table, torch in hand. She hadn't even noticed him there. With his free hand, he tore a leg off the bird and cooed with delight as he munched on the juicy meat.

"Ye don't know what I know? Do ye?" Ariel said, trying not to choke in her saliva.

"Why don't you tell me?" Munika said with a mouth full of meat, sitting back in his chair.

"No. Ye don't know if what I know is useful to ye. Ye just don't know." Was she making sense? If she heard herself correctly, she wasn't. Ariel sighed, pinched the bridge of her nose, and tried again, "Listen. There are things we know, and there are things we don't know. And there are things we don't know we don't know. And those are the things yae're after. Ye want me to tell ye these things. Well, let me tell ye right now, there are much better ways to go about it than this. Ye could've invited me for some scotch, for example."

Munika broke a piece of bread. *When did bread join the party?* "What's a scotch?"

"Whisky."

Munika considered this, chucked a beautifully roasted potato in his mouth and said, "I don't drink."

"Torturing people is much better, hey?"

Munika couldn't hide his smile. So much conceit in it. So much power. It drained her as much as the darkness.

"I'm ill. Soon there won't be anything left for ye to torture." Ariel made a point of showing her burns, red around the edges, a yellowish goo pooling in the middle. "I need medical care. Or, at least, sunlight."

Munika soaked a piece of bread in the fat of the tray and shoved it in his mouth, the fresh crust cracking loudly, echoing in the chamber.

Ariel's stomach shrank into a singularity. "Listen to me; I'm no use to ye dead. If ye let me out, we can work together. Ye get the boy, I get the book."

"I think I like you right where you are." He grabbed the leg again, gave it another big bite, and sauce ran down his beard.

"Then, at the very least, keep me alive. And please, for the love of all that is sacred, get me a toilet. Or a chamber pot, or whatever ye call it. This place's filthy enough to kill a healthy person from septic shock." Her words were quickly becoming a strain on her feverish frame. Was the room spinning? Ariel had to sit back on her straw bed, her vision coming in and out of focus, her hearing muffled. That wasn't a good sign. Death by fire would at least be quicker. Perhaps more painful but faster. "Give me some light, ye bastard. Open the darned window. What will I do with my power? Cut through the oil-soaked wood and hay? I'll burn. Isn't that the whole point of this cage?"

She had to stop for breath. The room slowed down, and only after some effort did her vision return to normal.

Munika stood by the bars of her cage, looking down at her. She hadn't realized he had walked closer. "Is this the show the great mages put on?" He sneered and bit into a peach. "Pitiful." He walked to the window in the back, tugged hard on the tick ropes, and the plank came loose. A beam of sunlight, upon which tiny specks of dust traveled and danced, covered Ariel's skin. Ariel bathed in its warmth, soaking, and diverting its energy first to her head and then to her wounds. She steadied her thoughts and steadied her wit. Her burnt skin itched terribly as new skin grew and puss oozed out.

Munika observed her, lost in wonder. *Is this a good enough show for ye?* Although it grieved her that she had given him any satisfaction, she'd managed to impress him. That should count for something, shouldn't it? Yet she felt utterly violated. No, she didn't *feel*. She had been violated—human rights stripped away like the pelt of a wild animal. She breathed in, each breath easier than the last—the sudden relief leaving her dazed.

"You're not from this world, are you?" Munika said. It was more of a statement than a question. Ariel didn't bother to answer, busy consuming as much sunlight as she could before Munika changed his mind. "Tell me, Leoht, how can one travel to other worlds?"

"Easy enough if yae're a mage. If yae're not, then yae'll need one."

"How does one become a mage?"

What was this now? How would he become a mage? Ariel herself didn't understand the requirements, and she was one. "I don't know. A tree gave it to me." There was no harm in telling him something, was there? Not any that she could think of, at least. The longer she held his attention, the longer the window would be open, and the more options would be at her disposal once he was gone. And at the very least, she wouldn't have to live in the dark anymore.

"A leohtre, I presume," Munika said, his gaze fixed on the light streaming through the small window. "Interesting story. You know, the common folk believe trees are alive. Not only alive but able to talk to one another, think, and dream, and aspire. Like men. What do you think?"

"It's true," she heard herself say. At least, that was what her memories suggested. And her late friend was as sentient as any person is. Of that, she was sure.

"I know it's true," Munika said. "Though I dare not say it to my subjects. Trees are a great blessing, and I must quench these religious ideas. Trees need to be seen as *resources* if we are to make progress in this war. Soon the Erosomita's republic ideals will infect this country, and the monarchic Aviz will fall."

Subjects? Did he see himself as king? Munika wasn't the king as far as she knew. But he did control the army. And by extension, he ruled the kingdom. Ariel understood the intricacies of his reasoning and realized the king of Aviz was Munika's puppet, whether his majesty liked it or not.

"What a great resource it would be to harvest a leoht's power."

A cold omen ran through Ariel's stomach. *Harvest.* The word gutted her. Had she doomed another leohtre by telling him her story? How could she have been so dumb, so shortsighted? *Stupid, Ariel. Stupid, stupid, stupid.*

"This has been the most *enlightening* conversation," Munika said and plugged back the window. The room was dark again, lit only by the torch at the entrance, shining on the barely-eaten meal. "I'll send for a chamber pot and fresh clothes."

A part of Ariel was almost grateful to have earned such comforts, but she quickly scolded herself for allowing such a cheap trick as behavior conditioning to work on her. Cheap but effective. If this carried on long enough, Ariel would eventually give him anything he wanted and get more in return, but never enough to buy her freedom. A shiver ran up her spine. No, she had to find a way out.

Munika took another bite of his half-eaten peach and tossed it to her.

Ariel caught it and stared at him. Ariel almost thanked him for it, and again, she felt disgusted.

Without another word, Munika left, leaving behind the torch and his lunch, purposely beyond Ariel's reach.

Ariel ate whatever remained of the peach. There was no shame in it. She was starving, and the sunlight wasn't enough to nourish her completely. She would always need food and water like a tree needs water and nutrients from the soil. She stopped abruptly, staring at the peach pit in her hand. She squeezed tightly. *Nutrients*, she thought to herself; there were plenty of those in the corner of her cell.

Ariel waited patiently to ensure Munika was far enough away, and no one else was coming. Every second was pure anguish now that Munika had foolishly given her the keys to her cell. She tore the straw bed into bits and mixed it with her scatological waste, making a cake of hay and poop and pee.

"I'm so sorry about this my wee sprout," she said to the pit and stuffed it in it. All she needed now was more water. She relieved herself on the straw pile. "So undignifying," she muttered, but she couldn't care less. She'd be out soon.

Her cell was heavy, but it wasn't attached to the ground; it just lay there by gravity alone.

Once she was sure no one was coming, she placed her hands over the pile and shone her light directly into the pit. A second later, it sprouted, worming out of the hay steadily. Two tiny leaves unfolded, waving and wobbling, reaching for her light. Ariel had to be careful—she couldn't waste any of it. She also had to make sure her peach tree grew in the right direction too.

The tree grew under her care until it reached about twenty inches tall and had developed a promising trunk. Ariel shifted the plant and needled it through one of the cage squares. Then anticipation grew in her. The floor around her became drier, but it just might be enough. There was plenty of moisture in that cellar. Ariel poured more and more light into her tiny peach tree.

The trunk thickened as the plant rose higher, caught the cane on the top of the square, and grew against it, pushing the cage up gently. Ariel gritted her teeth, afraid the tree wouldn't be strong enough. "Please, wee sprout, grow as strong as ye can. If ye get me out of here, I promise I'll come back for ye."

Did the little tree listen to her? It began to grow thicker, instead of taller. The cage creaked and scraped across the floor as it rose, the screeching noise echoing in the chamber. There was no time to stop now. She had one shot, and she would not have another. She was running out of light. The cage rose like a car needing a tire change. Her little jack-tree worked overtime, thickening and growing.

"That's it," she said, "that's it. Just a little more." Ariel could fit her hand under the cage now. The roots thickened and dug into the gaps in the stone. "Just a little more."

Wooziness came over her suddenly. Would she have enough light left in her? The tree started rising slower. That's when she heard the sound coming from the hallway. Someone was coming. Ariel pressed on. She could fit her arm through now—just a couple more inches.

She took deep breaths, the stinking fresh herb oil slashing at her nose and throat. But she needed those breaths. She squeezed her reserves dry and felt her legs bend like wet noodles as all her light fed the tree.

Another loud crank, her cell bending and buckling and sliding against the oil-soaked stone floor.

That's it. That was all she had. Depleted, she inspected the gap. It wasn't as large as she had imagined in her head. Could she squeeze through?

The tree's vibrant leaves bristled like a gust of wind had blown through, but no wind was there. Was the tree encouraging her? She could almost hear it saying, *You can fit! Just squeeze!*

Ariel lay on the ground and tried to slip under the gap, but it proved too narrow. Just barely. Only if she could—

Yes, that's it. Ariel stripped her stupid gown, rolled on the ground, smearing and rubbing the oil on her skin, and tried again. New light filled the entrance. Someone was coming. She was out of time.

Ariel pressed her head through the gap, the frame scraping against her scalp, then squeezed her shoulder. She squirmed and wiggled, and little by little, her lubricated skin slid through the opening like a human-shaped octopus. Her injuries burned like hot flames as they, too, scraped against the floor and the canes. One arm broke free and joined her head on the other side. She was so tired now she wanted to quit. Give up and just rest, or just die. But she was so close she could taste it.

The torchlight from the entrance grew brighter.

She used her free hand to push herself, but her grip kept slipping on the oil. Her other shoulder came loose, followed by her other hand, and with a big push that cut through her bare back, she pulled herself free. She got up in a hurry despite the pain and slipped on the oil-drenched floor.

Her bones creaked and cracked like an old boat sailing angry seas as she carefully got back to her feet, grunting with aches and frustration. Ariel lumbered to the window and pulled on the thick ropes. It was jammed. "Rats!" she snarled.

"Stop right there!" said a voice from behind.

She looked over her shoulder and found a soldier at the entrance, a bewildered look planted on his face and a torch in his hand. What a sight it must be to behold: an oiled-up naked lady and a tree lifting a heavy cage. Ariel held the ropes tightly, pressed a foot against the wall, and yanked the damned thing off. Light found her face.

"Stop, I said, or I'll drop the torch!" the soldier said.

Arie studied her situation. She could climb out the window in time before the flames reached her. But that would doom her little miracle tree. Her savior. She couldn't allow that to happen. Not to mention, Ariel had no idea how she would retrieve it, but that was a problem for later.

She had to stop that soldier from doing something stupid. She stepped to the side. "Okay, ye got me, lad," she said, then shot a searing sunbeam directly at the soldier's eyes and watched helplessly as the man dropped his torch to cover them.

The torch banged against the stone in a haze of sparks and, by a mere miracle, didn't touch the oil.

"I'll come back for ye," Ariel said to the tree and climbed out the window.

Chapter 32

Blue Heart

Ludik

They brought me food, a kind of stew, I think. Why should I eat it? I would hurl it the moment it touched my stomach.

At dusk, they came back. Soldiers this time, brute men who grabbed me by each arm and, even though I would've cooperated, dragged me out to the courtyard. The sky was the color of rubble and apathy.

The men shackled me to a wood pole, its bark still clinging around it, sap still trickling from its gashes. That pole had been a living tree not long ago. I wanted to be mad, to shout in anger, but all I managed was to stay still. Good enough, I suppose. Better than crying and begging for my life to those monsters. The chains dangled with the growing breeze while men heaped around me, odd expressions on their faces. I would have never expected curiosity from trained killers. Yet there it was. What were they so curious about? Was the prospect of watching a child die that entertaining? They spoke amongst each other, leaning their mouths to their fellow men's ears, anticipation in their demeanor. They were enjoying it.

The rusted cuffs bit at my wrists, coarse, tight, and hurtful. The chains were short so that if I tried to sit I'd dangle, knees bent, arms stretched, by the wrists. I did not want to cry, not in front of those cruel men, pointing and laughing at me. So when the rain fell, it was more than welcome, and with the rain, the cold began its familiar ceremony. It always started with my fingers, turning them numb and swollen, then my toes, my legs and arms. I tried to take my mind off it, but every thought reminded me of what I had lost, and worse, what I was about to lose. I found myself repenting the water I drank. If I hadn't drunk any, perhaps there would have been fewer tears. Or none at all. Was that how tears worked? They were made of water, weren't they?

Then there was the matter of hope. It clung to me like burdocks on ekkuh's feathers. It could happen, couldn't it? Mathew could still come and bring a firestorm with him. I couldn't care less if the castle burned. Let it melt. That's how I saw it.

When the storm worsened, rain poured like a waterfall, forcing the soldiers to huddle under porches and inside the buildings, the windows lined with scrutinizing faces. How could the suffering of a boy be of such spectacle to those people? When the first speck of hail pecked my nose, my joints were already cranky, and my limp legs trembled. The soldiers saluted Munika reverently as he entered the courtyard, seemingly oblivious to the rain and hail that began dotting the dark floor, eyes poised on me. All the water in the world couldn't wash the arrogance from his face. He said something, his mouth moving under his groomed beard. Then the arrogance gave way to a fake tenderness as he placed a hand on my shoulder and regarded me like he took no joy in what he was doing. As if torturing a helpless child was his duty and failing to do so would be an act of treason.

"Let me die with my boots on," I told him, and the tenderness in his eyes faltered. He seemed shocked or confused by my request.

A bright flash of lightning cast shadows in the yard, and I glimpsed an apology on his face in the brief light. A rumble reverberated through the ground and across my body. Munika gazed upon the heavens and back at me. His mouth moved again.

"I don't understand you!" I yelled at him, anger bubbling in me like wash in the spirit still. "I'm deaf! And your ugly beard makes it impossible to read your stupid lips! If you want to kill me, just do it! What's wrong with you? But let me die with my ordealing boots on!"

Munika cracked a smile like a proud father. Which festered

emotions in me, then continued with his speech. I had never been happier to be deaf.

I lashed at him, but the chains pulled me back, my face an inch from his. "I hope my friend burns you to dust."

Munika nodded, his smile unwavering, small ice pebbles clinging to his beard and melting. He solemnly patted my shoulder again and left me to die.

The rain and hail persisted as the wind picked up, plotting to skin me alive. My muscles shivered uncontrollably. And breathing air was like breathing oil. Thick and wet. I had been that cold before. Colder even. And once the initial shock was over, the dread mellowed and became soothing—even companion-like.

I thought of Brinn and our summer nights, lost in conversation until the first rays of dawn alarmed us into a day of labor and poor rest. And it was magic, and it was beautiful. And I would never see her again. The shackles, so rough at first, were now as soft as silk, and I eased into their support and hung loosely by the pole. The unpeeled bark scraped my bare back like tickling fresh water. Hail piled around me, in the yard and the roofs, and clung to my hair.

As time crawled by, I stopped trembling. *Finally!* I knew what followed. It had been chiseled in my brain through traumatizing experiences. The warm blanket of death. The last stage of hypothermia. Heimee wouldn't save me now. And what could Mathew do under so much rain and ice? So when the warmth came, I welcomed it.

If I had to die, this wasn't entirely inappropriate. Death by cold was as fitting an end to my story as death by old age. I wished I had spent more time with Brinn; made another batch of whisky with Heimee. But none of that mattered now; I would be with Mom soon, and our ordeal would be over. The cold had taken her. Cold and hunger and illness. And my peach tree, Laurin. Would I see her in the bliss as well? Would I see Dad? I missed them. I missed them dearly.

And yet, it was all untrue. The cold was not the culprit. The cold had no say in this, no more than a pleasant summer morning. My tragedy was the work of the man who stripped and shackled me. And of that damned mountain. One like the other, hearts of stone, lairs of evil. Cruelty upon this earth.

I felt Mom's touch, her warm embrace, her sweet scent, her lessons, and her smiles. She consoled me in my dwindling time. My life had been so painful and yet so hard to let go. The warmth blossomed in my chest like love: the tenderness of a parent, the care for a son or a daughter or a sibling, or a stranger turned kin. Then it spread, first to my neck and shoulders, tingling, and burst through my stomach, turning into a raging fire. It flooded my arms, and as it did, time sped up. The clouds whirled and tumbled above me, and the rain and ice took the form of a gentle mist.

My body became fire. I wanted to remove my clothes, but there were none to remove. Then the world shimmered in a pale blue light. It began in my heart and spread along the streams of fire within me.

Things are things, said a distant grumbling voice.

Uh? Things? What things? Who said that? I wanted to ask, but my vision funneled, blurred, and faded to black.

Chapter 33

Silent Night

Ariel

Ariel couldn't believe her eyes.

She had spent the better part of the day skulking about the inner layers of castle Lirterin looking for her belongings. It was an odd and austere building that resembled a prison more than any fancy European castle. Unlike the walls surrounding the city, the castle had no bastions. The whole thing was eerie geometrical, resembling a slanted pentagon; its defensive capabilities leaned heavily on the stone hill on which it was built.

It had been a puzzling day. No alarm had sounded, and no one came looking for her. She guessed that Munika understood how unlikely it would be for anyone to find her now. She found all her stuff stowed in a small shed not far from where she had fled. Her clothes were dirty, scorched, and tattered. And, thank God, her seed was there, too. Her relief was so intense she had to sit for a moment after placing the pendant around her neck where it belonged, clutching it tightly against her chest.

Once she composed herself, she found a nice little nook up on a rooftop, where she matched the surrounding colors like a chameleon and thought of a plan to rescue her little peach tree hero when they dragged Ludik out by his arms. The boy was completely naked, a gaunt expression of failure and defeat on his face. They'd shackled him to a pole right in the middle of the yard. Why would anyone go to such lengths to torture a little deaf boy? The pole itself seemed to be a new addition. Probably erected that very morning.

Soldiers gathered around the boy, and Ariel heard their mean jokes and taunts.

"Look at that. Burns half our town and now wants to cry. Do you want your mommy?" a soldier said.

"You get what you deserve!" shouted another.

They held Ludik in contempt for the fires of the previous days. Judging by the smoke she could still taste in the air, some small fires still lingered about the city. The rain would surely put a belated end to it.

After a while, the soldiers got bored or simply wanted to escape the falling rain and took cover. Murdering a little boy was easy, but god forbid if they got wet.

At that moment, Munika walked up to the shackled blond kid. Ariel couldn't listen to what he was saying over the pouring rain, but the general seemed rather amused. *What a foul man*, she thought. And without much ceremony, he left the boy there, exposed to the elements.

Ariel watched, anger building up inside her like a hurricane. She wanted to help him; she could probably create a distraction of some kind. Darken the whole thing or blind a few pairs of eyes. But how would she release and carry the boy out of there? She wished she had a helicopter and soldiers of her own—a modern army extraction team like in those American movies she liked to watch.

She considered a couple of ideas, but the day had grown dark quickly; the dim stormy light allied with her hunger and exhaustion made all her plans fall flat. From every corner, door, and window, soldiers observed the boy attentively. Maybe if the sun was up and shining, she could do it. But the sun had set, leaving only the storm in its stead and Ariel to watch the despicable spectacle helplessly.

An hour drew by, and not a soul left their post. All Ariel could do was watch that naive young boy lose his strength. The thought was so revolting she felt sick to her bones. Ludik dangled, arms stretched by the chains holding him; he didn't seem conscious anymore. Ariel had never killed anyone, but Munika was rapidly becoming a prime contender to be her first casualty.

Then the soldiers collectively lost their mirth, no longer enjoying the show. A murmur grew among them. They shuffled around, shoulders wobbling, exchanging looks. Ariel couldn't understand what the commotion was about. Were they somehow unaware of how this would play out? Were they expecting something different than an appalling act of cruelty toward a teenage boy?

And that's when it happened.

An eerie pale blue light permeated Ludik's chest reflecting in the sea of white hail. Someone shouted something, and soldiers poured out to the ward, spears in their hands, apprehension in their stares as they formed a line around the boy, ready to fight a monster, ready for battle.

Ludik's feet found the ground beneath them, and his arms steadily pulled him up. A white aura enveloped him like ionized air; sorrow his only expression. Ludik tugged on the chains which held him, and they snapped like glass. The ground around him froze, clumping the hail together. Tiny crystals sprouted like white mold spreading in a circle toward the soldiers.

The line of men took a step backward. A lightning bolt struck Ludik in his head, and the ranks toppled like dominos. Ludik, unphased by this, took one step toward the stupefied soldiers, desperately clambering back to their feet. Ludik raised a hand and every man in front of him became a pale, grim statue. The yard suddenly reminded Ariel of the terracotta army of Qui Shi Huang or, more terrifyingly, the cast statues of Pompeii.

Enthralled by the spectacle and mesmerized by the horror, Ariel couldn't look away—so much power. The soldiers at the back tried to run, but Ludik was on a killing spree. He raised his arm, and they, too, froze in place. The walls glittered with tiny crystals. The rain and hail stuck to whatever it touched, coating the frozen bodies. Ludik's light flared, and the crystals climbed up the walls, closing in on Ariel's position and forcing her to act quickly. Would she become his prey if she left her camouflage? What could a leoht do against that?

The crystals neared her. She gritted her teeth. Would she instantly freeze if it touched her? Better not find out. She got ready to jump away, legs tensing.

Then, like a flip of a switch, it was over. Ludik went dark and dropped to the ground, and the castle became eerily silent and motionless.

Ariel considered what she had seen and found it unmistakable. She had never witnessed it before, but she knew what it was. There, naked, surrounded by a blanket of white ice crystals and dead men, lay something that shouldn't exist anymore. Something thought extinct.

A dwinan.

Munika knew. But how could he have known? And where is he? Ariel surveyed the windows, where immobile men watched the drama below as if they had never realized their fate. Munika wasn't stupid. He might not have known what would happen, or he would have ordered his soldiers to stand further away, but he knew something perilous was afoot. He would be somewhere with a view, yet far enough from any real danger. Inspecting the highest vantage points, she quickly spotted him up on a keep, watching the onslaught. He was too far for her to distinguish great details, but she could see by how he moved that this had pleased him greatly.

"Ye bastard. I'm not going to let ye have him." Ariel got up from her position and slid across the wet, slippery shingles onto a balcony. A soldier was there, but his eyes were glassy blue, his limbs stiff.

"A couple more feet, and I'd be a freaking sorbet," Ariel muttered, inspecting the soldier. What was she doing? He could still freeze her, right? Regardless of her doubts, Ariel found herself running down flights of stairs as if they weren't there, dodging and jumping over dead men.

She burst into the yard, startling two soldiers inspecting the chaos of bodies. They were still for a second, and in the next, their spears pointed at her, ready to strike. Ariel didn't have time for carefulness and dazed them. Probably blinded them, even. The men dropped their weapons, groaning in pain, hands covering their eyes. Ariel almost allowed herself to pity them but couldn't spare the time.

Ludik stood on all fours, a faint blue tinge covering his chest. Ariel held her breath. The men wriggled, rubbing their eyes, stumbling closer when they, too, became ice sculptures right before her.

Ludik's empty gaze found Ariel.

"Don't," she said, lifting her hands in surrender as Ludik rose to his feet. "I want to help ye."

She winced and closed her eyes shut, both in terror and at her stupidity for crying out to a deaf person. Would she feel it? Would there be pain?

But death did not come. She opened one eye and saw Ludik move like a human glacier ever so slowly. Examining his face, Ariel noticed that he wasn't all there. Like he was, but also wasn't—a shadow of the former deaf boy. Would he listen to her? She didn't know sign language. She had to find something to write, but on what, and what with? Afraid that any sudden movement would trigger the lad, she took a cautious step closer.

Ludik looked at her with a pulsing aura. Ariel slowly dropped to her knees, hands in front of her. "Don't kill me," she whispered.

The blue light faded completely as his expression thawed, revealing the confusion and fear underneath, and he broke into a run. Ariel watched him scamper toward the outer gate and shot after him, keeping a safe distance, concealing her presence as best as she could.

Ariel crossed a wide tunnel and stopped. Dozens of soldiers gripped their spears while shouts came from afar to go after him, but they did not comply, barely even noticing her as she resumed the chase.

When she heard the guards finally acknowledge their orders, they had gained quite some distance.

Not long after they left the castle, Ludik slowed down, slanting his stride like a drunken sailor, until he stumbled on his feet and fell on the wet cobblestones.

Ariel approached him cautiously. His eyes were shut, and more importantly, his chest looked like any other regular chest. Ariel poked him gently at first, then shook him. Then a little rougher.

"This way!" she heard someone shout from afar.

Hastily, she hoisted him onto her shoulders, the weight of his body scratching against her burns and bruises, forcing her to feed on her light not to collapse. She had to leave the city, but she couldn't carry him all the way out. Even consuming all her light, it would be a tall order. The charred and broken streets looked like a scene from a war movie, but she recognized where she was. Kola's house, or what remained of it. Ahead, not far, she found a small stable. The outside was scorched black, but inside, it remained largely unscathed, and to her relief, she even found one of those feathered rides.

"Hey there, uh, feathery horse. Legged bird..." She winced at her awkwardness. "Look, I need yer help, okay." Ariel spun around so the ekkuh could see Ludik's face.

The ekkuh inspected Ludik, then squealed and tapped its talons gleefully against the hay-covered floor. For some reason it was happy to see him. Ariel looked at the ekkuh closely. There was definitely something familiar something about it. Could it be Ludik's ride? It began licking the boy's hair.

"Okay, good," Ariel said. "I'm gonnae break ye out of here, okay? Don't scratch me."

Ariel settled Ludik on the hay floor. She found a saddle quickly enough and wished she had a smartphone with her so she could watch a YouTube video on how to set it up. Were these bird saddles the same as horse saddles? She had no way of knowing; they looked identical to her. She quickly gave up on it and decided ropes would work well enough. It wouldn't be comfortable for Ludik, but it was certainly preferable to carrying him on her shoulders.

With a strength she did not know she possessed, Ariel got Ludik's body across the ekkuh's back and tied him up as best as she could, leaving some space for her. Ludik's head hung on one side while his legs draped over the other. It didn't look pretty.

Now all she had to do was mount the damned thing. She jumped on top and fell down the other side, landing on her back. Fortunately, the less-than-clean hay dampened her fall. She cursed the heavens and tried again. This time she held to her rope work and managed to stay on top.

"Alright, *yah!*" she said, but the bird didn't move.

Maybe if she kicked her hind legs with—

Ariel nearly fell again with the sudden lurch, holding on to her rope work and Ludik.

"Slow down!" she demanded. "Ohh! Ohh!" she cooed, which didn't work.

How was she supposed to turn? Luckily, she didn't have to. The ride seemed to know precisely the way out of the city.

Soon they were at the front gate, where a contingent of armed men awaited them. Ariel gave only a warning shot, leaving an amber scratch of molten rock at most soldiers' feet and cutting through the foot of an unlucky one who fell backward, screaming with pain.

The formation broke apart right before they passed it and into the safety of the night.

The feathered horse slowed down to a somewhat leisurely trot. If anyone else dared to get in her way, Ariel was furious and tired enough to commit murder.

She rode for an hour until the bird came to a full stop by itself. Ariel inspected the area she found herself in: far from the main road, with a rock face to provide shelter, clean of undergrowth, the ground was flat and not too wet, and not so far from there, she spotted two candlelit cabins she could rob. *Not a bad place to make camp. Or pass out.*

Ariel looked up through the canopies and found unfamiliar stars dotting the sky. The storm had come and gone. When did that happen? Storms didn't end so abruptly, did they?

Ariel pulled Ludik off the bird's back, and the boy fell like a sack of potatoes. Ariel winced at her clumsiness. "We wouldn't want ye waking up, would we?" With one careful step after another, she lay him on the forest floor. His eyes were closed, and his breathing was slow. Could a dwinan die of hypothermia? Of course not; that's what Munika had just proven. But maybe, if Ariel got him warm enough, he would return to normal—a conscious and reasonable human boy.

First, she needed to set up camp. Get a fire going and find some food and clothes for Ludik. Luckily, some whisky. Then she had to free her peach tree before someone chopped her down.

Her stomach growled so loud she thought she might wake the lad. But looking at him, that didn't seem likely. Despite the hunger, the exhaustion, the bruises, and the grime covering her skin and hair, there was no need to hurry. At least nothing was conspiring to kill her. Not immediately, anyway, and she had a plan. *Things just might start working out for me*, she thought. And if all went well, she would gain an ally. And what a powerful ally he could be.

Chapter 34

The Dwinan

Ludik

I PROBED my mind hoping to make sense of what had happened but found only fragments. Blue light, pain, terror; the warm blanket of death over my shoulders and the watchful stare of indifferent eyes. And cruel things as far as cruelty goes.

Was I dead?

No, I was still thinking. Dead people don't think, do they?

My whole body ached. I was... I was... had Munika taken me out before I died? Was all that just another excuse for torture? Was he coming back to torment me further?

I pushed through the haze; I had to get a grip on what was happening.

Something moved, rough and moist. Distant, foreign, yet—part of me? Yes. Something itched, some extremity...

I wiggled my toes, rubbing them against one another to scratch them, when I noticed the restrictive feel of fabric. I was wearing socks. A wisp of hope crossed my soul. Then the itch reached my eyes, and they opened. I was wearing boots—they were not my boots. I inspected my surroundings. A bonfire burned, warm and cozy, despite the smoke. Rocky ground, lumpy and damp, a poisoned treat for aching muscles. And a figure busy digging a hole. To her side was the ugliest peach tree I had ever seen, short and clunky, hunched and badly cared for; a thick branch had been sawed off recently.

Please! I'm telling you, the peach tree said, *I know you're tired, but this is not a good spot. I'll die of shadows. That's like dying of thirst but worse! This is what I get for helping strangers, a short life, an ugly trunk and the best spot to die in the shade. Just my luck. Would you mind moving your canopies a little once she settles me?*

How? asked another tree. *We're all terribly sorry, Sprout, but this is the way things are for us. It's bad enough that we have to see our sprouts wither under us.*

I squinted to clear my sight. Ariel. But how? Why? And why was she torturing a defenseless tree? More questions zoomed by unanswered. I should run. But where to? Where was I? And where'd the boots come from? Or the rest of the clothes I wore, for that matter? Simple, white shirt, brown pants, and red wool pullover. Did Ariel dress me? I wanted to get up and demand explanations, but my body refused any sudden gestures.

Had I been glowing blue? No, that's nonsense. The blue must have come from one of Ariel's spells. Why was I struggling so much with my memo—

Munika. The recollections of torture flooded in. He wanted something. He wished to see something, but what? Why did he shackle me and leave me to die? Why was I not dead? Did Ariel save me?

I helped you! the tree whined. *Leohirin, help me. Please, do not plant me here!*

Why would she save me? Most likely she wanted a hostage to use in exchange for Miranda. That made more sense. However, I wasn't tied to a pole, and I had clothes on—a massive improvement from my previous condition. Was running even an option, considering my stiff muscles? Probably not, and even if I could, she could just as easily slice me in half. I stared at my feet again. "Where are my boots?"

Ariel jerked and took two steps back, knees bent, hands in front of her as if ready to strike me down, and the ambient light dimmed dramatically, smudging the shadows cast by the fire. Her lips moved.

I tapped my ear, then gestured broadly around me. She knew I was deaf, right? She had to know. Right? Before I could state the obvious, the light came back, more intense than before.

Ariel's lips moved again. It occurred to me that I had never been that close to her, nor had I seen her in any situation other than a fight or outright running for my life. I studied her face. Short nose, oval face, and lips the thickness of a hay straw, too thin to read. It made sense; all villains have unreadable lips.

I sighed. "I can't read your lips. They're too thin."

At first, Ariel seemed surprised, drawing her finger to her mouth, probing as to reassure herself her lips hadn't fallen off. Then she grimaced and scowled.

"I'm not trying to offend you. It's hard to read thin lips, that's all. It's like having a beard."

Her scowl turned to a glare.

"Fine, be offended. I don't care."

After a moment, Ariel's eyes softened, and her expression was replaced by flustering as her eyes darted from side to side as if looking for something. After a moment, she threw her hands in the air.

I flinched involuntarily. Ariel's hands shot in front of her again like pressing on an invisible wall, and I flinched harder.

What could I do? Other than being sliced in half, that is. I drew quick breaths as Ariel moved slowly, crouching, lowering her hands. Was she telling me to remain calm? Why? What could I possibly do to hurt her? No. That wasn't it. Mathew and Brinn must have found me and were away for the moment, and Ariel was afraid I'd sound the alarm. But why was she planting a tree?

"She's here!" I bellowed anyway. "Ariel's here!"

Ariel drew a finger across her lips.

"Brinn! Mathew!"

In response, Ariel pressed her finger harder, grooving her lips and showing her teeth in a grimace, squatting further down and hunching her shoulders.

"Where are my friends?" I asked a milktree nearby. "Tell me, or I'll use you for tinder!"

Ariel's grimace was now back into confusion. Our impasse had reached full circle.

There's no need for threats, you dumb human. Your friends are west of the city searching for you. Oh, and while I have your attention, would you please shut that little stump up? I'm trying to rest here.

Who are you calling a stump? Wait a minute! Shit on my leaves and nest on my branches. You know treespeak?! the little peach tree said. *Please, I beg of you, have her plant me somewhere else. Force her if you must!*

I balled my fists and sighed in frustration.

I'll translate what she says for you! Wait, is it translating?

Nah, said another tree, a swirling mess of branches and long thin leaves, *to translate, you have to convert from one language to another. This would be more like repeating.*

I'll repeat what she says to you! said the peach tree. *But won't I be translating it into treespeak?*

I guess, but then he has to translate it back to his own language in his head. What a woefully inept system.

"It doesn't matter what you name it!" I said. "Interpret for me."

Interpret! said the swirling tree, *good one.*

Could you all be quiet? said the milktree. *I haven't cycled oxygen since the fires.*

Oh, shut it, said the swirling tree, *none of us have. We've been photosynthesizing moonlight for days now.*

Wait, said the peach tree, *aren't 'translate' and 'interpret' synonyms?*

"Focus. What happened to you?" I pointed at her branch.

She sawed it off.

I glared at Ariel. What an evil person she was, torturing a tree for pleasure. Ariel stared back at me, mouth open wide and furrowed brows.

She's asking who are you talking to? To know I risked my life for this.

"Risk her life or your life?" I asked.

Her life.

"What did she risk her life for?"

Uh, to save you. To avoid confusion, I'll say only what she says from now on. Just remember to talk her out of planting me here.

She rescued you, said the swirling tree. *No one is talking about what happened in the city, but whatever it was, it was worse than the fires.*

Humans never shut up about fire, and yet they are awfully silent about this. Anyway, she brought you here, made a fire to keep you warm and went out to fetch you some clothes. You ought to be thankful. Then she went back into the city and came back with this... this—the tree stopped as if pondering her words—*annoyance.*

"Rescued?" I scoffed. "When you find a coin on the ground, do you call it a rescue?"

Ariel's lips, hard to read as they were, spelled, "What are you talking about?"

I wasn't concerned if she found me a lunatic or not. In fact, I wasn't concerned about any opinion she may have of me. "Where are my boots?" I demanded.

Her mouth fell open.

She said, said the little tree, *are you talking with the trees?*

I gritted my teeth. "You work for Munika, don't you? I know that much. I want my boots back. I won't play your games until I get my boots back. Or you'd better kill me and be done with it. I can't take this anymore."

The tree repeated, *Me working for that jobby jar? Not in a million years. And I got you those boots, didn't I? So quit complaining about boots.*

I glanced at the boots covering my feet and had to look away, gritting my teeth before the sadness pierced my heart. "For Bastard's sake, stop hurting that tree."

The tree continued to repeat her words as if it wasn't even there and I was talking directly with Ariel. "I'm not hurting it. It saved me, and I'm saving it," she said.

The tree had saved her? Wait, did Ariel speak with trees too? No, that wasn't it. How could a tree have saved her? I shook the question aside. "There's too much shade, too much competition for root space, and the soil is too rocky. I could go on, but if you plant her here, she'll die."

Ariel covered her mouth with both hands and dropped to her knees by the tree. "I'm so sorry. I'm in a hurry, and I'm so tired. I should have thought of that. Oh, poor thing. I'm so sorry. Tell it I'm sorry! Her... uh... him. I don't know."

I was lost for words. What in the Bastard's name was going on? "She can hear you just fine."

Ariel patted the little tree's leaves. "I owe you my life. I'll find the perfect place to plant you. Don't worry." Ariel rubbed her face.

"If you don't want to hurt her, why did you cut off her branch?"

"To rescue it. It got stuck in the cage it helped me escape from."

Well, that sounded like nonsense. "What do you want from me?"

"I just want to talk."

"The light in the castle, was that you? That blue glow... Was that you? Why? Why would you save me after almost killing us all?"

The confusion was back on her face. It started with plain confusion then slowly wrinkled into stupefaction. Was that her only facial expression? Increasing degrees of bewilderment?

"You don't remember?"

"I..." The memories were so foggy, so distant. "I remember being cold. Munika, he was torturing me." I dry swallowed, the memory too hurtful to be summoned. "There was an eerie light. I thought I died, but then I think I ran. The tree said you brought me clothes and kept me from freezing. Is that true? Why would you help me?"

Ariel blinked. "Yes, that's precisely what happened. I saved you. What they were doing to you was wrong, and I put a stop to it. See, you don't have to hurt me."

"Huh? Hurt you?"

"Hurt me? Don't be silly."

"But you just said—"

"I know what I said. At least, I think I do. I'm not sure if the tree is translating this right. Also, I can't believe a tree is translating what I say in the first place. Rats, this day just keeps on giving." Ariel rubbed her eyes, then slumped. "I'm trying to make you feel comfortable around me. That's all."

"You want me as bait?"

"I can see how you'd think that. So I'll cut you a deal. If you want to leave, just go. I won't try to stop you. But I need you to listen to me. Alright?" Ariel pursed her lip, took a deep breath, and added, "Miranda needs to be stopped."

So that's what she was trying to do. Not only did she want to use me as bait, but also turn me against my friends. I wanted to laugh. What a dumb plan.

"She wants to save the world," Ariel added.

A snort came out of my nose. "This is ridiculous."

"You don't understand. Miranda wants to unify the world under one banner. Well, all worlds."

"That's awful. Can you even imagine that?" I tried to get up, but I guess I needed to rest a little longer for that.

"I appreciate your snark. Believe me, I do. But think about it. Unity is not so easily achieved. Unity is imposed. It's born of oppression. To save a world that doesn't need saving is to destroy it."

I scoffed. "That doesn't make any sense. Miranda is helping us—"

"Has she helped you? I don't think things have gone all that well for you since you met her."

"Things haven't gone well since I met you. As I recall correctly, you tried to kill us. Twice."

"I wasn't trying to kill you. I just want the book."

"All you want is power for yourself. You and Munika are peas in a pod."

"Sure. Tell me, Ludik, what do you really know about them? Mathew and Miranda. Who are they, really? You know what, just go. Off with you. You've caused me enough stress for today."

I got up. It wasn't easy, but I managed. "Just like that?"

"Yes. Just like that."

What kind of sick game was she playing? Instinctively, I took a step backward.

Her eyes followed my foot. "Just think about what I said. They're not being honest with you."

"I'll take my chances." Another step. Ariel did not move. Was she telling the truth? Was she really letting me go?

"Also, I lied to you," she said, eyes on the ground, shoulders slumping.

"I'm shocked." Another step.

"I didn't save you. You saved yourself."

I had moved at least four yards away, and the steps came faster now, one after the other. I glanced over my shoulder, ensuring I wasn't about to slam into a tree. "And how did I manage that?"

"It seems you're a dwinan."

"A dwinan?" I laughed. What was she thinking? "Sure."

I couldn't believe my eyes, you..." Her eyes widened as if she had remembered something important. "It all makes sense now. I think that's what she wants from you. Your power. Yes, that must be it."

"You're insane."

"Munika wants it, too. I don't know how he found out since even you don't know, but he does. That's why he left you out in the storm. He wanted to see it for himself."

I stopped walking, taken by trees whispering all around me.

A dwinan? they said, spreading from tree to tree like a continuous echo until the whole forest droned it in chorus.

We have no roots inside the castle, said the swirly tree. *But you were there! What did you see?*

"I was in a dungeon," Ariel replied. No, not Ariel. This wasn't a translation. It was the tree speaking for herself. *I saw nothing. But I heard. He froze everything in his path and walked out.*

I don't believe it, the swirly tree said. *The world hasn't seen a dwinan for thousands of years.*

I can't believe my leaves, added the milktree. *Could it be why the cold never killed him? It had so many chances? May my roots dry, can it be true?*

"Are you all insane? I think I would know if I were a dwinan. Do you want to know why the cold doesn't kill me?" Anger flared in me. If I had been so powerful, why hadn't I saved the ones I loved? "It killed my mother! And I have lived hand in hand with the cold ever since. It doesn't affect me anymore."

Leohirin's might! the trees kept saying. *A dwinan.*

Please, no need to be upset, the peach tree said, but no. Those words had to be from Ariel whose hands were up in surrender. "I wish you no harm. If you want to leave, just leave."

I found fear in her eyes. She was terrified of me. Could it be true? No, it couldn't be. I turned my back to her. Every follicle on my neck bristled. With every heartbeat, I expected a beam of light to cut right through me. I glanced back at her. Ariel sat on the ground, trying to be as least threatening as possible. Was she really so frightened of me that she would just let me go? It had to be some kind of mind game.

I hated her for it. I hated her with all my heart. I've had enough of this, and I'd rather die alone and cold than spend another second in her company.

An hour later, guided by the trees, I found my friends. Brinn hugged me to within an inch of my life, and Mathew patted my back repeatedly, pure relief on his face.

I sat by their fire and was pleased to learn they had food with them. I was utterly famished. And while I ate, I told them everything.

Chapter 35

Strange Power

Ludik

"So? What's this dynamo thingy?" Mathew asked Miranda.

He had torn another bit off Miranda to facilitate our conversations. Well, my whole life, for that matter. We had been on the road for about a week, heading toward Algirin. And even though we followed the main road, we actively avoided being seen or stopping in any place larger than Leftover. I was surprised by the number of Leftover-sized towns that had sprouted along the way. I'd never known that the interior of Aviz was home to so many. But it made sense. In a country that had been at war with its neighbor for as long as Aviz had, who wouldn't want to live away from the border?

"Considered by many to be the most powerful of the mage classes," Mathew read aloud and immediately interrupted himself, "Nuts, that is! Fyr is the most powerful. Everybody knows that. What could possibly best fire?" He scoffed before continuing. "Users can diminish environmental energy at will, allowing them, in theory, to survive extreme temperatures on either side of the scale, making them invulnerable to energy attacks—what a load of crap. Stop messing with me, Miranda. I'll return you to the library. Only God knows how much I have to pay in late fees by now."

Brinn's eyes widened as she processed what she had heard. "That's why you are so unaffected by the cold. That explains so much. Like how you survived the night Heimee found you. And how you pulled that boy from the frozen lake as if it were a summer day. And how you survived..." She trailed off. "How could you not know?"

I shrugged. "How could I have known?"

"I don't know, by feeling it?"

I shrugged again. "It's not obvious in any way."

Mathew took a deep breath. "It also explains how you survived that fire without a single burn. You and that little girl should be dead. If it wasn't for Brinn's insistence on making sure you were dead, I would have left you behind. I mean, no one could survive that fire, let alone unharmed."

"So you think Ariel was telling the truth?" Brinn asked. "What about the part about Miranda?"

"What about it? Every good lie is based on something truthful. Everybody knows that. Are you out for world domination, Miranda? See," Mathew pointed to a line on the page, "she says she is. Funny. You know, I never understood world dominance. What use do you have in ruling so many people by yourself? What's the point? I mean, it has to be exhaustive, doesn't it? We are only a group of four, and leading this group leaves me drained like the Sahara desert."

"You know I always enjoy your wisdom," Brinn said. "But when did you become our leader?"

"I thought it was obvious, really. I have the mission, and I have the power."

"One, your mission isn't the same as ours. We are tagging along so Ludik can find his mountain and because you sent the whole army of Aviz barreling down on his home. And two, I don't know if you have been paying attention, but Ludik could kick your butt if he wanted to."

"Oh, is that so? What's he gonna do? Make me put on a sweater? I control fire, baby. Fire!"

"He's unaffected by fire."

"My guess is that it'll still hurt. And can he breathe smoke? I bet he still needs oxygen, you know, to oxygenize or something."

"Could we stop talking about this?" I interrupted; the way the conversation had veered was making me sick. "How did I become a dwinan? Was I born one?"

Mathew read Miranda again. "Little is known about the origins of the dwinan power. It is believed to be a reminiscence from the days of creation, from a time when light, energy, and mass did not exist. The last dwinan perished during the Shatter thousands of years ago. And your library dues are ninety-seven dollars and thirty-five cents."

"Money well spent if you ask me," Mathew said.

"But you haven't spent it, have you?" Brinn noted.

"Ain't that the best money? I'm getting a lot for its value. Economics 101."

"Will I never make sense of what you say—what was that?" Brinn said, pointing at Mathew's belly.

"My stomach," he said.

We had been able to procure very little food ever since we'd escaped Lirterin. We'd had no supplies, and no Era. We avoided bringing the matter up as best as we could. Brinn had been able to buy some food at a small street vendor on Wrinkled Hill while we hid our faces in the woods, but even our pockets were empty. Luckily, we still had the two bottles of Heims, which Mathew wisely kept in his backpack. We could still sell those for a good profit, but in these lands, we probably wouldn't find anyone wealthy enough to pay full price—whatever that was—so we decided to keep them in reserve. Altogether, we had maybe two heads left, plus a bolt or two. Not enough to survive to Algirin and then further north into the Shatter. But one day at a time.

Could I starve to death? If I could survive freezing temperatures and waves of fire, would I be affected by something as menial as hunger? My stomach trembled and revolted inside my belly as if answering the question.

"What was that?" Mathew said, craning his neck to peer into the darkness of the woods.

"My stomach?" I said.

"No," Mathew answered. "Something's out there?"

"Where's Ariel?" I asked the trees.

You should probably run, came the response.

"Run?"

Mathew and Brinn both turned abruptly to face me.

It's coming.

"It? Not she? I don't have patience for a pronoun game!"

"Too late!" Mathew said.

Brinn pulled me by the arm toward a nearby tree and began to climb. I didn't ask any questions. I stowed the letter in my pocket and climbed after her. She stopped maybe six feet high and looked down. I tried to make it to her side, but the branches on that side of the tree didn't make it easy, and I snapped a couple before I found a good grip.

Ouch! said the tree. *You're hurting me, you rotten woodworm!*

"Sorry," I said.

Brinn was facing away, but I could see her mouth moving. I pulled the note out.

"Make me a firecracker and light me up; what in the world is that?"

"I can't see it. What is it?"

"You'll see it soon enough! It's heading toward you."

The whole tree shook violently, and I nearly slipped, snapping away a couple more branches. The branches fell on top of large antlers—at least four or five feet wide and four feet tall. They were connected to a face with four black eyes, reminiscent of a spider, except the beast had a gray snout, blistered with irregular lumps. Its body resembled a whisky barrel covered in thin brown spikes. It had stumpy legs ending on thick black hooves. The upper eyes were smaller than the bottom ones and moved independently, studying its prey—us.

The stuff of myths. Except this particular myth was right below us, trying to shake us loose from the tree. That was a fully-fledged borint.

The tree shook violently again.

A borint! I hate borints. Do something other than break my branches, you humans, or that four-legged cactus will ram me down. Then we're all compost!

"So much for being just a children's story," Brinn said. "Mat, I guess this would be a good time for you to prove your skill in combat."

"I'm not going near that thing."

"What a hero you are! Get down there and do something, or I swear to the Bastard I'll have your head—"

The tree bent with the next hit, breaking the branch I held on to, and my feet slipped. I fell backward, clinging tightly to the useless branch.

Oh, thank the light, I'm alive.

I landed on my back and got the wind knocked out of me. The beast's upper eyes moved furiously in every direction, but it didn't seem to have spotted me yet. I squeezed the paper in my hand, afraid to lose it. It's incredible the weird things one does under stress. What use would I have for that paper if I died? But I didn't want to have Mathew rip another piece of Miranda off. She made it very clear that she did not enjoy the experience. I hurried to my feet, but the fall and lack of breath had left me dizzy.

Then all eyes of the beast fixed on me. I found my breath quite quickly after that and dashed toward the next tree. I jumped at a high branch, thick enough to hold my weight and raised my legs to wrap them around it.

Mathew was a couple of feet above me, yelling something. I unclutched my hand a little to read the paper. "You idiot!" he said. "Why couldn't you have chosen another tree?"

"Shut up and do something!" Brinn said from the adjacent tree. I craned my head with great effort to look at her and gasped. Brinn's feet dangled in the air, squirming and kicking, her hands unable to keep their grip much longer.

"Mathew!" I said. "Do something. You're a fyr, for Bastard's sake!"

"And you're the Oh-so-powerful dwinan! Why don't *you* do something? That thing is terrifying."

The borint tried to pluck me off the branch with its massive antlers, but I was just out of its reach and could feel the tip of the antlers scrape against my back. Or at least that's what I think was happening; I didn't think to look down.

Mathew's eyes widened.

No no no no no no no, said the tree.

The impact shook Mathew off his branch and sent him falling directly in my direction. He slammed against me and the branch I held on to snapped.

I fell on my back again, Mathew on top of me. I was pretty sure that on any other occasion I would've passed out, but as it turns out, being in a life-threatening situation is a great incentive not to.

Mathew pushed away from me and jumped into a sprint. I guess the thrill of the chase was more attractive than me because the borint immediately took after Mathew.

Knowing he had nowhere to go, Mathew turned to face the creature and opened fire.

The borint seemed almost unperturbed and, with a sweep of his massive antlers, sent Mathew flying.

I rolled on my stomach. The fire wasn't completely ineffective. The borint seemed disoriented, its antlers partially on fire. Instead of taking advantage of the opportunity, Mathew was busy inspecting his body for injuries.

"Ah-ah! Missed!" Mathew said but quickly lost his courage as he noticed the borint getting ready for another charge.

FIRE! FIRE! FIRE! screeched the trees as some of their branches and underbrush caught on fire.

Mathew gritted his teeth and raised his hands. The borint became a living flame, and despite all that, it didn't slow down, not even a little. Mathew rolled out of the way before the borint hit him and said, "Ole!" then ran to my side.

"I think it's fireproof," I said as he stopped next to me and helped me up.

"Good job, Sherlock," Mathew said, panting. "Hey, Baskerville! Eat this!" he taunted the beast as fireballs rained down on it. The fireballs exploded, sending broken spikes from its hide flying in every direction. One stuck to Brinn's leg, and she grimaced with pain. Then she lost her grip and came falling like an overripe peach.

The borint shook the fire away, clearly not ready to call it a day, and noticed Brinn. Why bother with the fire starter human when there's another one ripe for the picking?

I don't know what I was thinking. Everything happened in slow motion, as if it was part of a dream. I'd begun sprinting toward Brinn before I even knew what was happening. Like a scene from Salamorin, a half-burning monster ready to kill a princess, and only he could save her. Coldness brewed in my chest. Pale blue and cruel. Guilt, sorrow, and regret boiled and bubbled, growing untamed until they were a force on itself that craved nothing but more of it to satisfy the void left in its wake. Consciousness fled my mind as the power took control over me.

No! I had to remain alert. I had to save Brinn. But the fire and cold within hurt so much that my mind wanted nothing to do with it. I was a menace, and I was dangerous.

Things are things, said a rumbling voice.

Those words... I had heard before. The blackness came, submerging me, and I almost let go, but a warm hand brought me back.

Let her warmth be.

Who's saying that? Was it my mind playing tricks on me?

I gasped for air, forcing my eyes open. "Brinn!" I called. "Brinn!" What if something happened to her? What if I did something *to* her? Please, please, Bastard, don't let this happen.

A *dwinan. Leohirin's light, it is true,* the trees said in trembling whispers.

Orange light flickered in my vision, then only blue. Then black. Another flash of orange. It was blurry but reassuringly there. I blinked and rubbed the blurriness away. I was conscious.

Mathew already had a fire going, the orange hue reflected on thousands of tiny ice crystals adorning the forest floor around me. The borint lay at my feet, looking directly at me with his four black eyes. It breathed slowly, all the grit and power gone from it. It was dying. Brinn!

I turned and found her sitting there, perplexedly examining the icy scene. She rubbed her hands in front of her mouth, blowing steaming breath to warm them up.

"Are you okay? Did I hurt you?"

She seemed puzzled by the question. "You saved me."

I held my face in my hands and almost cried. What if I had hurt her? The thought constricted my chest—what a horrible feeling. Brinn kneeled next to me and hugged me, guiding my head to her shoulder. I didn't fight it. The power, whatever it was, left me drained.

"What am I?" I asked as I returned the hug.

Brinn hugged me tighter. Mathew stepped closer and I looked at the letter.

“Well, look on the bright side,” Mathew said as he observed the borint take its dying breath, “I bet it tastes just like pork.”

Chapter 36

Treespeak

Ariel

Ariel had cleared the forest the day before and found herself roaming a land rich in farming fields and fruit orchards.

She patted the ekkuh's neck. "Over there, close to those trees? Looks like a good spot. What do ye think?"

The brown ekkuh bristled its feathers, clacked its beak, and without command, moved in that direction. "Aren't ye a clever horsey? You know, you look a little like Flora MacDonald. I'll call ye Flora if ye don't mind."

Ariel dismounted and promptly pulled a shovel from Flora's new saddle that she had fitted on a stable a few miles back, where she learned the beast was called an ekkuh, and got to work. Would peach trees and apple trees get along? She didn't know. She didn't even know trees could speak until recently. So it was all guesswork. What wasn't guesswork this time was the location. If other fruit trees grew there, a peach tree shouldn't have any problems. Probably. If only she could ask it.

"An easy job," she grumbled as she dug her stolen spade into the soil. "Was that too much to expect? Of course, it was. It always is. Nothing is ever easy nor simple."

Once happy with the hole, she untied the peach tree and settled it gently on its new home. After covering her roots and packing the dirt tightly, Ariel infused the peach tree with light, allowing it to grow new roots and straighten its trunk.

Ariel dusted her hands and wiped the sweat off her forehead, then took a Heims bottle and a Glencairn glass, or as they called it there, a thumbglass, from her pack and sat on the low grass admiring her work. "I'll come back later to check on ye, okay?" *If I survive,* she thought to herself. "I think ye look rather happy here."

Thank you, the tree said.

Ariel raised her glass and sipped at it. "Yae're welcome. Wait? What?" She listened attentively but heard nothing more. Ariel shrugged. "I'm going mad. It was only a matter of time, really."

You heard me?

Ariel perked up, turning her full attention to the tree. Nothing. Only a light snicker from the road. Looking over, she found two men riding an ekkuh cart, observing her. "Have ye never seen a crazy lady before?"

The men pretended to admire the landscape, pointed here and there, and shared firm nods of approval before moving away.

Ariel sighed.

A peach tree? Out of all the trees in the world, you had to plant a peach tree.

Ariel stood up in a heartbeat. "Who said that?" She squinted at the closest apple tree. "Listen here! This tree is a hero! Yae'll treat *her* with respect!"

Don't worry, Leohirin. I'll do fine here.

"This is so weird."

She was listening, but she didn't know how to listen. She concentrated, inspecting the trees closely. Again, nothing. Ariel pinched her chin in thought.

You're trying too hard.

"I definitely heard that," she said more to herself than to the trees.

How could she try less hard? How do you even go about it? She tried again. And again, nothing. "Is this like in The Hitchhiker's Guide? Should I throw myself at the ground and miss it? Do I not listen, and in doing so, I hear? Is that the knack to this?"

She cradled her face in her hands.

Is she always this crazy?

Most times, yeah.

"Hmm, I have to be distracted from sound to listen. That makes no sense. I can't shut my ears." Nevertheless, she was doing it. Somehow. After another sip, she asked, "Do ye know where Miranda is?"

Picaline.

"Picaline?" Ariel repeated. At first, she thought it was just nonsense, but, that name, she'd seen it somewhere. Ariel pulled a map from her bag and refilled her glass. There it was, south of Algirin on the other margin of the river Mare. Picaline. She sipped her stolen whisky in heavy consideration. "That's where ye cross the river into Algirin."

She listened attentively again, but the more she forced herself to listen, the less she heard. There was wind, the rustling of leaves like crashing waves, the chirp of birds happy in the spring sun, the trot of ekkuhs, and clanks of wheels coming from the busy road. She rubbed her eyes and sighed. She drank the remaining content of the glass in one gulp. Oh, that was good, like sipping Scotland itself, except it hadn't been made in Scotland.

Does she know treespeak or not? I can't figure it out.

I think she's just crazy.

She did lug that thing all the way here from Lirterin—that's just not right.

Ariel couldn't figure out which tree was saying what, and she was afraid to speak, move, or even breathe, lest the trees' voices fade again. It required incredible concentration not to concentrate, but she was getting the knack of it. And the Heims helped more than a little.

Does this mean we have to deal with that little stump from now on? I've known this peach tree for a good couple of minutes and already hate every leaf on her twigs.

Hey, she's the Leoht, right?

Did you just wake up now? Yes. She is.

Ah, that makes more sense. Definitely crazy, then.

Yup.

Yep.

Yeah, the trees agreed.

Is this what Ludik has to deal with all the time? Ariel thought. "Are ye always this provocative?"

She does know treespeak.

Yup. Seems that way.

Yep.

Hey, lady. Could you take your tree somewhere else? She's rather getting on my nerves.

Don't be silly. You're a tree. You don't have nerves.

Then how come I can feel all the vermin creeping under my bark?

"I'm sorry, Peach. I didn't know they'd be such lousy company."

No, no, this is great. We'll get along just fine. Hey, what did the tree say to the other tree?

Please don't.

Wait right here! said her peach tree.

All the other trees groaned and moaned together.

Please, Light, be merciful. I don't think I'll survive this.

Oh, but I have more! Tons more.

Listening to trees is not something she could put into words; she wasn't even sure how she was doing it. But Ludik had proved it was possible. It dawned on her she'd known how to listen all this time. Of course, her friend's memories! She was a tree; trees speak treespeak. It had been hiding inside her all along. All it needed was a little push, and by golly, she *was* doing it. And now that she was, she didn't seem able to stop.

Ariel looked north—over the horizon, where the plains met the river Mare and the port city of Picaline. If she hurried, she could still intercept Miranda again, and, more importantly, she could use the trees there to speak to Ludik on her behalf. Yes! That was it. It wasn't much of a plan, but it was a start. Ariel considered the singed bag tied to Flora's saddle. She had gone to immense trouble to retrieve that particular item. The last thing on her mind was to re-infiltrate Lirterin's castle, but it had to be done. And now, her not-much-of-a-plan had two parts, and she was eager to get going.

"Let's go, Flora," Ariel said, mounting the ekkuh. "If we hurry, we just may catch—arghhh!"

A shrouded figure popped into existence before her, making her jerk and fall over, landing with a muffled thump.

"Why?" she croaked. "Why can't ye be normal?"

Despite the direct sunlight, Alfred remained shrouded by darkness, as if his robes absorbed all daylight surrounding them. With a sweeping motion, Ariel turned his dark robes into a joyful blue, dashed with happy little yellow lines. His half figure was unsettling enough without dark ominous clothing.

"Why haven't you stopped her?" he said, voice like a howling wind slamming against a locked door.

Ariel fought to catch her breath. "Why? Ye dare ask me why, ye wrinkled bawbag! Ye nugget dunderhied! What about a simple heads up, 'Hey, Ariel, by the way, that American boy I told ye about, he's a Fyr.' And I would've been all like, 'Thank ye, Half, that's very helpful information. I'm sure it will come in handy and avoid me a lot of trouble.'"

She got so caught up in her rant she did not notice her slip. Would Alfred mind hearing his nickname out loud?

Half blinked a couple of times. "Feeling better?"

"No." Ariel crossed her arms. "What do ye want?"

"Benerik Strudaw."

"Is that supposed to mean anythin'?"

"I told him about your failures. He's on his way here."

"My failures? My failures? Yae've gotta be daft. This is all on ye! Ye can stop them with a flick of your wrist. But no! Let's send a completely unprepared agricultural advisor to save the bloody universe!"

"I can't," Half said, lost in thought.

"Yeah, ye said it before."

"Sad, isn't it?"

"Did ye scare me half to death only to tell me that you can't help me and that some bumpot is on his way? Well, when will he get here?"

"Soon."

"Bloody hell, Half. Yae're so considerate. Thank ye for being the wee ray of sunshine that ye are. Does he know what's at stake? Couldn't ye have found more help? I think this problem calls for as many hands on deck as possible, wouldn't ye agree?"

"The Shatter's only a fable to most, and most found me mad. Perhaps they're right."

"Perhaps they are. Tell me, *Half*," Ariel said while pulling herself up with the aid of Flora's reins and dusting herself off. "Ye sent me to fight yer battles, isn't that the same as fighting them yaerself? Am I not yer gun, so to speak?"

The happy blue covering his clothes dissolved like burning paper, and the darkness returned, spreading, infecting the land and the air surrounding them. Plants withered and died, replaced by a blanket of frost. Half loomed like a creature imbued with cosmic horror. Ariel shrank, her knees buckled, and she cowered.

When Half spoke again, his voice contained all the universe's anger and tragedy. "Why would I stop her? Why would I fear being whole again? Your ephemeral lives are the only cost. Some days I can barely deny the bargain it is. You're nothing but dust to me."

The looming darkness retreated. But when it faded, the sky was no longer blue, and the ground at least ten feet around Half was barren of life.

"With Miranda back at my side..." Half trailed off and shook his head.

Was he contemplating the doom of humanity for a booty call? "Hey," Ariel said, shooting upright and snapping her fingers, "snap out of it!"

Half regarded her as if seeing her for the first time and vanished, leaving only the scarred ground as proof he was ever there.

"Oh, yeah?" Ariel shouted to the heavens. "Yae're a coward. What love do ye think she has for ye? Yae're weak! Yae're a weak, weak man. All the power in the universe, and ye can't live life for yaerself. Yae're pathetic! That's why she doesn't love ye. She never has!"

Why did she always feel the need to scold the most powerful being in existence? Ariel gritted her teeth and got ready for him to return and answer her in kind. But he didn't. Was he not listening? Or was she right?

Chapter 37

Picaline

Ludik

Picaline was a mess.

We'd wanted to avoid large crowds, but Picaline was the only entrance to Algirin in a hundred leagues, and after eating nothing but slowly rotting borint meat for three days straight, we couldn't have cared less about caution. As it turns out, Picaline was such a colossal mess that hiding among the crowd was probably the safest place to be.

We crossed a vast area clumped with wagons, carts, tents, campfires, people, and people having parties that Mathew named 'the parking lot' and had barely taken two steps into the city itself, when the crowd ahead of us parted like a receding tide, allowing a man to run past while being chased by another holding a knife, who shouted, "I'm gonna murder you and feed you to the hogs!"

The commotion made a man wearing a bright yellow tunic bump into another by accident, and a fight broke out.

"Where the hell are we?" Mathew said. "The Wild West? Jesus!"

"It's very different from the rest of the country, isn't it?" Brinn noted. "Not at all what I expected."

"I don't think anyone expected... well... this," I offered.

On the bright side, Mathew was no longer the only dark person around. There were all sorts of people wearing all sorts of garments, from flamboyant and garish to plain and austere. A particular group wore only yellow, sticking out like yellow woodsorrels. Until that moment, Mathew had been the only dark-skinned person I'd ever seen, but there, on the streets of Picaline, they were as common as clouds in the sky.

Large crowds always mean street food, so that's what we searched for, being careful not to bump into anyone.

"Look!" Mathew said. "I can't believe it. Hot dogs!"

I followed his pointing finger and found a cart with a blue awning and a man selling sausages stuffed in some kind of white bread. Brinn and I offered no objections.

"Is that ketchup?" Mathew asked the vendor, pointing to a reddish sauce he kept in an iron pot at the corner of the grill.

"Nae, jirimari," the vendor replied.

"Can I try some?"

The vendor dipped a little bread in the sauce and gave it to Mathew. I didn't think it was possible, but Mathew became the color of the sauce.

"Holy shit, on a cracker! That's hot!" Mathew gagged and began sweating profusely. "Quick, water," he added, his voice a rasp.

Brinn watched him half dumbfounded, half amused as she passed him our water pouch.

"I'll have mine without sauce," I said.

We left the vendor with nearly all our money and proceeded down the street until we encountered an even more considerable commotion at the crossing station. The crossing station was a port where barges, big enough to hold about one hundred people plus cargo, called picas, were attached to cables that ran from four rotating towers on this side of the river to another set of towers on the other side of the river. The rotating mechanism pulled the cable along, tugging the picas across the river—literally, a pica line, as in a line that pulls picas.

"I give up." Mathew sucked air through his teeth and continued, "I can't think of a dumber name for this place. Jesus, my tongue is still tingling."

"Why?" Brinn protested. "It says precisely what it is. What's so wrong with that?"

"It lacks imagination."

"So what? Does everything need to be imaginative? Is everything in your world original?"

"Okay, maybe that's not the right word, then. It lacks creativity."

"Same thing. Well, I say, it adds creativity. It tells me it knows what it is and is not afraid to say it. Why would a random name be any better?"

Mathew failed to answer, and Brinn took the opportunity to plow through, "Not everything needs to be clever. And if you want proof of concept, all you need to do is look in the mirror."

"Ouch," Mathew said, rubbing his heart. "What do you think, Lud?"

I shrugged, too enthralled by the busy scene to care about the names of things. The departure lanes were packed to the top and beyond, stretching halfway across the city, made only worse by people arriving from the other side and crashing into the oncoming traffic. Garbage littered nearly every inch of the street, and ekkuh's and ox's droppings filled the rest. The smell aggravated with each passing moment.

"Oh, I know you agree with him," Brinn said at last. "I'm practically sure you named every rock in Heimee's land with cutesy little girly names."

I hadn't, but the thought had occurred to me once, apart from the cutesy bit.

"So, how do we get across," Mathew began, "the *pica line*? Shall we simply *barge* in?"

"No!" Brinn and I said in unison.

"Alright, calm your horses. What if you use your powers? Just walk over there and say, 'alright everybody, chill'."

At first, I stared blankly at him. Not in a mood to make jokes about my newfound power ever since a disturbing thought had occurred to me a few nights before: what if I killed my mother? It's possible, right? I was a dwinan, after all. Maybe I got too cold and—I couldn't bear to think about it. So I smiled meekly and changed the subject. "Well, we're not embarking today, not with this many people still waiting."

"Also," Brinn pointed to a small sign to our right, "did you see the prices? Two full tales. That's twenty heads. Per person! I could probably buy my aunt's bakery with that kind of money."

"They are also inspecting everyone who gets in," I pointed out.

"I can't see a thing with all this dust." Mathew shaded his eyes from the intense sun and squinted. "Where?"

I pointed to the heavily armored soldiers coercing the crowd into a somewhat coordinated line and inspecting every person, animal, and vehicle. As I glanced at the letter I kept in my hand, I asked, "How about it, Miranda? How do we pass the guards? Any ideas?"

Mathew and Brinn hovered over me, waiting to read the response. Mathew could easily have opened Miranda, but reading the note was faster.

Bribery, of course.

"Bribery?" I asked.

Bribery: the giving or offering a bribe. Bribe: dishonestly persuade (someone) to act in one's favor by a gift of money or other inducement.

"But if we had money," Brinn said, "couldn't we just use it to buy the ticket?"

Mathew held to the straps on his backpack, "But we would still have to get past the—"

"The Heims!" I burst. Of course, that's our ticket in. "You'll find them especially handy when in need of friend or favor," I repeated Heimee's words as I remembered them.

"What?" Brinn said.

"The Heims 39. We can sell one, or, better still, we use it to buy favor. Or, in this case, to bribe someone."

"Is that why you insisted on carrying these clunky things around all this time?" Mathew said. "How much are they worth? And if the answer is, 'that much,' why haven't we sold them yet?"

"I gotta say," Mathew said as we perched on top of a roof overseeing the chaos of the Pica Line below, "I like this plan."

"You do? Why?" Brinn said. "We're not setting anything on fire."

Mathew ignored Brinn and took out a bottle of Heims for the twentieth time, examining it. "Are you sure these bottles are that valuable?"

"I have seen how people lose their minds over the cheaper stuff.

Frankly, I have no idea how expensive they are, but not even Heimee drank them."

Mathew stowed the bottle away, turning his attention back to the departure lanes. Someone down there was bound to be our target, so we inspected our choices by commenting on which soldier looked more miserable and, therefore, more likely to accept our offer. And I have to say, it was a pretty fun afternoon. Bastard knows we needed one.

I know it's wrong to mock others, and I wouldn't like it if I was the one being mocked, but consider this, we were under a great deal of stress, and we weren't harming anyone. Not to mention that if I was going to let morals interfere, then I might also have a problem with the bribery we were about to commit in the first place. Bribery had to be wrong, hadn't it? Well, it was, at the very least, illegal. Is something illegal always wrong? Maybe. It didn't matter. It had to be done, and we were doing it.

"What about that one?" Mathew pointed to a bald woman wearing a black and red tunic, heatedly berating a soldier. "If she points a finger at him again, he just might punch her. That's not the face of someone who's enjoying his life."

"She's really going at him, isn't she?" I said.

"Kinda reminds me of Brinn."

"Yes, that's it!"

Brinn glared at us through the corner of her eye, but, amazingly, did not move her arms or quipped back. "She looks nothing like me."

"Oh, and the woman goes down!" Mathew said as the soldier finally punched her in the nose.

She held it as blood trickled down her chin and tears ran down her cheeks. The soldier looked down at her, obviously pleased with himself, judging by the vicious smile that slit his lips until the woman got back on her feet and punched the smile off his face. A minor skirmish erupted, with several soldiers rushing in to contain the problem before it escalated into a full-scale riot.

"On second thought," Brinn added, "I guess I do see the resemblance. Anyway, I think our Mr. Misery winner is the young lad at the end lane."

I had to squint to take a better look at the boy. Shoulders slumped, weary expression, trudging movements, not bothering to give a second look at the ongoing surge of contempt and aggression a couple of lanes down.

"Too young," Mathew said. "Our target needs to be older. Better chances he'll understand the value of our offer."

We nodded. If someone offered me a bottle of whisky, I'd puke faster than I'd accept it. So we kept looking.

"Ah-ah!" Mathew said. "There!"

"Don't point. Keep your hand down," Brinn said.

"Just look, the big guy with the red beard who just relieved No-Sympathy man in the vehicle lane." The man was so large that his armor had a tough time covering his belly; the chest plate was so far from the backplate I could easily fit through the gap.

"Why? Because he's fat?"

Mathew rolled his eyes. "No, look. He barely got in there, and at least six wagons drove by. Either he excels at his job or is super lousy at it. Or," he paused for effect, "he's doing it purposefully."

The man looked as disinterested in his job as a child doing house chores.

"And, okay, let's face it," Mathew continued, "how many fat soldiers have you seen lately? None right? I bet he receives bribes all day and that some of the other soldiers are getting a piece of the pie to remain quiet. Hell, I wouldn't be the least bit surprised if almost everyone in that queue had bribed him. Look at how they go."

At one point, a tall man wearing the yellowest tunic I'd ever seen—and that's saying a lot because I'd seen nothing else all day but yellow tunics—handed him something, a small pouch. The big soldier took it and went through the motions of inspecting the merchandise. He lifted the tarp covering the cart, barely glanced at it, and told the man to proceed—a stark difference from the previous soldier at the post who had a coach apprehended and punched the owner without hesitation when he complained. We crossed that one off our list.

After considering other options for the remainder of the afternoon, none were as promising as *Big Guy*. That's what Mathew called him, and the name stuck.

At sunset, the Pica Line closed, leaving many people still on the wrong side of the river, which was about to turn into a full-blown battle at any moment. Arms flailed, hands balled into fists, and according to Miranda: **mob shouts obscenities.*

As if going through the motions, a group of soldiers in a tight formation, holding spears and shields, left the barracks, and the commotion died down almost instantly. The armed men broke formation, laughing and patting each other on the back for a job well done. Clearly, that was the height of their day.

We left our little spot and followed Big Guy around for a while until he disappeared inside the barracks, leaving us with nothing to do but wait for him to come out and follow him some more. It wasn't like we could knock on the barracks door and ask if we could speak with Big Guy because we wanted to bribe him.

While we waited, I even gave the remainder of our money to a scruffy beggar who sat by the corner. I reminisced lightly on the days I tried to beg and quickly shunned the thought.

"Really? Our last money?" Mathew said as I returned.

I shrugged. "Why not? It's not like we can do anything with two bolts. And to her, it might be the difference between having a meal or starving."

"You have such a soft heart. Well, there goes that," Mathew said after another man left the barracks' back door. "He's not coming out. Maybe it's his bribe day off or something."

"And where do you want to go?" Brinn said. "Is there a party somewhere you've been invited to?"

"Brinn, we've been here for hours."

"By the way," I asked, almost as an afterthought. "What happens if he isn't, well, you know, corrupt?"

Mathew sucked air through his teeth. "Then we'll have a blast of an evening."

"I think that's him," I said, nodding toward the voluptuous man with a thick red beard who left the barracks and headed briskly toward the town center.

"Yup, that's him," Mathew said, rubbing his hands. "Alright, it's game time."

Chapter 38

Beggar's Day

Ariel

Picaline had no trees. A grand total of zero. Ariel tried to contain her frustration, but it was better to let it loose and be done with it. That was it, her last brilliant idea.

"What a mess," she said, contemplating Picaline's crossing station which had been named Pica Line probably to keep things simple. It was an odd place, to say the least. The whole country so far had been a reflection of her own, filled with rough, whisky-loving people. But arriving at Pica Line was like arriving at Heathrow Airport, apart from the medieval outlook and the lack of airplanes and metal detectors.

Ariel peered around, unsure of herself. How was she going to find those rugrats in that chaos? It was a lost cause, for sure. Ariel took a deep breath, which she regretted. The air was filled with dust and the stink of a gigantic litter box. She winced and coughed, then looked up, grunting in frustration.

Her frustration was short-lived.

On top of a small building, she found Mathew, Ludik, and the girl. Bran, her name was? Was Bran a boy's name? No, that was her cultural bias at work. Bran could very well be a girl's name here. But that didn't matter. The fools were right there in plain sight for anyone to see. What were they thinking?

Ariel inspected the area again and guessed that if she'd had any involvement in the chaos before her, she wouldn't have the presence of mind to look up. Besides, it's not like those soldiers feared snipers. But they could be victims to archers, no?

Ugh, her mind was all over the place.

She didn't have a plan, per se. All she knew was that she needed to reach out to Ludik. If anyone had the power to stop Mathew without straight out murdering the lad, it was him. There was little doubt about it. But what was Ludik, an honest to God dwinan, doing with Mathew and Miranda? Ariel understood now why Miranda wanted to keep Ludik in her company, but what did Ludik have to gain out of all this?

She should've paid more attention when she'd first found them. That didn't matter now; she still had time. Not much, granted, but perhaps enough. The good news was she only had to eavesdrop a little, and that meant sneaking around. Fortunately, that was the only thing she'd ever been good at, even before she became a leoht. She could build a better rapport if she could understand what drove the lad. *Great, now I'm using Munika's words.* And maybe, just maybe, she could avoid the calamity that would otherwise ensue.

Ariel patted Flora's neck. "Yer owners are almost as bright as I am." Ariel blinked and slapped her forehead. "I should probably get ye out of sight. I think I saw a stable on our way here."

Twenty minutes later, Ariel was back at the crossing lanes and breathed a sigh of relief when she found the three musketeers right where she had left them, enjoying themselves in congenial conversation. Not a bother in the world. So clueless. She inspected her disguise—deprived of attention as anything can be—drab clothes, shaggy hair, a little mange to her face, sitting at the corner begging for coin. Absolutely invisible and boring.

The kids perched there until sunset when they climbed down to the street and continued doing nothing. "I paid parking only until nightfall," she muttered to herself. "Will they charge me a late fee or simply sell the horse? Wait? Is he coming this way? Stop muttering, Ariel." *He is,* she thought to herself. *Could he have recognized me? Did a tree tell him I was here? There are no trees here. He did recognize me last time, despite my color change. But I'm sure I did a better job this time. Did I change my eye color? Of course, I did. Oh, rats. He's looking directly at me.*

"Here," Ludik said, extending his hand. "It's not much, but it's literally all we have. Maybe you can do better with it."

Ariel raised a trembling hand, which only added to her disguise, though she was trembling from pure stress. "Thank you, my son," she said with the roughest old lady-like voice she could muster while suppressing her Scottish burr.

"You're welcome." Ludik smiled at her and returned to his friends.

Ariel took deep breaths to steel herself. Then, mere moments later, they were on the move. Ariel followed them, adding a slight limp to her walk and pocketing the four gollings and three guillings she made begging, two of which came from Ludik himself. *Hum*, she thought to herself, *begging here is quite a profitable enterprise.*

It became clear after a while they were following someone, a fat man, it seemed. No, not fat, strong, she would say. Quite handsome, too. Groomed beard, rough around the edges, walking like he owned the place. Ariel wouldn't mind paying him a beverage. He looked like a strong teddy bear. She shoved the thought away; this was not a time for pleasure.

She followed the group until the large man entered a bar on the main street. Nightlife flooded every nook and cranny. What an odd place. Half city, half gypsy camp. Picaline was certainly full of surprises. The group stopped by the entrance of the bar, arguing. They didn't agree on something. And every time one of them ventured toward the bar, another grabbed him or her by the arm.

While they bickered, Ariel took the opportunity to change her disguise. Adjacent to the bar, she found a small dead-end alley filled with wood crates smelling like dead fish, reminding her of those American movies where someone always escaped by jumping a fence at the end or getting their arses kicked.

She came out with a much different look. Nothing flashy, but she did allow a certain amount of yellow. Many foreigners there wore yellow for cultural or religious reasons. She didn't really care why, but fortunately, the place was packed with them, making it easy to blend in. A small part of her, however, was upset about it. Yellow was her color, and she didn't enjoy seeing it so overused. She decided on dark skin, deep black eyes, and coal-like hair.

When she emerged from the alley, the kids were gone. They must've gone inside. She swung the door open, trying her best not to look hasty. A sign at the entrance said *Villy Vil*, written with what appeared to be ax blows. Other than that, at first glance, it was like any other bar. It even smelled of tobacco, rye, and spilled beer. What she didn't like was all the wicker. But now that she knew trees were sapient and plastic wasn't available, perhaps wicker was better than having everything made out of stone. After a careful look, the decor began growing on her. Lamps of every shape and size adorned the caned roof, which displayed distinct geometrical patterns like a monochrome kaleidoscope. Gifts from distant lands, including weird stuffed animals resembling either a tortoise or a rabbit, depending on how you looked at it, adorned the large stone columns supporting the roof.

Ariel walked straight to the bar, where all sorts of bottles surrounded a large war hammer hanging on the wall. "Heims, please," she said to the bald bartender. The man had shoulders the size of armrests from an old, upholstered sofa, a scar crossed his left eye, and a golden earring pierced his right earlobe. Several men in yellow tunics regarded her belligerently. Had she made some kind of error?

The bartender gave her the drink with pride in his eyes. "Nice to see a woman standing for herself, ain't it?" he said, sneering at the other men in the bar. "The lot don't let their women drink. Disgusting if you ask me."

"Will there be trouble?" Ariel asked.

The bartender nodded at the war hammer behind him and grinned, revealing an impressive lack of teeth. "No trouble, miss. Not on my watch."

"Cheers!" Ariel said, raising her glass and consuming the content. She slammed the thumbglass back down and motioned for another.

Ariel peered around the bustling bar and spotted the large man sitting alone in the back, a large mug of ale in his hand. What a dashing man. She walked closer, the Heims lighting up her mood, sat at a table within earshot, and waited. Her wait was short-lived because moments later, she heard Bran introduce herself to the man.

"Who're you?" said the large man in a deep guttural voice. A man's voice. "Whaddya want?"

"Name's Brinn," she said.

Brinn! Oh, that was it, not Bran. Well, that certainly made a little more sense. *Wait? Did it?*

"And I have something for you," Brinn said.

Chapter 39

Villy Vil

Ludik

"Aren't you a little too young to be offering yourself like that?" Big Guy said, examining her head to toe.

"What?" Brinn sputtered, nostrils flaring. "No!"

Mathew and I weren't far away, ready to intervene at any moment, but the rest of the bar seemed pretty angry about this woman who'd decided to have a drink. What a nerve on that one. A drink! There's just no respect anymore. So as you can imagine, our attention was a little divided.

"I kind of want to set them on fire. Just a little bit, you know?" Mathew said. "I understand it's their culture and all, but I've seen enough of this crap where I come from. A person should be free to do whatever they want."

"I wouldn't try to stop you," I said.

"Yuck," Brinn said. "No. Uh-uh, no way. And, also, yuck!"

The woman with black hair and yellow clothes glared at Brinn and scoffed for some reason. Maybe one of the men had said something to her, and she just happened to be looking Brinn's way. I know she scoffed because I was looking at her, not because I read it in Miranda's note. There was something about her, something vaguely familiar, and I couldn't quite place what it was.

"Yuck? Really? What else should I expect when a brat like yourself just waltzes up to me?" Big Guy said. "Whaddya want then?"

Brinn pulled the bottle of Heims out of a bag and presented it to the man.

Big Guy bulged his green eyes to the point where they nearly popped out of their orbits. "Where did you steal that from?" His hand jerked toward the bottle, but Brinn pulled it back in time.

"It would be a shame if I dropped it on the floor." Brinn stretched her arm out, bottle dangling in her fingers, eyes never wavering from his.

"Let's not be hasty, and do something we'll all regret," Big Guy said, not entirely losing his cool.

"My thoughts, exactly," Brinn said, tucking the bottle back on her lap so only Big Guy could see it. "I need safe passage across the river. Me and two others, plus one hundred heads."

Big Guy chuckled, took a long drag out of his ale, cleaned the froth from his beard with the back of his hand, and said, "Is that all? Passage for three and ten tales, for a bottle of Heims 39? You're either mad or desperate."

Brinn stared him down.

"You know, some might call this bribery."

"Yes—we've discussed that at length all day. And you'll accept it."

"Is that so?" He leaned forward, his belly pushing the table along. "Six tales and no passage. The money would be enough for you to buy your own passage in a more legal manner." He finished with a smug smirk that was kind of lost among his facial hair.

Brinn stared at him silently for a lingering, unblinking moment. "Twenty tales, plus safe passage."

"Where did she learn to be like this?" Mathew asked.

"Her aunt," I said. "She makes the most expensive bread in town, yet everybody buys from her out of fear of repercussion."

"That's one way to do business. Is the bread worth it?"

"I've had better."

"I see. Well then, pluck my feathers and call me a chicken—I'm glad she's on our side."

"Fine," Big Guy said, trying to keep his eager eyes away from the bottle and failing redundantly. "Ten tales it is. Who're the passengers?"

"No questions, remember," Brinn said. "And the price is twenty tales. Paid upfront."

The big guy let out a guffaw. Then seeing the resolve in Brinn's eyes, he leaned back, arms crossed, considering the proposition.

"I'm sorry. I seem to have wasted my time," Brinn said and turned to leave.

The Big Guy got up, almost flipping the table with his belly, and grabbed Brinn's arm. Mathew and I got up. The big guy shared a look with us and laughed. "Your friends, I presume. What's with all the secrecy? You're just a bunch of kids. Who are you running from?"

As if it had always been the case, Brinn lowered her eyes. "My father," she said. "He plans to marry me off against my will. I need to get away from him."

"And you stole his precious bottle. You don't know its real value, but you know enough. Smart girl."

Brinn held her stare.

"Alright, kids. You got yourselves a deal. Twenty tales, plus passage. But not upfront. Be there at the crossing come noon. If you trick me, I'll have you arrested."

Brinn extended her hand to formalize the deal. Big Guy shook his head. She withdrew her hand, understanding her mistake, and sneered at Big Guy so anyone observing the two would get the impression Big Guy had denied whatever it was Brinn wanted from him.

"Oh please!" said the dark-haired woman, standing up in a hurry. "Can't you see who they—" She didn't finish her sentence. A bottle ensured that when it hit her directly in her face.

The bar exploded.

I don't know how exactly, but in a matter of seconds, there were two factions. One side even had yellow uniforms. Chairs flew, tables flipped, fists shook—bottles, glasses, and ashtrays traveled across the air as the initial wave. And then the bodies clashed.

"Get behind me, kids," Big Guy said, smiling his teeth out. "And protect the merchandise; that's my ticket out of this ordeal. I'm sure I can get a fine promotion for it. Maybe a nice office spot on the northern bank. Wouldn't that be great?"

A man stormed Big Guy, wielding a chair. With one hand, Big Guy swatted the chair away, and with the other he slapped the light right out of the man's eyes. "What are you lot still doin' here? Scram."

Big Guy plowed through the mass of bodies. The girl with black hair was only then getting back on her feet, dizzy, confused, and defenseless. Poor woman, standing up for her beliefs and getting a bottle in the eye for it.

And that's when the hammer left its resting place. "Who wants a piece of Villy Vil!" bellowed the barkeeper, jumping on top of the counter and kicking a glass at a man's face. "Come at me, you piss-colored pillows!"

Chapter 40

White Star

Ludik

"I WONDER if anybody will ever drink that bottle," I said as we waited our turn in the queue at the appointed hour the next day. "Or it will just get passed on, from hand to hand, until the end of time because it's too expensive to drink."

The crossing station was in total chaos again. It was one thing to witness it from afar, and another to be right smack in the middle of it. There was so much pushing and shoving I gained a few bruises. Some people waited in line, while others tried to jump it, inspiring a whirlwind of obscenities, threats, and the fulfillment of said threats.

"How much do you think it's actually worth?" Mathew said. "Maybe we could make a fortune. Ride to Aureberg on a palanquin or something. Live as kings for a while. We should look into it. We have another bottle left, after all."

"I don't think we should say it out loud, though," Brinn said. "We're surrounded by ears."

"It's so loud in here I can barely listen to my own voice," Mathew pointed out.

"Lucky you," Brinn added.

"The line is moving," I said. "I can see Big Guy now, and I don't like the look on his face."

"I knew this was too easy," Mathew said. "He found out who we are, for sure. I mean, what did we expect? To fall in the dirt and come out smelling like roses?"

"Is that too much to ask?" Brinn said. "The line is moving again."

"Brinn, what do we do?" I asked. "Mathew can't use his powers here. And I don't know how to use mine."

"No one is using any powers because there won't be a fight," Brinn said calmly. "Let me do the talking and keep your mouths shut, or I'll shut them for you."

"I'll do you one better," Mathew said. "I hereby declare Brinn Kallak as our official spokesperson. Henceforth you'll be solely responsible for any negotiation that may occur now or in the future."

"That sounded very official, Sir Doller; thank you. I kindly accept the position. Now be quiet. We're next."

Big Guy motioned for us to proceed. Brinn handed him the bag containing the bottle of Heims 39 for inspection. Big Guy took it and peered inside. I swear time stood still while he contemplated his prize, then Brinn's face, then ours.

"I'm such a fool for not seeing it yesterday," he said between gritted teeth.

Brinn waited, her eyes unflinching, not even a blink.

"Off to be married, my ass. Deal's off."

"You may wish to consider the consequences," Brinn said matter-of-factly. "One, you can let us pass as agreed. We go on our way, and you get to live a better life. Two, Lirterin happens all over again. I'm sure you heard about what happened there. This place will burn to the ground, and it'll all be on your shoulders. If you survive, that is. In which case, I will make sure everyone knows about our little deal. What will your superiors say when they find out about your illicit ventures?" Brinn stepped closer like a mouse getting ready to charge at an ox. "You'll be sent to jail or some labor camp to live out the remainder of your days. And that's if you don't lose your head. My guess is this isn't your first infraction. Take the bottle, big man, and no harm will come to anyone."

He clutched the straps of the bag tighter, clenching his jaw. He glanced between the bag and Brinn a couple of times. "What's your purpose in Algirin?"

"Just passing. We won't be in the city for more than a day, and no one will ever know we were there. You have my word."

Big Guy squinted his eyes. "What happened after the fire in Lirterin? In the castle. No one's talking about it—it's like it's sacrilege or something."

"You don't need to concern yourself with that. You should be concerned with the safety of these people and your promising future."

"That bad, huh?"

Brinn said nothing.

The man took a deep breath, his eyes jumping between his brothers in arms and Brinn and then back to the bag. "Don't make me regret this."

Brinn stood still and opened her hand expectantly.

Big Guy produced a small pouch and deposited it in Brinn's hand. She smiled pleasantly, exchanged the bottle, and we moved along.

Once we'd cleared security and could breathe again, I used my breath to say, "Bastard's bother, I have no idea how you managed to keep so calm."

"Look at my hands." Brinn showed her palms. They were sweaty and trembled like she had been left outside on a winter night. "I think I need a change of underwear."

Mathew slapped her in the back. "That was impressive, girl. I thought we were done for."

After we cleared security, the lane led to a large pier with plenty of room to move around without bumping into anyone. People and animals waited their turn to embark before the big rotating towers, like upright whisky barrels, when something caught my attention. A lone ekkuh stood there with no apparent owner. I squinted. "Is that...?" I said. "Isn't that Era?"

Brinn's head turned so fast she might've broken her neck. "Where? Era!"

We dashed towards the ekkuh. Brinn inspected its feathers, beak and eyes and finally wrapped her arms around its neck. "It's her! It's really her! But how?"

How, indeed? Where had it been? How did you find us? My heart was a mixture of confusion and joy. I could only imagine Brinn's.

Mathew frowned as he inspected the animal. "This makes no sense."

"It is her!" Brinn said, jaw dropped and wide-eyed.

A hand swept across my shoulders.

I turned but found no one. I quickly checked my pockets, fearing being robbed, although I had nothing worth stealing on me. My feet kicked something on the ground when I turned. I inspected the object; something had been wrapped in what appeared to be a former bag of barley, and a note dangled from the knot tying it closed. *To Ludik*, it read.

I crouched apprehensively to inspect it. I flipped the note:

Consider this an apology,

Ariel.

A chill ran down my spine. I sprang upright, parcel in hand. I peered in every direction, scrutinizing every face and every movement.

Another hand on my shoulder. I jerked as I spun.

Mathew seemed confused as he pulled his hand away. His lips moved, but I had gone entirely deaf.

"She's here," I managed to mumble.

The parcel in my hand had a familiar weight and shape. No. May the Bastard strike down. I pulled the string, and the knot came undone, revealing its contents. The leather was smudged with soot, laces scorched, rubber melted on tiny spots here and there, and an encircled three-peaked mountain printed on the side remained clearly visible.

I forgot to breathe, the world spinning around me. But why? Why would she return them to me? Should I get ready to fight? Or get ready to hug her? Did it matter? I had my boots back, the last physical proof I once had a father.

Mathew drew his hands upward as if ready to strike. Brinn caught them and shook her head. "Come," she said. "We knew she'd be behind us. We can't fight her here and we can't risk drawing unwanted attention."

The tension among us was palpable as we walked to the pica. It looked a little like a colossal salad bowl. Heimee had a couple just like that one, though I couldn't remember ever eating a salad with him. The pica lowered a side ramp, allowing people and goods to disembark. Once the ramp was clear, we were ordered to board. The pica's deck was a mix of sawdust, hay and dung, in short, an extension of Picaline's roads. At the bow and stern, a thick cable connected the pica to the massive dark cable hanging above.

The picas traveled in a closed circuit. They came on one side of the line and turned to dock between the two towers, which would stop rotating and allow passengers and cargo to embark. Once the pica was full, the ramp was raised and locked in place, the towers resumed their rotation, and the pica trudged across the river.

Mathew came to my side after spending some time exploring the vessel searching for signs of Ariel. "I don't think she's on this boat. Jesus, this is giving me the heebie-jeebies. Are you alright?"

I nodded. "Are you sure she isn't here? She could still cut the cable loose and leave us adrift."

"There's little we can do about it if she does. I hope you can swim. Still, it's best if we keep our eyes peeled."

"Where's Brinn?"

Mathew looked back to Brinn who squeezed herself through the passengers, staring everyone down. "She's not satisfied. I don't blame her; Ariel is a chameleon after all. What's with the shoes?"

"My father made them. They mean the world to me—why would she return them?"

"Dunno. But hey, they're just shoes, man." He patted me on the back. "You know what? Forget I said that. I once had this Gameboy. It's a portable videogame—forget that; it doesn't matter. It was something I cherished. My grandfather gave it to me. My parents didn't want me to play video games, but he gave me one anyway. When he passed away, that was all I had left to remember him by. It was comforting to have it. Reminded me of him. And I was proud of him. He was a good man. Taught me a lot of stuff my dad was too busy to teach."

Brinn came to our side. "I checked everyone twice. She could be in the pica behind. What if she uses her light beam on us from there? And why would she return Era?"

"I hear ya. We'll be ready if she tries something," Mathew said, eyes doing another sweep around the vessel. "Anyway, I stopped playing with it after I got a DS for Christmas, so I stowed it away in a box. One day, my mother decided we had too much stuff and made a yard sale. She wanted to get rid of old furniture and toys I no longer played with. I didn't want to help because I wanted to hang out with my friends. It was almost a relief when I got home and saw my room empty of clutter. I had no idea I had so much junk. Then I noticed the Gameboy box was gone. Yeah... I flew downstairs to ask Mom if she had seen it. She had. She had sold it to Justin. Stupid Justin. Out of all the kids in our neighborhood, why did she have to sell it to him? I grabbed my bike and minutes later was at his house. I pleaded and begged. I even offered to buy it back for double the price. I told him what it meant to me and the story behind it. He refused to sell it back to me. I think he enjoyed my pain. A real scumbag."

"That's awful," I said. "What did you do about it?"

"What do you think?" Mathew said, raising his chin. "I stole his precious bike and dumped it in the river. He made an enemy for life that day."

"That's what I would've done," Brinn said. "After I made him swallow all his teeth."

"No doubt, no doubt," Mathew said. "Ah, let's quit moping, shall we? You have to come and look at this."

"Wait a minute," I said. "Let me just—"

"Yeah, yeah," Mathew said. "Just do it."

I put my boots on and tied the laces. Despite being scorched, they still performed their function. I stood up, feeling the familiar softness of the inner lining and the supportive rigidity of the rubber sole.

"The burn marks give them a wicked look," Mathew said.

He led us to the bow. We climbed some steps leading to a small platform that allowed passengers to look outside and found a spot large enough for the three of us at the rail. To the left, barges from the other line navigated carefree in the open waters. Beyond them, the estuary ran uninterrupted until it merged with the sea, where the water stretched farther than the eye could see. In itself, a humbling experience until I gazed ahead and faced the white bastions of Algirin piercing the river with all their might.

There it was: the capital of the kingdom of Aviz—a collection of large hills whitewashed with granite stone and gray shingled roofs, where aqueducts labyrinthed their way along the slopes or suspended by tall arches across valleys, taller than anything I could have ever imagined. I had read about Algirin in a book from Heimee's modest collection, but nothing could've prepared me to see it with my own eyes. With each yard we drew closer, the more impressive it became. The architecture, so simple at first glance, was astonishing. Unless one really committed, one could not distinguish the lines between each stone slab. Like the city had been carved from the hills it occupied and polished smooth by the Bastard himself.

"Why does it have to be so white?" Mathew wondered, taking in the view. "I bet it gets stupid hot in the summer. See there on the top?" He pointed to one of the hills. "That's the library."

"Those towers?" Brinn asked.

"No, that's the castle," I said. "That's where the king lives. Mathew is talking about that pinkish dome on the adjacent hill."

The library of Aviz was the only building in Algirin that wasn't white. It was said to contain more books than a man can read in one hundred lifetimes. "It's pink to symbolize the sunrise," I explained, "that only through knowledge can one find true enlightenment."

"Well," Brinn said. "Then let's try not to burn this one down then, shall we? I counted the coins, by the way. Ten tales."

"That's a win, right?" Mathew prodded.

"Oh, absolutely. I wasn't really expecting him to pay twenty when I first asked for ten. Next time, we know we can go much higher."

We shared smiles for a job well done, despite Ariel's looming threat, as I shifted my weight from foot to foot, adjusting to my boots and allowing myself to think that everything was going to turn out alright.

Chapter 41

Snowpory Pies

Ludik

"Damn," Mathew said, tapping the white cobbles with his foot. "I feel like I'm inside a microwave oven."

"Couldn't you just say 'oven' instead?" Brinn protested.

"No," Mathew insisted. "It's not nearly white enough."

"Wait," I said as I tied the pullover's sleeves around my waist. "A white oven? How does that work?"

"With microwaves. Aren't you listening? Jesus, how do these people live here? What do they do in the height of summer? Boil alive? And why is it all so steep? And where did they find so much marble?"

"It's granite."

"What?"

"The stonework. It's white granite."

"What's the difference?"

"I don't know, it just is."

"Alright, smarty-pants, then tell me why. Why go about all this trouble?"

"Legend has it," I began as we walked toward the stable, "a long time ago, the first King of Aviz married a princess from the northern lands, where today only the Shattered Mountains remain. The princess was sad because every winter, she missed the snow. In an act of love, he ordered the construction of a new city, built only with white rock. The stone had to be brought in from quarries a thousand leagues away, from the southern lands of Usturia."

"There are few things worse than a man in love," Mathew said. "I bet this act of love was all paid for in slave work."

"Nothing says 'I love you' like forced labor," Brinn said. "Hey, look at this." She pointed to a sign on a wall. It depicted a Stone ox defecating and his owner urinating on a corner. Beneath the picture, it read: *Severe fines will be applied to any and all defecating/urinating animals or people.*

"I kinda want to hang that on my bedroom door," Mathew said.

We passed a small market lining the outside of the inner wall of Alturin and found a stable. A man with curly gray hair and a thick mustache wearing a fleece coat came to greet us. "Nippy today, isn't it?" he chirped.

We exchanged astounded looks; we had landed not even five minutes before and beads of sweat already raced down our faces. The man examined us while rubbing his hands together. "You kids are gonna catch a cold." He blew into his hands.

"We're used to such low temperatures," I prodded.

"I have fine wool jackets if you're interested," the man said.

"I think we'll be okay," Brinn added as I winced at the thought. "I need a place for my ekkuh."

"Sure, sure. Of course, you came to the right place, miss. Will your beast require feed and grooming?"

"Sure."

"That'll be five gollings a day."

Brinn reached into her pocket, produced a tale, and handed it to the man. He gave her five heads back and took Era's reins. "This's one fine animal. You can see you've taken really good care of her."

"Thanks," Brinn said, patting Era's neck. "We'll be back soon," she whispered to her mount. "I promise not to lose you this time." Brinn struggled to let go. She had just gotten Era back. But time was of the essence. The faster we got to the library, the faster we would be on our way out and away from danger, especially with Ariel so close by. The thought of repeating the events from Lirterin was very much present and alive. Era and my boots were a good reminder that, well, she could be right behind us.

I tugged Brinn by the arm. "Hurry. Ariel must be watching us."

Brinn nodded, gave Era one last glance, and started moving. "Why would she return her?"

"It's probably a trick," Mathew said as he picked up the pace. "Lull us into a false sense of security, get closer, and pounce when we least expect it. I don't know what her plan is, but it's better to stay sharp." He pulled his bag in front of him and produced his sunglasses. "Ah, much better. Another minute and I would've gone blind."

We crossed a huge square, three times the size of Burrow or more. In its center stood a large statue of a man reaching for the sky. Though I had no idea who he was or what it meant. I could almost feel my skin sizzle in the direct sunlight aided by all that white granite, so we cleared the square as fast as possible. And things didn't get much better. After a small break from the sun, as we entered narrow streets filled with street vendors, the roads started to climb. It was easy at first, but the farther we walked, the steeper it got, as in I-could-touch-the-pavement-without-bending steep.

"I need a break," I said about an hour into Algirin's punishing streets. "My legs hurt."

"Already?" Brinn said. "It's not that bad. The people here do this every day."

"They're sick in the head, Brinn," Mathew said. "Don't tell me your legs don't hurt."

"They don't. Unlike you lot, I'm in good shape."

"Well, forgive me if I'm not stocky like you."

"Stocky? I'm not stocky."

"Sure. But I would rather get in a fistfight with three Ludiks than with you."

"Look," I intervened, "there's a tavern over there. We can rest and have a bite to eat. You must be starving as well; the last thing we ate was those sausages yesterday."

"Do you think I'm stocky?"

I think you're pretty, I thought, but I didn't say it. In all honesty, I never bothered to qualify her body type. So I shrugged.

"What is that supposed to mean?" A hint of fury crossed her eyes.

"Uhh," I said.

"Uhh?" she asked.

"Urgh!" said Mathew. "Girls are the same everywhere. Even a tomboy like you. Stocky is a compliment. I only wish I had half the stock you have. Now look at this," Mathew motioned to the streets above, "it's like a ski slope. If we fall from up there, we'll slide all the way down to the dock. Jesus, imagine how slippery it must be when it rains. These people are insane."

I wanted to disagree with him, but the building in front of us was clear evidence of the lunacy involved in the city's construction. You could enter the ground floor, climb six stories and still be on the ground floor. That's how steep it was.

We reached the tavern and sat at a table outside. We were high enough to view the building tops, the river, and Picaline on the other margin. A man wearing a thick jacket and a wool scarf came out to greet us.

"What are we having today?" he said as he shifted his weight from foot to foot, hands burrowed in his pockets. "Snowpory corantines are our specialty, and you will find none better in town. Can't come to Algirin and not try a snowpory corantine."

"Sure," Mathew said, and the taverner ran back in, disappearing behind a bead curtain. "Well, that was quick."

"What's this snowpor-thingamajig?"

"It's their specialty," Mathew said. "Didn't you hear what he said? Alright, listen up. I'm about to drop some knowledge. If a waiter tells you what to eat, you eat it, especially in developing worlds like this one. Restaurant staff love to play fools of their guests. It's a fact."

I looked at Brinn for help, but she nodded in agreement. "When customers don't take the bread I give them, I always replace it with one that fell on the ground or is evidently worse than the one they got."

"That's awful," I said.

Brinn shrugged. "Serve people all day, and you'll hate them, too."

"People are the worst," Mathew added and took out Miranda, laying her on the table. The pages went from blank to a detailed map of the city. A circle with a large arrow pointing at it said, *You are here.*

The taverner came out with three piles of food drenched in sauce. "Here you go," he said. "Would you like something to drink? Some mulled wine, perhaps? To heat up the soul a little?"

"We're fine, thank you," Brinn said.

"Mulled wine?" Mathew said as the taverner went back inside. "It's like a hundred degrees, and he wants to serve us mulled wine."

I stared at my plate. A meat pie cut in half with a healthy amount of fried potatoes and melted cheese in the middle, and all of it drowned in a brown, yummy-looking sauce. I temptingly cut into the pie, and oh, it was good. Meaty, but not too much, a perfect balance of spices, hints of something lemony, lemon thyme perhaps. The sauce was sweet and sour, thick and rich, like drinking a roasted steak. The potatoes were crunchy, and the melted cheese... was amazing. The pastry crumbled and crunched as I bit into it—a full-on gastronomical festival.

"Miranda," I said between mouths full. "What is this made of?"

A corner of the map dissolved into words. *Snowpories are a land bird common to this region. Its meat is too tough and sour to consume. It is matured until tender, then marinated in wine, lard, and a mix of local spices for several weeks until it gains its peculiar citric taste. The meat is slow-cooked for three days, mixed with mountain honey, and finally stuffed into corantine pastry and baked.*

"This almost beats a cheeseburger," Mathew said, barely breathing as he dug into his pie. "Almost."

"It's so meaty," Brinn said, pushing the plate away. "I need to order a salad or something."

Mathew and I stared at Brinn's plate.

"I didn't say I wasn't going to eat it; stay off my food," she warned.

"What are those kids doing?" I asked after we resumed our climb.

"I'm afraid to look down," Mathew answered. "I'm both standing and lying down at the same time."

"They aren't down; they're up. See, over there."

"I don't want to look up either."

Aqueducts ran both above and beneath us. Rows of arches stacked on more arches supported channels routing water to domed reservoirs strategically spread around the city. A group of children slid down a channel and disappeared into the reservoir near us. They came out dripping wet, ran uphill until they reached the aqueduct, climbed its side, and slid down again.

"That looks like fun," Brinn said.

"I think I'm gonna be sick," Mathew said. "Looking up is as bad as looking down. You guys go on without me. Fetch the book. I'll wait here."

"Oh, stop it. It's not that bad," Brinn said. "Stop hugging the ground. You look silly."

"Better silly than dead."

Brinn stuck her tongue out and blew out. "Sissy."

"I have vertigo. Okay? I hate climbing, I hate rollercoasters, and I hate water slides. I thought this would be easier, but I was wrong. It's bad enough I had to hang over a cliff for a day."

"Why did they build so many aqueducts anyway?" Brinn mused. "There's a river right there."

"They wanted fresh spring water," I said. "These aqueduct lines run for hundreds of leagues northwest, to the Shattered Mountains where the water is said to be purest."

"This city is a vanity project," Mathew said. "It's driving me mad. I thought it was cool and all when we arrived, but we've been here for what? Four hours? And I can safely say I hate it to my core. I can't wait to leave this place."

"Sure." Brinn winked at me. "Just don't think about it on the way down."

"Why would you say that? Oh, God, the way down. Oh, I'm gonna die today, aren't I?"

"The good news is," Brinn said, "we're almost there. Just another flight of stairs."

"Oh, just another, uh?" Mathew said. "That is the longest flight of stairs I have ever seen in my entire life!"

We sat by the reservoir, backs leaning against the white granite, cooled by the spring water inside, and admired the view while, occasionally, a group of wet kids ran past us.

"Still," I said. "It's a pretty impressive view." Where the ocean and the sky met, the world seemed to simply end. My mind struggled to make sense of it. "I wonder what it's like to sail the seas."

"It's like being stuck in your bedroom while being rocked from side to side for days on end while having absolutely nothing to do and absolutely nothing to see, eating only fish until our teeth fall out," Mathew went on. "Occasionally you'll fear for your life when a storm pops out of nowhere and rams you with waves as tall as mountains."

"The climb really soured your mood, *huh*," Brinn noted. "Why is there an aqueduct coming out from the hillside under the library?"

I shrugged. "Maybe it was easier to dig a tunnel. Many parts of the aqueduct system are tunnels." It was true, or so I'd read. The aqueducts of Aviz were the most complex in the world and a point of interest for visitors.

It took another hour of Mathew's complaints, but we reached the top. I was winded and exhausted. Only a handful of people climbed past us. All of them were tourists, regretting the moment they decided to visit Algirin if the look on their faces was any indication. Aviz had done a great job making me feel small and insignificant, but the library drove it through the heart. It towered six stories high, its dome impossibly round and wide. Simple yet so complex, it defied reason. Jaws hanging loose, we reach the entrance. Six pillars, resembling tree trunks and their branches, held a triangular pink roof adorned with carved leaves over metal doors so tall and heavy I had trouble believing human hands had built it.

A peach tree grew in the center of a large round patio leading to the library's entrance. It was odd to see a tree there, though I didn't know why until I remembered we hadn't seen any trees since we entered Picaline. (Not that I was complaining. It was refreshing to steer clear of their constant chatter.) Her trunk was bent and scarred, healed after snapping due to some kind of blow, and—"Laurin?"

Hello, my stubborn little boy who disobeys his mother.

Chapter 42

After All

Ludik

I hugged Laurin. The roughness of her bark pressed against my cheeks, digging indentations on my skin.

"How?" I mumbled.

I was found. I don't know. I'm only a peach tree; I should not have survived. None of the other trees did. Where our village once stood, nothing grows now. Erudites from the library came to study the phenomenon. They couldn't figure out how a whole mountain could have gone missing. I don't think they believe their own stories. Yet, they found me living and saw it as a good omen. So they brought me here. You were right, Ludik. I got to see a little more of the world after all.

"I'm sorry to interrupt," Mathew said. "But I'm a little confused about this since I can't hear treespeak, and until recently, I would have taken you for a lunatic if I found you hugging a tree. But have you been here before?"

I explained what Laurin had told me and that she had grown up with me in my backyard all those years ago.

"Today has certainly been weird enough," Brinn said.

This may seem odd, but I knew you were coming.

"You did?"

Yes, she told me. The leoht, Ariel.

"Did she harm you?" I asked.

She wouldn't. I may be the luckiest tree to ever live. I survived a cataclysm, traveled across Aviz, and have met three treespeaking humans in my life, one a leoht and another, it seems, a dwinan.

"She knows treespeak?" I asked.

"Who?" Mathew's eyes bulged as he stared at me. "It's Ariel, right? She beat us to the punch."

"She didn't know treespeak before," I noted.

She said she did not know how to until you showed her it was possible.

"Where is she?"

Inside.

"She almost killed us on several occasions."

Remember the stories I used to tell you? Remember the Worldroot tree and the cruel mage?

"Of course."

Miranda is that mage. Miranda's the one who shattered the world.

"What? That's crazy! Ariel's been trying to stop us ever since—Mathew, tell her. Tell her Miranda is good."

Mathew was reading Miranda as I spoke—light pulsating from the book, visible despite the bright afternoon sun.

My page was empty. Mathew was reading, his lips moved as he did, but no words formed. Mathew furrowed his brow and glanced at me. There was something odd in his eyes, a mix of feelings I couldn't tell apart. Fear, compassion, tenderness, hurt, guilt?

"Mathew, what's wrong?"

This world nearly ended when she was free. The shattered mountains were her doing.

Mathew glanced between Brinn and me. There was definitely pain in his eyes now; he was torn between something. His lips moved again, but I could not distinguish any words. Instinctively, I took to the letter.

Still empty.

"Mathew?"

Brinn began to seethe as Mathew spoke. She wasn't pleased with him. Then she punched him in the arm, but Mathew didn't seem to care.

He's going to set me on fire.

"That's preposterous," I said.

Mathew's eyes welled, and I found two words, all too easy to read on his lips. "I'm sorry." His expression turned to stone and out came the fire.

Chapter 43

Courage Within

Ludik

In a heartbeat, Mathew pushed Brinn to the side and lay fire between them. Then he turned his sight on Laurin, but I fell in between. The blaze hit me like a fall from a great height while a thousand daggers bit my skin. My vision blurred, and my heart screamed blue.

Things, said the distant rumble, *are things.*

What things? Bastard's bother, what is that? I didn't have time to mull it over. When the last tendril of fire vanished, Mathew was nowhere to be seen; an ice blanket covered the singed pavement and icicles draped from Laurin's twigs and leaves, and no fire had reached her.

Brinn lay on the ground, shock in her eyes.

"So Ariel's right?" I asked Laurin. "Miranda..."

Miranda's after power and revenge.

The weight of guilt and responsibility came crashing down on me. How could I move? *Could I save the world?* How? I had been so selfish, so childish, so foolish.

Her spirit, her energy, was contained and separated into several books and spread as far as men could carry them. If she collects them, she'll become powerful enough to break free. There'll be no one to stop her then.

"The book we came to get is part of her," I said to myself, remembering Munika's copy. It all made sense. I had been deceived. I sank to my knees, cold brewing in me. It was all my fault. Hadn't I helped Mathew, Ariel could've caught Miranda. Had I simply ignored that stupid letter...

Oh, I had been so blind. Blind with revenge and thirst for adventure.

A beam of light slashed through the roof of the library, leaving a molten scar of amber quickly fading into black.

Brinn slapped my cheek. Her lips moved too hurriedly to make sense of them.

She slapped my other cheek. I tuned in on her lips. It's been so long since I had to lip-read. "Snap out of it," she said.

I blinked. "What can we do?"

Brinn began signing. She was clearly out of practice, and she wasn't very good at it to begin with, but I could read it. "What do you mean 'what can we do'? Do the same as you did here. Absorb it, absorb more, absorb all of it. Suck all the power right out of him, out of *her*. We were tricked. How did we not see it?" Brinn slapped her forehead. "It all makes sense now; you said Munika had a similar copy. The book, it's not about defeating mountains; it's her. We must stop him from reaching that ordealish book. This is our mess, and we must clean it! Enough moping. You're a dwinan, for crying out loud."

She was right. But realistically, my powers were almost useless. Lazy, Miranda had called them. And I couldn't control them properly. The best I could do was to jump in harm's way and hope for the best. "No. We'll do it your way."

"My way?" Brinn's hand flew to her chest in disbelief.

"Yeah. We'll talk him out of it."

Brinn snorted. "He doused you with fire."

"But he's also being deceived, Brinn. He truly believes Miranda is his only choice. We have to help him, too. You saw the hurt in his eyes."

"You know I love when we do things my way, but this time I'm not so sure. I think ice fights fire better than words."

"Trust me." I took a deep breath and looked at Laurin. "We'll fix this. You have my word."

May the light be with you, my brave little boy who disobeys his mother.

Chapter 44

The Library

Ariel

Ariel finally found a tree. And what a tree it was. If Ludik were ever going to listen to reason, Laurin would be the one to convince him. Maybe her luck was turning after all. Maybe she would be able to do this.

She sat inside the main hall regarding the dome and the giant walls neatly lined with thousands, if not millions, of books. The mosaic-paved floor detailed the Bastard's Ordeal and Bliss. And, more noteworthy, the dome illustrated the story of Aviz and its greatest accomplishments, from the days of prosperity and construction of Algirin to the endless wars, forces of nature, and the mages of old who clashed like the wrath of gods and formed the Great Shatter; the following Therian wars, the civil unrest and the civil war that followed which brought the north to submission and the division from Erosomita and the southern kingdoms. So much history there, so much knowledge, and they'd put it all in the most inaccessible place in the country.

Ariel felt utterly appalled by it. She counted maybe seven other people inside. That was it. Maybe four were tourists who came in so tired from the climb that they gave no attention to the structure and its contents. And the rest were librarians. What was the point of all this?

A thought occurred to her. So simple, yet it hadn't crossed her mind before. She knew she was probably the worst person for this job, but darn it, at least she was trying.

"Excuse me," Ariel said to a bald man in a white toga. The man had tiny eyes, a pointy nose, and a perpetual expression of disdain. Guess librarians there liked to dress as ancient Greeks. "Do ye know who or what Miranda is?"

The librarian blinked twice at Ariel. "Who?" he said.

"Or what," Ariel replied.

He seemed to freeze, like a computer that's been given too many tasks at once.

She continued, "Ye know, a menacing mage from the old legends. The one who destroyed the world and stuff. Whose soul and energy were split between four volumes?"

"We have many books about the old myths. I could point you in—"

"No. I want *the* book. The one that is *her*."

The man froze again.

"Perhaps ye can refer me to a more knowledgeable colleague of yaers. Someone who might know what they're doing."

"I am one of the Masters; I assure you that I don't know what you're referring to, and if I don't, then no one does. And it's ill-mannered to disrespect a scholar."

"Well, yae're useless. The world is about to end, and ye could've helped save it. But ye didn't. You chose to be ignorant. I'd call it ironic, given yer status."

The man fumed but kept his temper. "If that'll be all, miss," he said with venom in his voice and left her.

"Yeah, run from the crazy lady. Ye won't be finding me so crazy soon enough."

The man didn't even glance back and disappeared into a separate room.

"Why does no one ever listen to me?" Ariel muttered. She sat on some steps and rubbed her eyes. How long would it take them to get there? She had been boiling in anticipation, but the anticipation had boiled away and was now reduced to tedium.

An orange flash came from the entrance, reflecting across the hall and into the library, sweeping away the boredom she felt in an instant, her senses back on full alert.

"This is it," Ariel said to herself. "Steady, this is yer last chance. Ye may die now. Urgh, stop it, Ariel. This is yer duty; no one else will do it. Right? Yeah. Okay. Sure. Ye can do this." She summoned all the energy she could muster for one decisive blow. She wouldn't get another chance. She had to kill Mathew. She didn't want to, but it had come to this. Could she do it?

Mathew entered the room running.

As light gathered at her fingertips, Ariel stood fast, blocking his way, intense heat prickling at her cheeks. "I won't let ye—" A torrent of fire fell on her, forcing her to dodge. She jumped to the side, but the power at her finger had passed the containment point, too heavy and too hot to bear or be absorbed back. She tried to aim but flinched; the beam left her fingers as fire licked at the flaps of her jacket, carving a line of molten granite across the dome, beheading several figures of ancient kings.

Mathew ran past her without a second glance.

Her heart pounded in her chest. She rolled on her back and got to her knees, bent on firing another shot, but Mathew was out of sight. It was over. What a pitiful final stand. "At least I'm alive," she told herself. "Rats, rats, rats!" she added, banging her fists on the floor. She had to get up. She had to go after him. But after so many failures, her legs simply refused to obey.

Several librarians rushed to where she stood, blankets in hand, to smother the little fires that caught on to the bookshelves and benches before they deflagrated into something unstoppable.

"What have you done?" the librarian master asked, hands on his head. "Insanity. Fire in a library! Put it out, put it out!"

Ludik and Brinn ran inside. *It's a little too late now,* Ariel thought.

"Go after him!" Brinn said to Ludik as her hands moved in sign language.

"What about you?" Ludik asked.

"I'll talk to her."

"Be careful," Ludik said and scampered after Mathew, down to the end of the domed room and out of sight.

"Your jacket's on fire," Brinn said as she approached.

Ariel looked down and found part of the seat of the jacket in flames. She tapped the flames out with her hands, cursing with each tap until the fire was out.

"I said—" a librarian began.

"Old man, we don't have time for this," Brinn snapped at him. "If we don't stop the guy that set this fire, there'll be nothing left but cinders." Brinn pressed a finger into the man's chest with each sentence, much to his disbelief. "Get ready to put out fires. Gather all the blankets and water you can. And most importantly, get out of our way."

"But, miss—"

"You heard about what happened in Lirterin? It's about to happen here! And only we can stop it. So tell me, do you want us to leave?"

For a moment, Ariel thought he would freeze as he did before, but his head twitched; he sucked in a breath and began issuing commands. "Gather blankets. Fill up every bucket, bottle and glass you can find. Move, move, move!"

"Why didn't you tell us the truth?" Brinn asked.

"Gee, it never crossed my mind," Ariel said, but even her sarcasm felt deflated.

"You tried to kill us. And then you burned half a city; I don't think that reflects well on your communication skills."

"Did ye stay behind just to scold me?"

Brinn pointed down the library. "We have to stop him from finding that book."

It was nice to hear someone offering her help, even if belated. "It's too late. He has a good head-start, and Miranda knows exactly where it is. Well, where *she* is."

"Don't give me that attitude. Do you think you're the only one having a rough day? We need to help Ludik."

"How? He's a bloody dwinan; how are ye supposed to help him?"

Brinn shrugged. "I don't know, but I'm gonna be by his side. You can mope there all you want, feeling sorry for yourself, or you can help us. It's up to you."

Ariel got to her feet. "I've tried so hard to stop this."

Brinn examined Ariel for a second. "I know. I lost quite a bit of my hair."

Those words took so much weight off Ariel's shoulders that she began to laugh. "In my defense, that wasn't me."

Brinn nodded. "Let's go. We've wasted enough time."

What a weird day, Ariel thought as she took after Brinn.

Chapter 45

Secret Entrance

Ludik

I ran past rows and rows of bookshelves, trying not to get distracted by the immenseness of it all and the magnificent dome. I wished I could forget what was happening and explore that wonderful place in full detail; find a little reading nook, and just read.

As I turned the corner into another long room, my minor concerns began boiling in my stomach. Aviz's library was the worst possible battleground. Whatever I did, I could not let it come to a fight. People craned their necks over their books as I passed them, and ahead others stared at a door at the far left of the reading area. I shot in that direction. Either I was going the right way, or I wasn't. There was nothing I could do about it.

I crossed the door and found a room so dark my eyes had trouble adjusting—bastard's luck. Then a thought hit me. Could I use my power? I didn't know how it worked, but it was about energy. In theory, I should be able to feel the heat. Use my power like one of Heimee's thermometers and see where Mathew went. He must've used fire to light his way.

I tried to focus. Oh, Bastard help me. *Urgh!* I grunted. What's the point of having power if I don't know how to use it? Shapes and shadows became clearer as my vision adjusted to the gloom. Two steps in, I tripped on what was most likely a chair and fell on my knee, scraping my shin. I caught movement from the corner of my eye. Then the room lit up. I turned to find Brinn with Ariel at her side. What a strange day.

"This is no time to tie your shoes," Brinn signed. "Get up."

With the room lit, I could see only one door at the far side of the room. I pushed the chair away and dashed through it. We climbed at least six stories down a spiral staircase, leading to a small room with a door hanging open—the lock blown to pieces. Beyond, we found yet another spiral. By the time the stairs spewed us into an oval-shaped space, I was so dizzy it was hard not to trip over my own feet.

"Where is he?" I asked, using my arms for balance.

Ariel said something, but her lips were like reading underwater. I took the letter out, but of course, it was blank. Ariel slapped the letter out of my hand, and as it fluttered to the floor, she incinerated it with a beam of light. Her lips moved again, reprehension on her face. Of course! Miranda would know where we were and be able to listen to us.

"Where did he go?" I asked.

Brinn tapped my shoulder. "She says he was here for sure," she signed. "She saw the firelight go out." The room was like being inside an egg, white and seamless, apart from the ceiling which funneled into some kind of round door.

"I wonder where it goes," I said, looking up.

Ariel filled the funnel with light, and at the top, black letters read *Waterway*. Ariel said something, "Not that way," I think it was.

I crouched, inspecting the ground, and that's when I noticed the hand smudges. A dirty hand had touched a square indentation. I got a good grip and pulled. It was cumbersome, but I lifted the granite slab enough to push it over the floor revealing some kind of hole. If it weren't for the smudges, I would have never found it. We shared a couple of glances before Ariel illuminated the interior. Inside we found a small ledge followed by what appeared to be a perfectly smooth chute with water running down it.

A knot formed in my stomach. "I think it'll be too steep and slippery to climb back up," I said.

"Only one way to find out," Brinn signed with quivering hands.

I took a deep breath, lowered myself to the ledge, and jumped down the slide.

Chapter 46

The Book

Ludik

My stomach climbed up into my mouth as I sped down the pitch-black tunnel. I pressed my hands and feet against the walls in a futile attempt to slow down, but the walls were not only wet but slimy too. Was I sliding into my death? If I crashed at that speed, I would, at the very least, break both legs.

I splashed into cold water and jerked, gasping for air even though my lungs were full, kicking against the water until I found footing. I steadied myself, taking deep breaths; the waterline reached slightly above my waist.

A fiery hand illuminated our surroundings. Mathew stood next to a strange pillar at the center of the oval room.

"Mathew," I said. "Whatever you—" Something slammed into the back of my legs, plunging me back into the dark water.

I came up, wiped my eyes, and saw Brinn. I helped her up and away from the tunnel's end right before Ariel splashed down behind her.

I spun toward Mathew again and trudged against the force of the water. We were in a circular room, the black walls shiny like glass. Mathew observed us, startled, his attention torn between Miranda, who lay open in his hand and us. He said something, but well, it fell on deaf ears.

On a closer look, I realized that the center pillar wasn't a pillar at all; intertwined wire mesh emerged from the water, as flickering sparks of light climbed up the metal lines, and in the middle, surrounded by copper bars, lay a book—*New and Old Worlds and How to Get There.* Little lightning bolts shot from the book, most connected with the wires, but a couple escaped the bars and licked the water's surface, leaving a tingling sensation on my skin and making my hair stand on end. I clenched with the queer feel.

Mathew moved his lips. "You can't stop this," I think he said.

"Mathew," I began, "what if Miranda is not who she claims to be? What if you're not saving the world but dooming it? I wish this weren't true, but it makes more sense than I can ignore. There is an ancient tale about how the Shattered Mountains formed. There was a war because one mage wanted to be all-powerful and dominate the world. That mage is Miranda. If we allow her to be free, there'll be wars. World-shattering wars! Isn't that what you are trying to prevent?"

Mathew sunk his head; Miranda clasped between his fingers.

"If I'm wrong, we come back, and we do this. Ariel can't harm us anymore. You proved that when you threw all that fire against me. She can't hurt me. You can't hurt me. I'm not mad, I understand why you did it. But please, put the book away."

Doubt flickered in his eyes, his hand wavering. He asked something, but I don't think it was directed at me. Ariel moved to my side. These cursed people and their stupid lips. Mathew kept glancing at me. What was Ariel telling him?

Mathew's lips stopped moving, and he stared. "Is this true?" I caught him saying.

The question caught me off guard, and my reaction was to say yes, but what was I saying yes to?

"He asked if you can save his world," Brinn interpreted. "Ariel said you probably could because you're a dwinan."

Me saving a world? How? I just discovered I had powers, and I had no idea how they worked. They came when I was in distress. Did I always have to be in distress to use them? There were too many unknowns. But Mathew's eyes beseeched an answer. "I'll try!" I said, and I meant it. What would be the use of having power if I didn't use them for something good? "I'll do my best."

Mathew slowly lowered Miranda as if she had become too heavy to hold, and for the briefest moment, I allowed relief to soothe my anxiety and—

Miranda exploded into a ball of fire and intense white light, forcing me to shade my eyes and helplessly watch as Mathew flew across the room, slammed against the smooth wall, and splashed limply in the water. The light died down, revealing a floating orb of flames and tendrils of light hovering above the water.

"Mathew," I screamed as I ran to his aid, water tugging at my legs. He wasn't moving, floating face down. I pulled his face above the surface, flipped him around and cradled the back of his neck. Something sticky and warm clung to my hand. Blood. He must've hit his head on the wall.

The fireball melted the wire mesh with ease, ember droplets falling into the water, where they fizzled out. Energetic slithering arms clawed out in a cloud of sparks, dancing and waving across the room, consuming the book's pages as my muscles twitched involuntarily.

A beam of light shot across the room, through the book, burning a molten ember mark at the far end, where I briefly noticed the shape of a small dark tunnel where the water slowly drained to. In return, a thick bolt of lightning struck Ariel down. The force made my body spasm and drop Mathew. What in the world was happening?

I pulled him back up. Was he even alive? How could Miranda so casually hurt his friend? The one who carried her around all this time and helped her with everything she needed. How could she be so callous? Despite knowing that Miranda, those orbs of fire and lightning wiggling excitedly in front of me, was the one who shattered the world, I couldn't believe it. I couldn't believe she would kill her only friend so freaking casually.

Brinn reached Ariel's twitching body and dragged her close to me. Why would she give Miranda one large target instead of two small ones? Oh, right! My power. I could protect them from energy blasts, and Miranda, as far as I could tell, was pure energy. She could always burn all the air and suffocate us, but I shook that thought away. I had to do something. But what could I do? Throw myself at her and hope for the best?

The balls of energy inched together, releasing ridiculous amounts of energy, pushing air and water away, stirring the room. Wind circled faster and faster, battering my eyes, and making it harder to breathe as the water slushed and whirled.

Through the corner of my eye, something moved. A shadow. It took me a second to make sense of what I was seeing. The darkness had the shape of a man. Long robes, black as night, a face straight out of the Ordeal, pale, hurtful and enraged. At first glance, there was a whole face, the outline of one at least, but so much of it was missing it made my spirit shrink even further.

The shadow lunged at merging energy spheres, and the room shook with incredible violence. Shock waves burst from the fight between the spheres and the half-man. With nowhere to go, the body of water whirled faster, dragging our bodies with it. I choked as it filled my mouth, and with horror, I glimpsed the gurgling violence gushing out from the tunnel we'd come through like a broken dam. The room filled, swirling our bodies around faster and faster as my chest burned blue and my vision blurred.

The dark figure extended a hand, dissolving a section of the wall, and the water took to it greedily, dragging us into the new-formed hole like bugs down a drain.

Chapter 47

Bastard's Ordeal

Ludik

My lungs cried out for air as I bumped and tumbled like a dead fish in a waterfall. There was no up nor down, only turbulence. Water froze around me in chunks and clunks, and I couldn't stop it. I was freezing our way out. If there even was a way out!

My lungs spasmed violently. Was this tunnel ever going to end? Was that light?

The darkness turned to day in a blink of an eye as the hillside ejected us with brute force. Water, chunks of ice and debris. I hit my shoulder on the wide aqueduct's channel. Blinding pain radiated through my neck and down my spine.

I gulped for air just in time to see the incoming reservoir.

The water cushioned our impact as we slammed into it. Disoriented, I kicked and flailed. I don't know how, but I found footing despite the dizziness and managed to stay upright. Brinn was conscious, pulling Mathew's limp head above water, while Ariel got on all fours with trembling arms. The reservoir's dome and wall had partially collapsed. Something told me that's what we were standing on.

I took in air greedily, trying to force the blue out of my heart. I looked up toward the aqueduct we'd slid through in time to witness part of the hill slide free, a torrent of earth and rock, barreling down our way.

The ground beneath my feet shook, and the water splashed with intense trepidation. I prayed to the Bastard for the landslide to stop. But it was no use; it wasn't going to stop. It was going to crush everything in its path.

This could not be the day I die. I still had a mountain to face, and I simply couldn't let my friends die. I reached in, and I touched the brewing cold within. And as I did, the power flowed in me, engaged and ready. A heap of sorrow and rage and pain and blue. It stung as I consumed it, forcing me to pass out. In the back of my mind, I knew I couldn't afford to lose the little control I had. What if I froze everything? What if I froze my friends? I closed my eyes.

Things are things.

When I opened them again, I could see them. I could see the energy of the water and earth, like a stream of light. I could touch it. Blue light erupted from my skin, painting the walls and glittering in the freezing current. I pushed harder, farther, leaning into the mass. The wall of death crashed on top of us, pelting our bodies with chunks of stone, ice and dirt. I bellowed. I fought for the right to live like I was fighting Aureberg itself with my bare hands. Energy ravaged inside me, uncontrollable, uncontained, unbound. The more I absorbed, the more water and earth I froze unto submission. I collected all my anger and fury and threw it at the incoming mass in one giant thrust.

I fell to my knees, panting, cold and drained. Then to the side, curling into a ball and wincing. Had it been enough?

The aqueducts had completely collapsed, and so had many buildings ahead, and in their stead stood a wall of ice and dirt diverging the still incoming water into the city. A large scar of brown soil covered a good chunk of the hill above as more pieces kept coming loose, threatening to collapse entirely.

I tried to stand but found that my body wasn't responding. Whatever I had done had taken a massive toll on me. Brinn seemed in distress, shaking Mathew roughly. I crawled to her side and grew pale as I read her lips. "He's not breathing," she said.

Was there anything I could do to help him?

Ariel limped to our side and motioned for us to step back. She gently laid Mathew on his back, propped his chin up, pinched his nose, and kissed him. I don't know what I was expecting, but a kiss wasn't it. She blew into his mouth, then laced her hands one on top of the other and thrust them rhythmically on Mathew's chest as she mumbled something, lips barely moving. One, two, three. Thirty compressions. She raised Mathew's chin again and blew on his mouth. His chest rose like a human water pouch, and she resumed the compressions.

"Is that a spell?" I read on Brinn's lips. "Staying alive?"

Ariel blew in Mathew's mouth again, and he jerked, eyelids cracking open, eyes swirling in their sockets. Ariel flipped Mathew on his side as he began to cough water out and suck distressed breaths.

The ground shook more violently than before. I gazed upon the hill again as a good part was ejected hundreds of feet into the air. And what remained liquified. The new landslide came crashing down toward us. I tried to reach in, but it was hopeless. I could not stop that. And we couldn't outrun it.

I felt Brinn's hand slip into mine. She looked me in the eye as if there was nothing else to see. I wanted to say I was sorry and that I did my best, but her stare told me she knew and that she'd forgiven me for failing. I gripped her hand tightly and gave the most reassuring smile I could conjure. We would be in the Bastard's presence soon enough.

A dark figure emerged in a swirl of shadows and smoke.

I blinked. And in that blink, everything changed. I still held Brinn's hand, and Ariel remained close to us, on her knees, caring for Mathew. But where before had been a broken reservoir, ice, and a crumbling hill, now was a street filled with people gazing ahead with dread and wonder. We peered around the white buildings, following the people's stare until we found the hill we had been facing in a blink of an eye before, far out in the distance. The mass of earth consumed the side of the city we had just stood on glutinously, and all we could do was watch as the tragedy we helped to create unfolded.

I felt empty, like all meaning in life had dispersed, and I was a shadow of a once-living thing. It couldn't get any worse than that.

That's when what remained of the hill exploded with spectacular force. A titanic cloud of fire, smoke and sparse lightning towered toward the heavens. A shock wave dispersed the clouds in a circular line, rummaged across the city and toppled us to the ground a second later, filling my eyes with dust.

I rubbed them, feeling the grains of sand under my eyelids. It was like watching Aureberg destroying my life before me again. But this time, there was no mountain. We were the mountain. We'd created this. How many Ludiks were born that day?

A dot of light flickered between blue, orange and white like a pulsating star as it shot up, away from the smoke and debris and stopped, hovering above the newly formed crater. Miranda.

A second later, a beam of dazzling energy connected her to the adjacent hill where the castle stood. The castle crumbled into pieces, tumbling down the hill and smashing into every building along the way. I watched helpless and in shock. Why would she do that? Hadn't she caused enough destruction? Then she streaked across the clouds, burning her path in the sky and vanished.

No. None of this was our fault. It was hers. And only we could stop her.

Chapter 48

Two Bolts

Ludik

No one cared about us. People flocked from every corner to remove rubble, collect the dead, and tend to the living. Every soul in sight dropped whatever they were doing and rushed to help strangers only because they were in need. Not just a fraction of the Algirin, no, but the vast majority.

The inner wall held the flood of destruction and demise from going past it, and we found the stable where we left Era intact. No one was there to deliver her to us, so we just walked in and took her.

That's when the news reached us through the crowd. The king was dead. Miranda had outright murdered him. But why? What could she possibly have to gain from that? Did she do it out of spite? Or to measure her newfound power? How evil can one be? And something else bothered me, something, well, *things are things.* When I used my power, someone was there with me—speaking to me. It was clear now. But who? Or, more distressingly, what? The thought gave me the shivers. There was one way to find out. I had to use my power again... without being in distress, that is. But I wasn't ready for that. Not then anyway, so I shook the thought away.

"We should go," I said. "Anywhere is better than here."

Ariel helped us hoist Mathew on top of Era. He didn't protest. His eyes were open, but he wasn't *there*. Remarkably, he still held to his bag, and the last bottle of Heims 39 remained intact.

By nightfall, we reached a small village, a collection of houses spread out circularly around a large Dendron, and found an inn nestled next to a large tree. The Yellow Roof, it was called, though the roof was made entirely of black shingles. That's when I remembered Laurin. Laurin! She couldn't have possibly survived. I wanted to believe she had. To mourn a friend is bad enough, almost unnatural, but to mourn a friend twice...

Around the inn, the word volcano was on everyone's lips. What happened could be misinterpreted that way, I guessed. But we still held our breath every time someone glanced at us. *They did it. There, they're the ones who destroyed the city and killed our king. Get them.* But as far as we could tell, no one gave two bolts about us.

The inn was like any other inn. Made of stone, whitewashed walls, wicker furniture and plenty of decorative wood. It smelled of food and flowers, for there were plenty adorning the tables and counters. A whole wall at the dining hall had a detailed map of all the pilgrimage routes slithering through the Leohtwoods. They had an available room for four, and after we settled in, we met in the dining hall and ate whatever was served to us. The dish of the day: snowpory corantines.

I regarded my nearly untouched meal. "How do we stop her?"

Ariel drank her third glass of Heims and gestured to the innkeeper for a refill. A pudgy man wobbled from the bar, bottle in hand. Ariel gestured for him to leave the bottle.

"We don't," Ariel said (or, more accurately, Brinn interpreted as best as she could) as she poured herself yet another drink. "To the end of the world." She raised her glass and downed its contents.

Mathew stared dead-eyed at the ceiling, where the stonework created a strange movement of gray colors, like a mosaic of clouds.

"What about that shadow man?" I asked.

"Half? Please." Ariel explained who he was and what kind of help we should expect from him with intense disgust. By the time she'd finished, Brinn was severely frustrated.

"It's too much to translate," she signed. "Are you sure you can't read their lips?"

"Very sure. Could we move outside? I'm sure the tree won't mind interpreting for me."

The tree, Houkin was his name, was tall and had needles for leaves—uncommon for the region but not rare. Pines used to be abundant where now lie the Shattered Mountains, or so legend says, and now only a few survive among the northern forests. Soon he would release so much pollen it would paint the roof of the inn yellow. Oh, Yellow Roof, I get it. Regardless, Houkin was friendly enough to agree to my request. There was even a table next to him for us to sit at.

"I found her in a library," Mathew started out of nowhere after we settled down, and Ariel had at least two more glasses of Heims. Mathew's eyes fixed on the stars above. "There's a big library in Boston where my aunt Kelly works. I used to spend time there after school. Anyway, there was this cabinet with dusty and flaky books. I wasn't allowed to touch them, so of course, I found every chance I had to do so. I knew Aunt Kelly would be mad, but hey, don't tell someone what not to do and expect them not to do it. *New and Old Worlds and How to Get There.* Man, what a long title, but filled with promise, though. While I tried to make sense of it, a flame sparked into existence and snuffed out in a blink of an eye. I was sure I imagined it. So, I pulled it out. I flipped it, intrigued. Its pages were blank. Then it burst into flames, nearly taking my eyebrows with it. I was ready to run, but words began to take shape on the page, 'Hello, Mathew,' they said, 'I have a proposition for you.' So I got the hell outta there.

"Aunt Kelly found out, of course. I didn't bother putting the book away where I found it. But for days after, I couldn't stop thinking about it."

"You didn't tell anyone?" Ariel asked.

Mathew gave her a prolonged side stare. "I promised my aunt I would never do it again and stole the book right after that. Miranda and I talked for hours on end. Together we planned to right the wrongs in the world. Then when I turned sixteen, she shared her power with me.

It was the single most amazing moment of my life. The kind of thing that little boys everywhere dream of. Superpowers. I became a superhero, just like in comic books.

"She convinced me that we had to go on a trip to Austria, in Europe. There we would find another book just like hers. It took much convincing for my parents to let me go, and I still can't believe they actually did, but I always had good grades and such. We also had a cousin living there, so that made it easier. I wanted to make my parents proud of me.

"We stopped for supplies. Miranda had a list. I filled my bag with flashlights, spare batteries, water bottles, a compass, a sleeping bag—anything an explorer would need. She led me across a forest to an unexplored cave. Crazy to think no one had stumbled upon it before. Inside, way deep inside, I found another book, just like she said I would. I opened Miranda next to it, and hands made of fire emerged from the pages and consumed the other book. Miranda then illuminated the entire cave. She told me people had taken her for a witch; that they feared her powers, and for that, they trapped her.

"Then we snuck on a train to Scotland and came here. My parents are probably worried sick, but I left to save the world. Surely, they would understand that, I thought." Mathew scoffed to himself. "So stupid."

Ariel shifted uncomfortably, her glass stopping before her lips. "That cow," she uttered.

"Not once did I doubt Miranda's words. Not even for the briefest moment."

"Mathew, I—"

He raised a hand to cut me off. "There are five classes, and she has collected only three. If we get ahead, we can still stop her. We need to reach the mountain before she does."

"But she can fly," Brinn noted. "How are we going to beat that?"

"Munika has a volume," I said. "It won't be hard for her to take that one." A thought occurred to me. "Do you think Miranda took out the king in exchange for Munika's book? Without the king, Munika can rule the country as he pleases."

Ariel shoved another glass of Heims down her throat. "It's possible. Then Miranda has four volumes and the armies of Aviz."

"The only question now is," Brinn said, "why us? What does she want from Ludik?"

A crushing feeling came down on me. "She was never after the mountain, was she?"

Mathew's mouth hung open. "Oh! Oh shit. Of course, that makes so much more sense. That's why she chose you to help me. She already knew, or at least suspected, you were a dwinan."

Ariel poured another glass. "I tried to warn ye, but ye wouldn't listen."

"You tried? Really," Brinn spat at her. "We didn't know what was at stake. But you did. You did, and you acted poorly. There is so much more you could've done. You could've been so much more persistent. But no, you chose to set fire to Lirterin instead of waiting for a better time."

Ariel was unimpressed and swirled the Heims in her glass, tongue wetting her lips. "I didn't know he was a dwinan until Lirterin. And I wasn't the one shooting fire willy-nilly. That would be the superhero over here."

"And?" Brinn shot both hands up in front of her. "What difference does it make?"

"You talk as if you have any idea of what I've been through. I did the best I could, alright? No one else did anything. No one."

"So we keep Ludik away from her," Mathew said.

"What?" I asked. "Why do I need to be kept away? It's not like she can pull the power out of me. Can she?"

"You must give it willingly, I think. Same way she gave hers to me."

"And why would I do that?"

"For starters," Ariel said as if it were the most obvious thing to do, sneering at Brinn, "she could threaten to kill this pretty little girlfriend of yaers. Or torture her. Would ye sit idly then?"

"That sounds more like a plan of yours," Brinn said and smiled back. "No wonder we're in this mess."

"I would never torture anyone," Ariel said. "And on that happy note, I'm going to bed. With any luck, sleep will make us a little wiser." She wobbled a little as she got up, and her steps weren't true as she walked away.

"Maybe," Brinn said. "But let's face it; sleep has failed you thus far."

"I'm sorry, Mathew," I said.

He waved me off. "I shouldn't have brought you into this."

"Despite it all, I'm glad you did." I remembered how we met, how that strange flying letter had hit me on the side of the head. It seemed so long ago. And weirdly, I missed Miranda and her letter. A small part of me wanted to forget the evil she brought onto the world and pretend everything was as it used to be. But nothing would ever be the same again.

Mathew chuckled to himself.

"What is it?" Brinn asked.

"I just remembered we promised Big Guy no one would ever notice we were in Algirin."

I know it was wrong, and it's a terrible kind of humor, but we all laughed. It was a miserable but mirthful laugh, enough to distract us for at least a little while. The laughter died down, leaving us to our own thoughts.

Dwinan, Houkin said once it was clear his services were no longer required.

"Yes, Houkin?"

The Mother of Light wishes to see you.

Chapter 49

The Whisper

Ariel

Ariel climbed onto her bunk, realizing she would regret her lack of moderation come morning. Those damned muskrats hadn't come up to sleep yet. Maybe that's for the better. It's not like she could face Brinn now. *Who does she think she is? This is why I hate people; always finding reasons to criticize me.*

Leoht, Houkin said from the window, breaking her thoughts.

"Houkin?" Ariel hadn't gotten used to speaking with trees, but now she didn't seem able to stop it.

The Mother of Light summons you.

"Who?"

The Leohtre.

"Why?"

I do not know.

"Okay... Where do I find her?"

You follow the fools.

"The fools, huh? I pity the fools." She waited for a moment to see if Houkin would continue and sighed. "I don't know who yae're referring to."

Ludik burst into the room. "The Leohtre, she wants to help us. We have to go."

"Houkin was just telling me something about following fools?" Ariel waited as Houkin interpreted her words to Ludik.

"He means the pilgrims," he clarified.

Brinn entered the room. "No one is going anywhere at this hour."

"Are ye this bossy all the time?" Ariel asked.

"You wouldn't believe it," Mathew said, jumping face-first into his pillow on the bunk beneath her.

"We're tired and broken, and some of us are drunk," Brinn said, arms akimbo. "We need to rest. We barely escaped with our lives today."

"But Brinn, we can't waste time," Ludik said.

"Do you think Leohtre is right around the corner? I looked it up on the map. It's at least a week away—walking nonstop. I know you feel guilty and want to do something about it. I do too. But we won't be much help to anyone if we tire ourselves out."

Mathew began to snore. Ariel admired that; she could never fall asleep on demand and always wondered how people did it. They made it seem so easy. Bastards. "It pains me to agree with her, but I do," she said.

Ludik fumbled with his hands. "Alright. Can we leave the window open, then?"

"No," Brinn said. "Get to bed."

The room spun around Ariel. She had definitely overdone it. To make matters worse, they would start another long-ass hike in the morning. But maybe there was still hope. After so many failures, she didn't quite believe it to be possible, but at least she wasn't alone anymore. At least, or perhaps, unfortunately. She would find out soon enough. Drowsiness washed over her, making her head heavy and sink into the rough pillow when someone shook her shoulders.

"What now?" Ariel spat, but her voice was rasp and groggy.

"Wake up," Brinn said. "Quickly!"

Ariel heard a slap followed by a heavy groan from Mathew.

Through the window, daylight flooded the room. Ariel tried to move the lump of bread left in a plastic bag for a week that was supposed to be her body and gave up. "It's too early."

"It's the middle of the afternoon," Brinn said. "You should look out the window."

Ariel commanded her legs to move—was she this sore the night before? She craned her neck and peeked outside. At least a thousand men wearing fireproof armor marched up the road.

"Rats! Can't a lass get some sleep?!"

"If we leave now, we might escape unseen," Brinn said, pulling Ludik off his bunk by his foot. Ludik fell to the floor with a thump.

"What was that for?" he cried.

"Soldiers, lots of them. Let's move."

Ariel stretched her limbs and cracked her back. "Calm down."

"Calm down? Do you remember the last time soldiers came at us? 'Cause I do, and it didn't go that well."

"I burnt a good part of my hair that day. A girl tends to remember that."

Brinn winced. "That's awful."

"Thank ye," Ariel said. "But yae're forgetting something."

"What?"

"This time, I'm on yer side."

Chapter 50

The River

Ludik

"Ariel," I asked her once we'd made camp for the night deep into the Leohtwoods and found a tree, Porin in this case, to interpret for me. "I had a letter from Miranda, you know, the note she used to transcribe everything everybody said around me." I fumbled with my thumbs. "It was very useful." Only some days had passed since we met, but it was hard to see Ariel as the killing monster I once thought her to be.

She gave me the side-eye. "So?"

I produced a piece of paper from my pocket. "I was wondering if you could do the same?"

"Sounds like a lot of work."

I pursed my lips. "It's so much more convenient than asking the trees to interpret all the time."

"Oh, the trees don't mind. Do ye, Porin?"

It's actually entertaining. We don't get much entertainment around here. There are only so many insults you can throw at humans before it turns tedious. Porin paused to let me know his turn was up and it was back to interpreting Ariel.

"See?" Ariel said.

I wasn't ready to let go. "Consider this. Imagine we come to a situation where there are no trees; you'd already have some practice doing it."

"I'll think about it," she said through a forced smile.

Well, it was worth a shot.

"How are we doing, Porin?" Ariel asked.

Not great. They'll be here before sunrise.

"That's it. They definitely know where we are. But how? Even if we are right and Miranda is in cahoots with Munika, the trees wouldn't clype, ye know, snitch, would they? I mean, they must know what's at stake."

I felt my stomach grow cold. "She's been torturing trees, hasn't she?"

Porin let his ruffling leaves speak for himself.

"Okay," Ariel said, folding her arms. "So stop telling other trees where we are. If they don't know, they can't grass up."

Not possible. We're not human; we share everything. But you shouldn't worry. These are the Leohtwoods. Light shines bright here, closer to Mother's leaves. We'll protect you as best as we can.

Light be seen! the trees chanted in agreement.

Mother Light herself is the most powerful leoht ever to exist. She'll cast eternal darkness on our enemies, and they'll never find their way out of the woods.

Light be seen!

"What are they saying?" Brinn asked, inspecting the canopies.

"Miranda has been torturing trees to find our whereabouts," I explained. "That's how the soldiers know where we are."

"Then tell them to be quiet," Brinn said, slicing the air with a knife hand.

"They're trees. It's their nature to share everything."

"Maybe they just need some incentive," Brinn said and stood up. "The fate of the world lies with us. We must band together and face this evil!"

Light be seen!

"So, If I hear any more about this nonsense," Brinn continued, "I will raise an army of lumberjacks and cut down every one of you!"

Light be seen... the trees chanted, less enthusiastically.

"Did that work?"

"You don't have the same effect on trees."

"That's because they haven't seen me with an ax."

Umh, Porin said, *a detachment of soldiers on ekkuh's back left Snottyfield. Two hundred strong.*

"Snottyfield?" I said. "That's about a day's walk from here. They'll intercept us for sure."

"This country has the best town names," Ariel mused as we got ready to move. "Just like home."

We walked through the night, none of us willing to risk making camp and having the soldiers catch up. The morning sun had breached the canopies by the time we reached the river Lore. Several pilgrims gathered at the banks, their flamboyant green and yellow robes grimy from labor.

The riders aren't far now, a tree warned.

I shared a look of concern with Ariel as we neared the riverbank and discovered why the pilgrims were stuck on our side of the river. The bridge had collapsed. Or, more worryingly, it had been destroyed recently.

"Can you hide us again?" I asked Ariel. "Like back at the Yellow Roof?" I didn't want to kill anyone, nor was I willing to use my power. I knew Mathew had no problems with it, but I was beginning to have my doubts about Ariel. The more I got to know her, the more I saw how soft her heart was, and I mean that in the best of ways.

Ariel said something, but we hadn't set up an interpreter yet. I should've thought of that before I asked her any question. Don't judge me; I was nervous.

Brinn tapped my shoulder. "Freeze the river, make a bridge," she signed.

I blinked. Could I do that? "I don't know how."

"You froze a landslide in place back at Algirin," she said, her signs coming out like laches. "Surely you can freeze a little water here."

I contemplated the river: fast current and at least ten yards wide. "I don't think it's possible. We have to swim across it."

Brinn grabbed my arm and tugged me toward the riverbank, which had the opposite effect from what Brinn intended. From up close, it was obvious how ridiculous her plan was.

"Brinn, even if I manage to freeze this area, the water coming from behind will... well, it won't work."

"Freeze a layer on top."

"I don't have that kind of control. Actually, I don't have any control. I'll probably end up making things worse."

Brinn looked over her shoulder at where the road disappeared behind the cover of the trees. That's when I noticed the vibrations from the ground. The riders had arrived.

Ariel and Mathew got into position, exchanging words, probably about their course of action.

"If you do nothing, those two will turn this forest to ash!" Brinn signed.

My mind raced, and my heart joined in. I focused on the river. I closed my eyes and thought of the happy days when Mom and I used to stroll about the countryside, of the evenings by the hearth, of the afternoons spent learning how to sign, of the nights when I climbed on my parents' bed after having a bad dream, and of how the mountain ripped all that away from me. It was easy for grief to fill me and for rage to ensue. That's how much I hated Aureberg. I couldn't wait to be done with Miranda so I could go after it. My mom's cold body pressed against my back—a vivid memory that unleashed fire across my spine as if someone threw hot oil at me, and my chest began to glow.

My vision funneled, my skin burned, and my heart poured light and pain. It felt like a thousand knives punctured my muscles and scraped against my bones. I fought to endure it, every conscious bit of me beseeching to give up—my vision blackening.

I breathed slowly, getting familiar with the pain. Then the colors around me shifted and inverted. Waves and strings of energy flowed in the air, the earth, the water, and the fish swimming beneath it. It rippled across the vastness of soil, trees, and underbrush, all of it teeming with living creatures and sparks of power. It was beautiful.

A being of light moved at my side. I could touch it. I reached it with my hand; it was like my finger had entered a basin of warm water.

Soothing and relaxing, a stark contrast to the bubbling pain in me. The body of energy fell to the ground, its hands up in surrender.

Leave her, a deep rumble said.

I drew my hand away, unsure. I turned around. Blobs of light galloped in like migrating lantern-swillows. I could reach out and breathe them in. Why did it feel so familiar?

That's when I remembered Lirterin as if it were happening again. A young boy naked and chained to a pole surrounded by statues of steel and flesh. No. It couldn't be. Ariel told me I hadn't hurt anyone. But their eyes—their terrified eyes. I snuffed out their lives as easily as blowing out candles.

With each breath, I absorbed the heat around me. That's where the pain came from; the stabbing needles were energy flooding in. I had to stop. I couldn't control it. What if I hurt my friends?

But I couldn't stop. *Turn away,* I screamed in my mind. *The river! Breathe the river!* I never knew rivers held so much energy. How could there be so much heat in cold water? I breathed in, and the energy slashed my body like a sword fresh out of the furnace, quenched in my flesh.

That's enough! I screamed inwardly. *Stop it!*

Let things be things, the voice said.

"Shut up! Shut up! SHUT UP!" I fell to my knees, my blurry eyes spotting shades of green and brown. Those colors dissipated and returned to normal. I had been foolish; I couldn't control this. I would never be able to control this.

Why were my hands and knees wet? Once my vision cleared, I saw why. A dam of ice, too rugged and clunky to cross, blocked the river's flow. The stubborn water slammed into it and overflowed onto the forest floor.

The being of light! "Brinn!" I found her on the ground, her blue clothes soaked, eyes filled with fear. No. That wasn't it. Not fear. Astonishment.

I stepped closer, and she flinched. "Brinn, I didn't mean—"

She rolled onto her knees, swirled, and hugged me. I felt her warmth, and it frightened me like nothing ever did.

"Get away from me!" I spat. "Get off me."

But Brinn hugged me tighter. What was she thinking? Had she not seen what I had done? Wasn't she afraid of me?

She released me from her embrace and signed, "You looked in terrible pain. I'm so sorry I pushed you. I love you, Ludik."

Stunned, I looked into her eyes. "Are you alright? Did I hurt you?"

"You didn't," she signed. "I just felt a little woozy, that's all."

Mathew ran up to us. "Good job!" I read on his lips.

Ariel came right behind him, and not so far away, soldiers dismounted, bows and arrows in hand. They nocked and loosed, and Ariel shot a wide beam, incinerating the arrows in mid-air. She spun around and slashed the rugged top of the ice dam with another light beam. The water coming from behind pushed the top layer out of the way, crashing downstream. I watched the newly formed ice road as Ariel spun back around and shot at the archer's hands.

Despite Mathew's hard lips, I read, "What are you waiting for? Go!"

Had they gone mad? As I watched the dam, chunks of it flaked off. It was a useless thing. There was no point in trying to cross it. "It's pointless," I explained as I watched the pilgrims flee upriver.

The archers halted their fire as a rider pushed past the line. He had a commanding face and began to say something but stopped; something in the sky caught his attention.

I turned to follow his gaze just in time to see a silhouette cross the sun. Was that a bird?

A lightning bolt struck the man's head, and he plopped to the ground.

The archers and riders observed their commander on the ground while his ekkuh fled from the scene. Another bolt struck another soldier, who fell to the ground, twitching.

The remaining soldiers shared looks of disbelief as another bolt struck another head, and in the next second, men bolted in every direction, away from the main road and into the cover of the trees. But that was of no use. The lightning followed them even through the thick forest. Then, a minute later, the flashes stopped. The only soldiers we could see lay motionless on the ground.

The bird flew over us again. I hugged Brinn and covered her as best as I could. Were we about to get hit? Wait. Was that a man riding the bird? Oh! No way! That was no bird. That was an aramaz!

Chapter 51

Flying Assassin

Ariel

"Well, ye must be my backup," Ariel said to the man that fell from the sky on the back of a freaking giant, four-legged bird. "Yer punctuality is astonishing." The man had gray hair and a long, braided beard, and eyes that were either tender or the embodiment of wrath. It was hard to tell. If not for his navy-blue flight suit jammed full of leather straps and metal buckles, he could be any Scottish farmer.

Ariel reminisced about a time when her life was simpler—days spent reading books in her cabin, feeding regular-sized birds, and petting her cat. She wondered if the Prentices were looking after Bubbles well. Ariel had been gone for so long that they might have given him away for adoption by now. She also missed taking farmers' money and how they'd tried to replicate her results the following year. But despite doing exactly what Ariel had advised, it never worked unless she inspected the crops personally. Oh, the dumb look on their faces once they saw their crops magically thrive into excellent yields was simply priceless. She loved to watch them scratch their heads over it. But in the end, farmers want profit, and with Ariel's services, that was pretty much a guaranteed, regardless of weather or soil conditions.

Sadly, those days were over. Now she dealt with teenagers, a half-man who could destroy the planet if he ever woke up on the wrong side of the bed, a witch made exclusively of energy who had definitely woken up on the wrong side of the bed, and now a bird rider. Yes, her life used to be simpler.

"Benerik Strudaw, at your service," the man said. He had a thick accent Ariel couldn't place—probably from this side of the roots. "And clearing out the mess over there is Hotcup."

The bird circled above, dashed downward, and let out another electric charge on some poor soldier's head. Wait! Hotcup? Was he being serious?

Mathew approached, eyes fixed in the sky. "Is that a griffin?"

"What's a *guiffun*?" Benerik asked.

"You know, a mythological beast, half eagle, half lion."

"Hotcup's an aramaz," Benerik stated matter-of-factly.

"It doesn't have a lion's tail," Ariel noted. "I thought Americans were all ignorant. How come ye know about mythological animals?"

"I'm happy to disappoint," Mathew said. "What about a hippogriff?"

"Again, no hoofs, and that's not a horse's tail either. It's all bird. Just more of it."

"Hotcup's not a bird," Benerik spat. "He's an aramaz."

Ariel glared at Benerik. "I had almost forgotten Half said someone was coming to help me."

Benerik's green eyes widened, and he let out a guffaw. "Half! Ah! That's a good one. Because there's only half of Alfred left. Ah! Wait! Does that mean you had *half*-forgotten about me?"

Great, he's an imbecile, Ariel thought.

Benerik cleaned the tears of laughter from the corner of his eye. "Well, seems like I arrived just in time."

Just in time? Ariel stomped the ground as she narrowed the distance between the two of them. "Tell that to the people of Algirin. I'm sure they are all celebrating yaer timely arrival," she said through gritted teeth, so close she could smell the bird stench on his beard.

"I was in the middle of an earned vacation in Borabumba. I flew here as fast as Cups allowed."

"Was Half too busy to teleport ye?"

The man removed his navy-blue wrinkled helmet. "I don't take kindly to blipping in and out of existence. Much rather enjoy the picturesque flight over here."

The fury in Ariel's eyes was enough to make Benerik go silent. Brinn came to her side, Ludik leaning on her. She, too, was fuming. *Better not let her talk, or we'll be here all day,* Ariel mused. "Alright, *Ben*. Can ye fly us to the other side?" she asked.

"Can't. Cups electrocutes anyone he touches," Ben said, stroking his beard regarding the river. "Apart from me, that is."

"I'm so happy yae've arrived," Ariel said.

Behind Benerik, a soldier groaned back to his feet. Benerik held up his hand and struck the soldier down with a bolt of lightning. "Ah! But as long as I'm grounded to Cups, he's harmless. We'll hop you over."

Ariel couldn't tell if she was happy or terrified about the prospect of having that beast ferry her over the river. Maybe both.

"Are those men dead?" Brinn asked.

Benerik glanced casually back at the men littering the ground. "Maybe. Electricity does not take kindly to the heart."

"Can your *Aramaz,*" Brinn said, making it absolutely clear she wasn't that impressed, "lift an ekkuh to the other side?"

"It's a pleasure to meet you too, miss."

"Cut the crap," Brinn spat. "I had so much of it lately that I need a week-long bath to feel clean again. Can it or can it not?"

Benerik whistled, and Hotcup descended from the sky like an arrow. The noise he made while flapping his wings to land was a breed between a helicopter and a bad theremin player. "*He* can. And we should hurry. There's a big mass of soldiers heading this way. Lingering here would prove very bad for their health."

Chapter 52

Holy Tree

Ludik

Despite the dire situation we found ourselves in, I had to pinch myself as I observed Hotcup: an honest to the Bastard aramaz that flew us across the river. An aramaz, just like in the tales of Salamorin. I couldn't believe it, no matter how much I gawked.

I had to pinch myself again when we came across a colossal tree—colossal being an understatement. Its trunk was so thick and wide that Heimee's house would fit inside it with room to spare; it towered toward the heavens, grazing the clouds. Its roots jutted and slithered, broad and bulky across the forest floor like a wavy sea. I didn't even know trees could grow so large.

"That must be the leohtre," I said while doing my best to fix my loose jaw.

Ariel shook her head. "That's not a leohtre," I think she said.

"Excuse me," I said to the colossal tree. "Are you not a leohtre?"

She won't listen, a voice like a whisper said, sweet and kind like a mother talking to her newborn child. Much different from all the other trees I've spoken to. *You're too short, and she's too tall.*

Ariel followed the words, eyes falling on a small, strange tree whose trunk swirled wildly like a corkscrew. Her bark was so rugged and cracked I could fit my fingers into the grooves. Her branches suffered from the same issues, slithering, and twisting into small, round leaves resembling fingernails. It was not a pretty tree to look at.

Loumirin protects me from the foolish pilgrims who come to worship her instead. I'm too old and fragile for the hands of man, all bent on taking a little of me home as a souvenir. Loumirin has grown above the chatter but, in return, has the best view a tree can hope for.

"'Same as man dreams of flying'," I repeated to myself, remembering Laurin.

Don't feel sad for Laurin, Ludik, the leohtre said as if she could read my mind. *She lived a full life. One that trees can only envy. She traveled, witnessed things no one could believe, and didn't die young for a peach tree either.*

"So she is gone." It wasn't a question, and the leohtre did not answer it. But I had reserved some hope for her; she had survived the mountain, after all.

Ariel's lips moved but we hadn't set up any tree to interpret.

Jorin please be Ariel's voice so our young dwinan can understand what she is saying.

Jorin repeated what Ariel had said, "We don't know how to stop Miranda. Perhaps you could give them leoht powers?"

Thank you, Jorin. My sweet Leohirin, we can only share our power once. And it must be with someone we care for deeply.

"Miranda shared her power with Mathew," I pointed out. "She can't possibly care about him. Can she?"

Some care differently than others. And for some, caring for the self leads to great sacrifices. It's the tragedy of greed.

"Why did you summon us here then?" Ariel pressed.

My impatient child, I see why my sister loved you so dearly. I'm old and wise and powerful. However, I'm still a tree, and I will never be anywhere else.

Ariel crossed her arms. "That's not what I meant."

Tendrils of pure light flew from a set of leaves converging on Ariel's chest. The seed pendant rose from her blouse and floated before her eyes.

There are few Leohirin left to carry out this deed and fewer even to earn my trust. Ariel, Leohirin, my kin, I, as did my sister, endow you with this responsibility. With that seed, you hold our future.

Ariel stretched her hand under the seed, and it gently settled on her palm.

Follow the light in your heart, and you'll know what to do.

Ariel contemplated the seed. "That's impossibly vague, you know that, right?"

And so is life.

Ariel rolled her eyes.

"Leohtre?" I said.

What a crude name. Call me Leanerin, Mother of Light.

"My apologies, Leanerin," I said. "Why now? I mean, why call us here then?"

Now is the only time. Time for adventure, for blunders, for joy, for sorrow, for victory and for defeat. A perfect time. Miranda heads this way as we speak. I'm a tree. Only here can I protect you.

"What can you do against her?" Ariel asked. "Can you help us defeat her? I mean, we got a lighten, a fyr, a dwinan, Brinn can probably scold Miranda a little, plus two leohts are better than one."

It is unlikely.

"But we must do something, no? Won't she burn this forest down if we sit idly by? And why didn't she come after us sooner, anyway?"

She's been buying the allegiance of the armies of Aviz. Erosomita lies in flames, and many of my kin burn. By ash and cinder, Aviz's war is won.

"That's not possible," I said, shifting uneasily. "You can't destroy a country in just a few days. Can she?"

Leanerin offered her silence as a response.

I shivered at the thought. "Then what can we even do? Did you summon us here only to let us know we're royally screwed? What's the point in that?"

I can't stop her, but I know who can.

"Well," Ariel said. "I don't mean to rush this speedy conversation, but perhaps you could've led with that. Who is it, then? Where can we find this person?"

Not a person, and you'll find him in exile, deep within the shattered mountains.

I felt the blood halt in my veins, a coldness lingering in my feet and hands. "No." I trembled. "No. No, no. No, no, no."

I tried to breathe, but the air refused to enter my lungs. Her words circled back and forth in my mind. The world spun fast and faster, churning, pulling my soul into an endless pit of unfairness and despair. A whirlwind of injustice. "Not *it*. It's a monster. It murdered my family! And you want me to ask *it* for help?"

Things are things, Leanerin added, almost as if it were the most natural thing to say.

My knees buckled under the weight of the words as a sharp pain stabbed at my heart. Those words. Those damned, horrible words.

Sorrow is your weapon. In pain lies a dwinan's strength. A cruel power, yes, but our survival depends on it.

"There must be another way," I pleaded.

I'm sorry, little dwinan. In the fights to come, we all have our sacrifices to make. Go now. I'll stall her for as long as I must. Do not fear the darkness, for it is a medium for the light.

And with that, the world dimmed, and the trees began to sing,

Oh, Oh, Oh, Two trees in a row
One became tinder. One became a bow
Oh, Oh, Oh, Three trees in the night
Two drew the bright. The other caught the blight.
Oh, Oh, Oh, Story of an oak,
one became a barrel. The other died of old.
Oh, Oh, Oh, Fall, Spring and Winter's light,
Summer left to splinter, Three trees in a fight.

Brinn and Mathew rushed to our side.

"I hope this was worth it," Brinn signed as flashes of lightning seeped through the thick forest. "Miranda's here."

Chapter 53

Fleeting Light

Ludik

A ball of light zoomed across the forest, cutting through the darkness Leanerin imposed on the world and shattered a nearby tree into splinters. Fragments of wood rained on us, while above the aramaz flew in tight curves, unleashing lightning between every dash and swerve.

Leanerin and Benerik did a great job keeping Miranda away. It's hard to fight in the dark, but Miranda was a leoht too, and the darkness didn't affect her much. We followed Ariel through the gloom as she cut a path for us to walk.

The trees before us were ripped from the earth, roots and soil, and flung our way. Ariel sliced a trunk in half while Mathew shattered another with a fireball. The wailing, the cries, the supplication of dying trees wrenched my stomach.

She's a togian too! screamed a tree. *We're doomed.*

Keep singing!

A curtain of fire dropped in front of us, cutting our path. My veins pumped blue, the dwinan ready to escape. Should we turn and fight?

Oh Oh Oh, fight in the dark

One on fire, one bereft of bark

Mathew pulled in the fire and tossed at the ball of light streaking above us. Another round of lightning fell on our heads. I saw it in time and breathed it in.

So much energy. I fought the darkness from overtaking my vision while pain erupted across my body. Yet something was different. A thin film of white light enveloped me, making it easier to remain conscious—a leoht's light. Leanerin was doing something to me.

The singing trees faltered as a massive chunk of land broke free from the earth and crashed with extreme violence ahead of us as we ducked and covered our heads, dirt and pebbles pelting our bodies.

I winced as I got back to my feet. "Darkness a stream," I sang, "Life a Show!"

That is not a battle song, a tree protested.

No, another replied, *but it's a song fit for a dwinan. New beginnings of a story long told.*

And all at once, the trees began anew, *It has never been this windy.*

"It has never been this cold."

Summer days will have me.

"With our wild Light to hold."

The song kept me sane—a song of a night long ago when I was doomed to die.

Rocks smashed the ground around us. Earth and moss slapped my face earning me a mouth full of dirt.

Then it hit me. It was true. Miranda must have gotten to Munika's volume. Togian, the tree had said. What could we do against such power? Would I be able to stop moving objects? I stopped the landslide. Would a flung rock or a wooden stake be different?

Benerik bent hard and dashed in our direction. I saw it; clearly, his energy was rough and spiky. A field surrounded him and Hotcup, their energies somehow linked, flowing in and out of one another, arching in peculiar ways, which reminded me of the inside of an onion.

A log homed in on Hotcup, who bent left to dodge but not fast enough; his right talons connected with the projectile, throwing them into a downward spiral barreling toward the canopies. The aramaz spun and spread his wings wide, pulling up, talons kicking against the treetops while Ben showered the skies with a barrage of lightning. Hotcup began leveling his flight, but too late. They crashed through the canopies, hitting branches and trunks, tumbling toward the forest floor.

Bolts from Miranda showered us as we ran toward them. They connected with me as I breathed the streams of electricity. The slithering power prickled every hair on my skin, seeping into my flesh and away from my friends. Brinn ran behind me, pulling Era by the reins, keeping close enough to have some protection against Miranda's blows but not so close that I would drain her energy. The poor ekkuh was so nervous, tugging at the reins to get away, but Brinn held them tight and close to its beak.

My leaves will be gleaming,

A beam of light nearly slashed through Brinn and Era had I not been exactly where I was. Again, the light felt different. Soothing, healing even. I shook the thought away; other things required my attention.

"In Loehirin's might to glow," I sang.

In the sky, darkness and light fought against each other, flashing like tormenting auroras. Leanerin fought to conceal us while Miranda pushed back. In a moment, we were dazed, while in the next, we were bumping in the dark.

Enough, you miserable tree! Miranda bellowed, and an intense white flash followed.

I turned, trying to gauge where Miranda was and got struck by a massive shock wave that crushed against my chest, sending me tumbling head over heels.

Darkness a stream, Life a show, the trees cried—a harrowing mournful cry.

Miranda did not waste a second and shot straight at us, hovering over the ground, toppling every tree in her wake.

I could taste her intent in the energy surrounding her. Thirsty and evil. Ariel and Mathew shot to my side and unleashed all the energy they had to spare. Benerik limped from behind and added a barrage of lightning in her direction.

But I could see the forces involved with great detail. They didn't even stall her a little. Her energy. So immense. So overwhelming. We would never escape it. Leanerin massively underestimated Miranda's power and paid dearly for it. We were all about to pay dearly for it. There was no way out. It was time to find out what a dwinan could truly do. I stepped ahead of my friends and steadied my breath.

"New beginnings of a story long told!" I sang with the trees as I threw myself at the wave of power in front of me.

And breathed.

Miranda smashed into me, and for a moment, it was like being inside a kiln and under a glacier simultaneously. And in the next, blackness blurred the edges of sight, growing, spreading, my mind splintering like the bark of the trees until I was but a point of pure excruciating pain floating in the void.

Chapter 54

Moonscape

Ariel

Ariel's mind fought to comprehend what she was seeing. The trees and land behind Miranda were like the surface of the sun—a raging fire so intense that it melted rock and turned entire trees directly into plasma. While on the other side, to the boy's back, the cold made her shiver. Air rushed in from behind like a hurricane converging into a fountain of blue light where Ludik stood. Around him, ice crystals formed and melted like a visual representation of sound waves. And the sound was abysmal.

Ariel kept her hands pressed tightly to her ears. Would she become deaf like Ludik? Or dead. Then deafness wouldn't be that much of a problem.

The pillar of blue light took a step forward. The crystals on the ground stopped melting. And the orb of pure energy dimmed slightly. It wavered, and in the blink of an eye, the raging fire and plasma got sucked into a single point so bright Ariel only managed to witness it because of her own power and shot away.

The lingering fires across the deadscape ahead mingled and twisted into fire-devils that whirled maniacally until they, too, died down abruptly, revealing Ludik. The lad wobbled, his knees buckled, and he fell limply to the ground.

Ariel panted, her ears ringing. That was a good sign, right? That meant she wasn't deaf. Right? She didn't want to be deaf. She would have to learn sign language and lip-read, and all of that sounded incredibly exhausting to her. Also, there was no doubt in her mind she would absolutely suck at those things. She had always been a horrible student. In fact, other than swindling farmers, she had always been terrible at most things in life.

The first flakes of ash tickled her nose. Absent-mindedly, she observed Brinn as she shot from her ekkuh's side, which lay on the ground, glazed eyes and tongue hanging out its beak, to her knees next to Ludik. Had there really been a forest in front of her moments ago?

Some noise overlapped the ringing. Good. Good. That has to be a good—

"ARIEL!" Brinn was shouting, holding Ludik's limp frame in her arms.

Ariel dashed toward Ludik and tripped over Mathew's legs. She took a moment to see how he was doing. He had passed out, but his chest was moving. She could worry about him later. Hurriedly she got back to her feet and kneeled over Ludik.

"Lay him down." Her words were muffled and distant, but she definitely heard them.

"He's not breathing," Brinn shouted.

"Lay him straight on the bloody ground!"

Brinn's face was a soup of scratches, blood, soot and tears as she lay Ludik on his back and moved aside, covering her mouth.

Ariel pressed two fingers on the boy's neck. No pulse. "No, no, no, no. Don't ye even..." she said frantically. "She is not dead, and we can't do this without ye."

Ariel laid him straight and began chest compressions. Wait! Was she supposed to start with mouth-to-mouth? Too late to think. Compressions. "Ah, ah, ah, staying alive. Staying alive. Thirty!" She lifted his chin slightly and breathed into Ludik's lungs. She placed her hands over his chest and began a second round of compressions as ash covered his chest, and Brinn gently wiped the flakes off his face. She sang the song as best as she could remember. Were those thirty? She forgot to count. She exhaled into Ludik's chest.

Brinn moved over to Ludik's opposite side and took his hand. "No, Ludik. Please—"

"Shut up!" Ariel spat. How did the rest of the lyrics go? She couldn't remember. She didn't even like the damned lyrics, but that was the song her CPR instructor had told her to use—something about a womanizer, what a joke. *Just sing the chorus.* "Ah ah ah ah, staying alive, staying alive."

Ariel pressed down on Ludik's chest harder. They had been so close to escaping, but then... then... she lost Leanerin. There was so much she wanted to ask her, and that stupid witch took that from her. Ariel hated that monster so much. So, so much. Miranda had made her leave her comfortable life to endure all this misery. Light spilled out of her without her knowing it as she pressed Ludik's ribcage so hard she felt something inside snap, making her hesitate for a beat. The instructor had told her it could happen and that patients can live with pain in their chest but not without a heart. The light poured out of her, like when she used it to nurture plants back to full health. She knew it didn't work on humans, but the light was comforting. And she needed all the comfort she could find. She needed *her* light, her friend's light, now more than ever.

The light seeped into Ludik's chest like a sponge soaking in water. Ariel stopped compressing. "Did ye see that?"

"What are you waiting for?" Brinn blurted. "Give him more."

Ariel looked up toward the heavens, where smoke and ash turned the day into a grayish hell, blocking out the sun. She had only seen such things in volcano documentaries. Closing her eyes, she let whatever light she had left flow out, down to the last wisp of it.

Ludik sucked it all greedily.

"Well, give him more!" Brinn urged.

"I'm out," Ariel said, panic creeping up her throat, dizziness and exhaustion taking their toll. "I'm all out."

"Then continue what you were doing!"

Ariel was so tired now. She took several steadied breaths, noting how sticky her mouth was from dryness, dust, and ash. She placed her hands on Ludik's chest and began compressions again, the strength fading from her arms. To compensate, she had to throw her whole body behind each thrust. Damn it, she forgot to sing. Was she in the right rhythm? Was she too fast? Too slow? Rats! Give him air!

She pressed her mouth into his and filled his lungs. She pressed her hands back to his chest when Ludik hiccupped. She drew her hands back and watched in absolute glee as Ludik coughed and struggled for a breath.

"Ye can do it!" Ariel nearly shouted. "Come on! Breathe. Yes, yes, that's it! Breathe."

Ludik gasped for air like an old car starting on a frozen morning.

"Yes, yes!" Brinn cheered.

Ariel hugged Brinn over Ludik's body. She hugged her back.

"Help me put him on his side," Ariel said. "We don't want him to choke."

Brinn helped turn the boy, and together they watched as his breaths came easier.

Ariel breathed a well-deserved sigh of relief. "I'm sorry about Flora," she said, "Era, I mean. I named it Flora when...."

Brinn looked at Era, her body resting on a patch of damp grass, splinters, and pilling ash. "She saved me," Brinn said. "I got too close and felt my strength bleed out. I don't know if it was on purpose or she just panicked, but Era pushed me away."

Ariel felt the drain too, but amid everything else, she barely minded it. *We're lucky not to be frozen statues,* she thought to herself.

"It's not his fault," Brinn said as she caressed the boy's golden curls. He saved us."

Ariel shook her head and regarded Ludik with a mix of pride and concern. "He hurt her. I think he hurt her badly, but she got away." Ariel drew in a heavy breath and swallowed a mouth of ash. She tried to spit it out, but her mouth was too dry. "I'm gonnae check on Mathew."

She almost didn't find him, as the ash had covered his entire body already. "Crap," she said as she wiped the ash off his face and turned him on his side.

"Let's not do that again," said a hoarse voice behind her.

A gray man and a gray beast approached, shuffling the gray flakes mounting on the floor.

"Happy to see ye alive," Ariel said, although she had completely forgotten about them.

"We don't die so easy," Benerik said, leaning on Hotcup.

"Yer leg's broken," Ariel pointed out.

Benerik glanced at it, bone sticking out of his leg. "Aye. I've noticed."

Chapter 55

Half Man

Ludik

Brinn brought the water pouch to my mouth. The water tasted stale and silky, and my tongue felt smooth and tingly, as if I had burnt it while drinking hot tea. But none of that mattered. I was alive. Somehow. The last thing I remembered was literally burning alive. Or maybe, this was all a charade from the Bastard, and I was indeed dead. I certainly did not feel like a living thing.

I think the sun was still up, but it was hard to tell with all the ash. I had never seen a sky like that. Evil and corrupted. Like everything else around me, I, too, was covered with a thickening layer of ash flakes. I reached out to touch it, smudging my hands and pants. I had taken the full force of Miranda's power; the same power that created this eerie landscape. I should definitely be dead.

"You shouldn't move," Brinn signed.

"I have to," I said. "She might be back at any moment. I can—" It hurt to talk, and I winced. "I can't—"

Ariel tapped Brinn's shoulders and said something.

"She says you got her good. She'll think twice before messing with you again."

Ariel gave me two thumbs up and a wide grin. I don't know how; she didn't look much more alive than I did.

"More water," I asked.

Brinn brought the pouch to my mouth again, and I drank a little more.

Mathew lay next to me, jacket hung over his head, supported by a couple of sticks so the ash wouldn't land on his face. Benerik and Hotcup leaned against the broken trunk of a tree. Benerik checked the bandages around his leg while Hotcup licked the gashes on his legs. The aramaz stopped licking and shared a look with me, and I swear he gave me a nod. I nodded back, and he got back to licking his wounds with his long whip-like tongue covered in white filaments.

"We thought about making a fire, but I don't think we'd stand the sight of it," Brinn signed.

I tried to smile. "Good thinking. Leanerin spoke of a seed. What was that about?"

Ariel shrugged, said something, then shook her head.

"She says she has a leohtre seed and has no idea what to do with it. Plant it once this is done, maybe."

I nodded. "I think I can move with a little help."

"You can barely lift your arms," Brinn pointed out.

"We can put Mathew on Era for a change." I tried again to smile, but it died on my lips as I noticed Brinn's and Ariel's glum expressions.

Ariel tapped Brinn's shoulders again and said something.

Brinn hesitated then signed, "Miranda consumed the air around you. Era suffocated." Her hands betrayed her words. I'd killed Era. I saw it in her eyes but didn't press the matter. I was a monster.

"I'm so sorry," I said, giving my best attempt at a hug. Brinn pulled most of the weight.

Soon, or an eternity later, night fell on us; although we barely noticed the difference, as ash continued to rain, tainting the world. Benerik finally made a campfire. We didn't like it, but we didn't have a choice, so we didn't argue. The fire required constant attention as ash threatened to smother it every few minutes. Benerik was in pretty bad shape, too; his face was a collection of cuts and bruises, not to mention a broken leg. I've got to hand it to him; he didn't grumble or complain about it.

I must have dozed off for some time because, between blinks,

Mathew was up. But it couldn't have been for long since it was still night. That, or the smoke had grown so thick that the morning light couldn't reach us. Everywhere we went, destruction followed. When would this end?

Mathew came to my side. I had never seen him that quiet. Nor the trees, for that matter, even the ones left alive. He sat there breathing along with me and nothing else. I wondered what was going on in that mind of his. Or if there was anything at all. Then he squeezed my arm, startling me, and pointed to a spot in the gloom.

A man in black robes emerged from nowhere. Only half of his face was visible in the firelight. *Dwinan,* he said, much like a tree would, except it sounded hollow and whispery.

Before he could say anything else, Ariel stomped her way to him, puffing ash with each step, hands balled into fists. She pointed a finger accusingly and began berating him.

I'll say it in treespeak so he may listen too, young Leoht. Your anger is but a consequence of mortality, he said. *I don't expect you to understand.*

Ariel fumed and tried to slap him, but he simply teleported away and reappeared over me. *Do you know how long a scaled worm lives?*

What kind of question was that? I was too broken to be intimidated by him. "Huh?"

Do you think about them when you run over their burrows? Or when you plow the land? How many of their little lives have you disturbed and even ended? What do you owe them? What do they owe you? Do you ever fear they'll come to avenge the ones they lost?

"What's your point?" I said, his ordealish look somehow less intimidating when compared to what we had just survived. "Ariel told me all about you. You could've fought with us. Instead, you hide in the shadows. Why even bother talking to us? Why did you save us before?"

He chuckled. *I have no peers in this world, young dwinan. Only her. If I hadn't lived through the shatter, I would have never saved you. And I would be whole again.*

"Whole?"

Miranda was everything to me once. Love has a strange way of creating false memories and altering one's reality. My scars, my halfness, were the price I paid for my betrayal, what it took to break her—to kill what I loved the most. Would you have remained whole? Would anyone? Power and love make the world; they make the sun shine brighter, the leaves grow greener, the oceans churn bluer, and they make life worth living, but when left untamed and unchecked, they corrupt and destroy all which they have created.

I have nothing left to create, only to mourn.

"But you helped us. You have been helping us. You sent Ariel, and you saved us back in Algirin. Why?"

In the library, she asked for my hand. I came so close to accepting it. Fill the void in me; heal the pain that has tormented me for lifetimes. For a moment, I almost gave in. You would've died, and the world would be left helpless and hopeless.

"You're a dwinan too?" I asked.

I am all.

"Ironic, huh."

A half smile crossed his half face.

I got up on my wobbly legs. Every string of muscle threatened to snap like stalks of hay, and I hugged him. My hands sunk in places where a body should be, but I did not care. He tensed at first as if hugging was an unnatural thing to do, then softly eased into it. "Thank you for saving us," I told him as I let go.

Did it help?

"I guess it did."

Then you know what you must do.

"I do. But I don't know if I can."

You're young. You still haven't been crushed by the weight of wisdom. Your concepts of morality still have hard borders. You'll find a way. Half looked up at the clouds of smoke and ash. *I saved the books, you know. Most of them, at least. I did not bother with Legislation or tax registry. I'm sorry I couldn't save the lives lost. There wasn't enough time for both. Maybe immortality has left me calloused toward the value of life. It's funny how sometimes our quest for good ends up causing such harm to others. It's funny, yet it's not funny at all.*

What would I have chosen? I love books, and I understand their power. The loss of knowledge would be like losing the lives of the people who have dared to invent, imagine and investigate. Which was the biggest loss? I could not tell and shrugged the thought away. "We need to get to Alturin."

So you will do it?

I averted my eyes. "It seems I don't have much of a choice."

Such a brave little dwinan. Here, take this. Half reached into his floating robes and produced a piece of paper.

I examined it. It was the size of a regular letter and had no writing on it. What was I supposed to do with it? I looked back at him in time to see his half-lips move, then back at the paper. It read: *May the silence be your blessing. Farewell, Master Ludik.*

In a moment, Half was in front of me, and ash covered the rest while in the other, a massive gate towered over me. To each side, the wall ran high and smooth from which bastions jutted out, piercing the land under the glittering light of a full moon. I knew that wall all too well. I turned around. The land ran flat almost to the horizon, dotted with gray boulders. I could almost see it, there in the distance, the refugee camp. I turned to face Alturin, its massive gate looming in front of me.

Before I could reminisce any further, my friends popped into existence around me like ghosts in the night. In the blink of an eye, we were sixty leagues away.

"No, don't you dare tele—" I read Benerik's words on my new transcription letter as he emerged, still leaning against the aramaz. "Narn!" He shook his fist. "You stupid—bah!"

"He should've done that the first time," Ariel said.

"Bah!" Benerik repeated.

"Who's there?" said a man over Alturin's gate holding a torch.

"I didn't see them coming, Oddik, I swear," said another head as it popped next to the torch. "They just appeared in front of the gate. One moment there was no one for miles, and in the next they were right there!"

"Ya're so useless. People don't just pop outta nowhere. Ya, and yar dumb stories. Why are they so gray? State yar purpose!"

"I'm Benerik Strudaw."

"Who?"

Benerik glared.

"Ah!" Oddik pointed at Benerik. "Got ya there, old man. Hannik, go get the lord."

"At this hour?"

"Just, urgh, Hannik, please just go."

"I know ya, always sending me to do what ya don't want to do. And I'm the one who gets in trouble."

"That's because I outrank ya."

"It's always the same excuse with ya."

"That's because it's not an excuse."

"Open the bloody gate," Benerik said.

"Sorry, Ben," Oddik said. "We're under orders not to let anyone in without the lord's permission. How come ya're all so dirty?"

An hour drew by. Far to the south, columns of smoke filled the horizon, reflecting the orange light of the conflagration below like a sunrise under stormy clouds. I thought I had put out the fire. Why were there new ones?

Mathew passed the time throwing rocks as far as he could, and Ariel joined him after a while.

"You got another magical note," Brinn said. "Aren't you worried? I mean, Half is hearing everything we say."

I shook my head. "I don't think he needs a letter to eavesdrop on us."

"Good point."

"Ben," said a head popping over the wall. "You look like crap."

"Thanks," Benerik said. "I feel like crap too."

"What do you want?"

"Food, care, a bath. Ale would be nice. Got a nasty wound that needs medical attention."

"Who're your friends?"

"Uh, let's see. The pretty lass there with snow-fair skin and blue hair is Ariel. She's a bit of a handful."

"It's a pity I'm out of light," Ariel added. "I would like to shed some on what a handful looks like."

"That was a good one," Brinn said. "You're getting better."

"Oh! Aren't ye sweet?"

"Shush, let me do the talking." Benerik made a swatting motion. "Katunik and I go way back."

"I'm sorry, Ben. From where I stand, I see fires everywhere in the distance. And I received distressing news about a large explosion in Algirin. The king is dead, and Erosomita's border lies in flames. What's going on?"

"I had nothing to do with it," Benerik said matter-of-factly. "I swear it was like this when I got here."

"Oh, please." Brinn walked to Mathew and dug through his bag. "Bastard be told, how much medicine do you have here?"

Mathew shrugged. "Not enough."

Brinn pulled out a square glass bottle with a honey-colored liquid inside. "Heims, 39-year-old reserve."

Lord Katunik observed Brinn sternly for a moment and disappeared behind the crenels.

"Ye had a Heims bottle with ye this whole time?" Ariel spat. "Are we sure we want to give it away?"

"Narn, you spooked the man," Benerik said. "On the bright side, I wouldn't mind a sip o' that."

The drawbridge trembled and began to lower, revealing the iron gate behind. When the bridge covered the narrow moat, the chess pattern gate raised.

"If it's talking that needs done," Mathew said, patting Ben's shoulder as they started crossing the bridge, "you let Brinn do it."

Chapter 56

Lord Katunik

Ludik

Despite our complaints, we were escorted by Lord Katunik and a group of armed and armored city guards up the streets and up the stairs of a tall keep. I wanted to lie down and die by the time we got to Katunik's office. The room was well-lit, with many oil lamps hung on the walls, and a modest candle chandelier made from an old cartwheel filled the ceiling. The round table occupying the center of the room was so large they probably had to build the room around it. The chairs were made of solid wood, which meant they were costly, to say the least and we were about to cover them with soot and ash and dirt. Tapestries depicting events and battles of long ago lined the walls, except for a small section dedicated to weapons; swords, spears, mallets, daggers, etc.

The Duke of Alturin's well-groomed face seemed somehow familiar, yet I couldn't quite place it. I had never met anyone with such high status. He wore bulky armor, made not with metal but many layers of fabric colored deep blue like a dying day. On the breastplate, his house crest glimmered in the candlelight, an aramaz shooting a lightning bolt over a tower. The tower was similar to the keep we were in, although I was too tired to appreciate Alturin's architecture.

"Thanks for this lovely hike," Ariel said, taking a keen interest in the weapons on the wall. She trailed a finger over the blade of a longsword, leaving a streak of ash on it. "It's exactly what I needed after everything that happened today. Are ye going to open that bottle or not?"

Katunik gave Ariel the side-eye as he circled the table. "Please, don't touch anything." He offered a chair to Ariel, who took the hint and sat down. Then Katunik turned to Benerik, "Why did you come here? You have always been welcomed in our city, but I don't know how well I should receive you under these circumstances."

"Well, Armrar, can't say I like the way we're being treated," Benerik said, stopping to breathe and motioning toward the crest on Katunik's chest. "I would advise you to remember how you got to where you are today."

"Is that a gentle reminder or a threat?"

"The latter."

"I should've known. You were never the gentle kind."

Benerik let out a guffaw and regretted it, wincing in pain. "Narn, don't make me laugh. I ache all over."

Lord Katunik drew in a deep breath. "Lirterin, Algirin, the king's death, reports that Erosomita fell. Entire cities lie in flames, and the border is all but abandoned; the war won."

"Wha—" Benerik tried to say, but Armrar interrupted him.

"And that's just the beginning. Munika sent me the strangest instructions and a piece of most puzzling news. It seems that Munika has called for the armies of Aviz to assemble. Every garrison in the country is now on the march."

Katunik paused to let that sink in.

"Where are they marching to?" I asked with a sinking cold brewing in my gut.

Katunik met my eyes. "You've grown quite a lot, young man."

That's when all the pieces came together. "Mink?"

He chuckled. "No one dares to call me that anymore," he said. "But I'll allow it. Tell me, what is a deaf boy doing in the middle of all this?"

"It's a long story."

"I expect no less." He glanced at the letter in my hand. "Why do you keep reading your paper when talking with me?" If he was annoyed, he did not show it.

"It's magical. It transcribes what people say so I can read it."

He furrowed his brow, decided to let it go for the time being, and said, "Two hundred thousand men march this way."

We shifted uncomfortably as a group. One of our best team efforts, I must say.

"That's preposterous!" Benerik protested. "The whole army? Why?"

Lord Katunik shrugged. "He didn't say."

"And what are these *strange* instructions?" Brinn asked.

The duke considered Brinn for a moment. "I have been commanded to arrest a deaf boy with curled golden hair at his arrival, along with instructions on how to execute a fyr and a leoht and to keep the strong girl alive."

"Ah!" Ben said. "That explains the armor. Personally, I wouldn't have gone with metal."

"It's not. It's better than metal, fireproof and..." Katunik paused, studying Benerik's grimy face "... lightning absorbing."

Benerik rolled his eyes and shifted in his seat in order to change the position of his broken leg.

My heart grew smaller with each beat. Were we about to fight our way out? I was too tired and weak, but looking over at my friends, they barely seemed bothered. Mathew busily cleaned his nails as if the conversation in the room meant nothing to him. Ariel had her eyes on the bottle of Heims currently occupying the center of the table. Benerik was hard to tell if he was having a laugh or about to kill someone, maybe both. Only Brinn and I seemed worried.

"Don't look at me like that," Katunik continued, surveying his audience. "In fact, I would have carried out my orders immediately, but alas, you arrived in the company of Benerik Strudaw."

"And a bottle of Heims." Ariel raised a finger. "If ye plan to kill us, at least give me the courtesy of tastin' it. That's all I ask."

"Why does Benerik's presence change anything?" Brinn pressed.

"Oh, Ben and I go a long way back."

"A bolt of lightning on a clear day," I muttered. I turned to Benerik, leaning to the edge of my seat. "You killed the old Lord of Alturin, didn't you?"

Benerik shrugged. "He had it comin'."

Brinn pinched her chin, then frowned. "Wait, that's how Lord Guilling died, too. Did you kill—"

Benerik shrugged again. "He had it comin'."

"How many people have you killed?" I asked.

"They had it comin'."

"So tell me," Lord Katunik continued, "why shouldn't I carry out my orders? I want to hear everything. Every little detail. You're not to leave this room until I do."

"Can we have some water?" Mathew said.

"He was going to open the gates anyway," Ariel said to Brinn. "Ye wasted that bottle."

Katunik ordered his men to fetch water and gently grabbed the bottle of Heims. He inspected the spirit like someone inspects a newborn child and took a seat. "Remarkable," he said. "The rarest of commodities. It's almost a shame to drink it."

Ariel seethed in her seat. "But we are, right? We're drinking it, right?"

Lord Katunik made no motion toward opening the Heims and settled it back on the table. Water arrived and served to us, our dirty hands smudging the clear crystal glasses. We were all ash, soot, dirt, and blood sitting at a lord's round table as if we were equals.

Brinn stared at me, and so did Ariel and Mathew. Were they waiting for me to start? Well, when would that be? When I found Mathew? That would take too long, but the lord himself wanted every little detail. And of course he did; immeasurable trouble surged on the horizon; he needed all the information he could get. So, I decided to start from the very beginning, with a stubborn little boy disobeying his mother.

I don't know how I found the courage to tell my story, but I did. It flew right out of me like the flood in Algirin. Ariel, Mathew and Brinn added their details here and there. While Benerik said a whole lot of three words in the process, "Bastard have me."

Duke Armrar Katunik, though he did not seem to believe most of it, listened to our story attentively without interrupting once.

"Then Half brought us here," I finished.

Duke Katunik's eyes flinched while he processed our story, then clenched his fists. "And you thought it prudent to come here and endanger my city? Why didn't this Half-character drop you off at the mountain and save us all the trouble?"

"I don't know, your grace," I said. Maybe it was because I'd explicitly asked to be brought to Alturin, but I decided not to tell him that. And, I mean, I couldn't be blamed; I was in no condition to face Aureberg.

Katunik wove his fingers and rested his elbows on the table, sucking in a deep breath. "My men said you materialized out of nowhere. I almost had them punished for such nonsense." He uncrossed his hands and leaned back on his seat, which looked as awkward in armor as it looked uncomfortable. "What need does such a powerful creature have of you?"

"As I said, she wants my power. Then she'll become invulnerable."

"So what do you expect of me?"

"We didn't ask anything," Brinn said sternly. "We need rest, tend our wounds, but if you've seen the smoke and ash covering the horizon... well, if I were you, I would give us all the help you can give."

"The king died. Munika runs the country now. That should be the greatest tragedy in our hands. Yet it's told as a side note. So here I am, torn between carrying out orders or having the armies of Aviz storm my city."

"Then you'll have failed me twice." There was a harshness in my words that I had never felt before, like the beat of a hammer against a stubborn nail. "Your camp failed; Alturin treated the refugees like cattle. Many died of hunger, and many more to the winter. You're as responsible for my mother's death as the mountain is. And there you sit, telling me how torn you are.

"I'm among the lucky ones. Heimee rescued me and took me in. Fed me. Raised me. Taught me much of what I know now. Made much of who I am. I owe him my life, my gratitude, and my loyalty. And yet, I sit here—heart hard as stone—knowing perfectly well that I can't save him. Because giving Miranda what she wants will cast a darkness the likes of which this world hasn't seen in thousands of years. She will burn everything to the ground to get what she wants. To her, the lives of others have no value." I regarded Brinn with all my love, I couldn't bear the thought of losing her, but under no circumstance could I give Miranda my power. "She'll torture and murder everyone I hold dear until I give her my power. So that's a sacrifice I must be ready to make for everyone's sake."

"You fear she'll harm Heimee?" The duke raised his chin and leaned forward. "The fate of a city hardly compares to the fate of one man."

"What about the fate of a country?" Brinn asked, hands slashing the air above. "Does it compare to the fate of a city? What about the fate of the world? Does it compare to the fate of a country? What about two worlds? Because that's what's at stake here. *Your grace.*"

The duke got up, pinched his chin and paced around the room. If he was angry at Brinn, he did not show it. "I wish our fathers would've swapped places the day you lost yours. Could he have known the mountain would move? Could Munika? How does a mountain even move?"

"It's a togian," Ariel said. "It's obvious, innit?"

Like the moon, I thought.

Lord Katunik returned to the window, surveying the city, the walls and the lands beyond. A thin blue line breached the horizon announcing another day's birth and revealing the magnitude of the smoke cloud. "You are in no condition to face the northern death," he said at last. "Healthy men are in no condition to face the northern death. The cold wind is so intense it drains the life right out of you. And I have been to the top of the Shatter many times. There's no mountain to be seen from there. Wherever it lies, it's too far for the eye to see. How do you know there's where it hides?"

How did I know? "Where else would it have gone?"

"True," Benerik said. "If the mountain had moved anywhere you find eyes, someone would've seen it, and the shattered mountains are as eyeless as anything can be. Perfect, if not the only place to hide a mountain."

"Does this mean you believe us?" Mathew asked, looking up from his nails.

"And what is your stake in all of this? You're not from this world, not you nor that malnourished soul over there," the Duke said, motioning to Ariel.

Ariel didn't bother to protest.

"Miranda betrayed me," Mathew explained. "She used me to regain her powers and then discarded me like an unmatched sock. I need to stop her. All of this is happening because I helped her. She promised me we would save the world, but instead, I helped her destroy it. She's my responsibility."

The duke walked closer to Mathew and searched his eyes. "Few things are more honorable in this world than a man who owns up to his mistakes. Ah, Benerik," the duke said with heavy eyes, "what have you brought to my front gate?"

"I brought hope, Mink. I brought salvation."

"Technically, he didn't do anything," Ariel added. "But hey, as long as yae're on board."

For the first time since we dropped the weight of two worlds on his back, the Duke of Alturin buckled. He closed his eyes, took a deep breath, and began unstrapping his armor, starting with the breastplate. "Damn you to the Ordeal for this. Can you fly the boy there?"

"Would if I could," Benerik said. "But I had to be carried up the stairs. And I cleaned the wound best I could, but I need surgery if I'm to, you know, survive."

"Could Ludik ride the aramaz, then?"

Benerik let out a guffaw that ended in a coughing fit. "Of course, if you intend to have roasted boy for supper."

"I'm contemplating the ruin of my city and the misery of war thrust into the lives of my people. Good people, happy people. Because, as you say, it needs to be done. If you aren't taking this seriously, perhaps I shouldn't either."

Benerik's mirth withered. "My apologies, my king. No, the boy cannot fly Hotcup."

"I'm no king," Armrar said.

"Forgive me again, but you are the next in line. And if you're going to war against Munika, then you'll meet him as his peer—and let's just say I know whose bust I'd rather see on the coins."

Katunik scoffed. "It's Lord Guilling's face on the coins, not the king's."

"Aye. Time to change that too."

"Well, Munika can have the world for all I care, but he won't have Alturin."

The room remained motionless until Mathew thawed it, "You know, Ludik's a dwinan; won't he be fine? I mean, he can absorb the electricity, right?"

"What?" Brinn spat. "You've seen the toll it takes on him. He nearly died today."

"Technically, for a moment there, he did die," Ariel added.

"Yeah, but that was against Miranda. You can't compare Miranda's power against a little electric pokemon."

Brinn's arms lost containment. "This is not the place for stupid references no one understands!"

"I understood it," Ariel said.

"Benerik, is it possible then?" Mathew asked.

I became dizzy with the idea, as if I had stood up too fast. *Alone. I had to go alone.* I had come this far because of the people that surrounded me, and I would have to leave them behind as they faced two hundred thousand men while I ventured into the shattered mountains to find the mountain that murdered my parents *alone*.

"I hadn't considered that," Benerik said. "My guess is as good as yours."

All eyes fell on me, and the room went still again.

When I failed to provide more information, the duke ended the meeting. "We'll talk again on the morrow after you've rested." He motioned to his men. "See them to their quarters. Have the maids awaken and get the doctor out of bed."

"Yes, your grace," said one of the guards, who promptly left the room while another motioned for us to follow him.

Katunik faced another man. I had seen him before, too, a long time ago. Infundibuliform face, listless eyes, an expression of casual informality. Balival was his name I believed. "How long until Munika arrives?"

Balival checked his notepad. "No less than ten days, sire."

"Wake the generals. I want a meeting within the hour. War marches our way. We should be ready to greet it."

"Yes, sire," Balival said, scribbling some notes on a notepad. "Right away."

Chapter 57

Good Bread

Ludik

Forgive the mountain. Forgive the mountain. Forgive the mountain.

Despite being utterly exhausted, having bathed, and lying on a soft bed, I couldn't sleep. My chest hurt like the ordeal, but that wasn't what pestered me most. Mom's words kept me awake, and the sun piercing through the blinds offered no help. Finally, I gave up. Careful not to open the balcony doors too much and risk bothering everyone with the flooding light, I stepped outside.

Brisk and refreshing morning air greeted me. Bastard, I hadn't noticed how claustrophobic the room was. I surveyed the horizon until I met Ariel's eyes, who sat there, legs crossed, basking in the morning sun. I sat next to her, Half's letter in hand.

"Couldn't sleep?" she said. "I'd be surprised if ye did. Here, let me help ye." She placed a hand on my chest, which was warm and kind. Light, gentle as warm water escaped her fingers, smearing across my chest like a medicinal ointment, but without all the greasiness. It enveloped my heart like a soft blanket and a warm cup of tea by the hearth. Soothing and lulling me into a new state of peace; my eyelids less heavy, my eyes less swollen, my chest less sore.

"How did you do that?" I asked.

"I have no idea. But it works on ye. Well, and me, of course. And plants."

I breathed a sigh of relief.

"What's troubling ye?" she asked.

"I'm not sure." I took a deep breath. "It's that... my mother told me to forgive the mountain. Then Half gave that speech about worms. Did he mean we are but worms when compared to a mountain? How is that supposed to help me? To be honest, I can't. I can't forgive that monster after what it did to us. I mean, would you be able to forgive it?"

Ariel turned to the smoke smudging the horizons far southwest. "I wouldn't have to."

"You wouldn't?"

"Of course not, dummy. Find the mountain, take what ye need from it, and save yer feelings for later. Ye can always return and exact yer revenge or whatever yae're after."

I mulled it over in my head. She had a point. "Once this is over," I said. "I'll get you a bottle of that whisky."

"I'll hold ye to that. Glad I could help. Now let's get some sleep. Light helps, but our minds still need rest."

Her light and her words eased my spirit, and soon after my head touched the pillow, I was out. When I woke up, the sun hovered low over the horizon, and fresh clothes hung at the bed's end: undergarments, blue shirts, straight pants.

"The best thing about medieval ages is that I don't need to use a bra," Ariel said, stretching her arms.

"What's a bra?" I asked.

"It's this torture piece of clothing that helps ye support yer diddies."

"What?" Brinn said with curiosity. "Why would you wear one, then?"

"Society kind of expects it of ye. I guess bras aren't all that bad. If ye have large diddies, it's actually helpful."

"They're a pain to unhook," Mathew added.

"Oh, is that so, Mr. Ladies Man?" Ariel said.

Mathew blushed, then turned toward the door, "Oh, good, the servants are here."

They led us to the dining hall, where Lord Katunik greeted us. "I have made an announcement this morning, and I'm pleased to say the city took the news rather well."

"Was there a scenario they wouldn't have?" Ariel asked as she took a seat. Several trays of roasted potatoes and meats occupied the center of the table, and the smell of honey glaze made my stomach growl.

"Yesterday, they thought the war was as far away as it could be. I myself, refused to send Alturin soldiers to the front line. Today they learn that the entire kingdom marches this way. To be perfectly frank, I expected much resistance. No one wants war. No one wants to see their children, siblings, parents, or paramours thrown at spears, swords, and arrows. Of course, even if they were against this, I still have the last word."

"Good thing the fate of the world is what's at stake then," Mathew said, filling his plate.

"The world's end is too vague a matter for the average mind," Katunik said. "The argument that won them over was Munika himself. The Alturians would rather see their city burn than have him rule us again."

"Jesus," Mathew said, dropping to his chair, "it's the same everywhere, isn't it? Don't get me wrong. I'm grateful they're on our side; I just wish they were for the right reasons."

"It is a tough tale to swallow," Katunik said.

"How's Ben?" Ariel asked.

"Surgery went well. He's lucky to be a lighten. A normal individual would probably succumb to infection."

"He's lucky I brought antibiotics," Mathew protested. "Make sure he doesn't drink alcohol while on them."

"That might prove harder than defeating Munika," Katunik said with a half-smile before turning his attention to me, eyes stern and commanding. "It's obvious the old fool won't be able to fly you to the mountain anytime soon." He left the implications to flutter around the table.

Katunik wanted to see if I could ride the beast. Without instantly dying, that is. Sure, no pressure. I wasn't too keen on discovering what being electrocuted felt like. I nodded meekly.

"Good. I have other matters to attend to. When you leave, don't be intimidated by the town's sudden interest. They know who you are and why you're here. Curiosity is only natural."

Six days remained until the armies arrived. I still reserved some hope for Benerik's quick convalescence, but my expectations dwindled with each passing day. To make matters worse, we heard from Ariel that Benerik drank as much whisky as she did, despite hers and Mathew's warnings and complaints of what a waste it was to use the only antibiotics in the world on an old crazy bat.

Hotcup, however, seemed, for all intents and purposes, fully recovered. There was no place large enough to put him in, so the aramaz was left to walk freely around town, though he seldom left the palace's courtyard.

"I think Ben is recovering well," I told Hotcup after Brinn and I left the palace on our way to explore the city. *Just not fast enough.*

The aramaz opened and closed his beak and ruffled his feathers.

"I don't know what else to tell you."

"The doctor says he'll keep his leg," Brinn added cautiously, but that didn't seem to appease the aramaz any further.

I had come to grips with reality. I had to fly the aramaz; there was no way of knowing how long Ben's recovery would last. I also had no way of knowing how long our trip would take, even if it proved possible. And on top of that, there was an even more pertinent question: Would that despicable mountain know what to do about Miranda? Every single one of those questions required me to gather a kind of courage and willpower I wasn't so sure I possessed, regardless of how many motivational speeches Brinn gave me. Still, I shrugged the doubts off my mind. There was no point in dwelling on them; the path forward was clear enough.

"Should I try it now?" I asked.

Brinn shrugged. "Now, tomorrow. It's up to you. I wouldn't be in a hurry to be shocked."

I looked at the aramaz. *Should I try it now?* Now there was a question that sent shivers down my spine. I should survive it. I was a dwinan. And I was, for intents and purposes, fully restored, physically at least.

Hotcup turned his face to see me better with his enormous right eye. *Are you ready to be electrocuted?* it asked. Was I prepared to tap into my power in order to survive said electrocution? Bastard, no.

As if answering his own question, Hotcup huffed and walked away.

"I'll try it later. Let me have today, alright? I promise we'll do it tomorrow." I had no idea if what I said was true or not, but I wouldn't have to wait long to find out.

"Sure," Brinn said. "But if you, as Mathew puts it, chicken out tomorrow, I'll push you."

"Thanks," I said rather unsurely.

We spent the morning meandering about the streets of Alturin. The city wasn't as big as Algirin, but it was at least twice the size of Lirterin and home to over two hundred thousand people. The Alturin masonry was, as in all Aviz's star cities, seamless. The shingles covering the city's roofs were brick-red, contrasting against the gray stone and green fields beyond the wall.

Most streets were narrow, reminding me a lot of Guillingsbaer, but paved with large smooth slabs of grainy schist instead of cobblestones. Strangely enough, I felt at home walking its streets. I remember how furious I was when I first entered Lirterin and somehow expected Alturin to provoke the same emotions, but it didn't. Maybe due to the familiarity with Guillingsbaer, minus the flood of preachers, or because I had seen it—if from afar—when I was a child. It was part of my story, and I had come full circle, and the city that rejected our entrance those many nights ago was now the city responsible for our protection.

Below, the narrow streets eventually led to large circular open spaces, like dusty water lily leaves in a red pond. And beyond those, the great wall, its bastions resembling a cogwheel, while outside, smaller triangular fortifications filled the gaps between them.

"It's quite a sight to behold," I said.

"It's easily my favorite city thus far," Brinn agreed. "It's not too dark, not too bright."

"Not too steep," I added.

"And not too hot, either. And the people aren't weird. You know what's strange?" she asked as she took my hand and continued walking.

"What?"

"I miss making bread. The feel of wheat and water turning from a sticky lump into a smooth dough. The smell of it too. Of yeast doing its work and of fresh bread as it comes out of the oven. It was a simple thing to do. I knew all the rules of the game, and there were hardly any surprises."

I read what she said, and a wave of nostalgia also took over me. I had the same feeling regarding making whisky with Heimee, and for the first time since I had left him behind, I knew that was exactly what I wanted to do with my life if we survived the days to come.

"I don't think it's strange at all," I said. "I miss making whisky too—none of this fighting or saving the world. You're right; life was simpler then. Sad, we were too naive to notice. Well, Heimee did warn me, though."

"Insistently," Brinn agreed.

We shared a laugh.

"There's a bakery there," I pointed out. "I don't think we'll find a distillery here, but bakeries are everywhere. Let's check it out."

"I think you're underestimating distilleries."

"I don't smell the cereal in the air. If there were a large distillery here, my nose would've picked up on it. Come." I pulled Brinn by the hand, and soon we were surrounded by the scent of freshly baked bread. The people inside turned to look at us, eyes screaming, *It's them. It's the mages.*

"Maybe we should leave," Brinn said, taken aback by the overabundance of stares.

Then I noticed a particular stare from a young man about my age, his face splattered with freckles behind the counter. "Ludik?" he asked.

"Graze?" I asked.

"It is you!" Graze leapt over the counter and hugged me, almost knocking Half's note out of my hand. "What are the odds?"

"Remote," I said.

"What brings you here?" Graze asked. "Let me guess, intrepid adventures."

"Something like that, yes."

He pursed his lips. "Oh! You are the—"

"We are."

"You? A mage?" he said, crossing his arms. "Now that's some skilled work."

"I like to think I'm a whisky maker," I said.

"Urgh. My father is always drinking that stuff. It's vile."

"It is, isn't it?"

"Then how can you stand making it?"

"A master distiller took me in; showed me the trade. I don't like drinking the stuff but making it has its pleasures. I see pottery wasn't your thing."

"Baking's not that different, but at least I don't have to do it with my dad."

"Graze, this is my friend, Brinn."

"Are you a mage too? Are you the one that shoots light?"

"No. I'm a baker. Just like you."

"Oh, you mages are such modest folk. Come, have a seat in the kitchens. I want to hear all about your adventures."

"I'm sorry, I'm kind of tired of talking about those. Would you mind if we hear about yours instead?"

"Well, you've got to give me something. It's not every day one of your childhood friends turns out to be a mage. Are you the one that shoots fire?"

"No, I don't know how to explain it... I make ice."

"Wow, crazy stuff. And you?"

"Still bread."

"It's true," I said, "although she's a natural politician, which in its own way is a superpower. This girl can talk her way out of anything. She's incredible."

Brinn blushed a little and decided to change the topic. "I was telling Ludik how much I missed baking bread, and he pulled me in here."

"So you know how to knead and stuff?"

Brinn pulled up her sleeve and flexed her arm.

Graze whistled. (I don't need to hear whistling to know someone is whistling.) "You're hired."

"Really?" Brinn asked.

"Well, I could ask Lokrik. He's the boss."

"I'm not looking for a job, but I would love to help you make bread. You know, to get our mind off things."

Graze smiled. "Gotcha. Come, I'll introduce you to Lokrik. I'm sure he won't mind some help. All this talk of war has made everyone particularly hungry."

Lokrik welcomed us into his kitchen with open arms. No doubt he was happy to see his bakery fill with clients trying to have a look at his new part-time helpers. It was odd spending the day making bread in the company of good friends while the world outside threatened to unravel at any moment. I wasn't protesting or anything. I accepted it gladly, like the gift that it was: good company and the simple pleasure of baking a good loaf of bread (and eating it too). The day after wouldn't be so simple or easy.

Chapter 58

They're Here

Ludik

"They're early," Duke Katunik said as he studied the mass of men seeping through the forest's edge, three leagues south of the wall.

"But it's impossible," Balival said, a collection of maps sprayed across the table. "No army moves this fast."

"Miranda is a togian," I said, remembering the trees and rocks she had flung our way during the Leohtwood battle. "She might have flown the men closer."

As soon as the army was spotted, Lord Katunik summoned us to a turret at the side of the gate, a forward command position which had been hurriedly set up that very morning when scouts first announced strange movements in the forest.

Below, people filed through the gate pulling their carts and animals inside.

"No one gets out," Katunik commanded.

"Yes, your grace," a guard in full battle gear said and left to convey the orders.

"They don't know of our intentions yet," Balival said. "We may use it to gain some time."

Katunik shook his head. "There's one last thing we should try. My friends, what say you to a little chat with the enemy?"

"What for?" Ariel said, lifting her eyes from the same collection of maps.

"Munika will soon find our gate locked to the like of his. He'll want to speak terms and persuade us to surrender."

"What if they use the opportunity to ambush you, sire?" Balival said, frowning at the idea.

"Munika isn't dumb," Katunik said, "He knows this city. He understands that if he aims at a coward's victory, the city will never be fully subjugated. He'll face rebellions for years to come and lose his foothold in the north. If it comes to a fight, he will have to show his strength."

"What about the mage, sire?"

"She ain't dumb either," Mathew said. "Too much can go wrong. Besides, why would she risk attacking us when there's a whole army of grunts to do it for her? Miranda will wait for the best moment to strike. After all, she has proven to be nothing but patient."

Katunik nodded. "Fine assessment, Master Doller."

"What are our chances of winning this battle?" Brinn asked.

"They're quite hopeless," Balival said in a calm neutral tone, like someone reading a shopping list. "We have the terrain, but their numbers are no match. We hold only with a force of twenty thousand. Should we succeed in repelling the first wave, they'll overrun our walls soon after. And they may choose not to fight at all and siege the city. We are cornered here while they have the whole country to supply them. In siege warfare, we don't stand a chance."

"But that's great," Ariel said, "that gives us enough time to... that's not happening, is it?"

Katunik shook his head.

"Not even a wee bit?"

"They'll want to force your permanence here, to help defend the city." Katunik paused, taking another long look at the army assembling further south. "Their rushed appearance only serves as proof of it. Master Ludik has repelled Miranda once, but if we want to defeat her for good, we'll need more. So here's the trick. He must both leave the city and show himself defending it."

Ariel's chin dropped. "Yer bum's oot the windae. How do ye figure that'll happen?"

"They need to see me fight before I leave," I said.

Katunik nodded, then faced Mathew. "How's Ben doing?"

"God damn it, Jim. I'm a mage, not a doctor," Mathew said, and when no one reacted, he continued, "Oh well, the meds seem to be working well enough, and he's a tough fellow. He left his bed this morning; said he wanted booze. Honestly, I gave up trying to reason with that coffin-dodger after he told me that a man shouldn't die with a dry mouth. He's still in pretty bad shape. But as he put it, 'It's but a shuttle job.'"

"Do you think he'll be able to fly the dwinan?"

"I wouldn't take his word for it."

Katunik pondered this development. "I see little to gain by having him fly off just to die."

"You think you can reason with him?" I asked.

"Benerik? No chance."

"I meant Munika."

Katunik shrugged. "We must go out there anyway and show to him that this won't be an easy victory. Might as well give it a try."

"Talking isn't my forte," Ariel said. "Why don't we ambush him ourselves? Kill him right there?"

"Miranda won't let it happen," Mathew said. "She needs him. We'd be forced to fight her right there in the open field. That didn't go that well for us last time."

"It didn't go well for her either," Ariel replied.

Mathew pursed his lips. "Yeah, but last time she didn't have an army behind her. We can't fight both out in the open; that's madness. You say we should talk with Munika, huh? I know just the right person for the job."

"No, no," Brinn said, waving her hands. "This is different. I can't lead this conversation."

"Why not? You have a proven track record for this kind of stuff. I think you should do it."

"You think the king of Aviz will listen to a Burrow's baker? You're mad."

Katunik laughed. "Don't worry, Lady Kallak. I won't hold you to it."

Balival shifted uneasily. "Sire, these are only children."

"Yes, they are. Children shouldn't have this much power, but, alas, this is our reality. They are our main weapons, and our fate depends on them. It is only wise to hear what they have to say. Wouldn't you agree?" Katunik held my eyes. "What say you, Master Ludik? Are you ready to face the man who had you tortured for his entertainment?"

Was this a test? To see if I was willing? It made sense, I guess. If I didn't hold against a man, how would I hold against a mountain? And in the end, did it really matter? Was there any other choice? No, there wasn't. A large part of me wanted this. I wanted to look Munika in the eye and let him know that I wasn't afraid. "Yes, your grace," I said.

"I'm coming too, then," Brinn added.

"I think we should all go, no?" Mathew said.

Ariel let out a sigh, "Is this a group thing? I don't do well in group projects."

"You don't do well in any project," Brinn added.

"Awa' n bile yer heid. When are we leavin', then?"

"See, Balival," Katunik said. "If every soldier in Alturin has this kind of courage, we may win this battle after all. Go have a word with Ben. See if his bold assurances hold any veracity. I don't care how fast Munika's army is, it'll take some hours before he forms ranks. And Master Ludik, I think this goes without saying, but don't try to touch the aramaz until we've met with Munika. After that, if Ben isn't ready, well, may the Light be on your side."

Chapter 59

Flight Readiness

Ludik

"Narn! I'm Benerik Strudaw, the flyin' assassin. I should be on Hotcup's back making quick work of those men out there, not here feeling useless. A single bolt to Munika's head and the witch is all that's left to deal with. Aye, I think we can take her."

We found Ben in a tavern outside the palace instead of, well, a hospital bed. The place was the usual stomping grounds of the army elite, but with the whole army at the wall, it was mostly empty, apart from us and the taverner's son, who wasn't much older than me and whose hands shook as he brought a tray with thumbglasses and a bottle of Heims.

"You can barely lift your glass, old man," Ariel said and downed the contents of her glass as the young taverner placed the bottle and glasses on the table.

"Water for me, please," I asked, and the boy nodded meekly.

"Water for me as well. We're about to face Munika. Should you really be drinking?" Brinn rebuked Ariel.

"Should I? Ah dinnae ken," Ariel said and refilled her glass. "But I may die soon, so I plan to drink as much as I can, thank you very much."

"Good point," Mathew said and poured himself a glass. "Cheers!"

Ariel and Mathew clinked their glasses and raised them to Benerik.

"Wow," Mathew said, shaking his head and wincing. "Holy!"

Ariel patted him on the shoulder. "First time?"

Mathew nodded, eyes welling profusely.

"Yer a lookin' a wee bit peely-wally." Ariel pulled Mathew's glass away from him. "Ye shouldn't be drinking at yer age anyway."

"Benerik," I said. "How do I fly the aramaz?"

Ben leaned against the back of his chair and took another sip of whisky before answering. "Firstly, don't call him *the aramaz.* He's not some witless creature. He speaks and has a mind of his own. I don't think he'll think kindly of you if you keep calling him 'the aramaz.'"

"I'm sorry. Hotcup," I corrected. How could such an intimidating creature be named Hotcup?

"He chose me, you know," Ben said, looking longingly at his glass as if that's where the memory lived. "I found him near Portos. Not far from where your village used to be but on the Erosomitan side of the border. The northern death hasn't been kind there also, but its people are resilient. What a rough bunch, and mean if you don't understand them, but also polite in their strange way. They'll insult the living soul out of you while offering you everything they have.

"I used to explore the wilderness outside town, close to the shatter. It drove my mother mad. My father struck me often on that account and many others. He wasn't evil, just dumb, resorting to violence easily. He loved me, despite it all; all he wanted was for me to grow strong. And that was the only way he knew how. I don't hate him. His teachings may have saved my life on several occasions.

"One day, I was out in the Ozezar Valley when the tiniest feathered creature came up to me. It caught me by surprise. Too small to be an ekkuh, even a baby one. Blue and white, never seen anything like him. Four kids were pursuing him. 'It went over there,' they said. They had sticks and stones in their hands and greed in their eyes. Probably thought they could sell the creature for a pen or two. That's about three heads, I guess. Anyway, once he saw me, he shrank, tail tucked under his belly, head low, body trembling. He was so afraid. Poor little guy; no one to defend him. I stood up for him and told the other kids to bugger off. 'Oh, yeah, what are you gonna do?' they asked. 'I'll make you eat your teeth for breakfast. And you sure look hungry.' They laughed like it was a joke. One stepped closer, 'Well, let me teach you how to count—' he said, stepping in front of me, chest wide. I punched his teeth in before he finished his sentence. Another kid lunged at me, a club in his hand. He hit me on the shoulder, and I fell to the ground. It hurt like the Ordeal itself. I swept his leg and hammered back. The other boys, stones in hand, ganged up on me. I kicked one or tried to, at least. Next thing I know, I'm on the ground getting kicked in the head. I thought I was done for. Little Ben and his short, useless life. But the little creature slid up to them and gently grazed around their heels. The boys went stiff and toppled like timber.

"The little blue creature stood there, as small as a loaf of bread, tapping his little claws, happiness in his large orange eyes. My head was pretty banged up, and one of my eyes had swollen to the size of a fist. The little guy came to me and lowered his head in a bow. I found it so amusing I bowed back. 'You're welcome little fellow, and thanks for the help too.' He stepped closer, offering his head for me to pat. Was I gonna go stiff like the other kids if I did? I don't know why, but I wasn't scared of it. So I did. And I went stiff.

"Unlike the others, I didn't pass out. Narn. It hurt, unlike anything I had ever experienced, but only for a moment. It was the only and last time it did. He made me a lighten that day, and our fates have been woven together since. When I came home, I told the story to my mother. She didn't believe me at first and told me she had no need for more animals around the house. But my father saw something else entirely: a son who'd stood up against bullies and defended himself. His son. He was utterly proud to see my face all banged up like a squashed blood orange. As a prize, he let me keep the little one as long as I cared for him and trained him. Mom sipped her hot cup of tea in silence. She didn't dare to dispute my father. 'I guess it does look cute,' Mom said. 'Kinda wanna snuggle with it like a hot cup o'tea.' Aye, I know it's a silly name, but regardless of how tough I was, I was still a kid when I named him. And it's not like he needs a mighty name to be mighty. So Hotcup stuck.

"My sister tried to touch him, and she got knocked out cold for days. No one dared touch him after that. So you see, dwinan or not, I don't know if you can ride Cups without me. I ground his power, and if I'm not there, it all goes directly through you. I don't know what will happen when you touch him."

"I understand," I said.

"At least you have guts; I'll grant you that," he said with a half-smirk. "If you manage to get past the shock, flying is another beast altogether. Flying in a straight line, it's not so bad. It's the turnin' that gets you. It pulls and pushes you, in and out. It can literally suck all the air out of your lungs and drain the blood from your head. Even now, on my best days, if I lose focus, I lose my grip. So be sure to be strapped tightly to the saddle. You'll have to wear my flight suit, but you're a tiny little fellow; the suit hanging loose is no big deal, but the safety straps won't fit you. It's unlikely that you'll have to perform any evasive maneuvers, so fly straight and leave the rest up to Cups."

"How do I turn?"

"Tell him," he said, then he frowned. "Hmm, perhaps that won't be so easy. When we're connected, we share our souls—with the burbling wind, there isn't much listenin' to be done. You'll have to find a way around that."

A soldier entered the tavern, sweat dribbling down his forehead. "The duke requests your presence at the gate, my lords."

We shared a long look among ourselves, and despite the seriousness of the situation, we burst out laughing.

"After you, my lord," Brinn said.

"Nonsense, my lady. After you," I said.

"I shalt henceforth be known as the lord lordness of Massachusetts," Mathew added, still not fully recovered from his whisky experience.

"That makes no sense, yer lord lordness," Ariel said.

"M'lady, how dare you?"

"My lords?" the soldiers said, confusion mingling with the sweat.

Ariel dumped a last glass of Heims down her throat. "Let's do it; let's meet this prick."

"Follow me, m'lady," the soldier said and led the way.

"Are you gonna kill him?" Mathew said as we walked out and left Ben to sulk on his own. "I mean, for leaving you naked in a dark cell?"

"The thought hasn't left my mind," Ariel said as we walked together toward our fate. "It'll depend largely on his behavior."

Chapter 60

Harsh Terms

Ludik

Duke Katunik was already mounted on a large black ekkuh with five other mounted soldiers when we arrived at the front gate. Next to the soldiers, stable men held four ekkuhs waiting to be mounted.

"Come on, do not dally," Katunik said. "Choose a ride. Best not to keep the *king* waiting."

The gate opened as we chose our mounts, and the bridge lowered over the moat. My heart began to beat faster. I couldn't show fear in Munika's presence. Was I up for this? It's normal to feel nervous when you ride out into a soon-to-be battlefield, no? I blew out a breath.

"Nervous, Master Ludik?" Katunik asked.

I couldn't even answer him.

"You don't have to talk, just remain still, and remember that nerves don't show unless your voice or your hands tremble. Keep your hands balled, and don't utter a word. Can you do that?"

"Yes, your grace."

"Hmmm, no trembling in the voice; perhaps you're not as nervous as you think."

"I left Ben with half a bottle of Heims," Ariel said. "I'd like to get back in time to help him finish it."

"Are you sure I can't immolate Munika on sight?" Mathew asked.

"It wouldn't be appropriate. And I don't think it would help us much. What about you, Lady Kallak, any ideas?"

Brinn held the reins of her ekkuh tightly, clearly distraught for it not being Era and said, "I'm going to ask for his surrender."

Katunik chuckled, and so did the men with him. "We're definitely in good company." He kicked his ekkuh forward, and soon we were out in the open, between the fortified walls of Alturin and the largest army assembled in the history of Aviz. But all I could think about was the refugee camp. There was nothing there now, of course, but I swear I could close my eyes and see it. Its white tents and reversed palisade among the green field and the scattered boulders stretching as far as the forest down south. Inside the city, it was easy to forget this place was a quintessential part of my story. Katunik had not been responsible for how ugly things got in the refugee camp. The man we were about to face was.

I caught Brinn's smile as she rode close to me. She had the warmest smile. I loved her. I did. Maybe it was young love, but love, nonetheless. And she loved me too; I knew as much, with all the green of the world. When this was over, we would go out, have some lunch, and I would even buy her something pretty like Heimee told me to, just for the sake of it. She nudged her head, telling me I should pay attention. I nodded and faced what lay ahead. I didn't want to, really. The little boy in me wanted to look away, run away, back to my mom and back to my dad. But they were gone. So, I wanted to go back to Heimee. Forget the world existed, forget the battles to come, forget Munika, forget Miranda, even the mountain. I would snuggle up in my bed with the window wide open and let the cold be a reassuring thing again, other than a weapon.

Munika waited on top of the largest ekkuh I had ever seen, with brown and golden feathers and orange eyes so large that, for a moment, I imagined it was another aramaz. He wore a dashing silver armor—a metal armor, *bold choice*—a white cape draping from his shoulders and a crown of Leohtre's leaves, like swollen green tears on his head—a gift from Miranda, most likely, to send us a clear message.

I had to grit my teeth. How could he defile such a holy creature?

Leanerin had given her life to save her line and our lives, and what remained of her was now a prop on a vile king's head. Ariel and I locked eyes, and we needed no words to describe our thoughts. *How dare he?*

Munika contemplated us, his expression serene, his soldiers slightly behind him. Seven, I counted, chests in the air and a thirst for battle in their stare.

I retrieved Half's letter from my pocket. The two factions stared at each other for a lingering moment. Munika's half-slit eyes and restful face exuded nothing but tedium. He always did manage to appear as if he had something better to do. Perpetual bored face. Even his uneven lips moderated whatever emotions lurked behind. His eyes fell on me as a small smile cornered his mouth.

"Ah! You brought the boy to me," he said. "You have followed your king's orders. Good for you, Armrar. I always thought of you as a smart man."

"I'm afraid you put too much confidence in my intelligence, *Mun-Mun*. The boy and his friends were a little tired of my interior decor and requested to come out for a stroll. That's all."

Munika chuckled and invited his men to chuckle along. "The duke never ceases to amuse me. I miss our little conversations, Mink."

"I cannot wholeheartedly agree."

"Very well, let's talk about what we can agree upon. You came out here, you must have something to say to me, or you would remain behind your locked gate."

"What do you expect from this?"

"The boy and the allegiance of Alturin. Is that too much for a king to ask?"

Katunik pinched his chin. "Those are pretty heavy terms. Could I interest you in a hot cup of tea instead? Peach, perhaps?"

"Don't play coy with me, Mink. You'll turn this into a tedious affair. Do you honestly believe you have a choice? If you disobey your king, only ruin can follow."

"You are no king. And if you take the city by force, every good man in the north will rebel against you, and you'll have a civil war on your hands."

"You put too much faith in the common people. That was always your biggest flaw. Fear earns more respect than kindness."

"I lead by example and character, and if you insist on this ludicrous attack, you'll find no kindness here. You'll doom your army, and for what? To satisfy a witch who intends to destroy all that man has accomplished? Miranda was divided and locked away for a reason. She will scorch the earth, brazen the skies, and there will be no one left to oppose her. No good can come of this. Why would you doom your kind to such fate?"

"How can you not see it? Haven't you heard the news? The war is won. In a single day, Erosomita fell; our enemies lie in cinders; our future forged by fire will be grand. And we will not stop there, Duke of Alturin. We'll end every war, every conflict. We'll wage one last war to end all wars. Man will live in peace, and life will flourish. And all you have to do is deliver a half-witted, deaf child to me and bow to your king. It doesn't have to be anything fancy; it only has to be public."

"A war to end all wars. Maybe my intelligence is failing again, but it sounds rather fallacious. How can you be so sure she won't destroy Aviz once she gets what she wants?"

"What use would be a world without men? There will always have to be men. Let them live in a world where our kingdom is her most faithful ally. We'll forge a new religion. One with a true and only god. So who are we to turn out back to the requests of a god?"

"If she's so powerful, why isn't she here? Why hasn't she taken the city already? What's stopping her?"

Munika scoffed. "She does not need to talk with petty men. Listen to me, Armrar, you cannot hope to win this battle. I brought two hundred thousand strong to your gate and a god. Your city will bow and deliver the boy, or it will burn." Munika paused, holding Katunik's eyes. "What is it that you seek? I can make this choice easy for you. Obey your king, and you remain the ruler of your city. I will not strip you from the title of Duke. In fact, I will give you more land, more power, and riches. I'll even give you a seat at the royal table. And your people won't have to suffer. No blood will have to be spilled, and no skin will have to crackle. Bow to me, Armrar, and let's end this madness."

The Duke of Alturin inspected the army ahead as the men formed ranks and prepared for battle. He glanced over his shoulder at his city, sadness heavy in his eyes. Only the slightest breeze filled the gaps around the silence. Was the duke considering it? The longer the silence stretched, the longer I feared his next words. What would I do in his place? To be burdened with the fate of so many. All for a little deaf boy. Cold grew in my chest. I contemplated surrendering myself. But no, that could not be. That would mean war on a global scale. The fingers of death would touch every nation and every soul until every remaining spirit lay withered or broken or dead.

Katunik observed me. And in his eyes, I saw shame. The Commander of the North, Duke of Alturin and a little orphan boy held the fate of the world in one stare. His head bowed slightly to me. "What a generous offer, my foolish uncle. It's almost a shame, but I must politely refuse."

My hands were steady, and my voice would not tremble. I wanted to say something, back up the King of Alturin and the northern regions of Aviz. Show that megalomaniacal lunatic that we would fight tooth and nail to preserve life. All life.

Brinn dismounted. All eyes followed her as she walked the five feet separating our parties, eyes poised on Munika's.

"We have the wall of Alturin and the courage of its people. We have not one but four mages on our side, including a dwinan," she said, hands dashing and slashing with fierce determination. "And we have beaten your *god* so badly she had to run and cower."

"What is this?" Munika scoffed. "A little girl speaking on your behalf?"

The grin on the duke's lips was of pure pleasure. "It seems so."

"I'm here to accept *your* surrender." Brinn glared at the King of Aviz, long and fiercely, until his eyes twitched and anger formed at the corner of his lips. Satisfied, she walked back to her ekkuh, remounted, and, without waiting for another word, spurred her ekkuh away.

Munika said nothing as, one by one, the members of our party parted and turned back on their ekkuhs. I stared him down until only Ariel and Mathew remained at my side—defiance in our eyes.

And that was enough. I needed no surge of brilliance, no great speech. Not a peep, not a word. I had power. A power they feared dearly, and I could defeat her.

Munika regained his detached demeanor. But it was too late. I saw it as clear as a blue sky—we could win this. The chances were slim, but not so hopeless after all.

Chapter 61

Time Bomb

Ariel

"Your grace, a word," Ariel said, waiting at the door of the turret being used as a forward operations command.

Balival looked up from the maps and shared an intrigued look with the duke.

"Your grace..." Katunik repeated as if tasting something new. "This ought to be interesting."

"I want to talk to ye about Ludik. In private, if I may."

Balival shifted around the room, making some notations on maps that had been nailed to the wall. "Balival is my right arm. Whatever you have to say, he can listen."

Ariel took a deep breath and nodded to herself. "I left something out of my story."

Katunik inspected her, clearly not pleased about surprises this late in the game.

"He, hmm..." Ariel began, unsure of how she would put it, but the growing impatience on the duke's face forced her to spit it out. "When we were in Lirterin's castle, the night Ludik escaped—"

"What about it?"

Ariel peered out the window. The lines of men stretched as far as her eye could see. "He uh," the memory came to her, still cold, still cruel, "he killed them."

The duke took a seat and invited Ariel to do the same.

"No, thank ye. I think I need to stand for this."

Katunik's impatience seemed to melt as he studied Ariel's discomfort.

"Something happens when his power takes over. It's hard for him to keep in control. The more he uses it, the harder it gets."

"I can't say I feel sorry for those soldiers," Balival said without glancing at her as he kept fixating on things on the wall. "To have a part in a child's torture is inhumane."

"That's the thing. He didn't kill only soldiers."

The duke shifted in his seat and settled his elbows on the table. "Go on."

The piercing memory stung her tongue as she drew in a trembling breath. "I didn't notice at first when we first escaped, but I returned to the castle after the... the bodies had thawed enough to fall to the ground. Munika's men had piled them outside. But the bodies didn't belong only to soldiers, but servants, maids, and house pets too—even the ekkuhs in stable. All dead. He killed everyone in those buildings close to him."

Balival stopped working and came to the table. Ariel did not see him fetch anything, but when he sat, he had a bottle of Heims and three glasses. "That's quite the tale. Why did you hold this information until now?"

"The wee lad doesn't know. At least, I think he doesn't know. And I'm not telling him. Grief is the major catalyst for his power. If he finds out about what he did, he may lose control all over again. I'm telling ye this now because I see ye plan to use him. Ye plan to use his power. Maybe yae'll ask him to make a demonstration before he departs, prove to Miranda that he's not going anywhere. Right?"

"We have discussed it, yes."

"Well, ye can't do it."

"Hasn't he proved he can control his power? He did not kill you when you faced Miranda in the Leohtwoods."

"He killed Brinn's ekkuh. She loved that beast. And Ludik loves

Brinn; he would never harm her pet. But he did. He sucked the life right out of it. I think we're still alive because of Miranda. She has so much power Ludik focused all of his on her. Brinn and I agreed to tell him that Miranda killed her ekkuh, not him—that it suffocated in the fire. Ye need to send him on his mission as soon as possible. Once the battle starts, he'll want to help. I don't know if he's dumb or brave, but he'll try, and he may kill us all."

Katunik let out a long breath and grabbed the glass of Heims in front of him.

"You should've brought this to our attention sooner," Balival reprehended in his matter-of-fact way.

"It wouldn't have made any difference," Katunik said. "He still needed to at least show himself to Munika and Miranda."

"Then we have to send the boy away," Balival suggested.

Katunik spun his glass on the table. "There goes our plan."

"Plan?"

"Miranda hasn't attacked because he is here. Or at least that's what we think, even though it doesn't fully explain it. Maybe there's another reason; maybe it has to do with the Northern Death and Aureberg. Even this all-powerful mage you spoke of, Half. Even he did not dare leave you at the mountain. If Ludik showed his power, he would buy us plenty of time."

"How?"

"Because if we are right, Miranda knows that Ludik must leave if we are to stand a chance to defeat her. And when he does, that's her window to strike."

"So if they poke at us and no ice comes out, we'll have to deal with her without Ludik's support."

Katunik nodded solemnly. "We hoped to widen our window of opportunity, but with this new information, it may not be worth the risk."

"It *may* not? I don't know about ye, but I'd rather die fighting two hundred thousand men and that hackit witch than have the light sucked out of me."

"There's a big rock headed our way," Mathew shouted as he ran into the room.

"What are ye doing here?" Ariel said.

"I followed you!"

The city rocked so violently that it toppled the glasses on the table. Ariel and Katunik both hunched down.

"Were ye eavesdropping?"

"Of course," Mathew said as if it were the most common thing to do.

Ariel ran to the window. Boulders were being plucked like pimples from the ground, then hung in the air just above the grass. A ball of light shone in the distance. One of the boulders rose higher, made a half circle over an invisible center and flung toward the city. Ariel followed the rock's trajectory. It would impact the middle of the city, not the wall.

"Urgh, ye reprobate bampot. I knew I couldn't trust ye."

"Really, you think this is the time for that? Miranda's bombarding the city, and your main concern is to reprimand me?"

The boulder struck an agglomerate of houses, red tiles and rock and dust shot in every direction.

"Tell all non-essentials to move further up the city and out of range," Katunik ordered. "And Balival, give the guard the good news—our wait is over."

"Right away, your grace," Balival said and was out the door shouting commands to whomever he found.

"I don't think we're safe here," Ariel said.

"Can't you cut a rock like that in half if it comes our way?" Katunik asked.

"I can, but then we'll have two rocks instead of one. We'll die all the same."

"I may be able to nudge it with a big enough fireball, but still, those things are coming in mighty fast," Mathew said.

"Then we might as well be outside," Katunik said. "I don't know about you, but I could use a stroll."

Another boulder smashed into the city, the vibrations spreading through the ground and up Ariel's legs, grinding at her knees. "But outside, we run the risk of getting hit by shrapnel."

"She wants to raise fear and dissent," Katunik said. "That's why she's targeting civilian buildings. I doubt she'll attack the wall at this point."

"What makes you say that?" Mathew asked.

"It's a good wall. Besides, this is where I have to be; show the men I'm not scared of this, and neither should they." With that Katunik marched along the allure.

Chapter 62

Single-handedly

Ludik

"Narn! What's with all the ruckus?" Benerik said, crutching his way out of the palace's infirmary and into the courtyard where I was gathering enough courage to touch Hotcup.

Hotcup eyed me with displeasure.

"Miranda's flinging rocks at the city," Brinn answered. "I don't think she can throw them this far. And you shouldn't be out of bed."

"The cowardly hag."

"What are you doing?" I asked.

"If she thinks she can bombard us, I'll show her some bombardment of my own."

"But, Ben, you can barely walk straight."

"Good thing I fly better than I walk, then."

I stood between him and Hotcup. "I can't let you do this."

"It'll only be a few minutes," he said, threw his crutches to the ground, and shoved me to the side as easily as one opens the drapes. He climbed on Hotcup's saddle. Sparks flew off the aramaz with its excitement. "Calm down, ya big, feathered pillow; I don't die so easy." He fastened the straps connecting his flight jacket to Hotcup's saddle, then patted his neck. "Are you up for a bit of reckless flyin'?"

Hotcup jumped over us, wings stretched wide open, and, in two powerful strokes, was airborne.

"He's insane," Brinn noted.

"We kind of knew that two seconds after we met him. Should we wait here?"

"Wait here? A sick man jumped on a mythological flying beast and decided to single-handedly fight the biggest army in recorded history and one of the most powerful mages to ever exist, and you want to wait here? No, I'm going down there."

I looked down at the city as another rock raised a couple of buildings in a cloud of smoke and destruction. "Down there?"

"Yeah, we have the duke's war ekkuhs. I'm sure they'll be fine under combat."

"I wasn't thinking about the ekkuhs, to be honest."

"So what?" Brinn's hands arched before her. "You want to sit on your bum until he's back? If he gets back."

I glanced at the mounts Katunik had given us that very morning. What a day this was turning out to be. I pocketed the letter and mounted up. "What are you waiting for then?" In my defense, I really don't know what we were thinking as we forged down the city while boulders wrecked anything in their path. With every impact, our mounts nearly lost their footing but never their nerve. What amazing beasts they were. Yet despite their nimble agility and hard focus, maneuvering in the narrow streets packed with people was no easy task.

A boulder impacted nearby, displacing air like being hit in the face with handful of sand, flooding the street with dust and shrapnel, painting the soldiers' blue uniforms gray. Despite the chaotic mess, they continued evacuating the civilians out of danger's path. The morning I'd lost my father flashed before my eyes. But this time, it wasn't fear I felt. I was enraged—clenching my teeth so hard they might've cracked. *Give her the whole Ordeal, Ben! Do it, or I swear by the Bastard that I will!*

Brinn turned her ekkuh into a narrower street where our rides barely fit, but at least it was empty of people fleeing for their lives. The courage hadn't left her stare, but it was obvious she had reached the conclusion that riding under a bombardment wasn't such a great idea after all.

We reached the base of the wall, where things were surprisingly calmer, and followed it to the gate. Not because we wished to warn the duke about Ben's actions, but because it was the place most familiar to us. Several ekkuh were tied there, waiting for their riders. I recognized Mathew's and Ariel's ekkuhs among them. We tied our mounts next to them and made it up the ramp.

I expected to find the allure crammed with men, but that wasn't the case. There weren't nearly as many as I expected. Were we that outnumbered? Brinn crammed her body into a merlon as I retrieved Half's letter. "Look," she pointed to a dark spec against a blue sky.

A sea of men marched toward Alturin, the sun gleaming on their armors like the crests of crashing waves. *May the Bastard help us.* Despite the cruel sight, the soldiers on the allure remained remarkably calm. Archers held their bows at their side awaiting command. Pikemen stood at ease chatting. And two men I recognized, Hannik and Oddik, were even playing a game of cards on large stone servings as a makeshift table. I stared at them in disbelief.

"Game," Hannik said. "Better luck next time."

"Hey, look," Oddik said, holding his cards, concealing the slight tremble in his hand. *So they were human, after all.* "I knew it. It is the potato boy."

"I knew it," Hannik agreed. "Potato boy."

"What are ya? A parrot?"

"Are ya the potato kid?"

"You're the soldiers that guided us to the refugee camp."

"Listen, potato mage. Ya stole my sword. Funny enough, Munika told us not to punish ya. And instead punished me."

I failed to see how that could ever possibly be considered funny under such circumstances, so I changed the subject. "How can you be playing cards at a time like this?"

"Helps pass the time," Oddik said, shrugging.

"Yeah, have ya seen those boys move, takes forever," Hannik said, sneering over the merlon. "We'll all be taking naps by the time they arrive."

Brinn waved to get my attention.

"Well, good luck," I said awkwardly.

"Ya too, kid."

"What's wrong with them?" Brinn asked as I got to her side on the empty merlon.

"They're nervous," Ariel said, appearing at our side with Duke Katunik and Mathew. "So if ye're here... does that mean Ben is flying the big blue bird?"

"We tried to stop him," Brinn explained. "Didn't even slow him down."

"Figured as much," Lord Katunik said, eye poised on the tiny speck flying high above the clouds. "Every year fishermen gather to fish these enormous schools swimming up the river Mare. Thousands are caught in the nets, and still, they don't give up. The further up the river they go, the more predators join the fishermen. The fish are eaten by the thousands, yet every year, they return to swim up the current, through the rapids, over waterfalls, and even over dry land if they must. Yet they show the utmost restraint when compared to that lunatic."

"Are we talking about salmon?" Mathew asked. "I love salmon."

"He's gonna doom us all."

The speck in the sky moved from under a cloud and came down like a hawk closing in on its prey.

"Wow! That's really fast," Mathew said.

Was he going to plummet to the ground? Had Ben lost consciousness? Hotcup pulled up tightly, showering the advancing army with lightning, tossing soil, grass and men into the air with the force of the strike. I had to cover my eyes with the intensity of the light.

The suspended boulders waiting their turn to strike the city dropped to the ground, and the orb of light shot away in pursuit as the Alturin's guard cheered for Ben. Benerik used their momentum to gain altitude again. Hotcup flipped on his belly and came back crashing down for another strike. Miranda left a streak of light as she zoomed in to intercept.

What was that man thinking? In one futile attack, he was throwing all our chances down the gutter. What if he didn't make it back? What if Hotcup was injured? How would I reach the mountain in time? By foot?

Ben shot a single bolt of lightning thick as a trunk. It struck the ground with tremendous force, causing a bright explosion that sent sparks to shower on Munika's forces.

"Alright, Ben, that's enough," Katunik muttered, but Half's letter registered it anyway, "Sound the horn! Sound the horn! Make as much noise as you can. Get that idiot's attention."

From atop the turret a man took a horn to his mouth. People around me winced, and I felt a tremor in my belly.

Ariel plugged her ears. "That's a loud horn."

Miranda was closing in. Ben cornered and shot in her direction; they were going so fast against each other that they both missed their marks, lightning and fire filling the air. Miranda came to a halt. Was she letting him go?

Hotcup tucked his wings and plummeted over the sea of men unleashing another curtain of bright tendrils that pelted the men below. They regained altitude and turned back to the city.

"That's it." The duke leaned so hard into the merlon that there was a serious risk of him falling over. "That's it. Come back over here."

Then the air above the field glimmered green, yellow, and purple.

"Get out of there!" I yelled. "Evade! Evade!"

But it was too late. An arch of fire, bright as the sun, climbed up in the sky like a fountain, burning the air around it into something else entirely. Faster than I could follow, the arch reached its zenith and bent, crashing down on Hotcup and Ben. The beam of blazing light didn't hit them directly, but even from that distance, I could feel the day grow warmer.

Hotcup and Ben shot to the ground faster than any maneuver they had made so far, then turned much faster than anything I could conceive. Hotcup himself became a ball of light as bolts and sparks emerged from him, adding more speed.

The arch of pure sunlight scoured the land, sublimating boulders, soil and grass directly into vapor.

Ariel had her hands over her mouth, but the letter transcribed her words anyway. "Oh, my god. It looks like a solar flare." She grabbed Katunik by the armor. "Order your men to take cover. If that thing even comes close, we're plasma. Vaporized! There'll be nothing left to worry about because we'll be dead."

"You heard the lady," he bellowed. "Get to cover."

Everyone did. Everyone but me. Brinn crouched behind a crenel, her eyes on mine. I won't let anything happen to her. The beam neared the wall as it followed the fast-moving ball of lightning. I stood on the merlon, took a deep breath, and called it. I was so angry already, so on edge. It came so easy now as if it had always been so. Memories of Mom and the day I felt her body stiff against mine flashed before my eyes. All I wanted was to find that damned mountain, not this.

The voice came louder than ever. From behind, over the Shatter. *Things are things.* Its reach encompassed and enfolded the land, not by touching but by being the land itself. *What is, is what was and what has to be. What is done, undone, and redone. It changes, and in changing, it remains the same. That's what things are.* Then I saw a colossal shadow, three peaks clawing the sky. *Things are things,* it said again, as if those words offered all the explanation necessary.

Aureberg. I'm coming for you soon enough, I promised.

Lumps of light and energy moved frantically around me, and silhouettes of light scrambled away. *Focus.* Miranda!

The tremendous beam chased Ben and Hotcup, sublimating everything in its path. And the colors, deadly and destructive, yet so beautiful and serene. Could I do it? Could I breathe such a force? What would happen if I did? Or worse, what would happen if I didn't?

I breathed in and pulled her stream of energy. It bent across the burning air and shot into my chest.

Chapter 63

Our Advantage

Ariel

"Brinn," Ariel shouted, but it was of no use. The noise Miranda and Ben produced was nothing short of an ear-splitting, reality-defying insanity that threatened not to crack her eardrums but her whole skull like an egg. She lunged toward Brinn as the heat built up around them. "Brinn!" Ariel said, but she did not hear her own voice, enthralled by Ludik's light.

She grabbed Brinn by her blue jacket and pulled her close to her. "Run!" she bellowed, though she could not hear it over the noise but broke Brinn's stupor. They sprinted along the allure, right behind Mathew and Katunik, who kept pulling and commanding his men to follow.

The heat softened. Ariel glanced over her shoulder at Ludik as tiny crystals sprouted at his feet. The air grew cold mighty fast, the stone behind them turning white as ice crystals flourished. Ariel ventured another quick look behind her as Ludik caught the arch of fire straight in his chest.

Ariel smashed into a heap of guards clogging the path. She fell and Brinn fell over her. A pair of hands, she could not tell whose, helped them up as the few men still running from the spreading white blanket crashed against them, knocking the air out of her lungs and squeezing her against the clumping crowd. Mathew pushed and shoved through the mass of bodies and armor, toward the closing ice. What was he doing? He pressed on until he squeezed himself free and flooded the allure with fire.

Brinn pushed Ariel roughly to the side and turned, elbowing Ariel in the nose. "Stop that, you over-proofed dough! Ludik has enough fire to deal with already!"

Ariel only heard her because Brinn's mouth was so close to her ear that she winced with pain. Brinn was right. More fire could throw Ludik over the edge of what he could handle. But would they freeze if Mathew didn't at least give it a shot? What a catch-22 they were in. How often had she come so close to dying in the last month? How could anyone be sane after this? Panic began to settle as more seconds passed between agonizing short breaths. Light gathered around her. The thundering sound came muffled now, distant like a jet fighter flying away from her at supersonic speeds.

Miranda dropped her spell. For a moment, it was like the sun had set. Instant and abrupt, even though the sunset was still hours away. The men slacked, and Ariel's lungs drank the air greedily. She choked on it and coughed. Brinn was at her side wincing and gasping for air too. Ariel blinked and rubbed her eyes as they adjusted back to normality. The ice had stopped barely a meter away. No one could've been sure if merely touching it was a death sentence, but she was thrilled they didn't have to find out.

The ice began to melt away immediately, like the first snows magically disappearing upon contact with the pavement. The guards regained their composure, returning to their battle positions. Oddik helped her and Brinn in the process. He said something, but her ringing ears were nearly useless when something else caught her attention.

Hotcup was—

"Ben fell from the saddle," Brinn shouted.

Ben's body hung loose; one leg bent in ways a leg shouldn't bend—foot stuck on the stirrup. Ben nearly hit a crenel as they flew over the allure and glided to a wide square not far from where they were.

Mathew ran to Ludik.

Brinn pushed Ariel to the side and nearly fell on the slippery stone as she rushed to her friend. Ariel took a moment to observe the battlefield. Lines of darkness, like chasms, scarred the land. A thick black gauge circled the dirt and grass across the moat and up the wall to where Ludik had been standing. And the advancing army was advancing no more.

"They retreat!" announced a soldier.

She found the duke as he inspected the receding waves of men. He panted, sweat dribbling down his face. His eyes were pale and distant. "We are but mere men cornered like mice in a battle among gods. May the Bastard pity us."

"Mink," she said.

He eyed her, a wisp of anger in his stare that quickly faded.

"Yeah, that's it. Yer grace." Ariel bowed clumsily.

The duke scoffed at her and then inspected his men. They cheered, patting each other on the backs, grins slashed on their faces. "They don't understand," he said. "This has just begun."

The sounds still came muffled. Ariel stuffed a finger in her ear and wiggled it as if trying to get water out after jumping in a pool but to no avail. At least she could still hear.

Armrar Katunik turned to gaze at the boy. Ludik lay down on the wet stone, drained and in serious pain. Ariel felt the blood drain from her head. *Stupid!* She'd gone to check on the duke instead of rushing to Ludik. The first thing she should have done was see if the boy was breathing and had a pulse. She was probably the only person on the planet who knew C.P.R. Why was she always this dumb? Last time, the boy had nearly died. How could she have forgotten about it so easily? She scolded herself mentally for it. Brinn and Mathew were at Ludik's side, and—

The lad was breathing, and to Ariel's surprise, he was also awake.

"Oh, thank God," she mumbled, rubbing her forehead.

"You there," the duke called to a guard near him. "Find out how Benerik and the aramaz are doing. Quickly."

"Yes, sire," the guard said and rushed away.

"I'll eat chilies and crap firecrackers," Mathew said as Ariel and Katunik approached. "That was insane."

"I think I get it now," Ludik said. "It's supposed to hurt. It has to hurt." He seemed feverish, his skin gummy and pale. "She's too strong."

Ariel knelt by his side and raised a hand to shut Brinn up before she started making demands. "I'm doing it," Ariel said, touching his chest with her light.

"Keep it," Ludik said. "Her power was mostly light. It affects me differently somehow. How is Ben?"

"Have some light anyway," Ariel said. "Hotcup seemed fine, but Ben..." her words trailed off like she could not tell them, "ah dinnae ken."

Brinn clutched Ludik in a tight hug, nearly twisting Ariel's hand in the process, forcing her to pull away. "I'm going with you. I'm going with you to the mountain."

It was almost comical how he tried to hug her back and still craned his head over her shoulders to read Half's stupid letter. Weirdly enough, the thing was still intact, and so were Ludik's clothes. Odd. "Not this time," Ludik said in such a way it left no room for doubt. "I know why she fears him. I saw her power drain over the shatter."

Well, that was an interesting thing to say. Everyone around leaned in to listen.

"There's a pull." Ludik looked over the rugged edge of the rock wall. "It's out there. So powerful it tugs on the fabric of the world, and it does not like her."

Katunik glanced at the Shatter and nodded to himself. "This is our chance then. If Hotcup can fly, you must leave now."

The guard Katunik had sent for news returned. "Sire, the aramaz doesn't seem severely injured. But the assassin's barely alive. They can't get him off the beast's saddle. Lourik tried, and, well, we think he's alive, but no one dares touch him."

"Thank you, Urrik," Katunik said. "Master Ludik, the time has come. You must fly the aramaz."

"Won't they notice the big blue bird not hanging around the city anymore?" Mathew asked. "I would think something's up if he suddenly disappeared."

An idea popped into Ariel's mind. "We can use this to our advantage."

"How so?" The duke seemed intrigued.

"Mathew's right. If they suspect the aramaz left the city, they'll know something's up. So, we build a decoy. A life-size replica of Hotcup and parade it around the city in plain view of our enemies. In our world, modern armies do it all the time to trick their adversary."

"Balival!" the duke bellowed.

Balival came to his side in a sprint. "Yes, sire?"

"Gather all the tailors, carpenters and artists you can find. Tell them they must build a life-size replica of the aramaz by morn."

"Sire?" Balival was perplexed. It was the first time Ariel had seen Katunik's second-in-command show anything other than calm and collectedness.

"It has to be able to move around and look alive."

Balival perplexion grew into incredulousness. He looked up as if organizing something in his head. Then he pulled the pencil perched in his ear and began to scribble furiously. He gazed at his commander one more time.

"Go, man!" the duke commanded.

"I'll see it done, your grace," said Balival and jogged away.

Ludik seemed out of it, eyes trailing the rugged edge of the shatter. "Am I a mountain?"

"What?" Ariel asked.

Ludik shook his head.

"Yeah, Lud," Mathew asked, placing a hand on Ludik's shoulder. "What're you on about?"

"I saw you fight the ice and Ariel pulling everyone away from me."

"It was just a precaution," Brinn explained.

"I know you're lying. What did I really do in Lirterin? Tell me, Ariel!"

"Listen, lad," Ariel said, laying the palm of her hand back on his chest. He had said he didn't need it, but Ariel didn't care. More couldn't hurt. "Ye did what ye had to do. Nothing more. Ye want to make this, right? Ye march up there, ye fly that glaikit bird, and ye find that mountain. It's an easy choice. Do it, or everyone dies. No more waiting around. Ben is out of this fight for good. So we're counting on ye. Leanerin's counting on ye. Two entire worlds are counting on ye." Ariel pulled the seed from her collar with her free hand and held it before Ludik's eyes. "I'm counting on ye. All my life, I've wanted to do the right thing but did not know what it was. Well, I do now. And ye do too. All yae've been through was just preparation for this moment. So who cares what yae've done before? This is yer chance—our chance—to do what's right."

"I couldn't have said it better," Brinn said.

"I think I have been hearing it all along," Ludik said, eyes glazed over the rock wall. "Aureberg. I don't understand it. Maybe Half's right, we're just worms to the mountain."

Ariel thought about it for a moment. It tumbled around her head as a grocery list would. What did it matter what the mountain thought? "Well, Ludik," she said at last, as she soaked Ludik's chest with more and more light, "if that's true, then it's certainly a very unfortunate thing."

Something changed about Ludik. First, it was like he had remembered something, and in remembering, his breath came a little easier, as if an immense weight had fallen off his shoulders. "Things are things," he whispered.

"What does that mean?"

"It's just something I heard. You know, Ariel, you're not as bad as I once thought you were."

Ariel laughed—a laugh that quickly infected her friends. Yes, they were her friends. How did that happen? They were mere children, not to mention enemies not that long ago, and now they fought side by side to save worlds. Maybe battles were always like this. "Yae're not so bad yaerself, laddie."

"Help me up," Ludik said, "I have an aramaz to ride."

Chapter 64

Easy-peasy

Ludik

"What are you waiting for? Unstrap that man!" Duke Katunik commanded as he dashed next to Ben.

"Don't, sire," a man said. "Don't touch the aramaz. Lourik was sent smokin'."

"Is he alive? Why is no one tending to him?"

"Marin touched him and went stiff—fell right at his side. We don't know what to do, but everyone's still breathin', so there's some comfort in that."

I was already walking to Hotcup before anyone could ask me to. "Alright, Cups, tell me what to do," I said.

Hotcup pointed his beak to Ben's foot. Then his large orange eyes were back on me.

"Just pull him free?"

Hotcup nodded. But, somehow, I sensed the sarcasm in his eyes.

I drew in a breath and let it out slowly. Ariel's light replenished my sored soul and body. Not that I felt refreshed or anything, but I was awake and ready. I neared Ben, noting that he was indeed alive, chest going up and down, but his leg was bent as if made of rubber. I reached out slowly, every piece of me screaming not to do it. I gritted my teeth and drew even closer. Just a little more. *It may hurt, but it won't kill me,*

I thought. *It may hurt, but it won't kill me. Forget about the two unconscious persons on the floor. They're not dwinans. You'll be fine. It may hurt, but it will not kill me.*

I grimaced and closed my eyes as my hand inched forward and touched the stirrup. Nothing happened—only a slight tingle on my fingertips.

My friends, the palace's staff, and the duke all stared at me, teetering in silence.

"I'm alright," I said. Guess being a dwinan has its perks. Relieved, I knelt to get a better handle on the stirrup and was sent flying through the air in a mix of light and smoke and pain. I hit the ground rolling, but it was not like I could feel more pain at that moment. Every muscle in my body contracted at the same time. Cramps galore. "Arrrgggg," I said. "Urghh."

Brinn came to my side, but her hands kept close to her chest. I had pocketed the letter but found, "Lud! Are you alright?" on her lips.

"Numb," I grunted. The numbness morphed into tiny worms wringing inside my flesh. It was not something I was eager to try again. But I was right. It didn't kill me. It didn't even knock me unconscious.

Ariel came from behind Brinn and said something. They argued a little, Brinn's hands shuffling about, Ariel pointing at my boots. I had no idea what they were saying and sure kept pointing at my boots a lot while everyone else looked at my hair.

Brinn began to sign, "The soles of your boots. They, I don't know the word she used—they keep the lightning from passing through."

"What does that mean?"

"I don't know," Brinn signed, and her hands shot over her head before she contained them again. "She says that as long as you don't touch anything else, you should be alright."

Ariel went over to Hotcup's unwilling victims and touched them cautiously. She then signaled the remaining staff that they were clear to approach. People flocked to the unconscious victims and carried them on stretchers to a building serving as a forward infirmary.

I got back on my feet, some muscles still spasming involuntarily but nothing I couldn't manage. Ben needed to be cleared from that saddle, the longer he stood there, the worse it would get, and he had been in that position for too long already.

I balled my fists and walked straight back to Hotcup. "Don't touch anything else," I muttered. "Don't touch," I grabbed Ben's foot and pulled, but it was stuck, "anything else." I pulled it up a little to gain some slack on the stirrup and twisted it free. I felt something crack inside his leg as I twisted his foot, and it came loose. Hotcup turned to look at his friend lying on his back as I crouched over Ben and touched his chest. I wanted to feel his breathing and heartbeat, but instead, I got zapped and flung through the air again.

I wheezed like I had been punched in the stomach by a battering ram.

Ariel was above me again. She was saying something as I struggled to breathe. I took out the letter and read: "Don't touch anything. How hard can that be?"

"Thanks," I grunted, "for the advice."

"This is much more amusing than I thought it would be," Mathew said. "It's like watching a live cartoon."

"Yae're clear to touch Benerik," Ariel said to the staff standing by. "Ludik discharged him already."

Omorik, the doctor, neared Ben and gently touched his wrist. You could plainly see the relief in his eyes as he let out the breath he'd been holding. "Steady pulse. Alright, bring a stretcher. Let's get him inside."

Katunik approached me as the doctor ushered Benerik to the infirmary. "I asked the staff to prepare supplies for your trip. Not much. I know Benerik always travels light. Camping gear, water, and some dried food. They'll bring it to you shortly. Master Doller, please relinquish your medication to the doctors."

"I, *uh*," Mathew said, scratching his head. "Ben has more than enough—"

Brinn shot him a glare so intense the hair on my arms prickled.

"Alright!" Mathew pouted. "But I'm keeping some."

"And you'll explain what they are for?"

"Yes," he said.

"That's a bonnie wee lad," Ariel added.

"Master Ludik," Duke Katunik continued. "I would gladly give all the time you need to get to know the aramaz, but time, as you know, is of some scarcity."

I nodded and ran a hand through my hair noting only then how it stood on end. What a weird power this was. "Alright, Hotcup, you know what's happening, right?"

Hotcup nodded, but his eyes were on his friend being carried inside.

"He's going to be alright," I said, although I could not know for sure. But Benerik had proven rather resilient. "Let's do it for him."

Hotcup turned his massive head and stared right into my eyes. It was the first time I'd seen him from that angle, and boy, was he a scary animal. I almost whimpered. Who am I kidding? I did whimper. His big orange eyes, over his massive sharp beak. Power or no power, he could snap me in half before I could say 'whisky' if he wanted to.

"Ready to fly over the shattered mountains and face the northern death?"

"Are you?" his eyes replied. Don't ask me how I know this, but trust me, that's what they said. Or maybe I was just projecting my fears on them.

I let out a long breath. "Alright. It hurts, but it won't kill me."

I gently stroke Hotcup's feathers—little sparks connected with my fingers, tingling and ticklish and warm to the touch. In the current, I felt something, emotions, sadness, and concern. They raged about the filaments of light connecting us. "He'll be alright," I said again.

Unconvinced, he said. It wasn't a word. Not really, more of a feeling. Was this how he and Ben talked?

Annoyance.

"I'm sorry," I said, examining the saddle up close. It wasn't like an ekkuh's saddle at all. It had handles everywhere, was long enough to squeeze one's chest against, and wasn't smooth. It was a little like touching a cheese grater. I probably required special pants to ride it. It would chafe the fabric of my trousers along with the skin on my inner thighs. "Are these pants enough?"

Amusement.

"I'll assume that's a no." I turned to the duke.

More people had gathered around him to watch the show. *Hey, let's watch the deaf boy die or something.* People flocked in, but, fortunately, kept their distance. Still, I didn't enjoy the attention at all. Then again, how could I argue? Their survival depended on my success, and after that first day of hostilities, tensions were high, to say the least.

I ignored them as best as possible and stammered when I finally addressed the duke. "I think I'll need a flight suit."

The duke nodded; maybe he had thought about it before because his reaction was nearly instant. He immediately motioned for a guard and gave him a command. The guard scampered away. I guess he went to find a tailor. If there were any left not working on the life-size replica of Hotcup. That's when I noticed several men drawing sketches of Hotcup. People were seriously on the clock.

"Alright, we don't need pants right now. We just need to prove that it's possible."

I placed a foot on the stirrup, grabbed a handle, and hoisted myself. I threw a leg over the seat, and there was much more contact. The tingle wasn't a tingle anymore. My whole body simmered, my teeth teetered, my hands shook, and the muscles in my back twitched. And it didn't stop there. It grew, through my thighs, my groin, and my butt as my skin turned into one single itch. It was hot and cold or something else entirely. One thing was for sure: it was impossibly uncomfortable. I couldn't take it any longer and had to dismount. I jumped off, landing with a hand on the ground. The discharge was so intense, I passed out for a couple of minutes.

I shivered on the ground for a while, just collecting myself as I regained consciousness, squeezing breaths in, a gasp at a time. Was that going to happen every single time? Ben had warned me it wasn't gonna be easy. What did I expect? Maybe if I used my power more actively. It was obvious that I was always using a little of my ability passively, but to ride the aramaz, maybe I had to be in full control. Whatever that meant. Ariel didn't want to tell me the truth, but I knew. Of course, I knew. Even though my brain worked overtime to keep that notion as abstract as possible, it didn't make it less true. I was a killer. I'd killed Era, too, and who knows how many in Lirterin. I knew it, yet it was as if the story belonged to someone else, and I was all too glad to keep it that way.

Ariel came to my side and motioned for me to produce the letter. "Take it easy. I know time is short, but take it easy."

"I think I have to use my power. My full power. But what if I hurt Hotcup?"

Ariel blinked, pressed her eyes shut and sucked air between her teeth. "If ye feel like yae're losing control, jump out."

"Easy for you to say. It hurts like being roasted in a kiln and then ground in a mill." But I found myself nodding. It just had to be done.

"I'm here if things get out of hand. Do ye need light?"

I shook my head.

"Alright then, gaun' yaerself," she said and walked back to the gawking crowd.

Pocketing the letter, I got ready to try again. I would love to tell you that I jumped on Hotcup and flew right out of there, but as the afternoon flew by in a soup of frustration, pain, and lightning, that seemed rather unlikely.

Frustration, Hotcup said right before I exited his saddle, doing my best to land on my feet without touching the ground. Often, my legs wobbled, as if I had been sitting on them for too long, lost strength, made me stumble and get zapped.

"I'm frustrated too."

Hotcup shook his head no.

"Oh, you're frustrated *with* me?"

He gave a little, *humpff*. It was definitely a *humpff*.

I had to tap into my power and use it. Hotcup understood that and was still willing to do it. He barely knew me and was putting his life in my hands. I did my best to acclimate to the pain, but it wasn't working. And as the first stars appeared in the sky, that became painfully obvious. I had to stop being afraid. Easier said than done.

There was talk between the duke and the others of whether it was best to cover the flashes with a large tarp or move the training inside. But where would they find so much tarp and sew it together in time, plus where would we find a room large enough to contain Hotcup?

Ariel came to my side and soaked my chest with light. If only I could take her with me. But that wouldn't work. We'd run through her reserves quickly, and she might not even be able to touch the aramaz, even if we managed to link. There were too many unknowns. Brinn came to Ariel's side.

"I know you're afraid of using your power, but I don't see any other choice. Do it, or I'll have to hit you in the head really hard."

"You're very kind."

"I do my best," Brinn said.

"She's right, ye know?" Ariel said. "Yae're being a wee bit too careful."

"Come on!" Mathew said from a safe distance. "This should be easy-peasy! What's the hold-up?"

"Are you sure you're ready for this?" I asked Hotcup.

Hotcup rolled his eyes.

"Oh, shut up. You think this is so easy. Well, it isn't. Do you want to see it? The power you were all running away from just a few hours ago? Is that what you want?" I climbed back on the saddle. "Be ready to shake me off, you hear," I said as the seething in my bottom began.

I clutched the handles tightly as the pain began its familiar growth. I clenched my teeth, drew in a shuddering breath, and reached into the ocean of anger, pain, and sorrow within, and the blue answered. This was it. My vision tunneled, the blackness involved me, and the colors shifted, inverted, flowing like flames and liquids, slushing and dancing, unquiet and untangled.

Hotcup morphed into a mesh of shimmering tendrils of light. The tendrils moved up through my limbs and took residence in me. *Don't breathe,* said a deep rumbling voice. *Things are things.*

I'm coming for you, you murderous monster.

Things are things.

The lightning filaments plowed through me, wild and careless. They wanted a link. They beseeched me for a destination and craved to be grounded in something. Not just something; they wanted the heart of a rider. With each beat of my heart, I pulled it in like rolling yarn into a ball inside my chest. A tug, a pull and my spine yanked, and my heart was lightning.

I took a tentative breath as my vision returned to normal colors. I sat on the saddle. The blue light in me faded, but the link had been established and the link held. I knew because I gravitated toward Hotcup, an invisible chain connecting our souls.

Joy.

"We did it," I said. "We did it!" I began to laugh. What a relief it was, I couldn't believe it. I didn't want to use my power because I was too afraid to hurt Hotcup, and with good reason. But that was all it took.

People clapped while the duke hurriedly told them to quit it, fearing the enemy could hear.

Brinn approached, holding a weird set of dark blue trousers reinforced on the inner thighs with rough black leather and a thick blue jacket with leather straps sewn across it.

"They didn't have time to make you one, so they tightened Ben's suit. He also broke all the straps, except the one around the waist, they sewed the others, but they also said they had no idea if they would hold." Boy, those tailors were having the most challenging day of their lives.

"Toss them over here; I don't dare dismount."

Brinn tossed the trousers. It was tricky to get my boots off, then my trousers, but I managed, then I put on the new trousers and slipped back into the boots. It certainly beat the alternative.

She tossed me the jacket next. It was heavy, but I was pleased they'd thought of it as I put it on. It was soft and cozy and warm. My power could keep me alive in the extreme cold, but it sure was nice to have some comfort.

Ariel approached with two large bags. "Supplies. I don't think this food will last ye more than four days, though. I don't know how much the bird eats, but judging by his size, it can't be just a wee bit. There's some water, some blankets, and a flint. I ran through it. It's the bare minimum."

I nodded. "It'll have to do." I busied myself, tying the bags to the saddle as best as possible. Once satisfied with my work, I fumbled about the straps to find which were still in good shape. I fixed the one around the waist first, except there were no punch holes for the buckle's prong to go through that fit my size.

"I need something to punch a hole here," I said as I fumbled with the buckle.

Ariel produced a dagger from her sleeve as Duke Katunik approached with Mathew at his side and tossed it to me.

The duke eyed the slim dagger and then Ariel. "I had noticed something was missing from my collection."

She shrugged. "I didn't know ye, and I was out of light. Ye really shouldn't keep so many weapons on display in meeting rooms. If anything, this is yer fault."

The duke made no effort to rebuke her argument as I tried to pierce a hole in the strap. The leather was rather tough to punch through, but I managed it with some twisting and wiggling. It looked more like a slash than a hole, but it would have to do. I had no intentions of making any complex maneuvers anyway, and it was best to get going as soon as possible. Many of the remaining straps suffered from the same problem, so it took some time to punch all the holes I needed. I tested it. The straps made my movements harder, as if stuck in a spider web, but they served their purpose well.

I held the dagger back out to Ariel.

"Ye can just drop it on the ground."

"Oh yeah, right."

Katunik watched his dagger clatter on the stone pavement, gave Ariel the side-eye, then turned his attention to me. "Take the stairs to the outpost at the top of Shatter's edge. Keep Hotcup out of sight. Do not fly until you're over the rock edge. May the Light be with you and the Bastard guide you. And any other gods that may be, may they help you as well."

"Yeah," Mathew said. "Godspeed. We'll hold the line until you get back."

I didn't know what to say. It somehow felt like a farewell, but it couldn't be one. The implication was unthinkable. "I'll be right back," I said, noting how lame it sounded, so I compensated with a smile I could only hope exuded a confidence I did not feel.

"Remember what I told ye," Ariel said. "Get what ye need; save yer emotions for later. There will always be another time."

I wanted to say, 'I'll try,' but that sounded peevish at best, so I nodded instead.

Brinn stared at me, her eyes stern. "To the ordeal with that. Take everything from it." And that, folks, is why Brinn should always be the one speaking. I grinned at her.

"Are you ready, Hotcup?"

Excitement. And before we prolonged our awkward goodbyes, Hotcup dashed forward up the streets at a speed I was not ready for and nearly broke my neck with the whiplash. I reached for the handles, even though the straps held me in place. We were doing this. I was going to face the mountain: the monster that murdered my village, my father, and my mother.

Hotcup sprinted through the streets, forcing people to jump out of the way as the wind battered my face. Minutes later, we passed the palace and climbed further up the city, zooming across the streets until we met the steep flights of stairs climbing up the rock wall. I held on tightly, afraid to fall back, despite the jacket straps that I hoped I had tightened well. I glanced behind as the city shrank at an abnormal rate. We jumped over the edge of the shatter, startling the group of guards at the outpost who ducked for cover. Hotcup jumped from boulder to boulder as if he did it every morning, then stretched his wings and took to the air.

Hotcup kept close to the ground so he wouldn't be seen over the edge while I, well, I was flying. I, the deaf orphan and master distiller apprentice, flew across the night on the back of an aramaz just like the stories I used to read.

I'm coming, Aureberg. It took me long enough, but I'm coming.

Chapter 65

Auld Lang Syne

Ariel

In all fairness, it was a beautiful day, despite the storm brewing west and that stupid army camped just outside. Still, Ariel was grateful for two things. One was the sun, bathing her in its power. The more sun there was, the better off they would be once the army advanced. And two, the army hadn't advanced.

"Why are they waiting?" the duke asked, observing the enemy.

Ariel shrugged.

"Maybe they're afraid of your fake bird," Mathew suggested. Mathew had spent the night and day contemplating his fingertips and sighing heavily. His eyes had lost most of the shine Ariel had seen when he was her main obstacle. They hadn't left each other's sides since Ludik's departure or even before that—since she saved his life in Algirin. "Where is Brinn anyway?" he asked. "She always makes a grave situation seem banal. She's like a walkin' Bob Marley song."

"She's off to bake bread with that ginger lad," Ariel replied.

"At least she has something to keep her busy."

"I don't like it," Balival said, resting a pencil back on his ear. "They're waiting for something."

"It's too sunny," Ariel said. "Miranda knows I could slash her army like a lawn mower. Ye see those clouds. I'm pretty sure that's Miranda's doing. I don't know how, but she's summoning a storm."

"Heavy rain would make my fire less effective, too," Mathew said while filing his fingernails, even though they were more than spotless.

The Duke of Alturin stared at the clouds for a long time. "Won't the storm affect her as well?"

"Only her leoht and fyr abilities," Mathew said before blowing on his fingers. "She can still fling rocks. Probably shower us with lightning until we're Kentucky fried chicken."

"So can Ben," Katunik said.

"Ben is out cold."

"But she doesn't know that," Ariel said.

"Master Doller's right," Balival said. "We shouldn't fall prey to false assumptions. She must have seen Benerik dangling off the aramaz. The decoy only assures her Ludik hasn't left the city yet. Nothing more."

Duke Katunik paced around the turret, hands clasped behind his back. "When the storm hits, she'll resume the bombardment."

"If I were her," Ariel said, "I would let the army pull all the work for a while. Weaken us before she joins the fray. She knows Ludik well enough. If she doesn't interfere, there's a good chance we won't intervene either. Cloudy skies and heavy rain will hamper our power, and with Ben out, this storm evens the battlefield."

"There goes our advantage," Katunik said and turned to Balival. "What do you think?"

"It's not all bad." Balival pulled his pen from his ear and underlined something in his notepad. "Heavy rain will make it harder for Munika's men to climb the wall."

"I need to get some air," Mathew said, leaving the room.

"I'll go after him," Ariel said and excused herself. When she got to his side, she found his eyes heavy and moist. Was he going to cry? Oh no. The thing she hated most about social interactions was consoling people.

"This world will burn, and so will mine, uh, well, ours. Because of me," he said.

Well, it serves you right, Ariel thought, but her mouth said something else. "So what are ye gonnae do about it?"

"I'll do what I can, but—"

"Exactly," Ariel said. "Don't whimper to me. Do ye think I want any of this? I also failed. I had a chance to fix this. Several, in fact, and I, too, failed. What do ye want to do? Grab a blanket and wallow in our misery?"

Mathew looked away.

Great, now I hurt his feelings. Alright, Ariel, change the subject, say something else. "Why would ye come here wearing jeans and a jean jacket?"

"What? Because they're too modern? You're wearing a bright yellow jacket, for Christ's sake."

"It's tweed, and I'll have ye know it's bespoke. There aren't that many tweed jackets with hoods. Worth every penny. Unlike yer H&M clothes, these are durable and actually protect me from the elements."

"Hey, these are Levis."

"Yae're wearing Vans. Were ye expecting to skateboard much around here?"

Mathew laughed. "Hey, what's wrong with Vans? I like them; they're durable and comfortable."

"That's because ye were so busy trying to look cool that ye probably never tried anything else."

"Ah! But I do look cool!"

Ariel sucked air through her teeth. "It's a bit too nineties for my taste."

By nightfall, clouds had taken hold of the sky, and soldiers took shifts sleeping along the allure.

Mathew seethed. "How can these people sleep?"

"They're soldiers. They've trained for this." Ariel looked up at the starless sky, threatening to rain cats and dogs.

"I guess nothing's happening, but still, c'mon."

"I wouldn't say nothing's happening. Things have worsened severely."

"You're such a ray of sunshine."

"Well, ye can always march up there and restart the fight right now. I'll wait here."

"Will you come with me?"

"Do ye have selective hearing or something? I just said I'd wait here. Although, if we attack now, we'll die quicker."

"You're such a Debbie Downer sometimes."

"Noted. I'll try to smile more often."

Mathew shifted uneasily, looking back at the rock wall. "Do you think he'll make it?"

"Ludik?"

"Yeah, it all seems so slim. Our chances, I mean. Since Miranda turned on me, I've been feeling lost. And now I'm only covering up with this fake courage when in reality, I'm scared shitless."

"No courage is fake courage, or all courage is fake."

"How do you mean?"

Ariel took her seed from under her collar and observed it. "To be courageous, ye first need to be afraid. If yae're not afraid, then there's no use for courage. To be in danger, to be *scared shitless* and still do what needs to be done, that's courage. It's not an emotion. It's an act. A deliberate act that goes against our most primal instincts."

Mathew pondered about it. "Are you sure?"

"If I weren't, then being brave would be as remarkable a thing as turning on the telly."

Mathew nodded to himself more than to her. "Never thought about it that way."

"That's because ye watch too many American movies."

Mathew chuckled. "Guilty as charged."

Ariel lay a hand on his shoulder. "I'm crappin' me pants, too."

Mathew regarded her, nodding slightly, then asked, "So what's with the seed? What's the story behind it?"

No one had ever asked her that. At first, the shock was like a bullet ripping through her heart. Then it became something else, a void that beseeched filling. "What are yer parents like?" Ariel asked, avoiding the topic.

"They're fine, I guess," Mathew said. "Good people, intelligent and hard-working. My dad always sends me to do menial tasks like shoveling snow in the winter or raking leaves in the fall. He says it's to build character. I don't know about that, though. Mom's sweet, and I miss her very much. She's the one who'd always pushed me to face reality as it is. Not to ignore the troubles of the world we live in. I think it's because of her that I took it upon myself to come here. And look at where it brought us."

Before she could watch him crumble under the weight of his own guilt again, Ariel stepped in. "I lost my parents when I was just a wee lass. I remember them, but the memory is so distant now they feel like an old dream. Just a mish-mash of random colors and scents. It's the scents that get to me sometimes. When I walk down the beach in Edinburgh and smell the fish and chips and sea breeze, I can almost be there with them. My dad throws me in the air while my mother reads her books while sunbathing. The water is always too cold for a swim. Dad buys me cheesy-chips, and the sky is always blue in my memories as we watch the seagulls play with the wind. Blue skies are a rare commodity in Edinburgh."

"What happened to them?"

"Car crash. I was five. I don't remember much of the following years. There was little light in my world—everything drab, mossy green, and worn-out nightgowns. I hated the orphanage. Not because of the institution itself, but because it reminded me, every damned second, that I was alone in a place built to stow orphans away."

Why was she telling him this? She wanted to stop, to ignore her past as she had done for so many years, but it kept coming. *It's this damn battle. Stirring everything in me.* Was she brave? Or was her bravery an escape, a figure she built around herself like a shield against grief? How easy it would be to run away, just like she had done all those years ago, and let the world burn for all it did to her.

No. That wasn't true. There were other little girls out there who still had their chance at a happy life. She had to, at the very least, fight for them. After all, she had just said it: there's no such a thing as fake courage.

Despite the long pause, Mathew didn't interrupt her, and before she knew it, the words poured out like an unstoppable flood. "I saw it happen. I was in the back seat, playing with this doll my maw had just bought for me, little freckles on her cheeks and blue wool for hair, while my parents checked something in the boot. We were going to see some aunt of mine. I had thrown a massive wobbly, so they had to stop and buy me that damned doll. A car swerved around the curb; its driver totally hammered. And I watched it as it crushed... I couldn't move for the longest time. Petrified. Some faceless people took me away, and I floated around from place to place for a while. Only saw my aunt once. She did not want a traumatized little girl—spoiled goods. I didn't make any friends; didn't even bother trying. Even the other orphans found me weird.

"I was twelve when I had had enough. I ran away. It was kind of easy, really. Orphanages aren't known for their security. It was a rainy day when I did, the staff ran after me, but somehow, I lost them in the woods. I had a bag with some juice boxes and crackers I had been saving. They ran out the same day. And that's when I experienced what being truly cold was. Yet, to be honest, it was the first time I felt a little alive in years. It kept me sane, somehow. So I grew wild. Hunting, foraging, stealing. Mostly stealing. Became quite the thief. Up north, in the highlands, there are plenty of holiday cottages. Some even look like castles. Plenty of well-stocked pantries to sort through.

"One summer evening, after a year or so of wilding, I noticed a distant light on a hill. There aren't any lights up there, only fog and cloudy skies. But when the skies open, they're magnificent, more stars than I could ever dare to count. That was such a night. I imagined someone camping there. Campers love to share food and are often not the kind of people who will rush you to the authorities. But the closer I got, the more obvious it became that there were no people there, only a light glowing behind a rock. Intrigued, I moved closer. Could someone have forgotten a torch? I could use a good torch. But when I looked over the rock, there was no light. Only a wee wrinkled bush. 'I must be going mad,' I thought. And I walked away, but when I glanced back, the light shone again.

"I looked back over the rock again. Nothing. Just that wee bush, mocking me. I walked back and forth a couple of times, and every time I walked away, the light would turn on. And when I got back, it vanished.

"I sat there with only the bush for company. Despite it being a bush, it was taller than any plant up in that part of the highlands. At that point, I had become a sort of expert in northern flora and had never seen a bush like that one. It was a sad sight to behold, withering and dying. Slowly but perniciously, the highland winds battered her life away. Leaves like pearls, shrunken and wrinkled, skinny twisting branches and a crooked trunk. The ugliest tree I had ever seen. 'Poor thing,' I told it, 'ye look a little like me. Broken and all alone.' The tree glowed. Faint but quick. On and off.

"I know this next part will sound absurd, but I dug it up. I took it up as a mission. I found a nice bag and a shovel and returned to the tree. I dug it up with plenty of soil to wet its roots and traveled south. The tree kept the dark nights bright with its soothing warm light. I didn't know if I had gone insane, but it felt right, ye know? We must have traveled together for months. There wasn't much communication between us. But either I was mad, or the tree had a mind. Either way, I kept going."

Mathew kept quiet, perhaps enthralled by her story, so still, he looked like a picture. Ariel sniffled and cleared her nose with the back of her hand. "We made it all the way to the Lake District. There is so much green there that it can make ye sick. Me and a stupid wee bush. I won't bother ye with our adventures along the way, and they weren't that exciting anyway. Eventually, I found a good place. It was an empty spot of land that no one seemed to be using. There was plenty of sunlight and good soil too. The tree grew faster than any tree should. Tall, green, and healthy. While life in Cumbria was a little more challenging for a sneaky burglar, I got by. Young little girls can get away with a lot of things. I stood by *her*. She was no longer just a tree. She was my true and only friend—the only person to shed light on my world since my parents left me.

"Two years later, some lavvy heid bought the land to build his house there. The tree had to go. But it had become too tall and heavy for me to dig it up again. I didn't leave her side, not even when I ran out of food or after the bulldozers arrived. The construction team waited impatiently, but no man wanted to be the one to remove a little girl from the plot by force. And I stood there defiant, hungry, and thirsty. I'd rather die than lose my only friend. Police and Child Services arrived soon after and made quick work of me. A man with a chainsaw stepped in. For him it was just a job, while for me, it was like watching my family being murdered a second time. 'Ye can't! Ye cannae kill her! She is my best friend, and I'm taking care of her. Please, please, I beg of ye. Don't kill her.' I bit the Child Service lady's hand and broke free. I lunged at my little bush and hugged her tightly. 'I'm so sorry. I'm sorry!' I bawled and screamed and screeched until my voice went out and my tears ran dry. The men, shaken by the spectacle, waited, but the lady from Child Services regained her composure and headed toward me.

"'I'm so sorry,' I said, and in response, my little bush shimmered with pure white light. A branch grew down and hung in front of me, and a tear of light dropped at its end. *Take it,* the light seemed to whisper. I plucked it gently, and the light formed a little shard of wood in my hand. The lady, the workers and the police officers took a step back, some taking their yellow hard hats in front of their chests.

"*Take it,* the light said again, and I, too, began to glow. I was warm and refreshed as if I had never gone on a hunger strike. I clutched her fiercely. It took the lady and two other men to pry me off, legs kicking them as hard as I could. They finally yanked me away, hands scraped and bleeding. I guess they blamed the event on their imaginations or a reflection of sunlight from a mirror or glass somewhere in the distance.

"And they cut my friend down."

Ariel took a moment to regain her wits, her story draining her as if it were happening again. "I was empty and miserable for days to come and back in some institution—on the float again. Then, on a dark night, while the rain battered against the window, its glass melting with age and the wood frame flaking and splintering, I began remembering things. Things that weren't mine to remember. Stories of light and darkness and stillness. Of hope and lack thereof. Of another world and of the roots connecting us. My little bush gave me the gift of her life's memories. I held on to that little shard, not knowing what to do with it. At first, I thought it was something to remember her by, but memories made it clear, it's a seed. She entrusted me with her future and bequeathed her power to protect it. After that night, I never had to endure another moment of darkness."

Mathew let out a long breath, and after a lingering moment of silence, he said, "Bloody crap on a cracker. I was not prepared for that."

It was funny watching him squirm. It was the first time she had ever shared her story. And despite its intrinsic anguish, Ariel felt good about it. Not like she was relieved, or a weight had fallen off her shoulders; no, the weight was still there, just a little easier to lift, and mirth took over her. She smiled at first, then snorted before laughter came.

"Hmm, hmm." Mathew puffed and made some clicking noises with his tongue. "That's about the saddest story I have ever heard. Why are you laughing?"

"I honestly don't know." She laughed some more. Oh, it was good to laugh.

Mathew smiled at her, and soon, he was laughing too.

When they quieted down, Ariel glanced behind her at the looming shadow of the Shatter—a reminder of what was to come if they failed. "Ye asked me if Ludik will make it. I know he will."

"What makes you so sure?"

Ariel smiled softly. "He and I aren't so different. Stubborn as they come. And if I learnt anything, anything at all, is that when it gets darkest, there is only room left for light."

Chapter 66

Long Hours

Ludik

Lightning flared around us as Hotcup picked up even more speed. Boy, did we fly fast. I didn't even know such speeds were possible. The wind battering my face made breathing a chore, like inhaling soup.

Hotcup wasn't going to relent. I just had to learn to trust him. I mean, he should know what he was doing, right? I regretted not having spent a little extra time to make proper holes in the straps. What if they tore? I mean, there were tailors everywhere. One of them ought to have a hole puncher with him and be able to bring it to me in a matter of minutes. But no, I had to leave immediately.

I tried to distract myself from the vertiginous speed at which we traveled with the view below. It was dead. A complete barren wasteland of canyons, rubble and shards of stones protruding like broken knives, illuminated only by the moon and Hotcup's flashes.

Despite my tense muscles, every time I tried to relax, the wind threatened to scoop me up from the saddle and toss me into the empty sky below and a less-than-pleasant death. Well, at least it would be quick.

Morning arrived in a heap of blinding glory. Crevasses creased the endless stone in crisscrossing patterns dotted by patches of snow and ice. How far had we traveled?

Interest.

"What?"

The horizon shot upward as the blood drained from my head and air from my lungs. My hands slipped from the handles, and for a moment, I wasn't touching anything, held only by the leather straps while the broken ones flapped about. The ground sped up toward us. Was I weightless? I had never experienced anything like that. Then I crashed onto the saddle like I had jumped from a roof onto it. It knocked the little air I had managed to suck right out of me, and my groin ached like I had been kicked there by an angry troll. Hotcup turned in a circle, pressing me further into the saddle, and my vision funneled. But something in the ground below kept me awake.

In a swift movement, Hotcup stabilized. *There.* But he needn't point it out. It was impossible to miss—a gauge in the land, deep and wide. Immensely wide.

Interest.

And it was. Clear as the day itself, something colossal had dragged over the surface of the Shatter leveling it.

"That's it. That's the mountain's trail! Follow it."

Relax.

"What?"

Tired. Relax.

"What? You've made me fight for every breath, and now you want to stop?"

There was no arguing with him. Hotcup veered downward again as my inners veered upward, then circled a few of the giant stone daggers jutting from the earth until he felt, *confident.* I didn't know what he meant, but it became clear when he made a sharp left and plunged somewhere, I guess. All the blood in my body rushed down, bloating my legs and hanging there for a split second, numbing my toes before climbing through my belly and chest, exploding in my head.

We landed in a fury of lightning and wing strokes. I jumped out, but belts pulled me back. I fought with the buckles as my stomach convulsed. I was going to be sick. I pulled free, fell onto the cold stone and got zapped. I was flung a couple of yards away, crashed against a clump of ice, landed on my face, and finally puked. I had found a whole new level of pain and wished for the Bastard to just kill me and be done with it.

"You can't..." I tried to say while on my elbows, emptying whatever was left in my stomach. I flopped on my back, breathing. Nothing more, just breathing for a while. I needed to breathe.

Hotcup seemed excited, turning his head almost a half-circle behind him, his beak opening at the sight of jerky.

"In a minute," I said, collecting my breath, my thoughts, and everything else. "In a minute."

After a lot more than a minute, I managed to sit up, and I was reasonably sure I wouldn't vomit again. Reasonably. Wobbly, as if the ground under me was moving, I reached for the bags tied to the saddle. "Urgh," I grunted. "I'll have to touch you to reach the bags. Then I'll have to either stand or get zapped again. I don't think I can sit back in the saddle just yet."

Hotcup's eyes glittered with amusement and cawed or something in delight.

"It's not funny," I protested.

Hotcup ruffled his feather and bobbed his head. That ordealing bird was laughing at me.

"At least someone's enjoying this." I took a deep breath and touched Hotcup. The familiar tingle itched on my fingertips. I unstrapped a bag and tossed him some jerky. I decided to stand and just drink some water, unwilling to ingest anything solid yet.

I paced around, careful not to touch the ground or get too close to the boulders surrounding us. Hotcup ate his food, rolled on his back and closed his eyes. Was he going to sleep?

"Hey," I said. "This is no time to sleep."

He opened one eye and closed it back again. I couldn't believe it.

"So that's how it's going to be, *huh*?" I looked around. Just broken earth and shards. Not a single bit of moss, lichen, not even a little bug of some kind. Nothing other than bare rock and ice. I couldn't sleep; I mean, where would I lay? I couldn't sleep on my stomach sprawled on that saddle. No way. But if I touched the ground, another shock would ensue. I didn't want that either.

"Wake up, you silly bird," I said. "We need to talk. You can't maneuver like that. I'm not Ben. You have to be gentler. In case you didn't notice, that was incredibly painful for—"

Hotcup extended his wing and knocked me over. I got zapped yet again.

"I hate you," I grunted.

Hotcup shrugged and relaxed completely. Well, at least now I could touch the ground without fear.

I couldn't help feeling familiar with that eerie landscape. The emptiness of it all unlocked something. Not exactly memories, but the smell, dry and old, reminiscent of the first rains on a stone pavement. It said something to me.

I couldn't sleep, of course. How could I? And, I mean, who would? Well, other than that sadist giant bird sleeping as if he had no responsibilities whatsoever.

It took hours, but I finally managed to close my eyes. Might as well rest for a little while. I wasn't going anywhere without that stubborn bird. And who knows what we would find at the end of that trail? Well, we would find the mountain, of course, but what would that imply?

The ground thumped. What now? I lay on my side and opened my eyes. Hotcup's large orange eyes stared right back at me.

"Go away," I said. "I finally shut my eyes."

Hotcup stretched his legs, wings, back and finally, his neck from side to side and began tapping furiously again.

"I hate you so much," I mumbled. "Why do you get to rest, and I don't?"

He motioned with his head toward the saddle.

I let out a sigh. There was no point in arguing. I got up, packed my stuff and the food he didn't eat, and retied it to the saddle. I climbed onto the saddle and prepared to relearn how to breathe. Pain and sorrow waited for me with open arms, ready to torture me into a dwinan. I tapped into them, and blue rose within. Vision blurred, and the colors faded into exotic shades.

The mountain was in front of me. Colossal. Powerful. Unyielding. *Things are things,* it said in a voice as deep as the earth itself.

I began to tremble. It knew we were coming. Of course, it knew. It always found me when I used my power.

Wait! He always found me! Oh, how did I not think of it sooner? I asked. Maybe he could just tell me now, and I could get back to my friends. Maybe this whole trip was a waste of time. "Aureberg! How do I defeat Miranda?"

What was cannot be again.

"Tell me!" I tried again and waited for it to continue. "You stupid monster. If you can't help me, I will kill you!"

Things are things.

Was this journey even worth it? I took deep breaths to calm my nerves and stabilize my power. The monochromatic color of the Shatter settled around me.

Hotcup twisted his neck to look at me. "I'm alright, Cups," I said, patting his neck, and strapped myself in. "Okay, I'm ready."

Sparks flickered in every direction as Hotcup opened his mighty wings, and three strokes later, we were airborne. For better or for worse, it wouldn't be long now.

Chapter 67

Toe Thief

Ariel

Despite the arrows, laser beams, floods of fire, boiling water, flying rocks, and the looming promise of death, the attackers crashed against the wall and hoisted their long ladders. They leaned them against the wall and climbed, only to be greeted by eager spears at the top. The heavy rain flooded the moat, but the marching men made quick work of it with hundreds of portable bridges.

Munika's army wore armor similar to the ones she'd seen in Lirterin, hardwood plates covered in a thick fabric. It vaguely reminded Ariel of Roman soldiers but browner. Resistant against heat and not too shabby against direct melee blows—the thick wood plates would stop an arrow. There was a lot of wood in that army, she realized. Any other day, it was probably the best choice of armor, but the heavy rain soaked the fabric and made their movements sluggish.

On her side, men, women, and even children ran up and down the wall and its access ramps resupplying the Alturin Guard with quivers of arrows, bags of water, and wood for the fires while a human cord delivered an endless supply of rocks to cast on the enemy—a well-organized bedlam. And, somehow, it all happened much slower than Ariel had ever imagined.

Soldiers weren't dying by the hundreds, and even the men climbing the ladders weren't in a hurry to jump over the merlons. No, most of the attacking force huddled, hugging the wall, shields raised, protecting them against arrow fire and falling rocks. Horns with different rhythms sounded, and every time they did, the army shifted like one gigantic organism.

"What are you waiting for?" Mathew asked as he poured fire down the wall. "Damn, their armor is tough."

"We're killing people," Ariel said numbly. She'd thought she was ready, but it's one thing knowing something will happen, and another being in it.

"This is no time for softness. If they get over the wall, it's over," Mathew said. "I know what you're thinking. That all of this is inhumane, but the simple truth is that it's either them or us."

Ariel looked away and shot a laser bolt. She knew she had hit something—someone—so what was the point in looking? The men were packed so tightly below, missing was an improbability.

"How did you miss that?" Mathew shouted.

Ariel was sick to her core by it all. "I'll be right back," she said. Mathew shouted something in reply, but she wasn't listening. A couple of arrows whistled by her. Enemy archers had gotten into position. A soldier in front of her screamed, an arrow stuck in his neck.

Mathew made it look so casual. How? The soldiers made it look casual, like line cooks in a busy restaurant. They were in a battle, yet it was like they were taking orders from their guests. 'Oh, would you like a quiver of arrows to the head along a side of deadly impalement? Very well, sir.' When a man died or was injured, his comrades pulled him out and carried on with their jobs. Ariel had only ever used her power for intimidation. She never even assumed there would be a situation when the sight of her cutting something in half wouldn't be enough deterrent.

She found herself entering the turret where Katunik gave his commands from relative safety. Katunik noticed her, eyes following her wobbling steps. "Lady Ariel, do you have news?"

She didn't. Why had she entered that room? She couldn't remember how she'd gotten there.

"Sire." A man entered the room running. "The forward defenses over the western bastion have fallen. The men are retreating but being harassed by spears and arrow fire."

Katunik sighed. "They're on their own. We can't..." Katunik spun on his heels and faced Ariel. "Can you shroud their escape?"

"Shroud their escape," she mumbled. That's it. Of course! That's what she could do. Help the others. She found herself nodding. Creating light drained her, but creating darkness was a different job altogether. With the help of the pouring clouds, she could darken a good deal of the wall if she wanted to. She nodded more firmly.

"Good."

"This way," the messenger called. Ariel got ready to follow him, but Katunik stopped her.

"Lady Ariel," he said. His eyes spoke what a thousand words could not. They told her he knew she wasn't firing back; he knew what kind of person she was. He did not add a measly 'we're counting on you' nor a 'give them hell,' no. Then his lingering eyes added, 'it's alright.'

She nodded again, clarity sharpening her mind. As she left the turret, she looked back at the city. The aramaz decoy from that distance was believable enough; those Alturin tailors and artists had outdone themselves. The fake aramaz spread its wings as if the situation at the wall was a tedious affair. Whoever the puppeteer was deserved a raise after this. *Everyone deserves a raise after this.*

"Lady," the soldier said, "quick now."

They sprinted along the allure, evading men as they fetched arrows, grabbed rocks, wielded long push sticks, and removed wounded or fallen soldiers out of the way. It was like sliding along an aqueduct of heavily armed and dying men.

"Where are you going?" Mathew asked as they ran past him.

"Help some men retreat from a forward fortification up west."

Mathew dropped the stream of fire he poured down the wall and followed suit. "And you weren't inviting me?"

Ariel slowed down a little to look at Mathew as he followed. Despite the fierce determination in his eyes, Ariel saw how alone he must have been feeling. These soldiers weren't his friends. Miranda abandoned him. Ludik was on a mission of his own. Brinn was baking bread—lunatic girl. And Ariel was doing her best to keep busy.

"Mathew," she said, trying to put as much meaning into her words as Katunik did with his stare, "I'm glad yae're here with me."

Mathew smiled. "You bet," he said, his usual nonchalant smugness, returning some color to his face.

Ariel had to admire the duke. Even in the face of certain doom, he held it together and had even taken a second to inspire her. Not only that, but he knew how to inspire her despite only knowing her for about a week, and he even inspired her to inspire others in turn. Maybe that's how battles are won. With charisma, and not iron fists. But what did she know about war? Until that day, her whole war experience had been based on films, documentaries, and history lessons, not any real-life experience whatsoever, and now that she had some, she was immensely glad to have kept it that way for so long.

The frantic composure that permeated the allure confounded her as they reached their destination. One of the forward forts had been overrun by enemy soldiers, and down the wall, a group of men in circular formation retreated to an empty slot at the base. Mathew pointed them out and immediately started shooting balls of fire to create some breathing room around the Alturin guards.

That section of the wall wasn't receiving as much attention as the sections near the gate. Ariel took a moment to understand the battle. She'd expected a lot more ladders. But that was not what was happening. The huddled men at the bottom of the wall, under constant fire—were they trying to cut through the wall itself? Why? That would take ages, but several groups were doing exactly that. And the fire didn't come only from above. The bastions cut the enemy line in sections, funneling them and exposing their flanks to the arrow fire.

Katunik had said at a previous battle meeting that since they had the numbers on their side, they might try to force all their resources into one section of the wall, leaving others vulnerable to ladder attacks. Which in itself was also insane. She had seen the ladders. They were tall enough for ten men to climb up at the same time. But that's not what was happening. In fact, the one thing she'd expected from a battle that was actually happening was the battering ram assault on the gate, and even that was more peculiar than what she'd envisioned. The drawbridge was raised, of course, and the moat was narrow but deep, so despite the constant fire, enemy engineers were building a bridge for the ram to get through. Absolutely insane.

"Ariel!" Mathew shouted, already fully committed to their new assignment. Ariel aimed a beam right in front of the soldiers harassing the Alturin guards.

"Wow! That's it! You must've cut the feet out of some of them," Mathew said, mouth agape.

Many of the enemy soldiers fell forward. Ariel had not intended for it to be a direct hit. She'd only wanted to create a line between them and the retreating force. *Hmm*, she mused. Killing was a problem, she didn't want that on her conscience, but incapacitating was something else entirely—as easy as kicking a burglar in the bawbag. Almost satisfying if she wasn't careful.

Laser beams escaped her fingers, one after the other; some men toppled to the side, while others hopped on one foot while grabbing the other. Mathew added his fire to the mix, and soon enough, a perimeter had been created around the men huddling under their shield roof and wall.

"How do we pull them up?" Ariel asked, but as she did, she noticed the spools of rope being rolled in. "Never mind. When ye lower the rope, I'll create a large enough shadow. Mathew, when I do so, make sure to keep a constant fire into that gap."

"Yes, boss!" Mathew said. "I think those archers over there noticed us."

Ariel examined the men below. How could Mathew tell anything apart?

Mathew pointed furiously. "There! There!"

Ariel followed his finger until she saw the bows, arrows nocked. They weren't such an easy target at that distance, but the men about to rappel up the wall would be. Ariel aimed carefully and relieved them of their toes. Does a person need toes to walk? She didn't have internet here to find out. She hadn't even bothered bringing her phone. There was no reception here, and where would she charge the damn thing?

Even Ben would most likely burn the device other than charge it. *Oh, well, better toeless than lifeless, I guess.*

"The ropes are in place," shouted the guard.

Ariel inspected the men, trying to find more archers, but after a couple of rounds of de-toeing, any man with a bow in hand felt the urgent need to replace it with something else. Ariel created a curtain of blackness around the men. Most of them made it up the wall and reported but a few casualties in their ranks—thanks to her.

The men began chanting her name. "A-ri-el! A-ri-el! A-ri-el!"

It was going rather well until someone bellowed, "All hail! Ariel Toe Thief."

And the chant continued as she and Mathew hurried back to the turret. "Toe Thief! Toe Thief! Toe Thief!"

"I know they mean well," Ariel said, a somber gloom over her frown, "but I'm not too pleased with my new nickname."

Mathew couldn't stop laughing. "Hey, you don't get to pick your callsign."

"This is why I hate people." But a part of her was proud. She wasn't a murderer. Not by choice, at least, and she wasn't a coward either. She was Ariel, Toe Thief. No, she would never like it. But that didn't mean she couldn't be proud of it.

"Where else is our assistance most needed?" she said as she barged into the forward command room. "I feel that perching over a merlon inflicting random damage isn't the best use of our abilities."

"That is certain," Balival said without taking his eyes from the table, shifting the position of several pieces on top of a map of the city.

"Then why haven't ye—"

"Because our dear duke felt it unwise to push the great powerful mages around before knowing how you'd hold in battle." Balival said it so matter-of-factly Ariel considered how he would look without toes.

Rats, I'm toe-thirsty now.

"Now that we know, I shall put you to good use," Katunik said. "Start by clearing the front gate. The siege engineers are nearly done with their bridge. It would be a shame to see their hard work go to waste, but alas, we wouldn't want to give the enemy a false impression of leniency, would we?"

She could hear the murmur coming from the generals in the room. "They're calling her Toe Thief," they said. She glanced at them but saw the absolute joy in their faces for having Ariel Toe Thief on their side and found herself nodding her approval.

"Yes, your grace," Mathew said and headed to the other side of the room where the allure led to the gate.

Ariel held Katunik's eyes for a moment, letting them talk for her. 'Thank you,' they said, and she followed her orders.

Chapter 68

Northern Death

Ludik

"How far has this mountain gone?" I knew from maps that the Shatter was large, like beyond imaginable. But it took flying over it at dramatic speeds, spaced with only a few short breaks, to even begin to comprehend exactly how large it was.

Hotcup slowed down dramatically, the cold consuming more of his energy than he could spare. That far up north, glaciers and snow covered the rugged remains of ancient mountains. It became so white it stung the eyes, with only sparse protrusions of bright blue ice, like giant gemstones, filling the emptiness. From that height, Aureberg's colossal groove remained as conspicuous as the morning sun.

Tired.

"I know, buddy. It can't be much farther. We're nearly at the edge of the world."

The day drew by, replaced by a garish glowing night. The northern lights outshone the stars and the moon, waving and dancing carelessly, reflecting their colors on the snow below. They dashed across the sky, contracted, and swept in every direction. It looked like wind, stellar wind to brighten our mood and guide our way.

Follow the lights, Laurin had told me all those years ago. And as I inspected the swirls of green, yellow, and purple, I noticed something.

They converged in the same direction. They descended from the sky together, joining on a single spot just over the horizon. Something big was out there. Something immense. "We found it."

Tired. Freezing.

I was freezing, too, I realized. Our hearts tangled, our energy flowing in and out of each other as we pumped it together; I could feel it dissipate. Our energy drained faster than cold temperatures could allow.

Cold. Unsure.

"Hotcup! Stay with me! Fly lower. We may have to land."

Sluggishly, compared with our previous hurry, Hotcup lost altitude. He didn't dive with his usual wanna-see-what-I-can-do; his breath was heavy and labored. We bumped into something, not hard but enough to stumble our flight. I looked around. We were too high to have touched the broken mountains below. We bumped again. The point where the lights converged grew, and its three peaks shone with all the colors of the rainbow.

Tired.

We jerked again. We weren't bumping into anything. It was Hotcup. He stumbled, ready to pass out. My vision blurred, and my chest added pale blue to the night. No, no, no.

Afraid.

Hotcup blacked out completely, and we fell like a brick.

"HOTCUP!" I screamed as the colors of the world shifted around me. I could see his energy now, so faint, exuding out of his feathers and streaming toward the mountain along the rivers of lights above. *It's sucking our power!*

I could barely feel his heartbeat now, his body limp. We began to spiral uncontrollably. "WAKE UP! WAKE UP!" I bellowed, but to no avail.

Hotcup tumbled and forced us into an uncontrolled spin. The force pulled me away from the saddle, increasing with each spin and each tumble. I gritted my teeth as I held on for dear life.

"WAKE UP!" I said, but the air in my lungs refused to stay still, clambering up my windpipe and out my nose and mouth before I could stop it. I clawed at the handles, but I couldn't hold a grip. We tumbled again and rolled on our backs as the straps tugged at my jacket violently.

It was difficult to judge the distance to the ground, but we didn't have much longer.

That's how easy it was for the monster to snuff us out. *What did it care for the lives of worms?* "HOTCUP! PLEASE!"

Hotcup opened his eyes, dazed and confused. He turned his neck to face me as if questioning why I had decided to hang loosely out of the saddle. Hotcup pulled his wings close. We stopped tumbling, but in exchange, we gained more speed, pushing me away from the saddle with increasing force as we barreled toward the ground. Hotcup didn't counteract the spin. He followed it, circling wider and wider.

What was he doing? The shoulder and side straps ripped from my jacket, throwing my whole weight into the waist belt. I got pulled backward, whiplashing my spine. I think I banged my head against Hotcup's tail, though it was all a painful blur as I whipped from side to side. I grunted, but I had no air to grunt with.

My arms weighed as much as an ox each as I tried to reach the waist belt. With monumental force, I grabbed it and pulled myself closer. With the bit of slack I found, I wrapped the leather band around my wrist just in time to see my slipshod hole tear apart. My body got sucked right out by the force of the wind, placing my entire weight on my wrist, breaking it, and popping my shoulder free of its socket. Blinding hot pain irradiated up my neck and across my body. And I fell through the air as Hotcup zoomed away.

I reached with my good arm for something, even though I knew I wouldn't find anything. By pure chance, I noticed how that helped stabilize my fall. I stretched my limbs as far as I could and came more or less into a stable position facing down, with my dislocated arm dangling beside me like a ribbon in the wind.

Hotcup circled before me, each cycle a little wider than the previous. And the ground grew closer. He kept circling wider, and with each circle, his wings opened a little more, and he reduced the rate at which he approached the ground. His eyes spotted me as I shot below him. The ground was mere seconds away, approaching mighty fast.

Would it hurt?

Searing pain exploded in my thighs as Hotcup dug his talons and snatched me from the air. He pulled up like a swing, swooshing upward and stalling our momentum before facing the ground again.

Hotcup raised the snow only a few yards above it and dropped me. I felt his talons leave my flesh with a sucking sensation. I must've passed momentarily after that. Hey, at least I don't remember getting zapped.

When I awoke, I still felt like I was falling. And crashing. Up and down. Up and down. The process repeated. Each jolt became increasingly more painful and heavy. My chest stuck. I needed air. I need to breathe.

Air!

I drew in a sharp breath, so fast and rough that I choked. But, oh, the air, it tasted so good. Hard against my teeth. I consumed more of it greedily, afraid that if I stopped, I'd suffocate again. Then, one by one, my ailments reached my brain. My thigh burned, my shoulder stung, my wrist prickled, and my chest, I must've broken a rib. But we were alive.

Hotcup stared at me, and once he was sure I was alive, he flopped on his side, panting.

I lay there for a long time, just breathing. Was breathing ever this good? I wanted to sleep, but even in poor conditions, I knew it to be a bad idea. I forced myself up, but my abdomen refused to cooperate. I had to roll onto my side and use my good arm to lift my torso. I came to my knees and saw the mountain. We were much closer than I'd expected. It didn't make much sense in my head, but when flying, distances get distorted that way.

I held my bruised shoulder with my good hand. *Will I have to learn to be left-handed now? Can I even? How's that the thought that comes to mind? I probably won't live long enough to heal, anyway. At least the cold stanched my bleeding thighs.*

Hotcup looked as bad as I, even without the injuries. "I still feel it. The mountain is tugging on us. You have to go." I watched the mountain again as it drank the northern lights.

Hotcup nodded. Even he was done with heroics, plus he was not a dwinan. If he stayed any longer, he would die. He looked at me and motioned to his back.

I shook my head. It felt like my brain slushed from side to side. "I can't turn back now. I'm too close. I've waited years for this."

He seemed frustrated with my answer, shaking his torso and thumping the snow with his talons. *It's pointless. You'll die here. We failed,* he was trying to say.

I understood him. I did. But I couldn't leave. Not that close. Not this close to *it*. No part of me bothered to ask, 'What will your death accomplish?'

Hotcup stumbled closer to me and touched my shoulder with his beak.

"Don't, you'll shock me."

But he didn't—*he's out of lightning.*

"Don't wait any longer, you fool. Go. Go back. Save yourself."

I saw it in his eyes, the petulant stubbornness of a child with something on his mind. There was something he wanted to do before he left, and I had to let him. Hotcup gently bit my shoulder.

"Have you done this before?" I asked.

He nodded with his enormous orange eye. I steadied myself.

It was over before I realized it. He pressed down on my legs with his massive talon and pulled my shoulder out and up with his beak until it clicked back into place. It hurt. It hurt a lot. But it was over before I could protest, and after the plethora of pain I had experienced, that one hardly registered.

Hotcup let go of me, my shoulder pulsating and whistling like an angry kettle. "Now, go. I'll find a way. I'm a dwinan, remember? I'll walk back, night and day, nonstop. I'll be alright," I said, but I had no idea what I was talking about. "Fly low. Aureberg's pull is weaker closer to the ground. I can see it."

Hotcup nodded, and three strokes of his wings later, he slid above the ground and disappeared behind a snowy hill.

I lay on my back. I knew my power would keep me alive; it preferred the lack of energy over too much of it. The lights danced before my eyes like rivers. And I felt *its* presence.

The dwinan in me painted the snow vaguely blue.

The sky... It contained so much energy! More than any river, more than Miranda. Whatever power created the light show above was unimaginable. What could possibly create that much energy? Could I reach it? I breathed in and tugged at a little tendril of green and yellow light. It curved in the sky and descended into my chest. It penetrated my skin like a warm summer morning and a motherly hug. It renewed me just like Ariel's light.

I staggered to my feet and faced the mountain. The snowy slopes, the ragged ridges, the three peaks, one slightly bent. The same picture printed on the side of my boots. "You destroyed my village!" I gritted my teeth and balled my fists. "You murdered my father." I felt replenished and radiant while hatred and wrath bubbled under my skin. "And you left my mother to die!"

The light streaming into Aureberg broke. The shimmering dancing ropes of heavenly beauty ascended back to where they belonged, and the ground trembled. Snow avalanched down Aureberg's side, and the world rumbled.

"I don't fear you."

Something lashed at me. It came from the mountain, wrapping and lifting me in the air. I didn't struggle.

The ground accelerated beneath me, and I gained altitude. Aureberg grew bigger and wider. *I do not fear you*. Energy surrounded me, pulling me, layered like an onion. I tugged at it tentatively and breathed in a little of it. It tingled like lightning, but unlike lightning, which feels hot and cold, this felt solid and liquid at the same time. Ariel was right; Aureberg's a *togian*.

I got closer and closer, high as its peaks. And before I reached them, Aureberg lowered me into a small plateau. My feet touched the smooth stone shadowed by his summit.

And there I was, face to face with the monster that had ruined my life.

Chapter 69

The Breach

Ariel

"They appear to be retreating," Balival said as he regarded the battlefield through the turret's narrow window.

Katunik made for the door, and Ariel followed with Mathew and Balival behind.

She took cover behind a crenel in case some toe-full archers were still out there. She peeked over the merlon as rain battered her face. She had grown used to it over the day—you can only get so wet. The men around them cheered and taunted the retreating army below. But something wasn't right. When Ariel imagined retreating troops, she imagined men running away in a hurry to clear the archers' range. That wasn't what she saw. It was perfectly organized, and men did not put down their shields or break their lines.

Katunik shook his head. "They've been at our wall for hours and have not made any convincing attack whatsoever."

Ariel glanced at the ram and bridge she and Mathew took down over the portcullis. *If building a bridge under fire and attacking the gate with a ram wasn't a convincing attempt, then what was?*

"They sat there under fire for hours, for what? Something's not right, Balival," the duke said.

"They were unprepared," Balival offered. "You can't move a quarter-million men in under six days and have a clear plan for victory. They may be testing our defenses. Study the weaknesses in our lines."

Duke Katunik wasn't convinced. "Does that look like a retreat to you? Or like they're getting out of the way for something else?"

"Ye think Miranda's going to try something?" Ariel asked.

Katunik leaned over the merlon to have a better look at the wall.

"Sire," Balival said, his hand lurching forward to get his commander out of enemy sight.

"Oh, relax," Katunik said, swatting Balival's hands. "No archer out there is inclined to lose his toes. And under this heavy rain, I don't think they'll be able to distinguish me from a regular soldier."

"Maybe they saw how pointless it was," Mathew said. "Those looney heads probably had enough. Heavy rain, rocks, arrows, boiling water, laser beams, and fire, and they got nowhere."

"They were mining our wall."

"But for what purpose, your grace? It's impossible to mine through or under our wall in a day."

The duke pressed his chest further into the merlon, craning his neck. "Balival."

Balival pushed a guard from the adjacent merlon and leaned in as well.

"There." Katunik pointed.

Ariel and Mathew squeezed into another merlon to have a look. There was a hole in the wall. About a meter wide, but Ariel couldn't see how deep it was.

"That's what they've been up to," Katunik shouted over the falling rain.

"At that rate, it'll be months before they pierce through," Balival said.

The army kept receding and out of range for the most part, yet they still kept their formation. Ariel understood Duke Katunik's concern. If they truly were done for the day, they would have broken formation at least.

Horns sounded in the distance.

Katunik frowned. "I don't like this. Evacuate that section of the wall."

"But sire—"

"Just do it, Balival."

Something caught Ariel's attention. A column of light descended from the clouds above. It widened dramatically, like the eye of a hurricane. Sunlight pierced through, glimmering in the wet grass, painting the falling rain in shades of gold and forming a rainbow over the enemy. Miranda was taking in light.

Ariel squinted to get a clearer view. In the center, an orb of light grew brighter, like a spotlight on a construction site. More horns blasted across the field. The mass of men began to part, leaving an empty path between Miranda and the hole they'd dug in the wall.

"She's gonna blast it," Mathew said. "That sleazy rotten bitch is gonna blast it."

"Get the men!" Katunik sputtered before he broke into a sprint. "GET THEM OUT OF THERE! GET AWAY FROM THE WALL!"

"Your grace, no—" Balival clenched his jaw in frustration and signaled for a man on the top of the turret, who sounded a horn.

"What can we do?" Ariel asked.

"We get out of the way," Mathew said. "Even Ludik had a hard time dealing with her previous blast. If she intends to blow the wall, no one's safe. She'll turn us all into those black stains you find inside an oven."

Ariel grimaced. "Thanks for the imagery."

The ground began to vibrate. In the field, Miranda's light grew brighter to the point it became blinding. Ariel shaded her eyes with her hand.

"TAKE COVER!" Mathew bellowed, but it was too late.

The ball of light shot through the field, displacing rain, soil, rocks and some unfortunate enemy soldiers who hadn't cleared the path, darting toward the wall.

To everyone except Ariel, that's what they saw. She noticed how Miranda's strike lost power quickly, dissipating and scattering almost imperceptibly over the city and the shatter, shrinking at least by half. But even half was catastrophic. The orb connected with the wall with insane speed and contracted like a beating heart before expanding, pushing the rain back like an invisible dome. The wall exploded into a million chunks of debris, flying in every direction.

The heat from the explosion lashed at Ariel's face, and the following shockwave blew her back against the turret like she was caught in a tsunami. Part of Ariel's brain was amused at the lack of noise; her ears rang, but only for a split second before everything went silent.

Chapter 70

Mountain's Hall

Ludik

A rock wall in front of me parted like someone opening the drapes. Stones and loose rubble slid down the mountainside, revealing a cave shining with an all too familiar color.

Follow your heart, and you'll find mine.

I knew that light. I knew it all too well. I entered the cave, unsure of what to expect. I didn't want to think about the implications of it. I didn't want to, but my brain had other plans. *Miranda gave her power to Mathew. A leohtre gave it to Ariel. Benerik got it from Hotcup. Where did I get it from? From whom?*

My legs wobbled as I limped across the corridor. The path upward was slippery and sinuous. The air tasted like spring water on a spring day and smelled of fresh laundry. Blue light permeated the smooth icy walls, brightened with each step until it revealed a large chamber where a sapphire crystal, large as a barrel, resembling a crooked egg, or more accurately, a heart, pulsed. The heart beat slowly, maybe a beat per minute or less.

Something old and rusty caught my eye. It lay scattered on the ground by the heart, throwing me back to the day I stole it from the refugee camp's armory and showed it to Graze.

My legs failed me, and I crumbled by the sword. My fingers titillated to the hilt, and I touched it. "I have been here before," I muttered.

Hmmm, Aureberg said in a low rumble, *Things are things.*

"You almost killed Hotcup and me."

I can see what is on the ground. Not what is not.

I gripped the sword tightly and white-knuckled and pointed it at the mountain's heart. "You murdered my family! Why?"

So many things to be, and yet this thing wants power and devastation. This thing does not want things to be.

"Munika?"

The mountain hummed in disgust. *A mere tool. I speak of a thing worthy of no name. Vile and brutal. Brought men hunting for my heart. That is a thing that could not be.*

A lump formed in my throat. "But you killed everyone!"

In Lirterin, I saw you. In Algirin, I saw you. A boy digs a hole, and a worm dies. Power does not move easily and deals with aftermaths arbitrarily. I regret what was. I regret many things. But power in an evil heart is a thing that cannot be allowed to be.

The sword became heavier and heavier until I could no longer hold it. It dropped to the ground. I tried to breathe steadily but buckled under the weight of remembrance. "You brought me here... why?"

A little thing lost everything, and knowing the cost, still kept being. Through cold and death, he demanded only justification. What a powerful heart you have, with the courage to shatter the line between resolve and stubbornness. How could I allow such a thing not to be? A boy who lost his mother and welcomed his own death.

My power shut down, and from the all-powerful dwinan that entered the cave, only the brittle shell of a bawling boy remained.

I gave you my heart. We are one thing.

"Stop it. Please stop." I was too weak, too frail to continue.

The mountain rested its case, and silence covered me. I thought I had experienced all the pains a man could live, and yet at the top of the mountain, I'd found another. I had been saved by the very thing that had killed my family and discovered their deaths were unavoidable—collateral damage in the grand scheme of evil. They died for nothing. I had held the culprit, the real culprit, in my hands. I'd spoken to her, befriended her, and helped her. And in doing so, I'd brought misery and war and death to so many. I was no better than the mountain.

I couldn't bear it.

What a stupid, naive little child I was. But how could I have known? It became harder to breathe. I couldn't move. Memories spun around me like specters, haunting me, taunting me, torturing me. I curled up on my knees, sobbing at Aureberg's heart. My life, ever since I'd lost my parents, had been a lie. I wasted all that time hating the wrong thing—the wrong being.

Chapter 71

The Crater

Ariel

Ariel awoke to the sound of thousands of men yelling and crying and the clank of metal against metal and wood and rock. It was dark, and her head threatened to explode with each heartbeat.

But in the darkness, a warm white light shone. She tried to move but found her right arm pinned by rubble. Only her left leg and arm had some wiggle room. She squeezed her left hand over her body for the pendant on her chest, the seed giving her light and keeping her alive. So small and so protective. She missed her friend dearly, even after all these years.

Ariel couldn't die. She had to do this one last thing. She had to plant the seed. *Rats!* She couldn't move, but she could send out a flare. Ariel erected her middle and pointing finger up at the stone slab covering her and shot a beam of light through it. A small burst. She didn't want to burn all the oxygen in her little tomb.

She shot again, but as her mind cleared, the claustrophobia gained space to grow. Another beam, and soon she was doing it every couple of seconds. She could not die. She didn't want to. She had to plant the seed.

"Help me," she croaked, her voice in splinters, "please."

She shot again, her breathing speeding up. She tried to move again, but she could feel her right leg swelling. Her head was about to crack at any moment from high blood pressure. It was no use. If she tried to cut her way out, she would just bury herself more.

"Ariel!" she heard a voice cry. "I'm coming! You! You there, yeah, yeah, yeah, you, come here. Help me dig her out. Not you, you sonuvabitch! Take this!"

From the little hole she'd carved, a bright orange flash came.

"You get back down there, where you belong! Quickly, get her out of there."

Another flash. Ariel could hear men removing the rubble from top of her. First, she felt her leg come free. Blood flooded in like raging fire. She winced. Her hip came next, then her right arm. The slab covering her head and torso rose and was pushed to the side by three guards.

Mathew came rushing into view. "Are you alright?"

Ariel blinked. The sky was still dark, but at least the rain had relented. "Urrgh," she grunted. "I don't know about my leg. But I think so."

"Good! Good!" Mathew said. "I need you to use your power."

"What?" she asked.

"Get her up; let her see it," Mathew commanded. There was a firmness to his voice she hadn't heard before. What had happened while she was unconscious?

Two soldiers helped her sit up. It was harrowing. Hesitantly, she bent her right knee, and it responded, even if swollen. She let out a sigh of relief. She had more lives than a cat. She tossed her arms around the guard's shoulders for support, and that's when she looked ahead.

Little fires had sprouted everywhere. And the wall, so impenetrable just moments earlier, lay broken. Where the explosion happened, it wasn't so much a hole but a crater. Chunks of the wall littered a vast area around it. And in the crater, men fought heavily. Thousands on each side. Thousands more waiting their turn in the churner. The hole could only fit a few hundred at a time.

"It's been like that for hours now," Mathew said. "They'll eventually get through. They have plenty of fresh troops." At their side, a ladder clanked against a merlon. Mathew dashed to it. "I told you to stay down there!" he said, pouring fire.

A man screamed in agony, voice fading progressively until it stopped.

"They're attacking from every side now. You have to do something."

Ariel wasn't sure she would remain conscious, let alone do something about anything. Her mind spun, and her leg throbbed. She started to gag. The men lowered her, and she emptied her already empty stomach. "I hate war," she croaked.

"Can you do it?"

"Do we have a choice?"

"We don't."

"Then I'll have to do it." Ariel sucked in a breath and almost threw up again. She focused on the light around her. There was no time for perfection. She just had to shut it all down.

"Warn the men," Mathew said to the third guard. "It's about to get really dark out here."

The man broke into a sprint down the debris-filled ramp.

Ariel drew in a bit of light surrounding her, just a wisp. It worked. Making a gloom at night had always been the easiest thing to do. But she'd never done it while on the brink of collapsing. And who knew how long she would have to hold the gloom until the enemy gave up, an hour? Two?

"Do ye have painkillers?" Ariel asked.

"I do," Mathew said, removing his backpack and reaching inside. "American ones."

"Not sure that's something to brag about, but I'm not complaining," she said as Mathew popped two pills onto her hand, then a third form a different flask.

"Here, milady," a guard said, handing her his canteen. She knew him. Hannik, was it?

Ariel took the canteen and swallowed the pills. "Alright. Let's do this."

Ariel sucked the light and a dark sphere blossomed over the crater. The light was dim and sparse, but even the littlest whisps mellowed her aches and strengthened her focus. Not like sunlight. Not at all. But every little help was welcomed.

The gloom spread. She was careful not to take so much light that she wouldn't be able to see inside. She just had to take enough so ordinary men couldn't. There was always a balance to be reached, but surprisingly, she was doing it.

Mathew poured fire down the wall at her side. "Just in case someone is trying to come up now."

The shadow fell over the wall and across the battlefield. Ariel tried to keep the gloom mostly to the enemy side, but some of the city would have to fall under the darkness as well. Soon, one by one, the clangs and smashes of metal and wood decreased until they stopped entirely.

"You're doing it!" Mathew said with relief. "Oh, thank God." He slumped on the floor next to her. "Are they retreating yet? I can't see a thing."

"Not yet. But they're definitely confused."

It took a little under an hour before the horns sounded the retreat.

"They're going now," she said.

"Finally," Mathew said. "I was almost falling asleep here."

The painkillers worked up to a degree. "Can I have more painkillers?"

"You gotta be careful. Think about your liver."

Ariel snorted. "Sure. And a drink. Do ye have a drink?"

"Again, liver. You shouldn't mix these with alcohol."

"Thank ye, Mr. Pharmacist. I'll take that into consideration."

"How's your leg?"

"It stopped throbbing. I don't think it's broken. Could I have more water, then?"

The soldier extended his canteen in the opposite direction.

"Hannik, I'm over here."

"Sorry, milady."

"A little more," she said as Hannik spun. "A little more. Almost there. Yes, thank ye." Ariel took the canteen and emptied it. She hoped she wouldn't puke all the water, but if part of her leg muscles died, her kidneys would be in overdrive trying to clean the blood. There were no IVs here, so she had to drink as much as possible.

"How long are you going to keep this up?" Mathew asked.

"Until after the last man is gone," she said.

"I'm so glad you're alive," Mathew said. "I thought you were dead. When I saw your beam, I came running."

"Thank ye. Ye saved me."

"Well, I guess we're even, then."

Ariel chuckled. "Yes, I believe so. The duke?"

"He broke his arm, and his face looks like someone tried to make wine out of it, but other than that, he's the personification of resilience. Gotta hand it to the man. He can really rile you up."

"He can," Ariel agreed. Then she looked up. "The clouds are thinning."

"Yeah. It stopped raining after the explosion. You don't want that hole to fill up with water. My guess is that we'll have clear skies tomorrow."

"Wouldn't that be something?" she said solemnly, knowing fully well that if the skies were clear, it could only mean one thing: they had lost.

Chapter 72

Blue Hearts

Ludik

We have at our disposal all the light in the heavens and not enough to fill the darkness in our hearts, Aureberg said as if that meant anything to me.

I wanted to cling to my hate for him—familiar and intimate—but I couldn't. Not anymore. Aureberg, too, had lost everything. I knew that now. His heart was my heart. I sat up, leaning against his heart, and found it surprisingly warm. I could feel his sorrow, as deep and vast as the stones that made him. It made me mad. My hatred migrated to someone new, renewed as I got to my feet.

"That wench!" I yelled. "That vile bitch! So much death! So much misery." I balled my fists so hard that my fingernails dug into my skin. "And for what? What could possibly warrant such a price?" My blood boiled, and in the next heartbeat, it began burning blue. I roared so loud I heard it like that crack of a mountain. I panted, and for the first time, I was in complete control of my power as it flowed through me, touching the fabric of the world. For the first time, I could see clearly as far as land would touch.

"What is the Shatter?"

That's not a name to be. A terrible thing of ineffable horror. A thing that was. A place where many things ended. My brethren, my kin. Here lies what's left of my kind.

I grit my teeth. There it is. He and me. Monsters of casualty, stepping on worms to do what's right. Victims of the same disgusting thing. Miranda.

"That's what it took to stop her?"

Aureberg didn't answer, but his heart dimmed. It was hard to believe that Miranda had been so powerful she shaped the face of the world and wiped out so many mountains. But not all was lost. Miranda no longer possessed that kind of power, or she would've had no problem killing me.

"I must stop her. Will you help me?"

It cannot be.

"Why?"

Things are things. And things end when I move.

"Things are things," I repeated to myself. But in repeating it, I refilled with rage. "I lost my parents. Many people did. Sons and daughters!" I stomped my feet, and flashes of blue erupted from my flesh, arching across the room. "It didn't stop you then. Why does it stop you now?"

More childless mothers. More motherless children. More broken souls. I do not want this. I want things to be.

"Nothing's changed. If we do nothing... we have to do something."

Aureberg rumbled. *If I move, we'll share that burden. Things will cease to be, and you'll become the mountain you always hated.*

I closed my eyes and gritted my teeth. It was true. Many would die if Aureberg moved, but how many more would perish if he didn't? I lost my parents so Miranda wouldn't become a dwinan. Regardless of how much pain it brought me, what would've been the consequences if he hadn't? What would've become of the world?

"I went toe to toe against her. I hurt her. But I'm just one dwinan. One small dwinan. Together we can do it. We can crush her." The words clawed their way up my throat. I didn't want to say them, but they came out in a fury of wrath and hurt. "You can't run away this time!" My eyes welled as I came to grips with my decision. "I'm the mountain now."

Aureberg hummed. *The earth will shake, and hearts will fade.*

I steadied my anger and unclenched my fists. "And if we lose to Miranda?"

His light diminished even more.

I took a deep breath. "That's our burden," I said, unable to contain the tears anymore. "I'm the mountain now."

I wiped the tears from my face and lay a hand gently on Aureberg's dimming heart. Warm and alive, I could feel its glacial beat against the palm of my hand and shared our heartbeats—not two, but one heart.

"I lost so much! Do you have any idea how impossible this decision is? I came here hating you with every fiber of my being just to learn that you had no choice. That my parents had to die for the greater good!" I laughed maniacally, unable to deal with it all. "And now you want to cower? I won't have it! You will move. I will move with you. You can't run away from this. This is where we stand and fight! We'll bring devastation to Alturin, yes. My friends are there, fighting that despicable thing as we speak. And we may kill them. I may kill them." I turned toward Alturin and felt my stomach twist: the wall lay broken. They wouldn't last long. "But that won't matter if we do nothing. It doesn't matter if we destroy Alturin or not. If we arrive too late, they will die regardless. Everyone will. For nothing."

Aureberg hummed and rumbled.

"I am the mountain now," I repeated, through grinding teeth, tears pouring out. "Your heart is my heart, and I command you to move!"

My heart is your heart, Aureberg said, as I felt the world as it shattered beneath me. *So be it.*

I closed my eyes as the weight of duty and sacrifice overcame me, settling in my young blue heart, and I let out a deep releasing breath, accepting my fate. "I'm the mountain now."

Things are things, Aureberg said, as the earth cracked with untamable noise.

Chapter 73

The Gods

Ariel

Ariel took another sip of water as she observed the withered Alturin guard. The men were exhausted. They had spent the night barricading the breach with everything they could find, taking turns to rest if they could. Alas, most couldn't, and so they worked, and time drew by, unwanted.

"What do you think?" Mathew asked. He hadn't left her side for more than a minute, gently waking her every hour or so. Ariel was pretty sure she wouldn't die in her sleep, but you can never be too safe with concussions. She glanced over her shoulder at the newly formed militias. A call to arms had spread across the city like wildfire, and people answered by the thousands, flocking to the squares where soldiers handed out swords and spears and shields. Able men and women of all ages teetered as they watched the dawn rise mercilessly. The city would fall, but it would not do so quietly.

Yet, Ariel found it absurd. "They're untrained," she said.

"People have the right to defend their land, no?" Mathew countered.

Ariel played with the thought. What would she do if an army invaded Edinburgh? She didn't live there anymore, but damn it, it was her city. Wasn't that exactly what she was doing already? Fighting for her world and all the cities in it? She had power, yes, but her training was mostly about tricking farmers into giving her their money, not war.

"Is that Brinn?" Mathew interrupted her train of thought.

Ariel peered into the square where the crowd gathered. Debris from collapsed buildings and parts of the wall littered the place. Ariel followed the crowd until her eyes spotted a girl in a pale blue jacket walking her way, with a ginger boy tagging along.

"Good job last night," Brinn said when she approached. "For a moment there, I thought we were in trouble."

"For a moment there, we were," Ariel replied.

A horn sounded. The enemy was advancing.

"Brinn," Mathew asked. "Why are you holding a baker's shovel?"

"It's called a peel," Brinn said, inspecting her tool. "Got tired of making loaves."

"Yae're gonna end up hurting someone with that," Ariel reproached.

"That's the general idea." Brinn sat next to Ariel. "There's no point in making bread if everyone will be too dead to eat it. Oh, this is Graze, by the way. He and Ludik are childhood friends."

"It's an absolute honor to meet you," Graze said, leaning on his peel for support. "I mean, mages! Wow!"

"Save it, lad," Ariel said. "If yer wee friend doesn't show up soon, we'll all be dead no matter how many bakers join the battle."

"Ludik's a survivor," Brinn said with more than a little annoyance in her tone. "He'll make it."

"Master Doller, Lady Ariel," Katunik called. His face was a bundle of bruises, his left arm wrapped in grimy bandages, and he leaned into a spear as he limped toward them. Balival strode along at his duke's side, looking haggard, more than a dozen cuts scratching his face like the drawing of a two-year-old who just found a red crayon. There was a grave air around them. Those were not the faces of good news.

"What happened now?" Ariel asked.

"The aramaz returned a few minutes ago." Balival re-opened a cut on his lower lip as he spoke and tapped the wound with a rugged cloth.

Ariel stood up in a heartbeat and regretted it. The dizzy spell became so intense she nearly fainted, and Mathew grabbed her before she fell. "I'm alright," she said. "A little woozy, that's all."

"What about Ludik?" Brin blurted, passing her peel from one hand to the other.

Katunik shook his head. "Hotcup arrived alone," he said, his voice hoarse and dry. "The safety straps are all broken. They must've torn during flight."

"So Ludik..." Ariel muttered to herself, unable to face the implications.

Armrar Katunik gazed over his city and subjects as they formed unorganized ranks.

"He's alright," Brinn said, thumping the butt of the peel. "I know he is. Ludik's a dwinan. He survived Aureberg and the long winter. I've seen him swim in a frozen lake to rescue a kid. He escaped from Munika's grasp. He jumped into a sea of fire to save a little girl and came out unharmed. He stopped a freaking landslide for Bastard's sake! And he fought Miranda twice and lived. You'd be fools to think a little thing like the northern death is enough to stop him."

"Lady Brinn, even a dwinan can't survive a fall from the sky."

"But we don't know if that's what happened, do we?"

"And how is he supposed to get back without the aramaz?"

Brinn shrugged. "He'll find a way."

"What about Ben," Ariel asked. "He can talk to the bird?"

Katunik's eyes grew somber. "I ordered the doctor to wake him. But even if he does and manages to talk with Hotcup, we won't have answers before the battle resumes."

"We have to give him more time," Brinn said with a slashing hand.

Katunik peered around at the people flocking to protect their city, indecision flickering in his eyes.

"Look around you, your grace," Brinn said. "The people are ready to give their lives for this. Even they understand how doomed we are if we don't stop her."

"Lady Brinn, where do you find such courage?"

"I'd gladly share some with you if I could."

Katunik chuckled at first, and then he began to laugh heartily despite his bruised throat. "That won't be necessary. In fact, Admiral

Munika, King of Aviz, sent a messenger earlier kindly asking for our surrender."

A lump formed in Ariel's throat. If the city surrenders, they'd become hostages to be murdered one by one until Ludik gave Miranda what she wanted.

"I told the great admiral I was very sorry for his mother. Even a whore shouldn't have to suffer such humiliating offspring."

"Damn!" Mathew let out a guffaw. "A yo-momma joke, really? Well, it's always a classic."

"Lady Brinn," Katunik said. "I see you've brought a weapon."

"I did, your grace. Can't wait to test it."

"Shall we?" Katunik said, turning to leave. "We mustn't keep the men waiting. Are you ready, Master Doller?"

"Born ready," Mathew answered.

"Good luck," Brinn said as Mathew helped Ariel up to follow the duke.

"Ye too, Brinn," Ariel said. "Be safe, if ye can."

Brinn smiled tenderly at her like they had been friends all their lives. "Don't let him do anything stupid."

"Hey!" Mathew protested. "Alright, you have a point. We'll find you once this is over."

Brinn nodded and left with Graze to rejoin their militia. About time; their conversation was starting to feel too much like a goodbye for her taste.

Ariel leaned on Mathew as they headed for the breach. The Alturin guards formed a line at the top of the crater's slope to take advantage of the high ground, leaving behind corridors where workers still brought chairs and tables and whatever other furniture or flammables they could find.

"I should find higher ground," Ariel said, inspecting the broken wall for a good nest to fire from.

"They need me at the front," Mathew said, taking Ariel's hand. "Will you stay with me?"

Ariel nodded. She would rather stay at the front in Mathew's company than safe alone. She was happy to have a friend that day. Even if that friend was a fiery murdering lunatic, and, in all fairness, it was a good day to be friends with a fiery murdering lunatic.

The crater somehow looked deeper and wider than before. The men had done a reasonable job clearing the dead, but many remained sprawled on the floor or tucked under debris. Ariel looked away, but Mathew pointed at the structures the men had built throughout the night. "Munika's men will have a hard time climbing it after I set it on fire."

"Your idea?"

"Nah," he said. "The duke's. The man's good at this. And I have to wait, too. Either they'll try to remove the clutter, and I'll light it up, or they'll try to climb over it, in which case I have to wait until a manageable group of soldiers climb through, and then set it on fire. Either way, there'll be a barbeque."

Ariel squirmed at that last word. "Please shut up."

"I forgot. You eat your steaks well done."

"I try not to eat steak at all, thank ye very much. And stop making food references. If we survive, I would like to eat again someday."

"The duke's gonna make a speech," Mathew said, pointing at Katunik, who climbed over a large chunk of the wall so everyone could see him.

The Duke of Alturin steadied himself on the uneven platform and contemplated his men. His city. His people. Despite his bruised face and the bandaged arm clutched to his chest, it was impossible not to be drawn by his stare. "Fellow Alturians, you have to understand what's at stake today," he began, his voice carrying far and wide. "The boy, Ludik, went over the Shatter, deep into the Northern Death. You saw his magic, a dwinan's power, the first of his kind in thousands of years. You may think he should've remained here to protect us, but he had to leave. Even he is no match against the wicked witch who threatens to kill us all. Out there, in the vast emptiness, is the answer to how we stop her.

"I won't lie to you. Ludik may never reach us back in time. He may even have failed his mission already, and we'd be none the wiser. I know it's bleak, perhaps futile. But I've met this boy and know he carries the fire and courage of thousand men in his heart. He will not fail us, and I'm prepared to give my life just to buy him a little more time." Katunik looked longingly at the advancing army, the noise of their march rising. They were getting close.

"This won't be like any battle ever fought by mere mortal men. This is a confrontation among giants. Beings of ultimate power, and dare I say it, gods." Katunik paused and held the stare of his people. "The very land, dead and broken, that stretches endlessly behind you came to be on a day very much like today when good defeated evil at an unimaginable cost. Today, you're not fighting for your commander. You're not fighting to protect our city or even to protect our families. Today we fight for the right to have a future, for us and for all mankind. If we fail, tomorrow dies with us! So heed me, my mere mortals! Take a good look at the men and women around you because today, you are to face a god together! Together! Together! And from now until the end of time, this day shall be remembered as the day when the brave people of Alturin faced a god and her evil forces and triumphed."

Armrar Katunik, Duke of Alturin, paused for a moment filled only with the heartbeats of an entire city, unsheathed his sword, raising it high above his head, and bellowed, "And by day's end, WE'LL BE GODS OF OUR OWN MERIT!"

The city exploded with the battle cries of every man and woman, swords clanging against shields and spears butting the ground.

Enthralled by the commotion, euphoria blew up inside Ariel, and she found herself crying at the top of her lungs along with everyone else, "TO THE GODS! TO THE GODS!"

Duke Armrar Katunik pointed his sword at the enemy closing in on the breach. "Forward into glory and a new pantheon. Man your stations! Form your ranks! To war with you and the legend you are!"

"Let's do this," Ariel said, hair bristling and soaking in all the light from the cloudy day.

"I'm glad you're here," Mathew said.

"I'm glad yae're here too, lad."

The invading army crashed against the barricade, breaking and chopping it down, advancing over the line of wood, wicker, and peat without a second thought.

"Now, Master Doller," Balival shouted. "Archers, nock! Loose!"

Mathew took a deep breath as arrows filled the sky above and flooded the crater with the largest flow of fire Ariel had seen him produce so far.

"Loose," Balival commanded again. "At will!"

The heat from the fire ahead prickled Ariel's face, so intense the Alturin line was forced to take a few steps back. The men that got through ran into the wall of shields and spears. Ariel wasn't sure if they were attacking or running from the intense heat. They clashed against the spears, and their cries died down.

Her stomach did a full summersault in her belly, and she emptied its contents.

"Are you alright?" Mathew asked.

"No, I'm not alright. I'm at the front line of a battle!" she said. "I need to get up there."

Mathew nodded and followed after her as the men cleared a path for them. The smell of smoke vaguely reminded Ariel of peated whisky. She could use some right about now.

Minutes later, as she and Mathew climbed the broken wall searching for a good vantage point, the fire began to spin. It whirled into a firedevil and shot upward, filling the sky where it scattered and vanished in plumes of dark smoke.

"Miranda," Mathew spat. "No biggy. Let's see who's more stubborn. Wait here." Mathew couldn't find a direct line of sight to reignite the fire, so he began climbing over large debris.

Behind the curtain of smoke, war cries erupted. Ariel peeked from the side and saw some heads as the first soldiers emerged, ignoring the heat and the smoke.

Mathew reached a vantage point and re-flooded the pyre, but seconds later, the fire shot upward to dissipate in the sky again. He tried again, and this time Miranda was even faster.

"It's no use," she yelled at him. "Save yer strength!"

Men cascaded down the heap of smoke and embers and cinders. Mathew climbed back down to Ariel's side and helped her up the broken wall. The invading soldiers ran over the barricade as if it weren't there, up the crater's slope and slammed against the Alturin line. It wasn't a fair fight. The hill gave the Alturians an obvious advantage, and the progress of Aviz was halted there. But Ariel knew it wouldn't be long before the tides changed. It was only a matter of time before the Alturin guard became too exhausted to fight while the Aviz line could replace their worn-down men with fresh ones.

If you're ever going to fight, it has to be now, Ariel thought. She didn't want to die, but she didn't want to kill those men callously. They were only following orders. They had no choice in this. Ariel heard herself roar and reached in for a madness she did not know she possessed, but it had to be done. There was simply too much on the line.

She drew in a deep breath and fired at the mass of men. She gathered what light she could and redirected it on the poor soldiers who fought for their king. Ariel cried manically as she slashed left and right cutting men in half, while Mathew threw balls of fire indiscriminately into the chaos. There. There was no going back now. She had become a murderer. Would she ever sleep again?

Enemy soldiers worked unrelentingly under fire to clear as much smoldering wood as possible so more soldiers could get through. Ariel and Mathew converged their fire on them. The plan wasn't to win the battle. The plan was to delay their victory.

Ariel hated every beam of light escaping her fingers, yet she unleashed them unmercifully. Mathew bellowed like a maniac, streams of flames raining down on the men, one after the other. It was brutal and unrelenting. As soon as a man died or was injured or retreated, another took his place; a vast expanse of men awaited their turn.

Hours drew by, and the clash raged on, and little by little, the Alturin line got pushed back. Then, some enemy soldiers broke through. A dozen men or so men dashed into the city and right into the militia mob. Was that a new tactic?

"The duke sure is full of tricks up his sleeve, huh?" Mathew said.

Another hole, another handful of Aviz's men trapped.

Ariel focused on her fire. Was she getting used to cutting down men? She did not want to think about it, so she shrugged the thought away. There would be a time to feel sorry for herself and the men she felled later, and that was the best-case scenario.

The Alturin guards took shifts at the front, rotating like a volleyball team. The Aviz's army did similarly, but their men were being dropped at a much faster rate. She had been churning beam after beam for hours now, and her stamina was draining. It didn't matter how much light she consumed. With each minute, she felt herself grow weaker.

Mathew's fire had lost intensity, too. When before, each ball of fire would blow away at least a meter square; now, it only harmed a man at a time. He dropped onto the ground panting and drank some water out of his canteen, beads of sweat dribbling down his forehead. "Will this ever end," he said. "Look at them. We barely made a dent."

Ariel noticed Balival waving a flag at her, the crest of the Alturin city, an aramaz holding a lightning bolt over a tower against a blue field. "Balival's calling us," she said. "There may be news."

They climbed down from their positions, circumventing the line of battling men.

"Benerik is up," Balival said as they approached, and then he turned to the line of archers at his side. "Keep firing, you fools! Do your arms hurt? Maybe I can still use them by cutting them off and throwing them at the enemy!"

The archers shook their arms, nocked, and loosed another volley.

"He's heading down this way. The old bastard has not an ounce of wit about him."

Ariel looked up over the ranks of militias and saw Hotcup coming down the street, Ben wobbling over the saddle. Hotcup's replica was still visible higher up. "Oh no," Ariel muttered. "Rats."

"What's wrong?" Mathew said.

"There are two Hotcups in plain sight," Ariel pointed out.

"I can't believe it," Mathew spat, hands on his hair. "That stupid bastard!"

"TAKE COVER!" someone shouted.

A bright flash blinded Ariel's view, and a wall of hot air swept her off her feet. Men blew into the air, torn like washcloths, raining down along with cinders and rock.

Mathew rolled on the ground and ended up next to Ariel. "She shot her own men down," he grunted. "She shot her own men!"

Ariel squinted at the front line. It lay in tatters. Bodies littered the ground, and wails and moans and cries and the crackle of a new dozen fires filled the air. The Alturin guard was no more. And no Aviz's soldiers either. Then, almost timidly, a few began to emerge.

"To the gods!" the militias bellowed.

Men and women armed with whatever they could find rushed to the breach from all sides. Brinn scuttled along, peel in hand, bellowing, "To the gods!" Graze right behind her, fear in his face but with legs fueled by courage. "To the gods!"

The call reverberated across the square as more and more people rushed in like an undying echo. "To the gods!"

Ariel rolled on her stomach and pushed the ground away from her. Why was he so shocked? Did he forget what Miranda did to him?

"Are you alright?" Mathew asked her, pulling her up.

"I'll live," she answered. *For now.*

Balival shot past them. "My king!"

Ariel found the duke on the ground, hands over his belly, a little ways ahead.

Brinn flung her peel and smacked a soldier's head. Her bravery impelled the whole militia to commit to the battle. Unorganized, no distinct line as they ran toward spears and swords. What a messy affair.

"Narn. The witch's comin'," a coarse voice said from behind.

"Ben! So nice of ye to join us."

"Ariel! I thought you needed some help."

Ariel closed in on him, swung her hand as hard as she could and slapped him across the face. The palm of her hand pulsated with pain. "Ye just killed us all, ye eejit!"

Benerik didn't bother to rub his face, cheek reddening. "Nah, the city's doomed already, and I didn't feel like dyin' on a bed. This is more to my liking."

"What about Ludik?" Mathew asked.

"Hotcup left him at the mountain," Benerik said without a trace of sadness. "There's no way he'll ever return in time. Might as well get this over with."

"Ye don't know that!" Ariel stomped her foot.

"Listen, sweetheart, Hotcup flew more than a thousand leagues. So unless your boy can fly, we're pretty much dead."

The words hit her like a sword through her heart. How could the kid be so dumb? Why would he stay there without any means of returning? Anger flared in her chest.

"Ye can barely stand," Ariel said in outrage. "Ye dumb bodach."

Benerik was all bandages and broken stitches, blood permeating the white cloths around his leg, and still, he left his bed only to crush their hopes and rush their demise. Stupid! Stupid! Stupid!

"Don't need to stand," he raised a hand and shot a running soldier with a lightning bolt. The thunder crashed across the square. "Just needn't lay."

Hotcup cackled and gawked, feathers bristling with electric sparks. He and Ben shot a few more bolts, and Mathew joined him. Ariel shook her head, and together, they stumbled toward the front line laying indiscriminate fire—a pointless last stand. There was nowhere to escape, but the civilians still believed they could make a difference. At least Ariel wouldn't die alone. So be it. Intense light shone off the broken wall like a new sunrise; above, the sky parted like the sea of Moses, revealing nothing but blue sky; and from the chaos and destruction, she appeared.

Miranda rose from the crater while Aviz soldiers cowered away from her. Miranda hovered inches above the ground, her body made of pure fire, light and lightning, waving and swirling, refracting like a living kaleidoscope. The ground under her broke and melted as she hovered above it.

Daylight fell on Ariel like a gift from the gods, though that might've been a poor choice of words. Still, she was grateful to see the sky right before she died. Miranda grinned as she mowed down militia lines, one after the other. Panic ensued. The brief flash of courage that had overcome Alturin's people faded like a blown-out candle. Only a brave few remained behind to fight.

"Stop it!" Mathew shouted. "Stop it right now!"

Miranda gazed upon him. "Oh, my young apprentice, my fire suits you well," she said in a voice of fire and destruction. "You can still join me, child. I owe you that much, regardless of what you may think. You are my favorite human. I won't take pleasure in killing you."

"Oh, is that so?" Mathew said. "Tough offer to refuse."

Ariel felt a lump clog her heart. Was he going to switch sides? It was only natural. What was the pointing in defiance in the face of certain doom?

"Tell me," Mathew asked. "Why all this?"

"A long time ago, I tried to do what was right, to create a world without wars. Instead of showing gratitude, they dismantled my soul, tore me into pieces, and trapped me inside cages to be forgotten. To lay there forever, only agony for company. What would you do if you finally broke free?"

"You know," Mathew said, "the problem is I wouldn't have terrorized everyone in the first place."

The remaining clouds began to scatter as if they, too, ran away from the world's end. The sun peeked between them, caressing Ariel's face. Thank God.

Miranda burst out laughing. "You naïve, child. The whole plan you concocted after we met is not so different from my own. Do you think you can show your power to the nations of your world and not start a power struggle? Men do not want to be saved. Men want war, even when they search for peace. Man needs conquering if they are to be subdued. Over fires and floods, I will transform this world. And yours."

"You're insane," Mathew said. "You'll be alone all over again. For what?"

"You presume I care," Miranda said. "You presume too much. Once I am whole, my dear Alfred will join me. And with time, even he will forgive me."

"Then why should I join you when I'm only a man?"

Miranda smiled. "Such fire in you. My dear Mathew, I do not wish men to be extinct. I wish them on a leash, and you can help me control them. By my side, you will be king, emperor, or tsar."

"Wow." Mathew smirked. "Now that's what I call an offer."

The conversation had dragged out long enough that everyone in condition to flee had cleared the vicinity. Mathew was stalling her! When had he become so cool-headed? Ariel had a glimpse of Brinn swirling with her peel in the background. If, for some unfathomable reason, they survived, she would have to buy everyone a round of the best Heims, even if she had to steal the duke's bottle.

"Oh, you think you are stalling me," Miranda said. "It does not matter. There is nowhere to hide. Aureberg stopped pulling; he fled again, like the coward he is. There is no hope left for you."

"Well, you may be right about that," Mathew said, glancing at the retreating people of Alturin. "But I can prolong theirs."

Mathew twirled his hands and shot a bolt of fire so bright and hot the rock under it glowed amber as it darted toward Miranda. Miranda spun the orb around her and sent it back to Mathew like a game of hot potato.

Mathew tried to swirl the orb around him, but it slipped, hitting a couple of buildings in a cloud of fire, dust and debris. Miranda shot lightning at Mathew, but Benerik caught it.

"You evil witch!" Ben said. "I ain't dead yet."

He and Hotcup charged up, unleashing a thick stream of lightning. Ariel drew in as much light as she could muster and shot at Miranda too. Miranda strained herself to control the attack as thousands of tiny rocks rose around her and shot at them like bullets.

"Duck!" Mathew said, breaking his attack and throwing himself on the ground. Ben created a wall of lightning enveloping Hotcup, deflecting or incinerating the barrage of projectiles while Ariel lunged for cover behind a large chunk of stone.

A rock caught Ben's left shoulder and pierced clean through, and he dropped his arm to the side. "Useless arm," he grunted, cauterizing his new wound with a flash.

Ariel and Mathew resumed their attack, while Benerik and Hotcup followed suit. The forces at play were so large and intense the shaking ground quickly evolved into an earthquake. Miranda swirled the mage's powers around, condensing them into a small orb of lightning, light and fire and shot it at the ground, separating them.

The world spun around Ariel as her body rolled and bounced across the square. Ariel gulped down sunlight to heal her wounds as fast as she could, knowing full well she should've been dead. Odd. With her power, she could see Miranda's energy being pulled away ever so faintly.

Why was the ground still shaking? Around her, buildings collapsed in giant plumes of dust. The world was so noisy it seemed like it would crack at any moment. A tremendous thunder exploded behind her. Part of the rock wall came loose, squashing the palace and most of the upper parts of the city in an instant. *Damn ye, Miranda! Ye disgusting cow!*

The rock beneath Miranda bubbled like the surface of the sun, and the sound viciously crippled Ariel's eardrums. Fire, light and lightning produced both symmetrical and asymmetrical shapes of circles and squares and parabolic lines like a mix of complex mathematical graphics.

Mathew, Ben, and Hotcup were still up and in the fight. How? They pushed everything they had left into one final desperate assault. Miranda strained to contain it as she spun the stream around her like a spool of energy.

One more time! Ariel added her light to the barrage. Miranda spun and shot the power upward. It arched over them, leveling whatever few buildings remained standing in its path. Ariel dropped to her knees, panting. That was it. That was all they had. Why was the ground still shaking? It shook so violently now she had trouble balancing even on her knees. And the noise. What was that noise? Wherever she looked, structures came down in clouds of dust and debris. There would be nothing left.

"An admirable attempt," Miranda said as she advanced over them. "Futile, but admirable."

Miranda lifted a hand, and Ariel closed her eyes. She expected death to follow, but instead, she heard someone shout over the noise, "Screw you!"

Ariel opened her eyes in time to see a spear vaporizing into Miranda. She turned as a peel struck her head.

"You cannot hurt me with those crude weapons," Miranda said.

Balival had another spear ready, legs trembling along with the intense earthquake. The duke lay by his side, gritting his teeth.

Brinn stumbled to her knees as she tossed her burnt peel to the side, "We're not afraid of you."

Miranda's glow began to drain faster, like the orb of light that blew up the wall. But this time, it didn't scatter; it twirled into a thin filament, shooting eastward.

The ground tossed Ariel in the air as the remaining buildings toppled like sandcastles, and the edge of the Shatter crumbled like a calving iceberg. She landed on her side, grunting with pain, mouth filled with dust.

Alturin lay in ruins.

That was when she caught the fright in Miranda's eyes. Ariel followed her gaze as a colossal mountain burst through the Shatter eastward, tossing the landscape up as if made of styrofoam. Clouds parted in its wake as dust and soil filled the air like heavy rain.

Miranda roared like a caged wild animal as large flakes of her power ripped out from her and into the mountain.

Something shot out from the mountain's top, quick as a hummingbird, glowing in a fierce blue light that even her leoht eyes struggled to follow. In an instant, Ludik landed on the square amidst flares of blue, raised his hands and consumed Miranda's energy.

The mountain's also a dwinan! Ariel realized.

Without hesitation, Ariel poured her light into Ludik. Miranda's power peeled away as she shrunk and screeched.

"You miserable deaf child," Miranda growled, then uttered in treespeak, *We are not done. Let us see how much you love that whisky maker of yours.* In the blink of an eye, Miranda shrunk to the size of a marble and, in a flash, slipped from Ludik's and Aureberg's grip and vanished, leaving only a streak of smoke in her path.

Chapter 74

Last Light

Ludik

"Never doubted you, Master Ludik," Katunik said, face sunken and sickly, contemplating his leveled city as Balival did his best to tend to the ugly wound in his abdomen.

I averted my eyes from the destruction surrounding me. *It had to be done,* I told myself. I bargained with the shame and guilt raging inside me, but to no avail. They tied a knot in my throat and pummeled my gut mercilessly. I gritted my teeth. *There was no choice.*

Brinn shot past everyone and clutched me in a tight hug. I hesitated at first. She was safe! Brinn was safe! A wave of relief abated over me, and it took everything in me not to start crying like a little boy. I wrapped my arms around her, pressing my face against the nook between her shoulder and neck, taking in her sweet smell, despite the sweat, grime and blood.

"I'm so happy you're alive."

"Me too," she said. Or I think she said. I didn't bother reading my note or even dare release her for a very long time.

"I have to leave," I said when we finally released and got a good look at her brave almond eyes. "I just have to get this one formality out of the way."

Brinn smiled gently, elation and grief fighting for a spot in her eyes as she caressed my cheek. Then she simply nodded.

"Aureberg!" I shouted. Though I didn't have to, even as a whisper would do. "Bring us the king."

The ground rumbled, and a tiny smidgen rose above the horizon. The army below tossed their weapons aside as they watched their commander float above them to land before Brinn with as much grace as a featherless bird.

"Well," Brinn said with as much disdain as her eyes could muster when Aureberg released him. "Seems like your god ran away."

Munika eyed her defiantly. "I surrender only to Lord Katunik."

"Ah, the thing is, *your majesty*," Katunik said through laborious breaths, "I'm in no condition to accept your surrender."

Munika snarled and lunged, but Aureberg latched on him and forced him to his knees. He struggled against the togian lines, but it was useless. Brinn stared down at the king of Aviz serenely, with a kind of patience and nerve I didn't know she possessed.

Munika stopped fighting to look at Brinn with as much dignity as a defeated man could have. "You stupid girl!"

"Ah!" Brinn raised a finger. "Lady Brinn Kallak, Baker of Alturin, please."

Munika's upper lip twitched.

"Give up, Mun-Mun," Katunik said and winced. "It's the only move you have left."

Munika Muril eyed Brinn hatefully. "Lady Brinn Kallak," he said through clenched teeth. "Baker of Alturin, I, Munika Muril, King of Aviz, supreme commander of the Armies of Aviz, surrender to you."

Ariel walked over to them. "I don't accept it."

A bright flash dazed me momentarily, and Munika Muril, King of Aviz fell limply onto his side.

"What the hell was that?" Mathew blurted, covering his mouth, his eyes in shock. "You can't murder a man after he surrenders."

Ariel's rage made her face muscles twitch uncontrollably. "How many lives—" Ariel gritted her teeth, then looked around at the destruction and countless dead bodies. "How many died because of him? Why does he get to live? All my life, I've done my best to preserve life—to be a good person. Even when I scam farmers, I leave them better off than they were before. I could've prevented all of this, ye know. I could've shot ye dead the moment I laid eyes on ye." She glared at Mathew. "Taken Miranda and tossed that cow to drown in the middle of the Atlantic. But I didn't. I didn't want to kill anyone. Because I'm not a murderer. At least, I wasn't until today. My hands are now covered in blood, because of Miranda and because of him. What's one more body in the middle of this mess? No. He does not get to live a life of exile. And I can tell ye with absolute certainty that this is the only life I took today that'll not bear heavy on my conscience. His crimes are impossible to forgive." She made a dismissing gesture with her hand and turned her back on Munika's body. "Besides, this way there'll be no doubts about who's king."

I didn't know what to feel about it. I didn't think I'd be able to do what she did. But then I remembered Munika was the one who made Aureberg move with instructions from Miranda. He was the one who treated the refugees like cattle. He and Miranda, not Aureberg, were responsible for my parents' deaths and countless others. Miranda!

"I'm going after her," I announced.

"Ye know it's a trap, right?" Ariel said.

"I know. But we weakened her enough that I may have a chance to take her out alone. We might not have another chance. I must go. I must go now. Hotcup, are you ready for another flight?"

Hotcup nodded his massive head. Vengeance, in his eyes. He wanted to hunt her down as much as I did. Then he turned, head low, to Ben, who sat against a part of a building, looking more dead than alive. "Get going, Cups. I'll be alright."

"Why don't ye take Aureberg?" Ariel asked as if it were a normal thing to say.

Before I could even conjure an answer, while flickers of anger sparked in me, Ariel continued, "Never mind. It's a dumb question. I'm going with ye. Well, what are ye waiting for? Wire the darned bird."

I smiled weakly. "I don't know if we'll make it through this one."

"Yeah, well, then ye won't have to die alone, innit?"

Gallows humor, not bad for, you know, the gallows. No one wants to die alone, I guess.

Brinn kissed me. On the lips. Despite everything that had happened, that stunned me. Only briefly, though. I wrapped my arms around her and returned the kiss.

"I know, I know," Brinn said, stepping back. And before I could say anything, she added, "Just try not to die."

"Quit it, lassie," Ariel interrupted. "We've wasted enough time."

I looked at Brinn one last time and nodded. Hotcup lowered himself at my side to make it easier to mount him. I jumped on his back and linked up. Only then did I remember the broken straps, but what could we do about it? "If you make any dumb maneuvers, we'll fall," I warned him. "Okay, Ariel, see if it works."

Ariel didn't tiptoe around it. She jumped on right behind me. "Great. I didn't die. Punch it, Mr. Sulu."

"Hold on tight," I said, vaguely wondering who Mr. Sulu was. "Let's go, Hotcup."

In the next moment, we were airborne and flying over the wall, surveying the extent of Alturin's destruction. What had they been through while I was gone?

"Things are things," I muttered.

We rose above the clouds, and I could feel Ariel basking in pure, unimpeded sunlight.

"Hurry, Hotcup, full speed, to Guillingsbaer."

Excitement.

Apparently, the last time we flew, he had been coy with his speed. Or maybe not having safety lines made it feel faster. But once he had my permission to accelerate, he ripped across the sky until I couldn't keep my eyes open anymore, and then sped past that. We flew so fast a bubble formed around us, and the air outside struck it with such force it glowed. Surprisingly, the win abated, but breathing was still a chore due to Ariel's tight embrace around my chest. I tried to shout that she was hurting me, but as Hotcup thundered across the sky, Ariel was as deaf as I was.

Not an hour later, Hotcup slowed down and descended beneath clouds. Flying above the countryside was much more pleasant than flying over the barren landscape of the shattered mountains. The distant details appeared to have been painted by a master craftsman: the little houses, the tiny hills, the miniature forests. Now I understood the appeal of flying. Below, thick lines formed an eight-sided star. We'd reached Lirterin. We had made it all the way back before sunset. My brain couldn't even comprehend that kind of speed.

"Follow that road through the woods; it leads to Guillingsbaer. You'll see a formation of smooth rock. Heimee's distillery will be there."

And then I saw it. The frigates scattered around a large patch of rock, sparse moss and low grass. "There, that tiny lake with the white building."

I was in awe. The distillery had been rebuilt. But what struck me the most was seeing Heimee's home. My home. The two boulders squeezing the house covered by dark shingles. Smoke came out of the crooked chimney. Heimee was home. Then my heart sank when I saw her—a little star shining in the land below.

She noticed us too. I know this because a second later, beams of energy shot in our direction. "Don't dodge. I'll take care of it."

Affirmation, was Hotcup's reply.

Ariel shifted behind me and tightened her grip around my waist.

Doubt, Hotcup reconsidered.

Oh no. I barely had time to hold onto the front handles before Hotcup turned into a spiral and dropped from the sky, seemingly aimlessly, until we were about a hundred yards from the ground. Then he spread his wings and regained control with a hard spin that nearly spat us out of his saddle, grazing over the rock and grass as lightning erupted all around us, leaving a trail of amber sparks in our wake.

"I said no dodging!"

We approached the house so fast I thought we would smash against it, but in a flurry of light and thunder, Hotcup came to a complete halt and dropped to the ground.

The sun chose that moment to start setting. Why? It was still far from the horizon a minute ago. Ariel dismounted and, without a second thought, scampered away. *Where was she going?* Had she suddenly decided to run away? That didn't make any sense. I dismounted

Hotcup, careful not to touch the rock or grass and provoke an unwanted discharge, and trusted my father's work.

Miranda hovered above the ground a few yards from the house, her body a raging fire, lightning swirls and flares of light, connecting her to the ground beneath like tentacles. And at her feet was Heimee, on his knees. He smiled at me, eyes filled, not with fear, but awe and pride. *It's alright*, they told me.

Hotcup stood by my side, shoulders hunched and piercing eyes.

"It's going to be alright!" I told him.

How confident of you, Miranda said in treespeak.

"Leave him alone."

Through the corner of my eye, I noticed Ariel scampering to the distillery. Did she come with me just to get her hands on Heims? I couldn't believe it. It didn't matter. I couldn't spare her the attention. I had one last mission to complete.

Miranda, too, glanced at Ariel unsurely, probably considering if she should stop her or not. Then, with a hint of a smile appeared on her fiery lips and she said, *Even your friends lack the courage to face me again. Give me your power, and I will spare them. I will leave this country alone. You have my word.*

"Your word," I repeated.

There is no need for you to lose another fatherly figure. Share your power with me, and I will spare those you love. Decide fast. My patience is not what it once was. Miranda took a more human form and lowered graciously to stand on her feet. The grass under her dried, curled, and burst into flames. She laid a hand on Heimee's shoulder. It was like watching a kettle boil as she burned through Heimee's clothes and seared his skin.

Heimee writhed in pain and plunged forward, rolling on the grass. I wanted to attack her, but I was scared she would kill Heimee before I got close enough. Heimee pushed the ground away laboriously with both hands, regaining a little composure, but grimacing with every crinkle on his face.

"I'm here. Take me." I goaded her, taking stock of her power, immense, big as a mountain. Bigger even. How could she have recovered so quickly? Aureberg and I had drained her badly in Alturin. How could I think to defeat her now? But I would have none of that; my mind was made up.

Miranda shot a bolt of lightning, unlike anything I had ever felt. It connected me to the ground. I breathed in most of it, but I was caught unprepared, throwing me backward. I tumbled across the ground, banging my head against a rock. Blood oozed from the gash and over my right eye as I tried to regain my balance. *I'll be ready for the next blow.*

Give it to me, she said. *And I will keep my word.*

But I didn't believe her, even for a second. Heimee gazed at me, and our eyes met. He may not know what was at stake, but he knew enough. He nodded to me, courage in his stare. He knew the end was near and gave me his permission to follow through.

"I love you, Heimee," I said to him.

"Quit whining," he forced his hands to sign. "I raised you better than that. I'm ready to meet the Bastard."

I closed my eyes. *I am the mountain,* I thought to myself. *I am the mountain.*

I surrendered to the pain and sorrow, to all the anguish in the world and shot toward Miranda. The colors inverted around me as my vision blurred, but I held on. I lashed onto her, breathing in her energy. It ripped across my body as if I was being torn apart.

She was fighting back. I felt her pull away, and I breathed deeper and harder.

Miranda showered me with bolts of lightning, attempting to push me away long enough.

Remarkable, Miranda said, and in return, she shocked Heimee. I had no way to breathe the bolt in time. But I couldn't stop. I had to follow through.

Was I sacrificing Heimee? Could I? I had to. I was the mountain.

Miranda added fire to the lightning with the strength of all the storms and all the furnaces in the world. But I kept my grip. I mustn't let go.

Her power flaked in large swats that nearly threw me off balance, smashing against me with tremendous force, consuming the ground around me, and peeling away my clothes; her power getting closer and closer to my skin before I could consume it.

So that's how it worked. That's why I was invulnerable. The energy never touched me.

Miranda latched on to one of the frigates and plucked it out of Heimee's house; layers of energy enveloping it as she spun it in the air.

What could I do?

The frigate lunged toward me at an incredible speed. I pushed to the side, but Miranda's barrage of lightning and fire nailed me in one place. She was going to squash me like a worm.

I noticed the strange layers flowing around the rock again. Could I breathe those? I tugged on them and bent them to the side as she hurled it.

The boulder missed me by mere inches, burying itself halfway deep, pushing the ground up and to the side like a rock breaking a lake's surface. The force of the impact sent me flying helplessly upward. Miranda took the opportunity and sent a torrent of dirt and stone under me to push me higher before letting me drop. The ground tumbled and zoomed before me as I spun. Dwinan or not, I wouldn't survive the fall.

Hotcup swooped in and grabbed me mid-air, piercing my shoulder with his talons. Miranda shot a fireball. Hotcup dogged the strike as I felt his talons rip through my flesh. A split second later, he dropped me on the ground. I rolled, and somehow, got to my knees, blood oozing from the open wounds on my shoulder. Despite the disorientation, I found Miranda, locked on her and breathed. Layers of power wrapped around the second frigate, but before she could pull it I breathed in, and the lines diverted to me.

Miranda dropped the power, but it was too late—I had her in my control. She wasn't going anywhere. Cornered, she doubled her efforts. The streams of energy poured in relentlessly. My clothes caught fire, and the scent of burning hair filled my nose. I felt my feet dig into the boggy soil covering the stone beneath. So much energy, I couldn't hold it. My skin boiled and flaked from my flesh. I bellowed, in anger and excruciating pain. Too heavy to sustain it, like trying to hold back a massive waterfall. She would snap me in two.

Enough of this! Miranda said as she moved closer. *Give me your power or die.*

I wasn't gonna make it. I wasn't even close. Not alive, at least.

Things are things, Aureberg rumbled across the earth. *I will come.*

"No!" I shouted.

You'll die, Aureberg hummed.

I didn't care. A mountain plowing across Aviz—how many more would perish if I let him? No. I had no idea if I could consume her whole, but I'd let her peel my skin and shred my muscles before putting out my blue heart if there was even the slightest chance that I could stop her by myself. No one else had to die but me.

"So be it." The air tasted metallic and of flames as I kept on breathing. I had to hold. I had to make it. The ground murmured and simmered. *Don't you dare move, you damned mountain!*

Things are things.

Miranda leaned on the togian lines to try and squash me, pushing me faster than I could diminish her strength while pouring more fire and lightning. I felt my knee crunch. I buckled, and she pressed me against the melting stone beneath. I was severely outmatched. What was I even thinking? How could I presume to defeat her?

No. I couldn't give up. I forced myself on my other leg and breathed harder. The wind was knocked out of me, and blood rushed off my mouth, boiling away under the intense heat. I looked at my torso. A spear of rock protruded from my abdomen, pinning me to the ground.

Miranda stopped her stream of power and floated toward me as I stopped breathing her power. My vision returned to normal. I barely managed to suck any breaths in. I had failed. Aureberg would have to finish the job. But at what cost?

You really thought you could do it, didn't you? Don't worry. I missed your vital organs. Share your power with me, and I'll stop your suffering. It's that easy. I'll even spare your friends.

"So many," I said with whatever wind remained in my chest, "contractions."

Miranda dragged Heimee across the dead earth and held him in front of me like a rag doll.

I'll start with him. Then I'll kill Brinn.

Sorry, Heimee. Sorry, Mom, I thought, hands over my belly as blood gushed out and my consciousness faded.

Miranda reached for the stone spear and pulled it from me. She inspected the blood, painting its surface, then melted the spear into lava right before my eyes. *You despicable, meddling—*

Her speech was interrupted by a huge flare of light that turned the world white.

Leohirin's might, Aureberg boomed across the land. *What a thing to be.*

Chapter 75

The Seed

Ariel

There was no time to lose. Ariel jumped off Hotcup's back. There was no point in telling Ludik her plan. He'd have to take that stupid letter out to read her words because, in Ludik's words, her lips were too thin. What a waste of time that would be.

Heimee on his knees was also a distraction. She couldn't help him even if she wanted to. And she did want to. That man was a genius—a treasure to be pampered and protected for as long as possible.

The sun hung dangerously close to the horizon; every second would count. If the day died before she completed her mission, it would all have been for nothing. Water. All she needed was water. Lots of it. Luckily, she knew precisely where to find it.

Ariel ran to the distillery at full throttle the moment she heard the first thunder behind her. She didn't look back. *No distractions.* She pushed forward, absorbing as much of the setting sun's light as she could. She would need every last string of it.

Another flash, another thunder. She had to hurry. Ariel cornered the distillery and found the lake. "Thank the lord," she muttered to herself. But what did she expect? That the lake somehow dried up since she had last been there? Ariel pulled the pendant right off her neck and inspected the seed. "We may die today," she said.

In response, it glowed reassuringly. Tears welled in her eyes. She had been through so much, and this was it, the final mission for her beloved ugly bush she rescued from the highlands. The battle between Ludik and Miranda was blinding and deafening, like standing in the middle of a bombardment. She shaded her eyes from the brightness, searching for a crack in the stone on the lake's shore. Pebbles jumped from the rock bed like popping popcorn. Something hit the ground hard, the force of the clash rippled across the lake's surface, and she felt her ears pop as dirt rained around her.

The dazing light abated. A crack in the stone. She had to find a crack in the stone. The clash resumed, and Ariel struggled to see as she groped the moist rock. "Come on! Come on!"

She searched furiously for anything and found nothing. Then the fight stopped abruptly. Ariel blinked, trying to shake off the daze. She looked over her shoulder and saw Ludik on his knees, and her heart sank as she understood what she was seeing. A pillar of stone impaled him.

Her hands began to shake. Was she too late? Her pulse ran wild, her breathing erratic. Was she about to have a panic attack? *Get a grip, Ariel! Save the lad.* She fumbled through the rocky ground, forcing her mind to keep sane.

What are you doing, you dumb lass? You're a leoht!

Ariel joined two fingers and shot a laser beam drilling a hole across the rock. Water welled in it, puffing steam as it cooled the melted stone.

It would have to do. She shoved the seed down the hole, covered it with both hands and channeled her light.

Chapter 76

For The Future I Shed My Past

Ludik

In a heap of light, I was brought back to life. Cold and refreshing, pure white permeated me. It circled and danced around my limbs and torso, reinforcing my blue heart.

This changes nothing! Miranda shot a beam of lightning toward the distillery, and without thinking, I caught it.

Why would she do that? I followed the intense lifelines of light rescuing me, expecting to find Ariel, but in her stead, I found a tree. A leohtre shimmering fiercely. How?

For my mother and your mother, take my light and make her pay, the tree said.

Yes. I shook my stupor away as her light soothed my wounds and washed away the pain like a powerful ointment.

You can do it, the light said. *She's all energy. Do it, Ludik. Do it for all the souls begging for vengeance. Do it for us.*

Miranda flared with anger and shot everything she had at the tree. But I caught it all, bending it in the air and into my chest. I was right. She was weaker. I could do this!

Do you think this changes anything? Miranda blared. She warped herself into a pinprick of light, but I snatched her energy as she tried to escape, and tenaciously pulled her power into me.

Refusing to give up, Miranda turned back to fight. I slammed into a wall of flames and thunder. She tried to reach for the frigate again, but I saw it in time. I pulled in the togian lines before she could heave the boulder.

You stupid child!

Light itself broke apart into rainbows under the magnitude of her attack. My tattered clothes flaked away. The rock bubbled under my feet. The rubber from my shoes melted like candle wax, and the leather peeled away as dust.

You will never be free from me! Miranda blared as she shrunk.

Her power diminished faster and faster until I was one with her energy. Too much for my body to contain. I was fire and ice. Light and lightning. And the force that bounds the universe together, and I consumed her whole.

I felt at peace as my power ceased, and every part of me began to tear and burst. I couldn't contain it all. It didn't matter. I did it. I'd stopped the woman who shattered the world. Blackness cast warm shadows and washed away all remnants of reality, and I found myself suspended on a vertical ocean where water didn't cling to my skin. The Bastard had come to take me to the Bliss, at last. There I found life as it once was. Bright and hopeful, filled with infinite opportunities and holes to be dug under fences. Dad worked on his shoes while Mom took care of the house chores. She noticed me before I escaped outside to meet up with Laurin and smiled. I stopped and returned the smile. "I did it, Mom. I forgave the mountain."

Chapter 77

New World

Ludik

The smell of whisky assaulted my nose. Just remembering its taste made my stomach flip. Yet, that wasn't what bothered me most. There was something else. Something in my ears. Was someone tapping them? *What was that?* I tentatively rubbed my right ear and heard a crackle. I groggily opened my eyes and found Hotcup lying beside me in Heimee's living room. *How did you get in?* Oh, right. Half the house was missing.

Rest, Hotcup said.

"Sure." My voice exploded in my head.

Heimee and Ariel stared at me from the kitchen, or what was left of it, at least. Something rasp rustled beside me. Hotcup cleaned his feathers with his beak, clacking. A calloused hand landed on my shoulder. I turned to find Heimee covered in bandages, but his smile told me everything I needed to know. He was alive! Then his lips moved while he signed with his good hand. I didn't catch any of what he said because sounds poured out of his mouth.

I sat upright, and it felt like someone dropped hot embers on my stomach, forcing me to curl with pain. My abdomen was completely bandaged together.

Heimee held me so I didn't fall off the wicker couch. Hotcup buzzed as his feathers bristled.

Heimee waved his hand to get my attention and signed, "Go easy. Magic mumbo jumbo or not, you were impaled yesterday."

Yesterday?

Ariel came into view. More sounds battered my ears. Was that Ariel's voice? Tears welled in my eyes. I couldn't stop them.

"I can hear you."

I listened to my voice. I had never heard it before. Slow and loud. I didn't understand what Heimee or Ariel were saying, and they were saying a lot. I focused on their lips, trying to make sense of it but it became even more disorienting. The words felt unfamiliar to me. I reached for my pocket to fetch Half's letter but remembered that it had burned away in the fray along with everything else. That's when I noticed my bare feet. The shoes burned away, too. I remembered it. But it didn't make me sad. In a way, I wouldn't have done any of it without my dad's shoes. He'd saved me even though he was no longer here. His innovation helped to save the world. And his shoes managed to find their way to me right before it all started, precisely when I needed them the most as if he had been there to guide me the whole time.

Heimee and Ariel looked puzzled.

"You can hear me?" Heimee signed and said. Actual words. From his mouth. Words that I heard. How? His voice was what I imagined waterfalls sounded like.

I nodded, and he hugged me, sending a searing pain across my tender abdomen. I failed to discern the words when he spoke again.

"I don't know what the words mean," I said. "I'm not used to them. It's been a long time."

Heimee pushed away and signed, "Are you alright? How's your stomach?"

"It hurts like it's on fire." I raise the bandages and peek through, expecting the worst. The skin was red around a nasty, whitish scarring tissue about the size of a fist right above my belly button, but otherwise perfectly healed.

"Ariel says the tree outside healed your wounds, but it still doesn't look great. You should take it easy for a while," he kept talking while he signed. It was beautiful yet disorienting.

Ariel said something, her voice like the flutter of a bird's wings before it smashed into a window. I don't know; I wasn't used to describing sounds. I shook my head numbly at her.

"She said," Heimee offered, "people who get some kind of hearing aid often have trouble adapting, but only for the first days. But forget that. How can you hear?"

"I don't know," I said. "But it's so, so..." Tears rushed out my eyes, and I let them. "I sound so wimpy." They felt great, and the little moans and hiccups I made while I cried only added to the emotion pile.

"Yeah, well, now you see what I had to put up with," Heimee said. He helped me up and walked me to the kitchen table. The constant noise of common things screamed at me. The thump thump thump of footsteps. The creaks from the wicker chairs we sat on. The rustles, swooshes, swishes, crackles, muffles and ruffles coming from clothes while we moved. I had no idea clothing was so noisy. It had never even crossed my mind to give it sound.

Ariel and Heimee reached for their half-full thumbglasses and clanged them together. I was mesmerized by the lot. Ariel said something else, the way she spoke, the inflection in her words, not like Heimee at all, almost like they spoke two different languages.

"Enough of this," Heimee said, getting up and taking the Heims bottle with him.

"*Mumble, mumble, something*," Ariel said with a frown.

"Relax," Heimee replied, then grinned widely. "Today is not the occasion for cheap stuff." He reached for the top shelf on the cabinet and grabbed a square bottle.

Ariel's eyes nearly fell off their orbits, and she... squeaked? I think that was a squeak. Or a squeal. "Is that...?"

Heimee returned to the table with three thumbglasses and offered me one.

I smiled. "Why not?" After everything that had happened, even I was curious about what such a sought after beverage tasted like. Heims 39.

"You earned it," Heimee said. He poured the amber whisky and pushed a glass toward me. I marveled at the sound of running liquid and glass rasping against the stone table.

Ariel could barely contain herself; I had never seen such excitement in anyone. She looked like a child receiving a castle as a birthday present.

"To saving the world," Heimee signed, then raised his glass.

"*Worlds*," Ariel corrected.

I was starting to get the hang of listening. Like sweeping the dust out of a long-forgotten skill. I raised my glass, and we clinked them together. I took a sip, and it was like a war broke out in my mouth. I forced my lips shut; I didn't want to spit it out in front of Heimee as the fiery liquid corroded my digestive tract. In the end, while a conflagration happened in my belly, I could feel some notes of biscuits and smoked honey, but at what cost? If I wanted a glass of water and honey biscuits, I could've served myself water and honey biscuits. Here's what I've learned, there's absolutely no difference between expensive whisky and regular whisky.

Ariel let out a long and pleasure-filled "ahhh," then smacked her lips together. There were tears of joy in her eyes.

After that, Heimee flooded me with questions. I answered them as best I could, but I needed time to process it all. Why could I hear all of a sudden? Did the light from leohtre heal my wounds and my hearing? I was grateful, don't get me wrong, but after a while, I began to wish I could turn it off. The noise was constant. There was no hiding from it. If I want to stop seeing, I shut my eyes. But I can't shut my ears. How do people ever sleep? For as long as I could remember, I'd wished I could hear as normal people do, but right then, I wasn't so sure anymore.

"I'm going outside," I said when Ariel's and Heimee's words slurred as if they had forgotten how their tongues worked. Also, it was hard to follow their conversation. I caught some words here and there, but for the most part, it was just like being deaf, albeit way more annoying.

Heimee lowered his glass pensively and rotated it with his fingertips. Now that was an ugly sound, glass grinding stone. "What? Are you waiting for permission? You have it."

I nodded and stepped outside. With half of the house gone basically all I had to do was stand up. A slight breeze rushed through, sweeping the ash in short waves. What a gentle sound. I'd forgotten the sound of the wind. Something else was different. The morning light was, what? Brighter? No, that wasn't it. I could see its direction like spider webs floating in the breeze. It could be an illusion made by lingering smoke or some other side-effect from the fight with Miranda, but no, I had seen similar lines when I went full dwinan.

I took my eyes off the rocky ground, singed and smoothed where it melted and resolidified. The space between the house and the distillery was crisscrossed with black scars and burnt grass—an alien landscape at my doorstep. But the biggest oddity was, well, the front door. It stood four yards up, at the top of the huge, upright frigate, half buried in the ground. And, of course, there was a tree shimmering in the sunlight by the distillery. She looked like Leanerin but younger. Her wrangled branches weren't so wrangled, the bead-like leaves wider and greener, and she was at least five yards taller.

She glimmered, and her leaves rustled as I approached—a sound similar to shuffling over the tabletop but smooth and soothing.

"So, what should I call you?"

Arielin. Ludikin didn't sound so nice.

That caught me off guard, and I broke out laughing, which hurt my belly. I sat against her trunk like I used to do with my peach tree, Laurin. May the Light be with her, wherever she may be.

"I couldn't have done it without you," I said as her warm light covered me like a blanket. The light was different. I played with it. A little like using my dwinan power, but different. I didn't breathe it in; I bent it as it flowed around me like water.

A leoht, Arielin said, surprise in her tone. *How?*

"What? You didn't give it to me?"

No.

"What about my hearing?"

What about it?

"Did you heal it?"

I don't think I did. But I gave you so much light I can't be sure.

I contemplated my hands; they felt hot and sweaty and connected to my stomach somehow. I was a little frightened and flinched when my hand burst into flames. I closed my hand quickly, and the fire disappeared.

"Am I..."

Arielin shook. *You have her powers.*

"Is that possible?"

I don't know, Leohirin, but I can see the lines stacked on one another around you.

"Oh." I decided not to play with the togian power. What if I lifted what remained of Heimee's house by mistake? And I avidly avoided thinking too much about it. What a strange new world I woke up to. How much could life change in a single day?

It's alright. There couldn't be anyone better to become a Hall.

"A Hall?"

A mage who wields all the powers.

"Like Half, huh? What about Ariel?"

She drinks too much.

And just like that, I was laughing again. "Can you see Alturin?" I asked when I could speak again.

I can. A cloud of sadness and uncertainty hovers above it. They don't know we won. What brave people you found.

"The bravest. Funny how I didn't use to think much of the Alturians. I thought them cruel and indifferent. Turns out I was wrong. I was wrong about many things."

Her leaves rustled in the soft breeze; it made a beautiful sound.

"Brinn!" I said. What would she sound like? I had to get back to Alturin. I tried to get up hurriedly, and it felt a little better than being stabbed. I sat right down. "Do you mind if I stay here a little longer?"

You'll always be welcomed under my shade and in my light.

Sometime later, I said goodbye to Arielin and headed back inside. Hotcup happily picked morsels of meat from a whole ham while Ariel admired the whisky in her glass, smelling it and sipping it gently. "We need to go," I said. "The people need to know we won."

Hotcup and Ariel shared a glance and looked back at me.

Ariel protested, but I couldn't understand what she said at all. Something about how she spoke was endearing and troubling at the same time.

Hotcup wasn't too happy about it, either.

"Benerik needs you."

Understanding. Tired.

I wasn't connected to him. Yet, I had understood him before. How was that—oh, I see, I was a *lighten* as well, of course. "I'm tired too," I said to him. "We all are."

"What's with the sudden hurry?" Heimee signed, studying me through half-slit eyes. "I know what this is about."

Ariel frowned slightly and asked him something. I think I almost got what she said. The inflection on her words was difficult to grasp, but I guess I just needed to get the hang of it.

Heimee stared at her and bobbed his head, glancing at me, then winked. "He's still a boy."

Ariel grinned widely, and this time I got what she said, "Ye want to see Brinn."

"That's not it," I said defensively.

Ariel stared at me.

I stared at her. "Alright, yes. But everyone else needs to know what happened too. They sacrificed so much; we shouldn't keep them waiting."

"Kennye'ven fly?" Ariel said before downing the remaining Heims 39. Okay, I could do it. I chewed on the syllables and somehow it became clearer. "Can ye even fly?" she had said.

I shrugged.

Hotcup got to his feet and stretched his back and neck while tiny sparks wormed between his feathers.

"I hate when he does that," Heimee noted.

"Yeah," Ariel agreed. "Sounds like someone tuning a guitar. Guess he wants to get moving too." It took a mix of lip-reading in conjunction with her sounds to decipher what she said, but I was getting the hang of it. She took a deep breath. "No crazy flyin', ye hear."

Hotcup yawned, then nodded.

"I hope this doesn't mean I have to find a new assistant," Heimee said, folding his arms over his belly. "It took years to make something out of you."

I grinned. "There's nothing I'd like more."

"Can I make whisky, too?" Ariel intervened.

Heimee regarded her with inspecting eyes. "We could use a feminine hand around the place."

"I'd only disappoint ye."

Heimee chuckled. “You have my undying gratitude. In fact,” Heimee headed back to the whisky cabinet and produced another bottle. “For the road. It’s not 39, but it’s quite a nice selection. Something to do with the barley that year or the strange barrels I put them in. I think you’ll like it.”

Ariel’s hands reached for the bottle as if Heimee passed her a newborn baby to hold. “Can ye be my dad?”

Heimee scowled. “This ain’t an orphanage. Off with you two.” Then we all laughed. He glanced at Hotcup and added, “Well, three. Ludik’s right. You shouldn’t keep Brinn waiting.”

Chapter 78

The Pyre

Ludik

We flew relatively slowly compared with our previous flight. Thankfully. As it turns out, being deaf wasn't such a bad thing when flying on the back of an aramaz, if you didn't have to hear the continuous gurgle of the wind wrecking your ears. Connecting with Hotcup was way easier—no more charge than undressing a thick wool sweater.

When we arrived at Alturin's outskirts, the sun painted Aureberg in shades of orange. Even though I had caused that, seeing a mountain where a few days earlier there hadn't been any was not an easy thing to comprehend.

"They've been busy," I heard Ariel scream behind me. I strained to understand her words, and, of course, I couldn't be sure I got them right, especially over the turbulence.

A corridor of torches stretched from the broken wall of Alturin to several large structures covered with the bodies of the fallen soldiers, and of course civilians too, while thousands gathered around it. Ahead, across the vast fields outside Alturin, hundreds of white tents dotted the land along with the silvery boulders. An ant trail of people extended to the forest's edge, disassembling the army camp and rebuilding it closer to the city.

The battle had made refugees of them all.

"Land by the pyres," I said. "I think I see the duke there."

"The king, you mean," Ariel corrected.

I pressed a finger into my ear canal, trying to shake the wind out of it.

Hotcup landed gently as a feather under the watchful eyes of thousands of people.

So he does know how to make soft landings.

I jumped off Hotcup's back and grunted in pain. I'd never realized we used our abdomen for so many things. Jumping included. I should deliver the news of our victory with as much dignity as a young boy could muster.

I approached King Armrar, who sat on a makeshift chair, Balival at his side. Not far behind, Brinn and Mathew, and Graze too, teetered in silence. The people suspended their breaths. They must've known we won just by my arrival, but they wanted to hear it. They wanted to taste victory.

The king stared at me while I averted the mob's scrutinizing eyes as best I could. Still, I could see the Aviz soldiers mingling in the crowd. Guess there was no reason to fear them now. They probably had already sworn allegiance to their new king. Right, Mink was the king now.

I reached King Armrar Katunik, Duke of Alturin, commander of the northern legions and the armies of Aviz, smiled at him, turned to his people, and hollered, "We did it. We won."

The king nodded cordially, almost as a bow, and despite the bags in his eyes, and his pale skin, he cracked a smile. Balival brought a horn to his lips and blew. Horns make a horrible, horrible sound. Why people use them is beyond me.

The crowd exploded. The noise of a quarter million people cheering thundered across the field, but the king did not cheer along. He leaned against a cane and got up, observing me intently. A heavy sadness shrouded his face. The cost had been too great for him to bear. It had been too great for us all. But to him and me, it was different. We had to make the hardest choices, and we would have to live with them.

"Aren't you fetching that letter of yours?" Katunik's voice was rasp and tired but firm and reassuring, like a fresh glass of water over a sunny day.

"I don't need it anymore, your grace," I said. "Uh, your majesty."

"It seems he's no longer deaf," Ariel explained. "Side effect from consuming Miranda."

"Please don't say it like that," I protested.

The king raised an eyebrow, then shrugged. "It's not the weirdest thing to have happened in recent times."

Hotcup gawked, eyes darting in every direction.

"Benerik is recovering, my friend," Katunik explained. "I don't know how, but he is. You'll find him in the field hospital by the main square."

Hotcup ruffled his feathers, jumped in the air, and flew away.

While distracted watching Hotcup take flight, Brinn tackled me to the ground. It hurt like being shocked by Hotcup, but despite the pain, I wrapped my arms around her. I was so happy to see her. "We did it, Brinn."

She sat on top of me. "I want to hear every detail." She tried to fumble it in sign language, but I grabbed her hands. Reading her lips had always been easy to me, but her voice was like birds playing in a summer breeze or a hot cup of tea and honey on a winter morning. Actually, that's not true. Her voice sounded like drunken sailors caught in a bar fight. Let's just say I hoped that I would never have to hear her sing.

"You have a beautiful voice," I said. No, that was not a lie. I did like her voice, no matter how brutal it sounded. No wonder people listened to her. "But you have to get off me. My stomach hurts pretty badly."

Brinn didn't move away and gaped at me. She covered her mouth and said, "I'll smack your head in if you're lying to me."

"It's true. I find it beautiful," I said with a wide stupid grin stamped on my face.

"Not that, silly. You can hear!" Brinn slid off me, in what was probably the worst way to do it, grinding her knee right over the sweet spot and pulled me up. I hugged her again.

She grabbed me by the cheeks. "You can hear!"

"Yes," I mumbled.

"You truly are a matryoshka doll of surprises." I turned and saw Mathew. "You sure she's gone?" His voice sounded like a drum set, deep and with tempo.

"I absorbed all her energy. There's nothing left of her except..." I was about to raise my hand and show off my new powers but thought against it. There was already enough to digest for one day, and I didn't want to divert more attention from the funeral.

"Except what?"

"Except for the devastation she left behind." I dodged the subject.

Mathew's lips curled inside, and he nodded heavily. "Yeah, there's that."

"I think the king is about to say something."

We watched King Armrar step onto a small stage in front of the pyres and contemplate his subjects as the day took its last breaths and torchlights took over. "Today, we shall not mourn. These brave souls gave their lives to protect everything. They saved the world. I will not pity them, and I will not grieve. I will celebrate and honor the heroes they are. Because of their sacrifice, we have a tomorrow. A tomorrow where we can rebuild, and the days will shine brighter than ever. A tomorrow filled with light, magic," Katunik raised his chin high and turned his gaze from the crowd to the new mountain filling the northern view, "and eternal friendship."

A soft rumble shimmied the ground beneath with Aureberg's answer.

The king bowed to Aureberg and faced the remains of his city before returning his attention to thousands waiting for his following words and finally to the fallen. "Thank you, Gods of Alturin."

"To the gods!" the crowd chanted. "To the gods!"

With a nod from the king, the men holding torches marched ceremoniously to the pyres and gently set them alight. The following silence was breathtaking, filled only by the crackle of burning wood and a soft breeze flowing east. Brinn clutched me tightly. I looked at her. We had done it. Against all odds, we had done it. Everything was going to be alright now.

Things are things, I heard Aureberg say.

Lights began to swirl over his peaks extending over the funeral, illuminating the night with hope and all the shades of the northern lights. Then the crowd burst into singing—The Bastard's song.

My fingers slipped into Brinn's as we contemplated the fire. She leaned her head on my shoulder, and we allowed the music to wash over us as the flickering flames consumed the bodies of the fallen gods but not their memory. I would later learn about the actual toll, about how many perished when I brought the mountain. A number far surpassing the casualties of the battle. Would I ever forgive myself? I squeezed Brinn's hand and sang along.

The wind swept the letters leaving an empty stool,
There she waited for him, willing to be fooled.

He handled useless tools and screamed useless words,
The time had finally come to do the things undone.
Roaming was key in finding promised land,
Mountains, snow and grit and withered distant hands.
But weakened is the mind as we stumble upon life,
And seas of opportunities among endless bitter strife!

Home away, Home away, Oh, what had he brought,
All he ever was turned into a new plot.

The wheels turned around. What were they about?
And smiles grew on his young youthless mouth.
Home away, home away, shining in his mind.
Home away. Home always. What a restless hindsight.

Home away, home away to shine in his mind,
Home away. Home always!
Where love remains, where sadness restrains, we'll leave the rest behind.

We celebrated throughout the night, sharing stories, chanting songs, reveling in our victory, and remembering the fallen. Emotions flared out of every pore, every word an anvil of the moment and every glance a flaming arrow igniting our hearts. We mourned and celebrated the cost of saving the world, along with a very expensive bottle of Heims.

Before dawn, after Brinn and everyone else had fallen asleep in our refugee tents and hard army cots, I flit under the moon's watchful eye. It spoke to me in a tongue I could not understand, but I nodded in consent as I made my way to Aureberg.

He lifted me to the plateau, and I followed the pale blue light to his heart.

You needn't come here. Whenever you touch the ground, we can speak.

I reached for his heart and planted my palm against it. "I needed to come. I still have something to tell you. I'm so sorry, Aureberg. I forgive you. And I hope you can forgive me, too."

Things are things. Berg means mountain in an old tongue. Call me Aure, and that's the only thing you should feel sorry for.

I leaned on his beating heart. "Maybe what we need is to forgive ourselves."

Aure rumbled. *Hmmm, a good thing to do. But if you wish to grant me a favor, I'll ask only this: things are things, and we should be wise to leave things be for as long as we can.*

"We will," I promised. "For as long as we shall live."

I left the mountain's hall with an immense calm overcoming me. A good calm, like an ocean which had never seen a storm or a heart that had never been broken. Aure offered to lower me back to the camp, but I declined. That morning, despite my aching abdomen, I climbed down Aure's face with bare hands and scraped skin. By sweat and by the company of my ghosts. Memories of what was lost and what was found. Of past and present, and future.

I climbed down Aure Mountain for the hymn of all that was meant to be.

And when I reached the bottom, dead and broken, resurrected and repaired, with the first rays of sunshine on my face, I held the truth in my heart: inside of every man, woman, and child, there's a monumental mountain capable of changing the world.

Epilogue

"Come on, wake up!" Ariel burst into my bedroom. "Heimee says we'll open the leohtre casks today."

"I'm going out with Brinn," I said groggily.

Ariel gasped. "Leohtre Edition! Remember three years ago, all the time we spent learning how to make barrels out of Arielin's branches? Today we'll know if it was worth it or not. And I bet whatever ye want that we're about taste something remarkable."

I sat in bed, bleary-eyed, wondering why that woman ever decided to live with us. "I haven't seen Brinn in months since she became the king's foreign affairs minister."

"Yeah, I still can't believe that happened," Ariel said. "This is a strange world indeed. I told her to open a pizzeria here, but no, if I want a pizza, I have to ride to Alturin for Graze's Pizza place. At least that's one baker who had the good sense of hearing what I had to say."

"You made pizza yesterday." A cat jumped on the bed. "Oh, get off me. Look at this. My bedsheets are full of fur now. Thanks, Bubbles. I can't believe you brought this thing from your flea-infested planet."

Ariel picked Bubbles up and stroked his chin. Bubbles bit her fingers. "Oh, stop it. Ye loved my world. Admit it!"

I did enjoy the experience, but I would never stay there. There was this box with images of other people in it, and you wouldn't believe the things I saw in it. Every day was an audiovisual assault on my sanity. And it was so crowded. Mathew stuck with us for another month while Ariel ushered us halfway across their world before we dropped him home. (Apparently, Ariel was kind of rich and paid for the whole thing. She also bought fake passports. You need those to get around. And for all intents and purposes, while on Earth, my name was Thomas Smith.)

No, I didn't take care of their heat problem. Brinn said it was a dumb move, so I didn't. And I think she was right. If I had removed all the extra heat from their *atmosphere* (uh, what a word), the carbon would still be there, and in a few years, the problem would return. And their *scientists* (I'd learned a lot of new words) would be left scratching their heads trying to redo their *climate models* (it was a barrage of new words), unable to explain what had happened to all the excess heat.

Our travels across Earth were interesting, but in the end, I just wanted to return home. There really is nothing like home. *Home away,* well, *home always.*

"It isn't the same thing when I cook for myself. Ye know, it still bugs me. The English language made it across the roots, but pizza didn't. Or hamburgers, or kebabs."

"How much fat is in those?"

"Plenty."

"I think I'll pass."

"What about sushi?"

I gagged. Raw fish wasn't my thing. I tried it once. I did. In Japan. It sucked. Ariel and Heimee ate plenty of it, but they also love whisky in ways I'll never understand, so there's that. Oh, I didn't tell you? Heimee went too. And Brinn. Apparently, when you travel the roots, you can take non-magical folk with you. We spent most of our time in what Ariel called cultured countries, which was her way of saying whisky-producing countries. Ariel and Heimee bonded heavily over their Whiskey World Tour and decided to join forces and rival the best whiskies from her world.

We made it downstairs where Heimee gave me a knowing smile while he set the table for breakfast and whisky tasting. "So when is the *missus* arriving?"

"Today," I said, then added, "and we're not married."

Ariel smiled and looked out the window. "Ye should look outside."

My head turned to the window so fast my neck cracked. Not a great sound. Brinn waved at me from the top of a sizable black ekkuh with yellow eyes and I was outside before I knew it. "Brinn! Where did you get that ride?"

"Oh, you mean this tiny thing?" Brinn said as she dismounted. "Autmon gave it to me after our conference. He's called Ingser. I think it means lightning in Erom."

I hugged her even before she'd turned completely. It was awkward, and I didn't care. She was getting more beautiful by the day. "Wait," I pushed her back. "King Autmon?"

"The one and only," Brinn said, placing her arms around my neck. She kissed me. "You should come with me next time."

"To tell you the truth, I'm still a little sick from traveling. Come, Heimee's setting up the table for breakfast."

We entered the kitchen after tying Ingser's reins outside.

"So, it's done then?" Heimee asked.

"It is." Brinn gave him a wide grin. "Erosomita and Aviz's economic union is formally established. Turns out those folks in Europe are really on to something. But to be honest, most of the time, I have no idea what I'm talking about."

"What matters is that they bought it." Heimee gave her a big hug. "Hear that, Ariel?"

"We're gonna make a lot of money," Ariel said.

Heimee watched her go, furrowing his brow. He shrugged and turned his attention back to Brinn. "What age are you now?"

"Seventeen."

"Seventeen, and you're brokering deals with foreign kings. You are truly one of a kind. Don't let it get to your head."

"Hey, King Armrar insisted."

"Any word from Ben?" I asked.

"Progress is slow," Brinn replied.

"It can't be easy to do a census on all mages," Ariel said. "Most prefer to hide their powers, unlike Mathew. By the way, did Ben fetch my mail?"

"Oh, right." Brinn took a chunk of letters from her bag and passed it to Ariel.

"Speaking of Mathew, what's that bottlehead up to these days?" Heimee asked.

"He's studying aerospace engineering and computer sciences," Ariel explained as she sat at the table perusing her mail. "He's still bent on saving the world. Can't believe I'm on another planet receiving mail ads from Lidl."

Heimee rubbed his chin. "Is any of that useful?"

"Lidl adds?"

"No. What Mat's studyin'."

"Well, yes. Whether he's smart enough to finish the courses or is just wasting my money, that's another question."

"Good for him. Well, enough chit-chat. Are you ready?" Heimee said, getting up. "I decanted it earlier." He reached for a small vial on the kitchen counter and poured its content into two glasses. The spirit wasn't amber as usual—it had a more yellowish tint, like lemon tea.

Ariel rubbed her hands together. "That's an interesting color." She added a few drops of fresh water to her glass, swirled it, then took a whiff. "Hmmm, Leohtre whisky."

They sipped it gently and then stared at each other, bobbing their heads for quite some time before settling on intrigued looks.

"What's with all the anis?" Ariel blurted. "And what is that? Clover?"

"Not what I expected." Heimee shoved his nose inside the glass.

"It feels like an ashtray had an affair with a liquorice plant." Ariel regarded her glass pensively. "Arielin won't be pleased about this. She was very happy to contribute." Ariel pursed her lips and gave it another sip. "I mean, it's not that bad once ye get used to it, and if ye get past the smokiness—definitely not whisky, though."

"This might sound mad," Heimee prodded. "But what if we don't peat the spirit? It might produce something remarkably fresh. A spring whisky, if you will."

"That's rubbish..." Ariel's eyes bulged. "Ye know what? That just might work."

I loved watching them talk about whisky, but I had other plans. "Alright, we're heading out."

Heimee regarded Brinn. "Make sure he doesn't get into trouble."

"Hey, I can take care of myself," I said defensively.

"That's what worries me."

We left to spend the day wandering around Guillingsbaer's streets. We went out for dinner and then to a music concert. And we danced. To music in all its glory. Not just the drums and strumming patterns vibrating in my chest but its full spectrum of notes and nuances. I couldn't have enough of it—always afraid my deafness could return as unexpectedly as it went away. Brinn was a horrible dancer, though, but I didn't care as long as she wasn't the one singing. Before we returned home, we sat by the lake where we ice skated all those years before, and Brinn regaled me with all her adventures. We fell asleep in the wild, in each other's embrace, under the soft, warm summer night's breeze with only the moonlight for company.

I woke up to a burning stomach. It spread quickly over my body like a wild fever, and I clutched my belly in pain. Was it something I ate? Images of fire and light flashed before my eyes. It felt wrong. It felt... oh no!

"Are you alright?" Brinn asked, startled.

"There's something wrong." I reached in, turning my heart pale blue to contain the conflagration, and as I did, I heard her as clear as the day we fought.

You stupid child, you will never be free of me.

END

Dear Reader

Thank you so much for reading *Ludik and the Runaway Mountain*. I hope you enjoyed it as much as I enjoyed writing it.

That said, it would mean the world to me if you could spare some of your time to **leave an honest review on Amazon or Goodreads.**

Books and writing careers live by their reviews, and without them, they're simply forgotten.

Stay awesome!

John

About the Author

John Ilho was born in Portugal in 1986. After a successful career as a chef, he put his knives away to pursue his lifelong passion for creative writing.

A passion that prompted the launch of *Don't Panic—It's Only a Novel*, a writing guide designed to help other aspiring writers hone their craft.

In fact, John talks about writing so much his wife told him that unless he has anything to say unrelated to writing, he should keep his mouth shut.

John currently lives in Norway with his wife and two sons in complete and utter silence.

For news and shenanigans, please visit:

www.johnilho.com

Printed in Great Britain
by Amazon

46460991R00283